Lakeland Lily

Lakeland Lily

Freda Lightfoot

Matador
9 Priory Business Park,
Wistow Road, Kibworth Beauchamp,
Leicestershire. LE8 0RX
Tel: (+44) 116 279 2299
Fax: (+44) 116 279 2277
Email: books@troubador.co.uk
Web: www.troubador.co.uk/matador

Cover photographs:
Steam Yacht: S L Osprey © Windermere Steamboat Museum
Girl: istockphotos.com

ISBN 9781783061563

British Library Cataloguing in Publication Data.
A catalogue record for this book is available from the British Library.

Typeset by Troubador Publishing Ltd, Leicester, UK
Printed and bound in Great Britain by TJ International Ltd, Padstow, Cornwall

Matador is an imprint of Troubador Publishing Ltd

Acknowledgements

I am indebted to Diana Matthews of the Windermere Nautical Trust for her assistance with research and for her splendid booklets, Lake Festivals on Windermere and Lake Windermere's Golden Jubilee. Also to her father, George Pattinson, for his excellent book, The Great Age of Steam on Windermere, which first inspired the idea. Any mistakes or liberties taken for the sake of the story are, of course, my responsibility and not theirs. Last but by no means least, thanks to the steamboat skippers who still operate these wonderful boats from the Steamboat Museum, Windermere, who told me their fascinating history and answered my many questions while I enjoyed several delightful cruises on the lake.

Chapter One

1909

'Lily Thorpe, if you don't come in this minute I'll batter your face with a wet kipper. See if I don't!'

The recipient of this dire warning made no move to respond, for she was entirely engrossed in holding her breath so as not to interrupt what must be the longest kiss on record.

'That was your mam,' the boy said at last when nature forced them up for air.

Lily, dizzy from the kiss, swept aside her shining brown hair and laid her cheek upon Dick's chest with a sigh of blissful contentment. For a long moment she lay listening to the rapid beat of his heart then lifted her face a fraction to give him the full benefit of her bewitching hazel eyes, glowing almost gold with desire, her tiptilted nose, and the bluntness of a deceptively demure chin which, he claimed, only proved how very stubborn she was. Lily meant to let him see that she would not be averse to the kiss being repeated.

Not, she admitted wryly, that the ash-pit roof from which strings of washing flapped, was the most romantic place in the world to experiment with these delightful new sensations. Situated at the bottom of a yard shared by half a dozen other houses besides her own, shovel-loads of ash from the fire were stored in the pit and used to sweeten the tippler privy next door.

But from its roof Lily could see beyond the huddle of narrow streets and overcrowded fishermen's cottages that made up The Cobbles, as far as the dark green fringe of woodland that cloaked the lower reaches of the Lakeland hills, the bare tops of the more distant peaks, and, if she stood on tiptoe, the glimmer of silver-bright water that was the lake.

Beyond the lake was the world where, one day, Lily meant to be: Rydal and Grasmere to the north, the busy towns of Windermere and Kendal to the south. To the west lay the snow-capped peaks of the Langdales, while to the east were the high fells of Kentmere. These were the limits of Lily's knowledge. She had never in her life stepped outside the boundaries of Carreckwater, though she took every opportunity to escape the pungent confines of The Cobbles, squashed as it was between Fisher's Brow and Old Martin's Yard, far from the more elegant quarters of the small town.

Lily hated The Cobbles and all it stood for. The sweet-sour stink of poverty gave a sense of hopelessness to the tiny overcrowded cottages. Walls ran with damp both inside and out. The alleys were infested with the kind of livestock nobody welcomed, and her mother fought a thankless daily battle against cockroaches. Each night the drunks would noisily roll home and by morning the stink of urine and vomit would be stronger than ever. Lily's single all-pervading desire was to leave The Cobbles for good.

She dreamed of making her fortune in the neighbouring village of Bowness. Of holding court in her own fine shop, perhaps a draper's and mantle-maker's, surrounded by silks and satins which she would fashion into much sought-after garments. These dreams made her life tolerable.

But she wasn't thinking of escape today. Nor had she any wish to admire the view. She wanted only to melt into Dick Rawlins's arms, to be caressed by his fevered hands and kissed into submission by his burning lips. How else was she to learn about life if she didn't experiment a little? She was fifteen, after all.

'Did you enjoy it?'

'What?'

'That French kiss.'

Lily considered for a moment. It had felt a bit awkward at first with his tongue in her mouth, but then something very strange had happened to other parts of her, which she really didn't like to think about. Mind you, the girls at the fish market had told her nasty things could happen to a girl after certain sorts of kisses. Was this what they meant? She'd hate to have to give up kissing Dick

Rawlins. Lily slanted a smile up at him. 'Happen I need to try it again, before I can decide.'

Taking hold of her shoulders Dick rolled her on to her back and without asking her permission to do so, stretched himself out on top of her.

'Here, you cheeky tyke, what you up to?' she demanded, pushing at his chest, though with little conviction.

'Don't tell me you don't like this either?' He made little movements up and down and even through her cotton frock and thick flannel drawers she was startled to feel his private parts rubbing against her, all hard and alarmingly large. Lily felt her cheeks grow hot and while she knew she should push him off, at the same moment she was too busy examining her own response and finding it entirely fascinating.

'It's all right, Lil. I won't do anything to you,' he grunted against her neck, and the sweat from him flowed inside the collar of her thin frock, leaving it all damp. 'Not till after we're wed, anyroad.' He chuckled, while Lily frowned up at the blue sky above his head and wondered if she dared ask what it was, exactly, that he would do to her then, and how it would feel?

She was no fool, nor entirely ignorant of sexual matters, she told herself. It wasn't possible to live in these streets and not gain some idea of the goings on between men and women. But it was a confused and distorted picture, filled with strange fears, whispered rumours, and unexplained gaps in her scanty knowledge. She'd asked her mother once, but Hannah's cheeks had grown dark red with embarrassment and Lily had wished the words unspoken.

'Fifteen is too young for such talk. You ought to be ashamed of yourself, Lily Thorpe. Go and wash your mouth out this minute.'

Hannah Thorpe was of the opinion that the less her young daughters knew of such matters, the less likely they were to get 'caught'. By which Lily understood her to mean, with a baby.

There were six Thorpe children, including herself, and it was still a mystery to Lily why her mother kept having them when she was so close to exhaustion much of the time. Lily had no intention of ruining her own health with a clutch of children, nor of spending her life washing, caring and cleaning up after them. So she needed to understand how it all came about, desperate to make sure she didn't fall into the same trap.

'Too much curiosity in you, girl. A woman makes bairns and a woman brings 'em up. And there are times when they cost her naught but pain and trouble.'

'Yes, but how? I mean, if they're such a trouble, why do you keep making more? And why do men keep giving 'em to you?'

'Because the daft beggars think only of themselves! Remember that, Lily. Men allus think they're in charge of everything, but theer's some things they can't do. Having a bairn is one of 'em,' Hannah had said with tart satisfaction, then added with a stern wag of one finger, 'you take care what you're up to, girl, and you'll be safe. And that's all I have to say on the matter.'

Thus the mystifying subject was closed, and Lily's curiosity remained unsatisfied, her thirst for life all the greater.

Despite her patched clothes, scuffed boots and underfed immaturity, Lily Thorpe was a sight to see. Her brown hair, which she attempted to screw up into a knot on top of her head, shone with health and vigour, and when released, fell into a heavy brown curtain about her shoulders. The whites around the hazel iris of her eyes glowed, the dark lashes curled enticingly, and the expression on her heart-shaped face seemed ever to be filled with impish promise. If there was little femininity to be seen as yet in the curves of chest and hip or the skinny limbs, they would come, given time.

Lily was not unaware of her burgeoning charms and since her mother meant to keep her in ignorance, felt bound to find the answer some other way. Dick, nearly three years older than herself, and therefore with considerably more experience, was in Lily's opinion the best person to satisfy these strange stirrings deep inside her. Particularly since they meant to marry one day.

They'd been walking out for some months and gone so far as to decide they were desperately in love and, as Dick himself said, 'meant for each other'.

At first they used to sneak away into the woods where Lily had let Dick kiss her as much as he liked, and once she'd let him touch the bud of her small breast. The experience had been so electrifying it had left her quite breathless and thrown her into a panic. She'd never dared repeat it. There was clearly more to this cuddling lark than she had appreciated.

Since then she had taken care to meet him only in public places. Lolling at the corners of the back street, snatching a bit of gossip in her tea breaks from the fish stall on the market, or this favourite place on the ash-pit roof – near enough to her own house to offer security yet with a sense of privacy. Folk never thought to look up, even as they passed by a few feet below them, and the roof was shielded by taller buildings on each side.

Her thoughts were brought back to the present by the voice calling sharply yet again, 'Lily!' But Dick was still talking so she took no notice.

'I won't ask you to take them off, as many a chap might.'

Lily was shocked into utter silence for a whole half minute. *Take off her drawers?* The very idea! Her mother had told her quite firmly never to take them off, even in bed, or she'd 'catch her death'. Lily wore them under an old shirt of her brother's which she used in lieu of a nightgown. If she could catch a cold in her own bed, to remove them while on the ash-pit roof would be an act of utter recklessness.

'Why would I want to, you cheeky tyke?'

Dick laughed softly in her ear. 'You're so sweet and funny, Lil, sometimes I could eat you all up.'

Lily gave him a sidelong glance from her flashing eyes. 'So long as you take care where you put those wandering hands of yours, you can kiss me as much as you like.'

He accepted the invitation readily, kissing her till her chin was rubbed sore, her jaws ached, and a hot ache grew somewhere deep in her belly. When he rolled off her with a great grunting sigh, he left her with an unexplained need, like being thirsty on a hot day, though not half so unpleasant. Lily was sorry he'd stopped. She'd enjoyed the weight of Dick's hard body against hers, the moist excitement of his mouth and his teasing hands. Trust her mother to spoil it, shouting down the yard in that common way.

Propping her chin in her hand, Lily gazed down upon him, seeing how his long lashes lay closed in an adorable crescent on the smooth skin of his cheeks. His fair hair was all tousled and boyish, pale pink lips partly open to reveal the glint of good white teeth, rare in these parts. Oh, how she loved him! The memory of that burning need rose sweet and strong in her, bringing a fresh spurt of pain between her legs. It all felt so shockingly dangerous that Lily deemed it prudent to occupy her mind with other things. She had no intention of getting 'caught' and being trapped in The Cobbles forever.

'Are you going to talk to my dad tomorrow, like you promised?'

'What about?' Dick teased, in the kind of voice which meant he knew only too well but wanted to hear her say it. Lily flushed and pretended to slap him.

'That you want to wed me, soon as we can.'

'Sooner the better, if you carry on with other chaps the way you were with me just now,' he said, his face so serious that it took a moment before Lily appreciated he was still teasing her. She tossed back her heavy hair and lifted that stubborn chin.

'Happen, if you don't look sharp about it, I'll change me mind and marry someone richer,' she told him rather sniffily, as if she had a queue of suitors lining up in her back yard, just waiting for the chance to marry her.

'Happen there's more interesting ways of choosing a husband than seeing how much money he makes.'

'Such as?'

'The way he kisses for one thing. You still haven't said if you enjoyed it?'

Lily recognised his sudden vulnerability and laughed at him now, ignoring the question. 'Oh, there's so much we could do together, Dick. Go anywhere we want, make our fortunes.'

'I wouldn't want to leave the Lakes.'

'Me neither, but there's better places to live than this hole. We deserve better, and we could get it. You as the best carpenter in the district, me as a dressmaker.'

'Nearly a carpenter,' he reminded her, half laughing at her

eagerness. 'I've a few years of learning to do yet. And you haven't even started.'

'Who's fault is that? Not mine. Oh, but I mean to! That's the whole point of you speaking to my dad. Then he'll see that we mean to stay together, mean to make something of our lives and go up in the world.' Anxiety crept into her voice. 'He'll agree to find the money for my apprenticeship, I know he will, if *you* ask him. Five bob a week I earn helping Mam on the fish stall, most of which she takes back for me keep. And I hate it – all that filleting and gutting. There's got to be more to life than that. You and me could be so happy together.'

He looked vaguely troubled, feeling events rushing away from him. Much as he loved Lily, and he *did* love her, at barely eighteen he had a long way to go before he could support a wife. He'd really rather enjoy the present. He pulled her close and started to kiss the curve of her throat. He'd heard somewhere that was a sure way to please a woman. It certainly seemed to work with Lily as she sank weakly against him.

'Lily!'

'Oh, lord, there she is again. It's no good, I'll have to go.' Lily sighed with exasperation. She really shouldn't still be at the beck and call of her mother, not at nearly sixteen.

Then she was pulling away from him, tidying her hair and straightening her skirt, her voice all bossy and anxious.

'Mam'll want me to put our Kitty to bed, I expect, or see Emma and Liza wash behind their ears.' She punched him playfully in the chest. 'You're lucky to have no brothers and sisters. When Dad, Jacob and Matt get back from their afternoon stint at the boatyard, there'll have to be hot water poured for them to wash, tea brewed and food on the table before they go out on the night fishing. I have to wait hand and foot on me own brothers, for all they're younger than me, just because they're male.'

Dick only laughed, as if he found her vehemence amusing.

'It's all right for you. All you need do is wash your hands and take your boots off and your mam'll have it all done.'

'You should be making my tea, not my mam. Would you

complain then, Lily Thorpe, when it's me you're waiting on?'

She pulled a face at him. 'I said I'd be your wife, not your servant.'

Dick grabbed her tightly round the waist and rolled her over to the very rim of the slate roof, making her squeal with delicious fear and excitement at his complete disregard for their safety. It was perhaps the wildness in him that she loved best. Once, he'd stuck them both into potato barrels and rolled them down Claife Heights. For a dare, he'd said. He'd won, of course. Lily had been covered in bruises for weeks.

'Who says there's a difference? You've promised to love me for ever and obey my every demand.'

'What demands?'

'These for a start,' he said, kissing her again and running the palm of his hand right down her thigh to her knees where the hem of her skirt had rucked up.

She yanked it back down to her ankles, cheeks bright. 'I never promised owt of t'sort, you cheeky tyke. You made that up.' But her protests were weak, her teasing eyes enticing, small pink mouth opening and closing in pretend outrage, inviting him to make further onslaughts on her virtue, if he dare.

It would have taken a stronger man than Dick Rawlins to resist. He gave a low growl somewhere deep in his throat. 'You're a witch, Lily Thorpe, that's what you are.'

'Am I?' she enquired, with an air of manufactured innocence, and no small degree of pride.

'Oh, I do love you, Lil. I'll wait hand and foot on you, if you like.' As he reached to kiss her again, Lily's heart soared with pleasure. He was her man and he loved her. Tied to her mother's apron strings she might be but these few snatched moments with Dick made a dull life beautiful and exciting.

'Lily? Are you down there? I'll not tell you again. If you don't come in this minute you won't go to this Water Carnival you're so set on. You can stop at home and read what the good Lord has to say on the subject of obedience.'

'Oh, heck, I've done it now. She's got her Puritan voice on.' Lily was thrusting Dick's eager hands away, hitching up her long skirts and scrambling down from the roof as fast as she could. She flapped a desperate hand at him. 'Oh, do go home, Dick. It would be dreadful if I couldn't go tomorrow. I've been so looking forward to it.'

He dropped lightly down beside her but when he would have gathered her in his arms yet again, Lily thrust him away. 'Get off with you. You've promised to take me out in a boat tomorrow, remember. And to speak to my dad.'

Snatching her hand, he kissed the back of it. He'd seen a picture in a magazine he'd read at the Working Men's Institute of a Frenchman doing exactly the same thing, so thought he might as well try it on Lily. He was a great one for showmanship. Made life a bit more interesting, it did. He certainly didn't care to get too serious about it. Except for Lily. He'd do anything for his lovely Lil. He meant to impress her tomorrow too, with his skill with the oars.

'I'll show your dad what a good boatman I am.' In the hope he'd look kindly upon him when later Dick made his request. Assuming he plucked up the necessary courage.

'It's me you have to please, you daft lump. Not me dad.'

Dick wasn't so sure. He felt sick to his stomach at the thought of facing big Arnold Thorpe. Not a man to mess with, wasn't Arnie. Everyone knew that. One of the most experienced fishermen on the lake he was a big brawn of a chap. Loved boxing and cock fighting and would take a gamble on anything that moved, for all he had a wife who was a Card-Carrying Methodist. Arnie was a hard man, and protective where his family were concerned, Lily in particular.

'He won't give his most precious daughter away to any Tom, Dick or Harry, now will he?' he said, and they both collapsed into a fit of giggles at this old joke between them.

'Lily! If you don't come in this minute I'll come and drag you up this yard by the scruff of your neck!'

Spinning on her heel, Lily ducked beneath the flapping sheets pinned on the washing line and ran, stopping only briefly with her hand on the sneck of the back door. 'You'll meet me on the jetty?'

'Aye, Lily. I will.' Then Dick blew her a kiss, just to finish the romantic interlude with a suitably extravagant gesture, and swaggered off down the back street, whistling.

The Thorpe family rowed the short half mile in the family fishing boat to where the water carnival was to be held. Arnie and the boys had given it an extra thorough clean, and decked it out in ribbons in honour of this special day. All six children, including Lily, were hardly able to sit still for excitement.

The town was humming with people in their best summer dresses. Flags and streamers were everywhere, with much splashing and squealing coming from the lake, everyone enjoying the fun.

Besides the sailing races there were always plenty of games for the children: musical chairs at the water's edge, balloon bursting, eating buns on cycles, tent pegging and apple bobbing. Lily didn't think herself too old for such fun. Not quite yet. For the more adventurous, there would be home-made raft races and lots of other silly water games which resulted in the contestants getting a proper soaking if they were anything like her twin brothers.

Later there might be a sham sea battle with mock explosions and clouds of smoke as if in a real war. Then the winning side would storm on to the other team's island and everyone would cheer.

Lily knew her father would take part in the fishermen's boat race, and likely win it as he so often did. After a picnic tea, which they would take together beneath the trees, they'd loll about and recover from their adventures for a while. Then would follow the grand firework display. It was worth coming to the Water Carnival for that glory alone.

The uncertain Lakes weather had been known to spoil the day in the past, for all it took place in early summer. Lily was delighted that this particular June day was perfect, with a merry blue sky and hardly a puff of cloud, the striped Egyptian cotton sails of the small boats dazzling in the sun. When the figure of Dick emerged from a stand of trees a few yards from the water's edge, Lily's happiness was complete.

Her three younger sisters, Liza, Emma and Kitty, were running in dizzying circles around Hannah, too excited to keep still. Jacob and Matt, her twelve-year-old brothers, were busy helping her father tie up the boat at the jetty, arguing furiously as their eagerness to escape and savour the delights of the carnival made them clumsy.

'You'll ask him now, right away?' Lily whispered to Dick, and the sight of his death-pale face told its own tale, bringing a giggle bubbling to the surface. 'He won't eat you.' Lily held the certainty of all treasured children that she'd have to commit cold-blooded murder before Arnie Thorpe fell out with his favourite daughter. Dick did not share this somewhat naive viewpoint.

'I wouldn't count on it. I'll ask if I can take you rowing first.' This would give him the chance to test Arnold Thorpe's mood before he put the more important question. Lily pouted, but as her father approached turned it quickly into a smile and gave a furtive nod of agreement, meant only for Dick's eyes. But Arnie, as he was often heard to remark, hadn't been born yesterday. If a lad was standing around like a bit of wet water weed beside his pretty daughter, it wasn't hard to guess the reason. Still, not a bad lad, Dick Rawlins. And if he was a bit lacking in the brains department, Lily had more than enough to spare for the pair of them.

'Now then, Dick.'

'Mr Thorpe.' Dick swallowed the lump of terror that had lodged in his throat and wiped his hands on the seat of his trousers. The man seemed even bigger than usual, if that were possible. 'I wondered, happen, if I could take your Lily – if you had no objections like – out on the lake?'

Arnie considered Dick very solemnly for a moment and then looked at his daughter. 'She's only just got off it. You're not taking her home the minute she's arrived, are you?'

Diverted by this unexpected remark, Dick stood nonplussed, cheeks starting to fire up. It was Lily who saved his embarrassment.

'He means out in one of the hire boats.'

'Oh, from the posh new rowing fleet. A fishing boat not good enough for you, is that it?'

'Stop teasing him, Dad. He's saved up.'

'Aye, one shilling and ninepence,' Dick said, recovering valiantly and puffing out his chest with pride. 'So I can afford to pay for her.'

Arnie's brown eyes crinkled at the corners with suppressed laughter. 'Oh, well then, if thee's a rich sort of chap, happen I should drop all opposition. What do you say, Mother?'

'I say, stop plaguing the poor lad and let everyone enjoy themselves.' Then Hannah started handing out small brown paper packages. 'Here's your dinner sandwiches. I doubt we'll see hide nor hair of you till teatime.'

'Four o'clock,' Arnie said. 'On the dot. Anyone who's late will have to suffer the sharp end of my tongue in consequence.'

No one, it was agreed, would risk that.

There were some initial moans and groans as Hannah insisted the two younger girls remain with her and baby Kitty. Jacob and Matthew beat a hasty retreat before anyone should suggest they do likewise.

'Well, get on with it, lad,' Arnie chivvied poor Dick. 'Or them boats'll all be taken afore you get there.'

Thus galvanised into action, Dick and Lily walked sedately along the shore, a good six inches apart. Only when they turned a corner and believed themselves out of sight did they reach for each other's hands. Arnie and Hannah, peeping at them between the trees, exchanged a smile and did likewise.

Less than ten minutes later Lily was reclining against the red leather cushions in what she considered a suitably ladylike pose. Unlike many of the young men recklessly showing off their inadequate skills to their sweethearts, Dick had handed her in and walked the length of the row boat without putting either of them in any danger of capsizing. Now he had a firm grip on the oars, his well-muscled arms flexing beneath his best summer shirt. Some of the toffs wore smart blazers but since Dick did not own such a garment, he'd tucked a neckcloth in the form of a cravat into his shirt collar to mark the occasion, and his one pair of brown boots were polished to a mirror brightness.

The sun was hot, and Lily adjusted her ancient straw bonnet which she hated, despite the new green ribbon trimmings meant to heighten the colour in her hazel eyes. She wished she owned a parasol like the fashionable young ladies and their mamas. These exemplars of loveliness occupied the long narrow steam-yachts which sailed majestically up and down the lake; the kind of glorious vessel owned by every rich family who occupied a mansion on the shores of Carreckwater, each vying to outdo the other in opulence.

These people had usually made their money from cotton in Lancashire, or shipping in Liverpool, and could afford to display their wealth in the finest teak, pine and oak craft. Far grander than a hired rowing boat, they were sleek and stately with embossed velvet upholstery, walnut panelling, even carpets and white marble wash hand basins. Lily had caught glimpses of these wonderful floating palaces when Arnie had been helping out with some refitting. He did occasional work for Hadley's boat builders, which helped to eke out his low wages from the fishing, and had sneaked her aboard for a peep. The memory of such unbridled elegance had lived in Lily's mind ever since.

One was approaching even now, sun glinting off its brass fittings, the chatter of genteel voices, merry laughter and the chink of china tea cups echoing over the lake as the ladies took tea beneath a pretty blue and cream fringed canopy. There was the papa in his top hat, the engineer in his flat cap, and the women with their wide straw hats skewered with giant pins so they didn't blow off in the wind.

Somewhere far away on the shore a band had struck up a jolly tune and a voice was calling passengers to board *Lucy Ann,* the Public Steamer, smartly decked out with strings of flags, for the next lake cruise to one of the islands or the Fisherman's Inn for luncheon.

'All aboard! Next sailing in ten minutes. Hurry along there, please.'

Lily's lips curved into a contented smile as she watched the jostling crowds in their bright summer dresses, some hurrying to take advantage of this offer, others strolling along the promenade or enjoying the sun on the wooden benches that stood before the

Marina Hotel. She was much happier here with Dick, and the steamer already seemed crammed with people.

Emboldened by his success over the boat trip, Dick was saying, 'So I've decided to talk to your father, man to man like, the minute we finish tea and before the fireworks start.'

'Let's hope you don't spark off any fireworks of your own!' Lily giggled, but for once Dick only looked troubled and paused in his rowing while he considered her quip.

'What d'you reckon he'll say then?'

'Oh, don't look so worried. He's in a good mood. And he likes you, I know he does.'

Lily let the fingers of one hand trail in the water as she offered Dick her most radiant smile, hoping he was watching as she pressed her young body back against the cushions. 'Make sure you tell him we don't want to wait too long. Next summer would be perfect. I'll be nearly seventeen by then. And don't forget to mention our plans. See this frill on my petticoat? I did the crochet trimming myself.' She twitched up her skirt, managing to reveal a good two inches of slender ankle as well as the lace edging.

Dick was enchanted. He had not, in fact, missed a nuance of these flirtatious gestures and wondered how he would manage to resist this adorable girl for as long as a year. The sun had burnished her brown hair to a glowing chestnut, worn loose to her shoulders beneath the straw bonnet, and on her delicious nose was a scattering of freckles brought out by the sun, that he had a desperate urge to kiss. The outline of her long legs and slender hips, curving enticingly beneath the cream print frock she wore, made his necktie feel suddenly too tight about his throat.

He almost forgot they were in a boat and he was rowing it as his gaze wandered downward to the peaks of her young breasts against the thin fabric. The sight of these wondrous delights put him in such turmoil he very nearly lost all control.

'By heck, Lily,' he said, in a small choking voice, 'you're a real cracker. I'll do me best to persuade him, I swear it.'

Thrilled by his ardour she blew him a kiss, puckering her lips into such a delightful pout that Dick could resist her no longer and the recklessness in him surged to the surface. In the next instant he was on his feet, making the boat rock madly as he reached forward to steal one sweet kiss before rowing her out to Hazel Holme and maybe managing to steal a bit more.

Lily squealed with delight at his daring. 'You'll have us over, you daft lump!'

But he only laughed. It was in that moment that he happened to glance up. Something alerted him. A shadow? Someone shouting or dropping a tea cup? But it was too late. By then the steam-launch was upon them. He could almost see his own slack-jawed surprise as he was catapulted into the air, his ears filled with the terrifying sounds of splintering wood as the slender rowing boat was sliced into two neat halves. And endless screams carried up into the true blue sky.

Chapter Two

'All my best china broken! Not a single cup left intact. Completely ruined. It really is most dreadfully upsetting.'

Edward Clermont-Read gazed down upon his wife with appalled disbelief registering on his usually pleasant, moustachioed face. 'Nay, Margot, the loss of a young man's life is worth far more than a few pots.'

'They weren't pots, they were the finest bone china. Please don't use such common expressions.'

Edward stood corrected. 'Even so. That poor young man...'

'We cannot be blamed.' The pitch of Margot's voice rose as she struggled to hold on to her quick-fire temper. 'He was standing in the boat, like the fool he evidently was. I saw him with my own eyes. If he'd been paying proper attention to what he should have been about, he could easily have got out of the way.'

'Now don't get yourself into a lather.'

'I'm not in a lather!'

'Well, I'm sure George will be heartened, if a little surprised, that you champion him so adamantly, my love,' Edward said with some asperity.

'George?'

'He's the best chauffeur-engineer I've ever had, and devastated at having caused such a tragedy.'

Since it had never entered his wife's head to defend the man, a servant after all, who had actually skippered the steam-yacht *Faith* into disaster, Margot opened her mouth to say as much and then snapped it shut again. Edward could be ridiculously egalitarian. He never had managed to shake free from his roots.

She rose with self-conscious elegance from the chaise-longue in the drawing room of Barwick House to which she had repaired after the accident and jerked the bell rope that hung by the marble fireplace. 'I long for a restorative cup of tea. I'm surprised you didn't think to order a pot for me when you saw how dreadfully upset I was.'

'I saw you were concerned for your crockery,' he said tightly. Her eyes glinted beneath narrowed lids.

'Make fun of me if you will, you dreadful man, but that service was especially commissioned and monogrammed with the *Faith's* name. It cost a small fortune, and are you not always telling me to watch the pennies, as if we too were st-silly peasants?' She'd almost said 'still poor'.

Edward gazed upon his wife in helpless despair. How could he go on loving such a selfish, snobbish creature? Yet he did. He adored her. He loved every hair on her beautiful and expensively coiffured head. Every gesture of her plump, ringed hands. Every movement of the exquisitely gowned and, though she might deny it, increasingly matronly figure. She may no longer be the fresh, slender, eager young girl he had married all those years before, but she had nerves of steel, had been as ambitious as he and as anxious to drag them, step by painful step, up the ladder of success. In short, the best helpmeet a man in his position could have had. He'd been damned lucky to have her and he knew it.

Not once had she complained, no matter how hard he'd had to work, however many long hours he'd put in at the warehouse. There'd been times when they'd wondered if his freight business would survive a harsh winter or a particularly bad debtor. Yet not for a moment had she doubted his ability to succeed; never been anything but impeccably dressed and, in his eyes at least, gloriously beautiful.

Building this fine house on the shores of Carreckwater had been the pinnacle of their joint achievement. It proved they'd arrived. They'd often rented a place on the lake, as was fashionable, for the entire summer, but now that they owned their own small mansion, Edward didn't mind in the least commuting to Manchester from Windermere every Monday morning when he could return each Friday to this proof of his success.

17

So if his wife was now hell-bent on being accepted into the highest echelons of society which Carreckwater, and the County, had to offer, could he blame her?

Dear Margot would permit nothing to stand in her way, certainly not a distinct lack of return invitations from the local arbiters of social acceptability.

The *Faith,* now sadly battered, had been the key meant to open many doors, since it admitted them as members of the exclusive Carreckwater Yacht Club. Edward was even considering sponsoring a prize himself at next year's regatta.

He had taken great pleasure in designing the craft and believed it to be a fine vessel, if he said so himself. Not a steamer on the lake possessed a taller mast, even if he rarely ran a sail up it. But then, he knew a thing or two about boats. They'd been his passion for years. He also owned a neat little launch in Liverpool, and was considering buying himself a small sailing yacht on the Isle of Wight one of these days, exactly as Ferguson-Walsh had done.

He'd naturally left Margot to choose the furnishings and fittings: blue leather upholstery, blue and cream silk panelling, and all the tasteful fol-de-rols considered essential for gracious living aboard a yacht.

He watched her now, pacing her drawing room, fretfully folding and unfolding her hands, and knew it wasn't so much the china which bothered her as her injured pride. Margot cared deeply what other folk thought of her. Too much so, in fact. And if the Gowdrys, the Dunstons, and most of all the Mrs Lindens of this world should decide that it was the Clermont-Read's vessel which had breached the unwritten code of the lake and caused the terrible tragedy, all hope of attaining the status Margot craved, not to mention a suitable catch for her wilful daughter, would be gone. Even now he could hear the two of them discussing the effect of the tragedy upon their social lives. 'We really haven't time to sit here endlessly talking round the subject,' Margot was saying. 'We're expected for lunch with the Ferguson -Walshes.'

'Damn it, Maggie, we can't go out to eat ham and fancy salads with the Ferguson-Walshes as if naught has happened.'

'Don't be coarse, Edward. We can't let them down. It wouldn't be polite. And don't call me Maggie.'

'There might have to be an enquiry,' he said, desperate to escape this particular duty. He couldn't abide Clive Ferguson-Walsh, for all he strove to match his wealth. The man thought he owned the town just because he was a J.P. and had been Mayor more times than any other member of the town council.

Margot stared at him. 'Enquiry? What are you talking about?'

'I'm saying there'll no doubt be an enquiry.' Once having got the idea into his head he was reluctant to let it go, although privately Edward doubted anyone would have the nerve to tackle him on the subject when it came to the point. He may not yet have reached Ferguson-Walsh's stature but nevertheless was recognised as a man of substance these days. But if he could use the threat gently to browbeat his wife into obedience for once, he would do so.

'What sort of an enquiry?' Anxiety sharpened her features and she looked, in that moment, all of her forty-three years.

'To see who was at fault. We'll have to stop in. The police may call.'

'Police? In my *house*?'

'In any case, we'd be best to lie low for a day or two. Out of respect.' Edward moved to his humidor and, lifting the lid, took his time selecting, sniffing and rolling a cigar between thumb and forefinger while his wife and daughter struggled to curb disappointment and mounting hysteria as all their plans fell about their heads.

'We have the firework party tonight.'

Edward frowned. 'I don't believe you're listening to a word I say, the pair of you. I reckon I'm still master in my own house, and I say it wouldn't be right.'

Selene got shakily to her feet, and her voice when she found it was oddly shrill. 'But what about the ball tomorrow? I must attend that. I'm perfectly sure that Philip Linden will sign my card for every dance which etiquette permits.'

'But of course you must attend, darling,' Margot reassured her. 'I wouldn't hear of anything different. Nor would your father.' She threw a challenging glare in Edward's direction but he merely clamped his teeth about the butt of his cigar and drew gratefully and deeply upon it. She was indeed the most vexing of wives, yet he couldn't help but admire such single-minded resolve.

But then his darling Margot had worked as hard as himself over the years and deserved her reward. If it meant he had to suffer, and pay for, all manner of balls and picnics, gowns and gee-gaws, for eighteen-year-old Selene to find the right husband, so be it. Only not now, not after this accident. Never let it be said he wasn't a man who knew what was right and proper.

'I know what's right and proper,' he said, needing to air his thoughts. 'It might do us damage.'

And if his only son failed to appreciate the worth of his achievement, or the effort required to keep his fortune intact, choosing instead to idle away his days, then ... No, that was a worry he hadn't the strength to face today. He had enough on his plate with this pantomime. By which he meant the behaviour of Margot and Selene. You couldn't class the death of a fine young man, for all he came from the poorest district in the locality, as anything but a tragedy.

Pictures of the horrific scene had scarcely left his head since it happened and Edward doubted they ever would. Was it only an hour since? It felt like a lifetime. There was no doubt the young man's carelessness was largely responsible for the tragedy. He'd been far more interested in his young companion, which Edward did not wonder at, since she had an unusual and striking beauty about her.

'Edward, I really do not think you appreciate how much effort we have put into preparing for this ball.'

'That girl...' he managed.

'Never mind the dratted girl, I'm talking about our own darling Selene!'

There was a furious rustle of skirts from the window-seat where Selene had slumped, to gaze morosely out upon the ruin of her dreams.

'Did you see the surprise in that girl's eyes as her half of the boat sank?' she said now with peevish satisfaction. 'I swear it was the funniest thing I ever…'

'*Selene!*' Much as he might love his family and make allowances for them, even Edward's patience had its limits. 'Have you no sense of decency, girl? No taste?'

'Don't turn on your daughter simply because some careless young man has scraped our new yacht and damaged not only our best tea service but probably our place in society. We are *ruined.*'

As Margot defiantly lifted her plump chin, she caught Edward's ferocious gaze. She had never been a woman to resort to sal volatile and didn't intend to start now. Even so, there were times when a little assumed weakness could pay dividends, so she lowered her head and sniffed dramatically into her lavender-scented handkerchief. 'I grieve for the young man's poor mother, of course, Edward, but refute the charge that we are to blame for the accident.'

'We must bear some of the responsibility. We were the other party involved.'

'The innocent party.'

'How can you say so, until there's been an enquiry?'

'There'll be no enquiry, you silly man. Who would *dare*? Damn you, Edward, I believe you wish to make me ill.'

There was a long and dreadful silence in which nothing could be heard but the doleful ticking of the grandfather clock. Then the door opened, very slowly, as if whoever entered had waited an age for this very silence to give her leave. Betty Cotley, their youngest and newest maid, crept in with a huge silver tray, crossing the room as if it were a desert and she longed only to drop her load and scurry back to the sanctuary whence she'd emerged.

'Shall I pour, ma'am?'

'No. Leave it. A cup of tea is the last thing I need. That isn't going to solve anything.'

'Very good, ma'am.' But when she was about to take the tray away again, Margot slapped at her hand and the maid did indeed scurry away.

'We'll have to attend the funeral, of course,' Edward said into the yawning silence.

'Indeed we won't.'

'It'd be the proper gesture. In the circumstances.'

Margot, for once, poured her own tea, hoping it would soothe her nerves. 'They'll say it proves our guilt. That we are admitting blame.'

'Balderdash! We must send a wreath and a card. Show due respect to an innocent young man.'

'That innocent young man, as you call him, was alone in that boat with a young woman. Some hussy or other. And no doubt they'd been drinking.' She handed her husband a cup.

Edward sighed. 'It was barely ten o'clock in the morning, Margot. How on earth could you conclude that they had been drinking?'

'Why else would he be cavorting about if he wasn't drunk? He'd have seen us otherwise. It's not as though we are small. The *Faith is* the largest steam yacht on the lake.'

'Apart from Mrs Linden's,' Selene reminded her.

'Very well, yes, apart from hers.' Irritated by her daughter's untimely reminder, Margot's temper flared hot and acid. 'I'll not be told what to do by a clutch of stupid peasants who spend their time drinking and forn—' She stopped, rouged cheeks shot crimson with horror at the crudity she'd been about to utter.

For a second she'd forgotten that she was no longer Maggie Read, only daughter of a humble tailor, but the scented Margot, beloved wife of the once up-and-coming and now splendidly arrived and well-to-do merchant, Edward Clermont. Together the Clermont-Reads made a formidable partnership which neither had regretted making.

Not that she had ever been as poor as that young man and his flighty piece clearly were. They positively reeked of poverty. You could almost smell it in the limpness of the girl's cotton frock, bought no doubt from one of those dreadful hand-me-down rag stalls. Goodness knows when it had last been washed. The poor, in Margot's opinion, should be locked up or have the decency to keep indoors out of sight of decent folk. The girl's straw bonnet looked as if it had been sat upon, and no sign of a parasol. Even from the deck of the *Faith,* Margot could see quite clearly how outrageously the girl had flirted with the young man, lifting her skirt to reveal *bare* ankles, would you believe, above common black boots. No better than she should be, that little madam. Dear me, no. She and Edward may have had their hard times but they had never lacked for taste or propriety.

As for Selene ... 'My sweet darling girl's future is in ruins,' she railed. 'Along with the family good name. Can't you see that, you stupid man?'

Edward sucked on his Havana and remained impassive. 'I see that you think so.'

'I was perfectly sure that Philip Linden would offer for Selene at some point during the festivities. Now it will never come about.'

'I'm sure our clever daughter will find a way around the set-back,' Edward declared, and Margot only just managed to stifle a scream of frustration. Tantrums rarely worked with her vexingly phlegmatic husband.

'I shall take to my bed,' she declared, in the injured tones of a woman who has been driven to the limits of her endurance.

'As you wish, my dear,' Edward quietly remarked. 'Pour me a drop more tea, Selene,' And reached for a piece of his favourite shortbread. Uttering a silent oath beneath her breath, one which Maggie Read had used often but Margot Clermont-Read had long since forsaken, she sailed from the room with the last scrap of her dignity intact and took out her fury on her pillow.

Lily felt her life was over. Despite the fire in the small grate she felt so cold in every limb she was sure she'd never feel warm again. The noise and bustle of her family floated over her head as if they existed in some other time, some other place, and had nothing to do with her at all.

'Come on, the lot of you,' Hannah was saying. 'Sit up to the table. We must eat.' She started laying out knives, a modest wedge of cheese and a dish of home-made pickles. 'Slice that loaf, Liza.'

'Oh, I'm no good at it. I cut it too thick. Why can't our Lily do it?'

'Because I've told you to do it.'

The two boys were squabbling over which of them should have the single slice of fat pork left over from the previous day's supper. Arnie settled the matter by bestowing it upon his own plate.

Seeing that her eldest daughter hadn't moved, Hannah pressed a hand on her shoulder. 'Come and eat, lass. You've sat there for nigh on two days, not eating, not sleeping, doing naught but weep. It'll do you no good.' But Lily turned her head away, not wanting to listen to the usual family banter, and certainly with no desire to eat. A great pain occupied much of her breast and sealed her throat off as tightly as if it were in a vice. Every part of her felt numb and the effort to move, even to feed herself, was well-nigh impossible. It seemed somehow a betrayal to poor Dick, who would never sit at a table and eat again.

'I know it seems like the end of the world,' Hannah murmured. 'But the pain will pass in time.'

Lily did not for a minute believe this, so remained silent. Hannah sent a mute appeal to Arnie, but he was spearing pickles with his knife and paying no attention to his wife. She tried again. 'You have to keep up your strength, lass. You've hardly eaten a thing since – well, since it happened. Everyone's been hurt by this terrible accident. I do understand how you feel, love, but life goes on.'

Lily could hear her mother's words, the sort everyone uttered in such circumstances, and was grateful for her sympathy. But deep inside she knew that she did not understand at all. Nobody could. Hannah hadn't lost the man she loved, the man she had meant to marry. And then her mother committed the ultimate sin.

'I'm sure the Clermont-Reads, toffee-nosed though they may be, are every bit as upset as we are,' she said, in her rough but kindly way. 'And young Dick was always a bit of a gormless lad, bless him.'

Lily was on her feet in a second. 'How can you say that? You weren't even there. You know nothing about it. The Clermont-Reads don't give a toss about folk like us!' Tears spurted, hot and fierce. 'They've ruined my life. If Dick was a bit of a madcap, what of it? He was young and good and kind, with all his life before him. And I loved him. We were going to get *married*.'

At which point Arnie lifted his head long enough to take an

interest in what was going on. 'Married? Don't talk daft, girl. Enough of this. You're too young for such notions, our Lily. I'll tell you when you can get wed.'

'Oh, will you?' she said, defying her father for the first time in her life and feeling a strange satisfaction at the startled expression that registered in his blue eyes. Then she was shocked to see them narrow and harden.

'Aye, I will. And I'll tell you who to, an' all.'

'Listen to your father, Lily,' Hannah soothed. 'I know you liked young Dick well enough. He were a grand lad. But you'll find someone else. You're young and will love again.'

'Can't you understand? I don't *want* anyone else. *I want Dick.* And now he's *gone.*'

Bursting into tears Lily fled noisily upstairs to the tiny room she shared with her younger sisters, the sound of her father's voice echoing angrily after her. 'Come back here this minute, girl. You'll not speak to your mother in such a way.'

But she did not go back. She paid him no heed at all. Nor did she speak to any of her sisters as later that evening they crept into the room and silently got ready for bed. So far as Lily was concerned, her life was empty, happiness vanquished, and she wished at this moment that she too were dead. What did she have to live for without Dick to love her? She'd never be a dressmaker now, never make her fortune and live in a fine house with a loving husband beside her. Probably never marry at all. Instead she must somehow find the strength to attend his funeral and watch them put his beautiful young body into the cold dark earth. She shuddered, and the pain in her chest expanded, filling her entire being with an anguish which robbed her of the very breath of life, her dreams turned to dust like that which filled the old ash pit.

This thought reminded her of their last sweet love-making session on that very roof, of how he'd laid on top of her, pushing his tongue into her mouth, and a new fear started. What if the rumour were true and such kissing did get you a bairn? What would she do then? The tears spurted afresh, hot, unstoppable and horribly silent.

Emma said, 'I brought you a cheese and pickle sandwich, our Lily,' thrusting a much squashed piece of bread in her hand. Two-year-old Kitty dabbed at the tears on her face with a damp flannel and Liza brought her a mug of hot tea from which Lily took two sips then left it to go cold. Only the warmth of her three sisters curled close about her like spoons in a drawer brought her the comfort she craved. And then at last, after two sleepless nights, Lily slept.

The simple interment of young Dick Rawlins took place two days later. Lily stood in the stiff breeze of the churchyard, eyes red but squeezed dry of tears as she watched the bearers carry the plain coffin to its final resting place. The small cemetery was packed with silent women in unrelieved black, turned green from long years of service, and men in hard bowler hats saved specially for this purpose. The rooks cawing in the lattice of branches above almost drowned out the minister's words, and Lily thought the sob wrung from Dick's weeping mother at her side as the first clod of earth rattled on to the cheap wood would live with her for the rest of her days.

There was no wake, no funeral cake, not even the money to hire the horse-drawn parish hearse, nor any exchange of chatter and happy memories. Paying the laying-out woman, gravedigger and minister would put Dick's family into debt for weeks. There was certainly no money to spare for cold meats to feed those who came to grieve with them. Nor was it expected. This tragedy was too keenly felt, the boy too young for anyone to have the heart.

Duty was dispatched as quickly as possible, words of sympathy issued, and then the grieving woman was borne away by her family and friends and everyone hurried back to their own home or workplace, dabbing at their eyes and blowing their noses. For the next few days at least they would exhibit a touch more patience towards their own loved ones.

Lily was the last to leave, lingering by Dick's grave to drop a wild rose she'd gathered specially on to his coffin. It seemed a pathetic offering in comparison with the enormous glass bowl of waxen lilies and white gardenias which had been sent by the Clermont-Reads. Though hers was offered with love, she told herself, not guilt as theirs undoubtedly was.

As if spirited up by this thought, she found herself joined by a dark figure in greatcoat and tall hat.

'Miss Thorpe?'

Lily lifted her chin, gaze hostile, and was surprised to see grey eyes filled with sympathy fixed upon her.

'My card. Should you ever require help or assistance in any small degree, you have only to ask,' Edward Clermont-Read told her.

Anger kept Lily silent, the scent of the graveyard yews becoming in that moment so overpowering she felt suffocated. How dare he? As if he could atone with money for having killed poor Dick.

When Edward had gone, Lily sank to her knees and, finding the card still in her hand, thrust it into her pocket. For a long time she fixed her burning gaze, unseeing, upon Dick's grave, determined not to break down, not to give Edward Clermont-Read the satisfaction of witnessing her weakness. At length the choking sensation in her throat eased sufficiently for her to put her thoughts into words.

'Goodbye, my love. I'll never forget you, Dick, for as long as I live. I swear it.'

'I don't wonder at it. He were a right grand lad.'

The voice made her jump. Lily saw first a pair of patched black boots, from which protruded stick-like legs beneath several layers of indistinguishable clothing. Then the legs bent, and beside her squatted a girl of around her own age. Dark, curly hair hung in straggling rat's tails about a small pixie-like face, from which a pair of moist dark eyes regarded Lily with candid interest. The end of the small pointed nose was red, as if it had been blown a good deal.

'Who'd have thought we'd lose our lovely Dickie?'

Lily stared at the girl. 'Your lovely Dickie? I didn't know Dick had any sisters?'

The girl seemed to think this hilarious. 'Bless you, I ain't his sister. Me an' him was, you know, friends.' She winked, then seeming to realise what she had said, fresh tears spurted and she let out a great howl of anguish. 'Oh, lordy.' And plopping backwards on to the turf by the graveside, the girl brought out a big red handkerchief and buried her face in it. 'I can't believe he's gone,' sobbed the muffled voice. 'How will we manage without him?'

Lily felt a bit odd inside. Who was this girl? What did she have to do with Dick?

'Friends?' she ventured. 'What sort of friends?'

The small face emerged screwed up with pain, then the red handkerchief was used to scrub away the remaining drops of tears. 'Oh, don't you worry none, Lil'. You don't mind me calling you that, do you? Only I feel as if I know you already, him doing naught but talk about his darling Lily. I know you loved him. But I loved him too. As a dear friend, you might say. He were right kind to me, even though he telled me over and over that you were his girl. D'you see?'

Lily wasn't too sure if she did see, or if she were missing some vital piece of information. But the girl had evidently cared for Dick, or Dickie as she affectionately called him, and clearly grieved, as Lily did, over his death. Well, perhaps not quite as she did. The girl had made it plain Lily's own relationship with Dick was special.

She was right. However would Lily manage without him? Then it was she who was weeping, sobbing and hiccuping as if her heart were broken, for surely it was, and the girl was holding her close against a chest even flatter than Lily's own. Patting her shoulder as if she were a young child.

'There, there, don't take on so. I didn't mean to upset you, lass. Dick wouldn't want you making yourself ill, now would he?' When the red handkerchief had been pressed into further service and the tears were all mopped up, the two girls exchanged tremulous smiles.

'I'm Rose. Rose Collins.'

'Hello, Rose. I'm Lily Thorpe. Oh, how silly. You already know that.' And they grinned at each other.

'Well, we've summat in common, anyroad,' Rose said. 'Our mothers must have thought we both looked like flowers.'

28

'I'm no pale and peaceful lily.'

'And I'm no pretty pink rose.' Rose grinned widely. 'But then, we both loved that great daft cluck who's gone to his untimely end. If in different ways of course.' The huge dark eyes, almost too large for her small pointed face, narrowed into slits of anger. 'I don't know about you, love, but I'd like to see someone swing for what happened.'

'Me too,' Lily admitted, realising on the instant it was true. 'Steaming along in their great yacht without a care for other folk.'

'Aye. Bloomin' toffs,' Rose said with feeling. 'Think they own the lake, they do.'

Arms about each other, the two girls began to walk down St Margaret's steps and along the shingle to the old boathouses, sharing the damp handkerchief from time to time. Swept along by the emotion of the day Lily opened up her heart to this sympathetic stranger.

'Dick was the love of my life.'

'Aye, I know.'

'We were going to be married. Happen sooner than we planned, what with me mebbe carrying his bairn.'

Rose stopped in her tracks. 'Nay. Ee, you poor lass. Dickie told me how you was to wed, but he never said aught about that.'

'He didn't even know.'

Intrigued, Rose linked arms with Lily. 'Tell me all about it? Happen I can help. You never know.'

As dusk gathered and a breeze filtered down from the high fells, cooling the deep wooded valley and gently ruffling the slate surface of the lake, Lily poured out the pain of her longings and secret fears about the things her own mother had never fully explained. As Lily talked, she plainly revealed her naivety, and the gaps in her patchy knowledge.

'So when did you last see the curse?' Rose asked, bewildered, as well she might be, by Lily's tale.

'What curse? Curse of what?'

When this was explained, which took a good long time, tied up as it was with more intimate facts of life with which Rose was easily familiar but which held more surprises than Lily was prepared for, she learned the full extent of her ignorance. It turned out she was in no danger at all of having anyone's baby. Not only because she and Dick had never actually done anything likely to bring one about, but because so far as Mother Nature was concerned, Lily's malnourished body was still that of a child. Somehow this upset her even more than an unwanted pregnancy, for all her mother would have scalped her alive had it been true.

Now Lily forgot her vehemence about not wanting to be shackled by children. She forgot how they had dreamed of escape and making a fortune together. For now she would never have Dick's child ever, any more than next summer she would be his bride? The Clermont-Reads had denied her all of that.

Her darling Dick was dead and gone, and she'd never see him again.

It was in that moment that Lily made her pledge. One day, no matter what the sacrifice, she would take her revenge. She took Edward's card from her pocket and ground it into the mud under her heel.

Chapter Three

1911

Over the next two years Lily and Rose became almost inseparable. Lily never enquired into the true nature of Rose's relationship with Dick, nor did Rose ever fully explain it. They were content to enjoy their burgeoning friendship and bring what comfort they could to each other.

Rose had recently come to live on Fossburn Street, quite close to the churchyard where the two girls had met. And if, on the occasions when Lily visited, there were more comings and goings than seemed quite normal for a modest cottage, she made no comment upon the matter. None of the many men who tramped up the narrow wooden stairs in their heavy boots made any trouble or stayed very long.

Rose's mother Nan, rake-thin and little more than a girl herself, had a pretty face beneath a thatch of none-too-clean red hair, soulful eyes and a big laugh.

After her latest visitor had gone she would come downstairs in a silk dressing-gown, as if she were a music hall artiste, and sit and roll her own cigarettes, a habit which Lily considered dreadfully daring and modern. Then she'd prop her slippered feet on the brass fender and blow smoke rings while she passed on the juiciest bits of gossip she had picked up, and describe her men friends with such hilarious accuracy it made the two girls weep with laughter.

Nan was more than generous. Lily did not fail to notice that unlike her own family, who survived mainly on thin soup and bread when the fish weren't running, Rose and her mother ate well.

Lily was sick of fish. Even on those rare occasions when the catch was a good one, the best part of it – the char – was sold to Agnes Lang, who potted it in fancy little pots and packed them off to London to be enjoyed by the well-to-do. The Thorpe family lived mainly on eels, small perch and brown trout.

'Here, lovey, go and buy three pennyworth of meat and potato pie from Mrs Edgar's Cook Shop,' Nan would say. And off the girls would run to the corner shop where a fat old lady with a toothless grin stood sentry over a huge pot from which she doled out platefuls of the best steaming hot meat and potato pie Lily had ever tasted: the pastry golden and crisp, the meat succulent and tender. It made Lily's mouth water just to stand there and breathe in the appetising aroma. Or they would buy Cumberland sausages, fat and spicy and dripping with hot fat.

'We'll take a drop of stout to wash it all down,' Nan would say, sending Rose running next to the Cobbles Inn with a jug.

Nor did she worry about tidying up the mess when the delicious meal was over.

'We'll see to it tomorrow,' was her favourite phrase. Oh, so unlike my mam, Lily thought, only too aware that Hannah could never sit still for a minute if there was a cup to be washed or a hearth swept.

Arnie was fond of telling his wife: 'If the good Lord himself were to come calling you'd tell him to wipe his feet first.'

'He wouldn't need to be told,' Hannah would say, at least able to laugh at herself. 'He'd have more sense than to come in with dirty boots on, unlike some chaps I could mention.'

But for all her mother's cheerful disposition and Arnie's good heart, Lily told her parents little of her new friend's home life. Hannah would not have approved of the goings on in Fossburn Street. Rose was polite and quiet on her frequent visits to the house in Carter Street, for all she was an odd little creature, and her innately cheerful nature seemed to be good for Lily, so she was accepted at face value, with no enquiries made into her background – never a wise thing to do in this district, in any case.

Hannah made over a warm coat for Rose when winter came. She'd meant it for Lily, but the other girl didn't seem to possess such a garment. Arnie helped her to find a job working on the greengrocery stall at The Cobbles market every Wednesday and Friday. Rose could hardly believe her good fortune.

'By heck, a proper job with money in me pocket every week, and a good coat to keep the cold out. I'm right glad I met you, Lily. And your lovely family.'

'I'm glad too,' she said.

'I don't want to end up like my mam, you know.'

'Neither do I.' And the two girls smiled at each other in perfect understanding.

'It's changed my life it has, to have a friend like you.'

It seemed to Lily that the day Dick drowned her whole world too had changed, but unlike Rose's, not for the better. Their friendship was the only thing which had kept her sane. Not only had she lost her dearest love, but she felt the chains of The Cobbles weigh heavy upon her.

The subject of her apprenticeship to a Bowness dressmaker had only once been broached.

'You'll have to ask your father,' Hannah had said, looking sad and troubled when Lily had ventured to make her request. It had seemed so much harder to ask without Dick beside her for support.

Arnie's response had been entirely predictable. 'Your mother needs you on the fish stall. How would she manage without you?'

'Our Liza could help more.'

'She's too young, nobbut ten, and can't add up for toffee. Anyroad, what good would dressmaking do you? Mixing with your betters. No point in getting above theeself, young lady. I hope I'm a man who knows his place.' Arnie sat on his stool in the back yard and applied his full attention to mending his nets, the subject closed so far as he was concerned.

'Don't you want me to better meself?' Lily demanded.

'How would you do that, pray? Thee's good enough as you are. There's naught to be ashamed of in being poor. We do an honest day's work for an honest day's pay and don't hanker after aught we can't have.'

'Yes, but...'

'Lily!' He flung down the half-mended net in exasperation. 'Don't you think I've troubles enough, without listening to yours? The Board of Conservators are hell-bent on putting an end to commercial fishing in this lake. They say it's been over-fished for years and stocks are running out, and it's true it don't support us like it used to. I have to work at boat building, odd jobs, aught I can lay me hand to.'

'All the more reason for me to get out of anything to do with fish,' Lily stubbornly persisted. She could hear Mrs Adams next door, shouting at her two sons. She'd be out in a minute to complain to Arnie about how wicked and lazy they were. The yard door creaked open and Bessie Johnson staggered in with a sack of wood she'd collected.

'Evening, Arnie.'

'Evening, Bessie. Winter here already, is it? And here's me thinking it were nobbut summer.'

'Found a tree down, out in the woods. Waste not, want not, eh? I like a li'le fire of an evening.' The old woman shot Lily a piercing glance. 'You all right, lass?'

'Yes, thanks. I'm fine.'

Oh, but she wasn't fine. She wasn't fine at all. How Lily ached for a bit of privacy. A place where a person could have a conversation without being under the scrutiny of every prying busybody. Where ceilings didn't drip with damp and you didn't spend half your time scrubbing the stench of urine from the yard flags.

'Well then, if you're fine, you can help me with this lot,' Bessie told her.

By the time Lily had helped the old woman stow her load of rotting wood in the stinking little cubby hole under her stairs, the Adams boys were rolling around the yard engaged in a bout of fisticuffs which it took their father's and Arnie's combined strength to bring to an end before they killed each other. Lily's hatred for The Cobbles was magnified to enormous proportions. She must get out, she really must. She was in danger of losing all her dreams simply because she'd lost Dick.

Arnie calmly returned to work on his nets, and Lily to her argument.

'I'd bring good money into the house if I had a trade at me

fingertips.' But somehow the fight had gone out of her. She felt so utterly powerless, so overwhelmed by her situation, that she knew it to be useless.

'Aye, in about seven years happen, if we survived that long.'

'Why won't you help me to escape?'

Arnie's mouth trembled as he looked at his wilful daughter, and his pale blue eyes held such an aching sadness that it pierced Lily to the heart. 'Don't you think that if I had the money to buy an apprenticeship, or whatever else you'd set your heart on, I'd do it? But I haven't the money, Lily, and never will have. It's a struggle to get by each day and put enough food in our mouths. So what's the point in wishing for what thee can't have? Be happy with what tha's got. That way you don't go mad.'

Lily acknowledged defeat. There was nothing to be done. No escape. Only she couldn't be happy with what she'd got, that was the trouble. She wanted so much more.

Arnie took his troubles to the pub. Whilst he respected his wife's abstemious nature, he didn't share it. Being Church of England himself, he'd never signed the Pledge, and didn't intend to start now. He and Hannah had come to an agreement early on in their married life, to live and let live. He never went home rolling drunk, not like some he could mention, so didn't feel guilty. Not that he had the money to get drunk even if he had the inclination. He'd certainly little enough tonight, but he liked coming to The Cobbles Inn. There was a warm, friendly fug about the place, for all the filthy straw beneath his feet and dubious cleanliness of the tankards. He fastidiously brought his own because of it, though he was ready enough to join in any bit of fun that went on here: cock fight or bare-knuckle contest, a bit of crack with his mates. And he wasn't averse to betting a bob or two each way, if he had any to spare. A little matter he failed to mention to his wife.

'Aught on tonight, Jim?' he asked the landlord, who jerked his head in the direction of the back room by way of reply.

'I'll happen look in later.' Arnie ordered his usual half of bitter and, leaning against the bar, sank into unaccustomed gloom.

He'd give anything to make Lily happy. She *deserved* to be. Such a bonny lass, and so young to suffer grief. He felt so fiercely protective of her, the pain was almost impossible to bear at times. Why didn't she see that? He'd buy her the world if he could afford it. Didn't she realise that if he could see any way to get her out of The Cobbles, he would? Drat the place!

'Should have been razed to the ground years ago,' he growled out loud.

A deep chuckle came in response to this fervent declaration. 'I don't know, the beer's not that bad.'

The man at his elbow, for all he seemed little more than a boy, had the sort of physique Arnie would not have cared to tackle alone on a dark night. He had thick eyebrows that almost met in the middle, dark hair, and a swarthy complexion which hadn't recently seen a razor. Dressed in a navy pullover, he had the air and bearing of a fisherman, but Arnie knew them all, there being so few left, and this man wasn't one of them. But he seemed friendly enough, and the hand grasping the handle of his jug looked as if it had seen a fair day's work.

'I wasn't talking about the beer. It was the whole place I meant – The Cobbles,' Arnie explained.

'Ah, I see your point.'

'No drains, gutters broken, only water from a pump in a shared yard, and walls that thin you can hear 'em stir their tea next door. Been here hundreds of years it has, and should be burned to the ground.'

'Won't do it though, the landlords, will they? Wealth is power, and mustn't be weakened by consideration for those who labour. But times are changing. The bosses won't always have it their own way. Some of us are fighting back.'

'How do you mean?'

'Take me, for instance. I've got meself a good job working on the Public Steamer. It's only taking tickets but then I'm young yet, just twenty-one. I've plenty of time, and you have to start somewhere, eh? I mean to go places.'

Arnie laughed. 'Working for the steamer company, the only place thee'll go is round the lake!'

'You can mock but I've served my time on bigger ships and I've a bit put by. I'm on my way, I tell you.' He pointed a finger at the grimy ceiling. 'I have plans.'

Arnie looked more closely at the young man, at the set of his jaw and the determination in his blue eyes. 'Aye, happen you will an' all.' There was a tinge of new respect in his voice. 'You're not from round these parts then? I don't seem to recollect...'

'Monroe. Nathan Monroe. I've been away for a good while. But, aye, I was born in the middle of this rat's nest of streets, the smell of refuse on me doorstep battling with the sweet scents from the fells above, so I understand how you feel. It's criminal this place wasn't flattened years ago. With the elegant new villas built all along The Parade, you'd think they'd want to clean up these poorer areas, wouldn't you? But no, profit is all. The landlords don't give a damn whether The Cobbles is a good place to live or not.'

'Aye, you're right there.' Arnie sighed. Landlords seemed to be the source of all his problems. Only last week his had come knocking at the door yet again in the shape of Percy Wright, the ferret-faced and persistent agent. Lily might resent the fact that Arnie had refused to complain to the Clermont-Reads over young Dick's tragic accident, but how could he? It was to them he owed rent. He took a swallow of his beer, depression settling still further.

The young man was still talking. 'All they care about is making Carreckwater comfortable for themselves.'

Arnie looked doleful. 'And now we've got steamers, posh houses all round the lake, a town band, women on bicycles for God's sake! Even electric lamps in our streets that frighten our old folk who fear they'll leak and kill 'em in their beds.'

'Ah, but that's all for the good of the tourists, Arnie,' the young man said, as if they were old friends. 'They'll provide the profits which could make us all rich, if we play our cards right.'

'Well, the fishing's going nowhere, is it?' He gave a harsh little laugh, and recklessly ordered a second half so he could sink his troubles in his beer. He would have liked to buy the pleasant young man one too, but wasn't sure his pocket could run to it.

'How's Lily?'

The abrupt change of direction took him by surprise and he spluttered into his drink. 'Who?'

'Lily. She is your daughter, isn't she?'

Arnie wiped the froth from his chin and peered at the man through narrowed eyes. 'How do you know our Lily? Come to that, how did you know my name?'

Monroe laughed. 'Went to the same Dame School, didn't we? Mrs Jepson, I'll never forget her. She used to point at a big map on the wall with a long stick, and knock us on the head with it if we talked.' He chuckled. 'Mine was pretty sore by the time I left. Right old slave driver she was. So, how is Lily? I remember her as small and skinny with two long brown plaits.'

'Aye, that were her all right.' Arnie grunted, and wiped away a sentimental tear at the recollection of his schoolgirl daughter. 'She's had a bit of a disappointment. Getting over it now like, but slow.'

Arnie told him all about his lovely daughter and her problems, flattered by the young man's sympathetic attention.

Then, having talked himself out, and the beer having mellowed his mood, he slapped Nathan on the back. 'Come on, Monroe. We've chewed on enough problems for one night. I'll give you a game of dominoes. See if you can beat me.'

'Or take good money off someone else?'

Arnie grinned. 'Aye, that too, if thee likes.'

At three o'clock each afternoon, Selene Clermont-Read took a drive out in her gig. Particularly on a day filled with sunshine, as this one was. She rarely had a specific destination in mind, the object being primarily to show off her expensive equipage, painted a tasteful burgundy, and of course her own beauty. She took great care always to choose a stylish gown which would enhance to perfection the smooth slope of her shoulders, the fullness of her fine bosom and the delicacy of her features. She changed at least three times a day as it was essential to wear the most suitable gown for any occasion.

Equally important was the choice of hat, which should attract attention without appearing too ostentatious.

Today she had chosen one of plaited straw, suitably wide-brimmed and trimmed with artificial silk roses in pink, green and lemon to match her gown of ribbed lemon silk. The dress itself was slim-fitting, much decked about with drapes, bobble trim, and dozens of non-functional buttons. The more intricate the style and complicated the cut, the more expensive the ensemble – a vital consideration when wishing to impress.

Selene enjoyed driving the gig herself since she felt a woman alone attracted far more masculine interest. Besides which, she never doubted her own skill at anything to which she'd set her mind. Since anyone who was anyone would also be driving about Carreckwater at this time, it seemed perfect sense to be seen along with them.

On this particular day, the sky pearl-bright with sunshine, she drew up outside her favourite mantle-maker's and waited for the lady of the establishment to come out, after which she might be persuaded to step down from her carriage and take a cup of China tea in the small parlour set aside for this purpose, while they discussed the line and fabric of her next ball gown.

It was while Selene was waiting, with a certain degree of impatience, that her attention was caught by a bustle all around her.

Crowds were beginning to gather, chattering excitedly, running downhill in the direction of the lake. For a moment Selene almost decided to ignore what was evidently peasant hysteria when she heard a sound like an angry insect, and recollection of a half-overheard breakfast argument between her mother and brother returned. Margot had wished her son Bertie to stay within doors that afternoon since guests were expected, and he had been even more determined to go out. Something to do with a new invention.

A voice at her side asked, 'Would you care to step inside, Miss Clermont-Read?'

Selene paid it no heed. The excitement of the hurrying crowd was irresistible and, briskly urging her mare into a trot, she left the dressmaker standing open-mouthed in front of her shop.

Moments later Selene had joined the crowds by the lake, her gaze as riveted as theirs upon the strange machine humming high in the sky.

It comprised two broad wings held together by a fragile network of bamboo poles. Making erratic progress over the lake it emitted the most peculiar noises. Selene scrambled down from the gig and tossed the reins to an urchin, sternly bidding him to hold the horse which he eagerly agreed to do. She hurried away, very nearly breaking into an unladylike trot.

A large crowd had gathered at the end of the pier. Two boy anglers stood open-mouthed, rods forgotten in their hands. A boatman scratched his head in bemusement and one woman was actually kneeling and praying in a gabbling frightened voice while the crowd jostled each other for a better view, putting several people in danger of being tipped into the lake.

Selene came to a halt beside two girls a year or two younger than herself. They were dressed in striped cotton blouses and plain blue serge skirts, clearly the sort of young women who should be at their work some place rather than gallivanting about the pier with their heads turned skyward. Though, admittedly, so was everyone else's.

'God love us, what is it?' said one.

'I don't know but it looks as if it might be made from matchwood,' remarked the other.

There was something vaguely familiar about one of the girls but Selene did not have time at this juncture to study her. She was far too alarmed by what was happening above. Could it be her brother, up there in the waterplane? Was that what the argument this morning had been about? He was mad enough. And if it were, poor Mama would have a heart attack for sure. Margot had great plans for her darling Bertie. Seeing him ending up head first in the depths of Carreckwater wasn't among them.

The small plane's engine seemed to stutter and cough, and a gasp of horror erupted from the watching crowd as it dropped several feet. Then the engine kicked into life and the little plane swooped up again on a general expulsion of deeply held breaths. Selene was appalled to find she was actually perspiring. How dare he do this to her? How dare he risk his life for a moment's excitement. What was he thinking of?

'It's called the *Water Hen*. Rotary engine's a five-cylinder Gnome and the front elevator rod comes direct to the joystick.'

The young man's voice, filled as it was with cheerful self-confidence, was only too familiar and Selene pressed a hand against the thumping of her heart, closing her eyes in a silent prayer of thanks.

'*Bertie!*' She turned upon him, ready to unleash her fury for his frightening her half to death. It was then that she saw he was not speaking to her at all, but to the two girls she had noticed earlier.

'No chassis,' he was explaining with many gesticulations of his finely shaped hands. 'No protection against the weather. Takes off from the surface of the lake, don't you know, and uses castor oil. Damned clever, eh?'

'You seem to know a good deal about it,' said the girl with the laughing eyes, and as she turned her face up to his, pale-skinned for all she wore no bonnet on the thick brown hair piled on top of her small neat head, Selene knew on the instant who the girl was and where she had seen her before. She snapped shut her parasol and was beside Bertie in a second.

With one mittened hand Selene angrily tapped the ferule of her parasol upon the wooden boards of the pier. 'If this plane isn't about to take a nose dive into the lake, and you along with it in a daring bid to get your name in the *Chronicle,* you may drive me home this instant, Bertie.'

'Selene! I didn't see you there. Wasn't it wonderful? Did you see the take-off?'

'No, I'm glad to say I didn't.' Wishing to put herself above such childish pleasures. 'It was not wonderful in the least to be scared half to death. The fear of believing it was you up there in that ridiculous machine has quite jarred my nerves and left me utterly exhausted.'

Brown eyes shone with sudden excitement as he laughed. 'Me? Fly in the waterplane? What an idea! Wouldn't I love to have the chance, though?' He cupped a hand over his eyes to watch as the tiny machine swooped and shivered over the shimmering lake, making a bumpy landing that had the crowd following its every movement with 'oohs' and 'ahs' as it slid from side to side and finally sank to a halt in the water. 'He did it! Down safe. I might ask the owner, a Captain Wakefield, if he'll let me go up with the pilot next time.'

'Don't you dare!' Selene's fist itched to knock some sense into his handsome young head, but with some difficulty she managed to restrain herself. It didn't do to lose control before the lower classes.

Catching the direction of her disapproving gaze and laughing at it, Bertie said, 'I haven't introduced you, have I? This is Rose and Lily, would you believe?' He laughed, as if it were the funniest joke in the world. Selene allowed her gaze to flicker momentarily over the two girls, thereby dismissing them, and her upper lip curled in displeasure.

'I believe I have run across Miss Lily Thorpe before,' she said, with acid satisfaction at her pun.

'Have you, by jove?' Bertie was delighted. 'When was that?'

Lily was frowning, not making the connection quite so quickly as Selene might have expected, or even hoped. No one, in Selene's opinion, should ever forget her, once having gazed upon her beauty. But Lily Thorpe clearly had, or at least was pretending not to remember. 'I'm not quite sure...'

'This is my sister, don't you know? Selene Clermont-Read.' Selene watched as the girl's eyes widened as realisation dawned, and then darted from one to the other of them as if she couldn't quite believe it.

I see. I-I hadn't realised.'

Selene sniffed in disbelief and abruptly turned her back upon the girl, addressing her brother directly. 'My carriage is on the promenade, Bertie, and I haven't all day. Pray hurry. Mama will be waiting tea, and the Ferguson-Walshes are expected, if you recall.' And gathering up the ankle-skimming hem of her gown, she spun upon her heel and swept away without a backward glance or further explanation, her modish button boots tapping on the wooden boards.

It was only when she had settled herself comfortably back into the gig, having given the urchin a halfpenny for his trouble when he had hoped for a sixpence, that Selene realised Bertie had not, after all, hurried along beside her. The foolish boy still seemed to be deep in conversation with those two trollops.

She slapped her whip against the leather seat in a furious outburst, startling the temperamental mare with the sound so that she had to force herself to sit still or the silly creature would bolt. Selene battened down her impatience as best she might while her gaze burned up the distance between herself and the trio on the pier.

It was the very same girl, no doubt about it. The hussy who had caused all the trouble two years ago and robbed Selene of the chance of catching Philip Linden.

Mama had point-blank refused to go to the young man's funeral, of course, but Papa had kept his word and insisted it would be unseemly for them to attend the Carnival ball. So it had been Lucy Rigg, not herself, who had danced with Philip. And Lucy it was who had become his wife, leaving Selene still unwed at twenty since Carreckwater was not exactly bursting with suitably rich young men. The fault for that tragedy lay here, with this slut who was even now flirting outrageously with her impossible brother!

What was she saying to him? How Selene wished she'd stayed so that she could hear what it was they talked of with such earnestness. Oh, why hadn't she dragged the stupid boy away, forced him to escort her personally, instead of flouncing off in a fit of pique simply because the girl had forgotten her? Well, she couldn't go back now. It would be too demeaning.

She was on the point of driving away in a flurry of temper when she saw the trio turn and begin to walk towards her carriage. What was Bertie thinking of? Why didn't he tell them to go away?

Then one of the girls – Rose, was it? A gnomelike creature with huge eyes and straggly hair – reached up and kissed his cheek, which seemed to delight the stupid boy. Then, turning, she skipped away in a most common manner. Thank goodness! Selene thought. Now if only the dreadful Lily Thorpe would do the same. But she did not. Worse, she hooked her hand in a proprietorial fashion around Bertie's arm and walked right along beside him, with the kind of rapt interested expression upon her lively face as she gazed up at him that was so often recommended in the *Woman At Home* magazine.

Mama is perfectly correct, Selene told herself, almost tearful with suppressed rage. The creature is common beyond belief. Without doubt a harlot.

Seconds later, to her very real horror, Bertie was actually handing Lily into the gig.

'You don't mind squeezing up, do you, Selene? I've asked Lily to come to tea.'

Chapter Four

Lily couldn't believe her good fortune. Any other day of the week would have found her with her sleeves rolled up, hands all red and swollen and stinking of fish. Today, because of the excitement over the flight of the *Water Hen,* she had been permitted a half-day holiday. As a result she had met Bertie Clermont-Read.

She knew exactly what she meant to do. The idea had come to her on the instant Rose had left them, and he'd told her how he dreaded the prospect of afternoon tea with Dora Ferguson-Walsh, a dull, plump girl whose charms were located largely in her father's pocket book.

'How fortunate to enjoy such treats as cucumber sandwiches and cream sponge,' Lily had gently chided, though making sure her lips curved into an enticing smile. 'You wouldn't find them in our house.'

He grinned at her, his boyish good looks making him far more approachable than the rest of his family. Frizzy, slightly sandy hair framed a smooth, untroubled forehead, rather like a halo about his head – though not for one moment did Lily take him for the angel a fond mama might wish him to be. The glint in his brown eyes told quite the opposite tale.

'Do you enjoy cream cakes?'

'Adore them.' Lily had never tasted such a delicacy in her life.

'Well, I dare say I should enjoy them too, if Dora were as jolly as you. She is so worthy, always busy with her Good Works. All she ever talks about is the pleasure she finds in serving others, and how a happy marriage is a man's salvation, if not that of the whole nation.'

'Poor Dora.' She slanted a glance up at him through her lashes. 'She'd make you a good wife, of course. Which I'm sure must be a serious consideration for any young chap.'

Bertie rolled his eyes in good-humoured disbelief. 'So Mama constantly reminds me. For my part, I'd rather have a pal for a wife. Someone who knows how to enjoy life, and have a good time.'

Lily had put back her head and laughed, aware as she did so how his gaze lingered upon her pink mouth, taking in the white evenness of her teeth, and down over her throat to the rise and fall of her breasts, now satisfyingly full.

'I say, why don't you come too?' he'd said, a slight breathlessness in his voice. 'We could have ripping fun. And it would show dear Mama that I won't be bossed about or dragooned into early matrimony.'

'Does she boss you about?' Inside, Lily felt a surge of jubilation. The invitation was even more than she had hoped for. She only had to accept and he would take her, one of the faceless poor, right inside his splendid home, to confront the very people who had so heartlessly ruined her life.

'Of course. Adore the old thing, but once she gets a grip on a chap it's hard to shake her off.' He beamed at Lily. 'Do say you'll come. What a lark!'

She giggled. 'Your mother wouldn't let me through the door. I'd never feature on her list of suitable candidates.'

This of course had the desired effect of appealing to his sense of chivalry, and Bertie puffed up his chest in indignation. 'Just let her try and stop you! A chap has some rights, despite all this suffrage business which tries to make us seem like worms.'

Lily laughed, partly to show she would never treat a man thus, but also because she knew little about suffrage in any case. Besides which, he really was quite amusing. Lily decided she might even come to like him, and for an instant suffered a twinge of conscience over the plan rapidly forming in her head even as she smiled and cast teasing glances to enrapture him. She could change her mind, even now. Did she have the courage to sit in Margot Clermont-Read's parlour at Barwick House and tell her exactly what she thought of her? Did she want to remember the loss of her beloved?

Lily and Dick should have been married by now, living happily together as man and wife, he the best carpenter in the district and she a dressmaker, well on the way to making their fortune. Lily's heart swelled with remembered pain. Making an extra effort, she put the memories aside, brightened her smile and politely accepted Bertie's invitation.

If Lily sensed the freezing reception emanating from Selene, she made no comment upon it.

Bertie told Lily that tea was always taken in the little parlour. But as the maid showed them in, 'little' was not the word which sprang immediately to mind. Hung with dark landscape paintings, each one the size of a small door, on its pale blue walls, the entire room seemed filled with sofas, chairs and assorted tables, not to mention people. Even Lily in her ignorance could recognise the carpet as oriental, and so thick she dared hardly walk upon it.

'You could fit the whole of our li'le cottage in here,' she whispered in Bertie's ear, making him laugh. She struggled to curb a sudden desire to tidy her hair, smooth her skirts then turn tail and run.

Selene swept past, chin high, and headed straight for two inoffensive-looking young men who were balancing cups, saucers and plates as they perched on spindly chairs. At sight of her, they almost overturned the chairs in their haste to be the chosen one, each vying to pour her a cup of tea and fetch an almond slice. Lily felt a bubble of laughter surge recklessly within her as Selene sank upon a chair with several tortured sighs and a hand pressed dramatically to her brow. The young woman clearly enjoyed melodrama.

'Bertie darling, you're late. Come here and kiss me at once, you naughty boy.' A woman of statuesque proportions seated in a crimson brocade chair by the marble fireplace lifted her hand in regal fashion. Her round face and rather sandy, fashionably frizzed hair marked her as Bertie's mother, even if he hadn't surprised Lily by doing exactly as he was bid. 'Sorry, old thing. Went to see the *Water Hen*. Gripping stuff.'

Margot was not, for once, listening to her son's excuses. Her small dark eyes had fastened upon Lily, lips already thinning with disapproval that such a dishevelled creature should be allowed to enter her drawing room uninvited. 'And who do we have here?'

'This is Lily Thorpe. She was given an unexpected half-day holiday because of the *Water Hen* and adores cream cakes, so I invited her for tea, as a treat.'

The silence which followed this artless introduction was awesome. Anyone with less stamina or reason to stay put than Lily might very well have chosen this moment to offer their excuses and depart. She stepped forward, tilting her chin, and smiled at Margot.

'Surely you remember me, Mrs Clermont-Read? We have met once before. Though why should you remember? I'm sure it seemed of no consequence to you at the time.'

Had anyone dared to gasp, they would certainly have done so at such audacity. Selene fanned herself furiously. Margot silently seethed. Bertie, oblivious to the freezing atmosphere, pushed forward a chair.

'Make yourself comfortable, Lily, and I'll fetch you the biggest cream cake I can find. Milk or lemon in your tea?'

If she had derived any pleasure from this encounter, her enjoyment was soon about to fade. Margot, after all, was in her own drawing room. This was her home, these were her friends, and she was certainly not going to be put down by some young upstart from The Cobbles.

She made no attempt to introduce the girl to her other guests: Mrs and Miss Ferguson-Walsh, Felicia Morton-Cryer and her devoted mama, and the two young Heddington boys. Instead, she turned slightly in her chair so that Lily was not in view, was in fact slightly behind her, excluded from the ensuing conversation.

This ranged from the Royal Family, especially dear Mary of Teck, to the latest exploits of Lord Lonsdale, known as the Yellow Earl. Then moved on to the likelihood of war.

Margot declared her complete opposition to the very idea. 'I cannot abide this alarmist view that our sitting rooms are about to be invaded by Russians or Germans. The country wastes near half our taxes on arming us to the teeth, yet who would dare start a war on England's fair lawns?'

'I believe they'd hope to fight it elsewhere, Mama. It might be quite a lark. We'd soon see them off.'

'War is not a football match, Bertie,' she snapped. Then more sweetly to her guests, 'As my dear Edward often says, there is nothing to be gained by scaring peaceable folk in their beds. He is perfectly certain, and I agree, that there will be no war.' She sipped delicately at her China tea, satisfied that no one, not even the British Government, would dare to disagree. An unhappy silence fell as everyone considered the consequences if she were wrong.

'But I suppose we must be prepared,' Edith Ferguson-Walsh ventured. 'What if Armageddon should truly come?'

Lily thought the poor woman might faint clean away, so venomous was her hostess's answering glare. 'What do you know of the matter, Edith?'

'Why nothing, nothing at all,' the poor lady hastily demurred, wishing she'd never opened her mouth, but being the kind of nervous individual who must always fill a vacuum with words, however ill conceived.

'Are you saying that I, as a fond mama, should prepare to send my only son to the trenches?'

'Indeed no, Margot.'

'But you claim to be an expert on military matters. Is that the way of it?'

Lily thought the hapless woman might burst into tears.

'Dear me, no. Taking care of my darling Clive, and making sure Dora's future is settled, takes up all of my time. I'm sure I wouldn't dream…' she wavered, fading into breathless silence, and shot a meaningful glance in Bertie's direction. 'Indeed. Marriage, dear Margot, is as you know my whole world.'

'An admirable sentiment,' Felicia's mama fervently remarked, silently urging her own daughter to move closer to Bertie, who was unfortunately too busy gossiping with one of the Heddington twins to notice.

'Of course,' Margot put in, 'no one should embark upon such a serious venture unless they have the funds to do so. To my mind marriage should be the sole prerogative of the better classes who know best how to conduct themselves.'

Try as she might, Lily could not let this pass. 'Are you saying that the poor should be made to live without the blessing of marriage?'

Margot addressed her reply to the plaster frieze above her mantelpiece. 'I believe it better for all concerned if the poor remain single.'

'To provide an army of servants for the upper classes, I suppose?'

'The dearth of good servants is a severe problem, it is true. Too many, I am forced to say, do not appreciate how fortunate they are to be taken into a good Christian home.'

'Meaning we – the poor – have no feelings?' Lily felt herself grow hot with agitation, even more so when Selene gave a chirrup of laughter.

'For all you've suffered a grievous loss, Lily Thorpe, it hasn't taken you long to begin enjoying life again, now has it?'

Lily stared at her. 'It's taken two years,' she protested. A lifetime wouldn't be long enough. But she didn't say as much. She had her pride.

'What has taken two years?' Bertie asked, puzzled. 'What on earth are you all talking about?'

'Do be quiet, Bertie. You weren't there.'

'Oh, you mean the accident? That's ancient history.'

'Certainly the less said about it, the better,' was Margot's tart reply, and she concentrated on pouring fresh tea, handing out delicacies from the many-tiered cake stand.

Lily had never seen so much food in all her life. Cucumber sandwiches, as expected. Thinly sliced bread and butter with tiny dishes of strawberry jam. Scones and almond fingers, and various pastries filled with cream, which disappeared in one bite and simply melted in the mouth.

'What do you think of our cream cakes, Miss Thorpe, since Bertie avows you an expert on the subject?'

To her very great annoyance, Lily felt her cheeks fire up, tried to swallow a piece of flaky pastry which caught in her throat, and began to cough.

'Dear me. Pray use your napkin, Miss Thorpe, if you are about to spit and splutter. We never use a spittoon in this house.'

Bertie stepped eagerly forward. 'Leave her be, Mama. Gone the wrong way, has it? Shall I get you some water, Lily?'

'No, no. I'm all right.'

'You live in The Cobbles, if I recall correctly?' Margot persisted.

'Yes.' Furious with herself, Lily would have given anything to say otherwise.

'Yet you are accustomed to eating such treats every day? You surprise me. I wouldn't have thought they went with cabbage soup.'

Lily flinched, wishing in that instant she had never ventured into this dreadful woman's fancy drawing room. But however much she might long to say that yes, her mother made cream fancies every day and they always ate at least three each for tea, she couldn't – nay, *wouldn't* – pretend to be what she wasn't. That would be denying her heritage. Yet not for the world did she wish to admit the fact that this was the first time she'd ever tasted one in her life. Before she'd found some way around her dilemma, Bertie, bless his heart, spoke up for her.

'Stop your bullying, old thing. I told you I'd brought Lily here for a treat. Now let her enjoy her tea in peace.'

Margot smiled with the satisfaction of a woman who knows she has found her mark. 'Of course. And she must indeed enjoy it. We have so much it really doesn't signify. Half of it will be thrown away as it is. When the servants have had their pick, that is.' Her laughter trilled out and the assembled company tried a few stiff smiles. Then, swivelling in her seat, she addressed Lily more directly.

'You must send your mother round with a basket tomorrow, dear, and we'll find a few leftovers for her.'

Despite this inauspicious start to their friendship, and the huge gap in their respective lifestyles, Bertie and Lily continued to meet, albeit in secret.

As promised, he did take a flight in the *Water Hen,* coached by the pilot, a Mr Stanley Adams. The trip took place during the day while Lily was working at the fish market. But she could hear the buzz of the plane high in the sky and once caught a glimpse of it as it soared over the lake.

'Against the rules of nature,' was Hannah's opinion. 'What it must cost to fly that thing for one afternoon would keep us for month, I don't doubt. Pity the rich haven't summat better to spend their money on.'

Every penny her mother earned, including most of Lily's wages, went into buying food the likes of which Mrs Clermont-Read didn't even know existed. Stale bread at least a day old, bruised fruit and vegetables, cracked eggs, and sometimes on a Sunday, as a change from tatie pot or the hated fish, they would have bacon bits bought cheap at the Saturday market.

So Lily made no mention to her mother of her budding friendship with the young man now soaring over Carreckwater in a crazy machine.

But she did manage to sneak off from home at every opportunity, leaving more of the household chores to her sisters. Lily wasn't quite sure where all of this was leading, or even what her aims were in striking up this friendship with Bertie Clermont-Read, but fate had brought him into her life and she was eager to let their friendship continue, if only to see what came of it.

He took her out and about with flattering regularity. He would walk her over Loughrigg Fell or down to Skelwith Force where they would paddle in between the great stones and splash each other, squealing like children as the ice-cold water chilled their bare feet.

'It's wonderful to be out with a gel without all that fuss over chaperones.'

Lily would laugh, as if she understood perfectly the restrictions of being middle-class and rich. And if sometimes he held her hand, he made no attempt to kiss her. Lily wasn't quite sure whether to be relieved or disappointed about this.

On her day off he'd drive her down winding country lanes in the gig, which was such a great thrill Lily would almost wish her family could see her, looking so grand and elegant, like a real lady.

They would travel along by dry-stone walls and white-washed cottages with their circular Lakeland chimneys. She would enjoy the glories of pink weigelia, showy rhododendron and the purple clematis and sweet honeysuckle that tumbled over garden walls. Sometimes they would walk through the woods, the scents of yew and laurel, pine and beech, all around them. And between the latticework of branches could be glimpsed the broad flanks of the hills, misted pale in the distance or lit with a glorious patchwork of sun and shadow.

Never once did Lily refuse an invitation from Bertie. Why should she? She enjoyed any excuse to get out of The Cobbles.

'I don't intend to spend the rest of my life in that dreadful place,' she told him, with what she believed to be the right degree of haughtiness. 'I deserve better.'

'Course you do, old thing.'

'I have plans.'

'Knew it the moment I clapped eyes on you.'

She told him all about her ambitions because Bertie made such a sympathetic listener. 'Over these last two years I've saved hard.' She kept the amount secret, fearful he might mock. One pound and two shillings in an old tea caddy, hidden under the floorboards beneath her bed. 'I want enough to rent a small house of me own. In the smart area of Carreckwater, naturally. Or mebbe Bowness or Windermere. Then I'll buy a sewing machine and set meself up as a dressmaker,' she told him.

'Splendid. I'm sure you'll achieve it, Lily. You're such a dashed fine person.'

She wasn't sure how she would acquire the necessary skills for this grand ambition, even if she found all the money, but Lily did not in any way allow this to daunt her. She'd had plenty of practice at hand-sewing, hadn't she? Helping her mother make hookie rugs, turn and patch bed sheets, and crochet blankets from scraps of wool made out of pulled back socks and cardigans. Lily felt she was an expert on thrift but privately admitted she'd a lot to learn about style.

'I don't care how or what I do, so long as it's respectable and earns me a good living, d'you see? And from the look of the posh gowns the young ladies wear who stroll along The Parade, dressmakers must do well enough.'

'Absolutely,' Bertie agreed. 'I shall send Selene to patronise you.'

Lily made no comment upon this anticipated honour.

Then one day she managed to save enough to buy herself a blue print frock from the rag market. It was far too big for her, of course, but several late nights spent stitching by the light of the gas lamp turned it into a neat new gown for herself. She unpicked the waistband, took in the bodice and sewed the whole lot back together again. Then she trimmed the hem and elbow-length sleeves with a deep blue braid.

'By jove, you look splendid,' Bertie told her as she twirled and preened herself in front of him on their very next outing. She'd begged her mother to let her finish work early for once. Lily knew she shouldn't ask, for Hannah had seemed even more tired than usual lately, but she'd arranged to meet Bertie behind the old boathouses and was desperate not to be late. Now he sat on an upturned boat, his eyes devouring her.

'I'll set you up myself, if you like?' he generously offered, impressed by her skills.

'*Bertie*, the very idea! What are you suggesting?' And her merry hazel eyes laughed up him, making him blush, as she so loved to do. Lily found it alarmingly easy to embarrass Bertie, and sometimes felt a pang of guilt at the way she took pleasure in so doing.

'Steady on, you've got it all wrong. I never meant anything of the sort. Nothing, you know – improper, dash it.'

So upset was he she should interpret his offer as a proposition that he slid, all arms and legs, down the hull of the boat and landed in a heap on the grass, gazing ruefully up at her. 'I mean, there might the sort of female who – well, I dare say there are – only, a chap wouldn't dream of asking a girl like you, Lily.'

She put her hands on her hips and laughed at his panic. 'I know you wouldn't, you daft haporth.'

Then she went and sat beside him, enjoying the warmth of his body beside hers, breathing in the clean expensive tang of him and feeling a long-forgotten sense of power stir within her. Bertie Clermont-Read was potty about her, and would do absolutely anything she asked, Lily was perfectly sure of it.

'You've always shown proper respect for me, Bertie.'

'I should jolly well hope so!'

'I appreciate that. A lot of men wouldn't, bearing in mind where I live.'

'What's that to do with it?'

'You're not ashamed of me?'

'Absolutely not.'

A teasing glance. 'Haven't you ever fancied a kiss?'

'What sort of question is that to ask a chap?'

'You've never tried.'

'Wouldn't want to scare a gel, would I?'

Lily chuckled. 'Who says I'd be scared?'

Then she cupped his face between her hands and kissed him full upon the lips. The kiss wasn't half so exciting as the remembered delights of Dick's lips, but not by any means unpleasant. When she broke away, he was blushing all the more.

'You're a dashed good sport, Lily.'

'And you're a good, sweet man.'

The devil of it was that this was entirely true. How could she set out to take revenge on such a kind gent? But then it wasn't the gallant Bertie she wanted to take her revenge on, was it?

Lily had asked him several times if she was ever to meet his family again.

'If you're not ashamed to be seen with me, and if I look so fine in me new frock, mebbe your ma would approve of me now? I am your girl, aren't I, Bertie? Should I visit again, and see how it goes?'

An expression of anxiety crept over his boyish features. 'Why would you want to do that? Mama was pretty rotten to you the first time. It's true she can be a funny old thing. Bit blunt, and all that. But means no real harm, of course.'

'Course not,' Lily generously agreed. But privately wondered what was the point of walking out, assuming you could call it that, with Bertie Clermont-Read, if it didn't give her the opportunity for which she most longed: to get even with his family. In what way exactly she meant to achieve this, Lily wasn't sure. But she ached to ruin Margot's life, as the woman and her family had so heartlessly ruined hers. 'We may get on better with further acquaintance, you never know. It takes time, after all, to build friendships.'

Bertie considered the delicate machinations necessary to make a friend of Margot and his usually smooth brow wrinkled with worry as his fingers plucked at strands of grass. Even his smattering of freckles seemed to stand out in alarm at the very idea. It certainly wouldn't be easy, but he surely owed it to Lily at least to try. She was his best pal, after all. And he'd no wish to fall in with Mama's plans, not at any price. His brow cleared as an idea came to him.

'We take the *Faith* out every weekend. You could come on one of our picnics. We go to one of the islands, and in September an especially long trip to Kelda Bay. Mama loves picnics and is always in a good mood then. I'll ask if you can come too.'

Lily squealed her delight, and, flinging her arms about his neck, impulsively kissed him again. This time his arms came about her and they both fell back into the long grass, fully engrossed in the activity for some moments. It was hard to know who was blushing the most when they were done.

'I'll take you with me anyway, whatever she says, damned if I won't,' Bertie decided, gasping for breath.

He insisted on walking her right up Fisher's Brow to the end of her alley, which he'd never done before, promising that he'd fix it up for September, even if he couldn't manage it earlier.

Lily watched him go, her mind busy. September was two long months away, but she didn't mind. It would give her time to think and plan. Now she turned and started along the sunless street, her boots clattering on the cobble sets.

Bertie hadn't exactly said she was his girl, had he? Yet she must be, otherwise why would he agree to risk her meeting his family again? Trouble was, for all he was a lovely man, did she really want to be his girl?

It was true that she'd enjoyed his kisses, but she'd best take care.

It was vital to her plan that she stay in control. Hadn't she come one step nearer to her goal today? It was long past time for herself and the Clermont-Reads finally to settle their differences.

Lily was filled with sudden nervousness at the thought of seeing Margot again, and had to stop for a minute, leaning one hand on the wall till her heart stopped its racing. She must get a grip on herself. This time she must be prepared for the woman's acid tongue.

And hopefully Lily would also meet Bertie's father. She'd never forgotten her feelings as he offered her his card, as if grieving could be settled like a business transaction. There were a good few things to get off her chest when she met up with Edward Clermont-Read again. Oh, dear me, yes. Though how she would go about it, she wasn't quite sure.

Lily skirted a group of young children playing hopscotch on a patch of broken paving stones, their bare feet slapping in the overflow of water from an open sewer. She turned into Carter Street, and as if he'd been conjured out of her thoughts saw Percy Wright, the landlord's agent, picking his way between the puddles towards doors which shut fast and were locked before ever he reached them.

Lily couldn't help but smile, knowing no one would answer when he knocked. If the dratted man had called on her mam again, she hoped Hannah had done the same.

'Hello, Lily.'

She managed a smile. She would have hated Percy Wright in any case. Local sidesman at the Methodist Chapel, his spare body, wrinkled face and high-pitched way of speaking always made it seem as if he'd swallowed a mouthful of prunes.

'I can't get an answer at your house. Tell your ma I'll be back on Friday. We ain't running a charity.'

Lily said nothing, knowing as Percy Wright did that the house could not be empty at this time of day. Hatred warred with her fear that the family was once again slipping behind with the rent. How long before they were turned out on to the street, as others had been before them?

She recalled a conversation she'd had with her mother long since. It was one winter when ice had broken the ceiling rafters in the bedroom and they were all half frozen in their beds. Lily had asked if Hannah had never yearned for something better.

'Be thankful for what you've got, that's my motto. I came here as a young bride, happy and willing to make a home for Arnie and me. He's been a good husband, not like some who drink and gamble all their wages away. I've had my children here and, praise the Lord, managed to bring them all up healthy. I won't say it's been easy but I've no complaints. What more could I ask for than that?'

Lily could think of a dozen things but had the good sense not to say so, Hannah's view of The Cobbles being entirely different from her own. 'You could at least get the landlord to mend the roof.'

Her mother had looked away, lips tight, folding her arms across her chest and rubbing them, a familiar gesture whenever she felt uncomfortable. 'Mr Clermont-Read is a busy man. I'm sure he has better things to concern himself with than our situation. I'll get your father to see to it.'

Even as the young girl she'd been at the time, Lily had been aware of the sense of bitter defeat in her mother's attitude. She could still remember the hiding behind closed curtains, the fear when someone did a moonlit flit and were never seen again. The hopelessness which Hannah concealed with a staunch pride.

How could she have forgotten? Edward Clermont-Read, landlord of The Cobbles. And Percy Wright, his ferret of an agent.

Lily didn't move till he reached the end of Carter Street and turned into Drake Road. No wonder nothing was ever done to help the poor souls who had to live in this awful place. She strengthened her resolve to enjoy her revenge all the more. She would talk the whole thing over with Rose at the very first opportunity. Her friend would help plan a good strategy. Tugging her shawl close, Lily came to her own back door, stepped over a puddle and hurried inside. She saw at once that trouble with the rent was the least of her worries.

Chapter Five

'Late again, madam.'

Lily flushed with guilt as Hannah pressed a hand to her back, a gesture indicating her very deep weariness, then burst into a fit of coughing.

'I'm sorry.'

'Where've you been? I wish I knew what you got up to half the time while I'm trying to make ends meet.' Hannah lifted the tin laden-can full of hot water from the kitchen range and Lily ran to help. She'd forgotten it was bath night. The girls, Hannah and herself always took theirs on a Wednesday; the boys and Arnie on Fridays.

'Here, let me bath our Kitty. You look worn out, Mam. Go on, put your feet up for a bit.'

Hannah had never felt more peculiar in all her life, but hated to confess it. Weakness was a sin in her book.

'When have I time to put me feet up?'

Lily would take no arguments. She sat her mother down with a mug of hot, sweet tea and then went in search of her three grubby sisters.

Four-year-old Kitty was first, giggling infectiously as she scampered to escape Lily's ministrations.

'I don't want me hair washed. The soap stings me eyes. Oh don't, our Lily!'

Laughing, Lily caught her, and once the squirming infant was safely seated in the zinc bath tub before the fire, scrubbed her from top to toe with red carbolic soap and a soft flannel. The child's hair was washed with the same soap and combed with a fine tooth comb afterwards.

'Ow, you're hurting me.'

'You don't want no biddies in your hair, do you?'

Hannah leaned back in her chair with a thankful sigh. 'Ee, Lily, what would I do without you, girl? I've no energy for this lot tonight.' But she was aware that she still hadn't received an answer to her question.

'Are you going to tell me then?'

'Tell you what?' Lily chased a giggling eight-year-old Emma around the kitchen table, captured her and set about scrubbing her in the same manner.

'You know full well. Where is it you go off to whenever my back is turned? Got a new boy friend, eh?' Hannah smiled as she sipped her tea, sincerely hoping that it were true. For there was nothing she'd like better than to see her lovely daughter wed to a fine young chap.

'Don't start, Mam.'

'Why won't you tell me?'

'There's naught to tell.'

A screech from Emma as Kitty aimed a swipe at her sister with the flannel brought Lily's attention back to the task in hand. Later, while Liza took her turn in the bath, old enough at ten to wash herself, Lily dried the two younger ones and dressed them in their nighties, set warming by the fire. Made from old flour sacks they might be and, if you looked closely, still bearing the imprint of the maker's name, yet they'd been washed so often they were soft and warm to wear.

'You'd say if there were?' Hannah persisted, her eyes half closed, watching the proceedings as she lay back, trying to relax.

Lily glanced at her mother, thought how pale she looked, how exhausted so much of the time. For all Lily loved her sisters and brothers, she really didn't wonder at it. Hannah never stopped for a minute, not from dawn when she got up to make breakfast for them all to the moment she fell back into bed at night after a long day of cooking, washing and ironing. And that was on top of minding the fish stall. Which only made Lily even more determined not to end up the same way.

'I've told you, I mean to have me own business one day. Something grand in Carndale Road happen, or even Bowness or Windermere. I stand by that.'

Hannah's eyes opened wide, and pride mingling with concern

softened the next, seemingly harsh, words. 'Ee, Lily, don't talk so soft. Dreams are dangerous things. Give up with 'em, lass. They'll only make you dissatisfied with life as it really is.'

'They give me hope.' She turned to her sisters who were rolling together on the rug like a pair of puppies. 'Come on, you two, time for your dose of sulphur and treacle to keep your innards clean.' Despite more groans, this was eventually achieved, followed by a mug of hot tea and slice of bread with a scrape of dripping by way of supper for each girl.

After she'd got them to bed, Lily and Hannah both took turns in the bath, a hasty all-over wash before the water went cold.

Then Lily ladled out the zinc bath tub and hung it back on the yard wall. But there was still work to be done, and tired though she may be, she worked extra hard to catch up on her missed chores, making sure that Hannah rested some more.

She scoured out the swill baskets which were used to hold the fish, and set them to dry. Then she boiled kettles and prepared the men-folk's supper almost single-handed. Her father would be tired from working on the boats all day, aided or rather hindered by his two sons, and yet he would still go out on his night fishing.

Considering she'd sat still long enough, Hannah set about wiping the cottage down with damp cloths, as if it weren't already clean enough. She swept the floors, shook the hookie rug, wiped down the range and polished the brass fittings with pride, bringing it to that pristine cleanliness which could only be achieved by constant and daily attention.

Lastly Hannah wiped away the black mould which clung to the walls, knowing it would be back again the next day.

'The worst thing about housework is that it'll all have to be done again tomorrow.' She laughed, but it sounded forced, even to her own ears.

After watching her for a while, noting the lines of strain at the corners of her mouth, Lily took hold of her mother's arm and gently shook her. 'I told you to sit down and put your feet up.'

'I've had 'em up.'

'Why don't you have your supper now, Mam, then go on up to bed? I'll see to me dad and the boys.'

Hannah stared at her daughter as if she'd gone mad. She couldn't remember ever going early to bed in her life. 'Ee, I can't, our Lily, much as I might like to. I have to finish up in here. Needs must when the devil drives.' And shaking scouring powder all over the sloping wooden draining board, she began to scrub. As she did so, a cockroach ran across it and she captured it in her cloth to toss it into the fire where it hissed and cracked. Lily shuddered.

'God almighty, I wish we were out of this stinking hole.'

'Lily! I'll thank you to keep a clean tongue in your head or I'll wash your mouth out with this carbolic.' Stiff-backed, Hannah wiped her hands on the sacking apron that covered her black dress. In all Lily's seventeen years, she'd never seen her mother wear anything else, save for Sundays when she put on her 'best' coat and hat in a rather dull olive green.

At last satisfied with the state of her sink, Hannah crossed the small living-kitchen and taking a candle from the hook on the end of the mantle-shelf, lit it from a taper and disappeared into the dark scullery hole under the stairs. This was the place where the family washing was done. It had one small window looking out on to the backyard, and its stone floor was often littered with earthenware bowls full of clothes left to soak, so they'd be easier to rinse out when Monday came round.

Stifling a sigh Lily reached for the bread knife and started to hack the loaf into huge doorsteps, thick enough to please her greedy brothers. Then she set the soup to warm and gently stirred it, her mind replaying the kiss Bertie had given her. Where would it all lead? And what would her mother say, if she knew?

'Will you hand me the dolly blue, Lily?'

'You're surely not going to start washing now, not at this time of night?' The idea wasn't too far-fetched, though Hannah had such a fetish for cleanliness and 'getting things done' as she called it, that it was not unknown for her husband to return from a bit of crack with the lads to find his wife still washing or ironing at close on midnight. When her mother did not come back at her with her usual biting response, Lily said no more. She'd lost this particular argument too many times to try. Then the sound of a crash made her drop the soup spoon and sent her running into the depths of the scullery-hole.

'What is it, Mam? Have you hurt yourself?'

Hannah was sitting on the floor in the gloomy half darkness holding her head, her face a mask of pain. 'It's all right, don't take on. I banged me head on that low beam, that's all. You'd think I'd know it was there, wouldn't you? After all these years.'

The beam in question was at an angle on the side wall, some distance from the sink where Hannah was working. 'How did you manage to hit it?'

'I don't know, do I? Must have lost me balance. I've not been right since I had that cold. Can't get rid of this cough, I can't.' The cough started up again just as the back door sneck rattled and both women looked at each other as they heard the tread of men's boots. 'Help me up quick, your father mustn't find me like this. He'll never let me hear the last of it.'

As both women emerged from beneath the stairs into the light and warmth of the kitchen they saw that Arnie was not alone.

'I've fetched a mate to take supper wi' us. We can stretch to another mouth, I suppose?'

'Aye,' said Hannah at once, and hurried to examine the contents of the soup pan, hoping Arnie wouldn't see the flash of worry which must have come into her eyes. There'd be just enough if she didn't have any herself. Then Lily's voice hissed against her ear, 'I'm not hungry, Mam. Sit yourself down.'

'Why choose today to bring home one of his lame ducks?'

Lily smiled, for nothing would prevent Arnie setting out to help all and sundry. He'd give the coat off his back if someone asked for it. She squeezed her mother's hand in sympathy and urged her towards the table. 'Go and talk to him. I'll serve and say I've eaten with the girls.'

'But...'

'Do it.'

For once Hannah did as she was bid. If she'd felt a bit queer before she'd put those tea cloths to soak, she felt a whole lot worse now. Her chest felt on fire. A bowl of hot soup would set her up a treat, so she accepted it gratefully.

After she'd served her mother, Lily turned enquiring eyes to the visitor, now helping himself to a slice of bread without even being asked. Surreptitiously she studied his profile. Dark and unshaven he wasn't too bad-looking, if you didn't object to a slightly crooked nose and the most glowering brows she had ever seen. He smelled clean enough though, she thought, with some relief. Not all Arnie's friends were so particular. This man smelled of fresh air, tar, and some indefinable masculine tang which wasn't in the least unpleasant. But then as she handed him a bowl of soup he turned to offer his thanks and she saw him full face.

'Nathan Monroe?'

He grinned at her. That same wide, wicked grin that had once given her the shivers and kept her awake many a night as a young girl. 'The very same, Lily Thorpe. You remember me then?'

'As if I could ever forget!' She slammed his soup bowl down in front of him with a thump, sending tiny splashes scattering over the rim on to the wooden table top. Nathan simply continued to smile, which angered her all the more.

Arnie was chuckling as he watched his daughter's reaction. 'He told me he went to your school and remembered you well. So go on, tell us, lass. What did this young rogue do to put you in such a paddy?'

'He spent his entire schooldays taking every opportunity to plague me. Pinched my skipping rope, hid my school books, once put a frog in my lunch bag…'

Lily's twin brothers snorted with laughter and she scowled at them both to no effect.

'He'll be a bad influence on those two, I tell you that much. Always fighting over something or other he was, and got the cane more times than any other boy I can think of.'

'I remember pulling your plaits,' Nathan remarked mildly, his gaze lingering on the curling tendrils which lay upon Lily's shoulders. 'I never forgot their beautiful chestnut colour.'

She didn't trouble to respond to this flattery, simply pushed the thick swathe of shining hair down her back where it bounced and rippled, crackling with vibrant life, entirely ruining the small gesture of defiance.

'I remember him tying me up behind the old boathouses one dinnertime, and leaving me there alone with the water lapping about my feet. I was still there when Mr Adams came for his boat over two hours later and set me free. I don't think I'd ever been more scared in all my life.'

But Arnie did not, as she'd expected, come to her defence. Instead he looked from one to the other of them then gave a shout of laughter. 'By heck, you were a one, weren't you, Monroe? Well, boys will be boys. No wonder he asked after you, Lily. I can see why.'

'He was the school bully,' Lily said, the outrage in her voice as strong now as it had been on that well-remembered day, nearly ten years ago.

Matt and Jacob were giggling so much by this time, Hannah was desperately trying to shush them, but Jacob at least was determined to have his say. 'You should have stuck up for yourself more, our Lily. Maybe he thought you were a cissy.'

She did not join in the general amusement at the idea of her not being able to defend herself, but handed out the rest of the soup in condemnatory silence. As a child, Nathan Monroe had scared her rigid. Big and wide-shouldered even then, his broad face carrying a perpetual scowl, she had lived in fear of what he might do to her next. But she wasn't a child any more, and nor was he, more's the pity. He looked more intimidating than ever as a grown man, even sitting down. But no one would bully her now.

'That teacher always seemed to have it in for me,' he said, lifting his spoon.

'And no wonder,' Lily replied crisply.

'Well, you'll have to forget your argumentative past,' Arnie was saying, slurping at his soup. 'I've offered Nathan a bed. He's stopping on as lodger for a bit, till he finds hissel a place of his own.'

It was as if her father had struck her. Throughout her entire life she could always depend upon him taking her side. Now, for some reason, he was taking the opposite view. Lily felt betrayed. 'You've said he can stay *here?*'

Hannah quietly asked, 'Where will he sleep?'

'He can sleep with us,' Jacob offered, and Matt eagerly nodded in agreement. This was one lame duck who sounded like good fun to have around.

Nathan laughingly shook his head. 'There's no need to put yourself out, you two. I can sleep down here.'

'In the kitchen? Where? There's no bed and it's a slate floor.' Hannah was shocked. 'Nay, lad, we can't let you do that.'

'Find me a straw pallet and a blanket, and I'll be right as ninepence. I want to cause no trouble.'

At this he let his eyes slide till they met Lily's, warm and intimate, as if they were lifelong friends. But she and Nathan Monroe had never been friends, and never would be if she had anything to do with it. For a long moment she held the gaze, determined not to be the one to weaken and look away as she had done so often in the past. But the sheer intimacy of his smile unnerved her, as it always had done, and the expression in those blue eyes said more than she cared to read. At length she did turn away, cheeks stained with colour.

'I've already eaten and I'm tired, so I'm off upstairs. Good night.' Then she stuck her nose in the air and left them.

The long weeks of summer were more difficult than Lily could ever have dreamed possible. The presence of Nathan Monroe in the house completely changed her life.

He always seemed to be around: sitting helping Arnie mend his nets or lines in the yard, taking the boys out in his boat – up to no good, she wouldn't wonder. Once he took them on the steamer, the full length of the lake. For a mere ticket-collector he had the cheek of the devil. But then, hadn't he always?

Worst of all, his eyes followed her every move. Lily was aware of him watching her, or felt as if he were, the whole time. But whenever she glanced up, ready to berate him for harassing her, she'd find him absorbed in some innocent task, not paying her any attention at all. But she knew that he did. She just hadn't caught him in the act yet.

Infuriatingly, Hannah liked him almost as much as Arnie did. Wouldn't hear of his leaving. But then he was the perfect gent with her mother. Lily knew she should be glad of that for Hannah was not herself. She seemed pale and distracted half the time, so tired she often stumbled over her words, and far more willing than usual to leave the work to others.

All of this meant Lily found less time to sneak off and see Bertie. Vexing as it might be, her anxiety for her mother, and worries that Nathan Monroe might spy on her while out with Bertie, caused her to be circumspect.

She escaped when she could, but too often was forced to leave a note behind the boathouses, their favourite meeting place.

More often than not it would simply say, '*Can't get away.*'

And he would leave one for her. '*Never mind. There's always September and Kelda Bay. Don't forget.*'

As if she could. Lily thought of little else. Throughout her long days working at the fish stall, and as she struggled to cope with the never-ending stream of tasks involved in keeping nine people confined in one small cottage clean and fed, her mind would escape to the promise of that glorious picnic which awaited her in the coming autumn like a golden glow on the horizon. A magical dream just waiting to come true.

She contrived endless conversations in her head with the Clermont-Reads. Some of them witty, some clever and sharp, others cool and gracious. But in all of them she came out on top, getting the better of Margot's acid tongue every time. It was most satisfactory.

She talked to Rose about her plans one day during their tea-break behind the vegetable stall, and was surprised and hurt by her friend's lack of enthusiasm.

'Aw, forget it. Bertie Clermont-Read isn't the man for you.' Rose chewed happily on a potted meat sandwich as she sat perched on a pile of old cabbages which, judging by the smell of them, were well past their best.

But what their eating place lacked in comfort was more than made up for by the view. The shores all about the lake were green and lush, tiny wooded inlets starred with red campion and garlic flowers. Soft curving bays with shingle beaches harboured brightly painted wooden boats. Towards the northern end of the lake the gently rolling countryside, flanked by swathes of steeper fells, became more rocky and sheer. Beyond these the countryside grew ever more rugged up to the high fells and craggy mountain peaks.

'But I like him,' Lily said. 'He's amusing, and fun, and very kind.'

'And safe, I know. Every girl's dream. A quiet man to do her every bidding.' Rose sidled closer to offer a dab of mustard, which Lily gratefully accepted. 'How about this other chap then, the one what's living in your house? Nathan Monroe. What's he like? Bet he isn't so safe.'

Lily's glance was withering. 'I hate him. I've always hated him.' She told Rose of her childhood experiences while her friend listened, wide-eyed.

'Nay, that's naught,' she said at length. 'Worse happened to me every day in Workington. Why, once I was turned upside down in a water butt and...' But seeing the warning in Lily's eyes, thought better about pursuing this particular argument. 'Well, happen he's calmed down a bit now he's full-grown. And he's certainly done that! I've never seen such a strapping, broad-shouldered chap. Quite handsome in his way.' Again she caught Lily's glowering look and concentrated on wiping her smeary fingers on her apron. 'But go on, what's he like to live with?'

Lily's cheeks flushed and she almost choked on her sandwich. 'Live with? Rose, you make it sound as if we were slept in the same room, which we don't.'

Rose giggled, wriggling her hips with delight, which unfortunately disturbed the rotting cabbage leaves and had both girls screwing up their noses at the resulting odour.

'I wouldn't say no though, would you?'

'He's despicable. So pernickety he drives me mad – always

cleaning his boots. And he likes his clothes pressed and ironed with the creases in just the right places. Anyone'd think I was his servant!'

Rose gave a wry smile. 'Sounds like a man with standards.'

'He's a slave driver who uses women for his own ends. He was a bully when I was eight and he twelve, and he's a bully still,' came back the fiery response.

Rose widened her eyes. 'Whoops, sorry I spoke.'

Two cows stood ankle-deep in the water, relishing its coolness, while a gentle breeze gathered strength, frothing and slapping at the waters, sending yachts scudding and playing havoc with a clutch of rowing boats tied up alongside the wooden pier. Both girls giggled. There was always something entertaining to watch on the lake.

'Happen he learned all this tidiness when he were a sailor on them big ships. That's where he says he's been these last few years, isn't it?'

Lily looked even more scathing and sniffed with disdain. 'If you can believe that. Personally I suspect he's spent the time in a far less salubrious place.'

'You don't mean...'

'I do. He always was a trouble-maker. I reckon he's served time somewhere he'd rather not mention.'

'What, in prison?'

'Where else? Otherwise why has he never come home, even on a visit, for nigh on eight years?'

'There could be any number of reasons.'

Lily tossed her head, not wishing to hear anything which might change her view of this odious man. 'He once caused me a lot of grief, and I never forget folk who do that. Anyroad, I've no wish to talk of Nathan Monroe. It's the Clermont-Reads who interest me. What am I to do about them?'

'There's naught you can do. They have life all sewn up to suit themselves. Like I say, forget them, Lily. You'll only end up hurting yourself.'

This was not what Lily wished to hear. She explained to Rose how they had ruined her life, how Edward Clermont-Read owned the very house in which they lived and had never lifted a finger, so far as she knew, to help improve life for his tenants in The Cobbles.

'He's only concerned with his own comfort, and profits. The whole family is.' Lily got to her feet, too agitated now to sit still, hands on hips, hazel eyes flashing fire. 'Did I tell you how Mrs Clermont-Read spoke to me? As if I were dirt.'

Rose sighed and nodded. 'Only hundred times or so. You can tell me again, if you want to, but it won't make no difference. They have money and you don't. And with money comes power. Don't you ever forget that, Lil.'

If Nathan's ears had been burning while the two girls discussed him, he gave no indication of it as he studiously performed his duties at the ticket office. He clipped and handed out two tickets with his most winning smile to a couple of middle-aged maiden ladies. It was their fourth cruise this week, largely due, Nathan was sure, to his own flattering charm.

Trade this afternoon was slack, but he prided himself on the positive efforts he was making to encourage business. He'd displayed two new posters, and sent a young lad round town carrying a sandwich board announcing a short evening cruise around the lake.

The proprietor of the Steamship Company, Captain Swinbourne, had certainly made no efforts in that direction, nor ever would, if Nathan was any judge.

At four the man himself opened the ticket office door and nodded to Nathan. 'That's the afternoon run over. We can take a break now.'

'We're not full yet for the evening cruise. Don't you want me to stay open, see if I can get a few more?'

Swinbourne shook his head. 'Waste of time. There'll be nowt doing for an hour or more while everyone has their tea. We'll do the same. Get the kettle on and I'll find the cards. See if I can win back some of yesterday's losses.'

'Right,' said Nathan with a smile. 'Whatever you say, governor.'

Margot Clermont-Read sat in the little drawing room with her diary on her knee, making plans. They concerned her precious son and heir, Albert Frederick Clermont-Read. Despite an agonising pregnancy and traumatic childhood years in which poor Bertie had been sickly and ailing, he was now proving to be worth all their efforts, in Margot's eyes at least. She found him sweet and charming, with a rakish sense of humour. And if he didn't work quite so hard as his father would wish, why in truth should he? There really wasn't the need for it, not any more. The family riches had been made, the future could take care of itself, could it not? Style was the necessary requirement now, gracious good manners and position in society, rather than driving ambition. All the former assets Bertie possessed in abundance.

Edward had always been a bit hard on him because of the boy's greater degree of sensitivity, but Margot knew that all her beloved son needed was a good wife to care for him, and provide her with grandchildren.

Selene was making little progress in this direction so all her hopes rested on Bertie. And it looked as if her efforts might be paying off.

The summer season had been most satisfactory. Several young ladies had caught his eye, though admittedly none quite suited, for one reason or other.

Millicent Gowdrey, for instance, was completely lacking in grace. Felicia Morton-Cryer talked in too loud a voice, and Sophie Dunston seemed a positive recluse. The one thing they all had in their favour, however, was money. Without exception their parents were quite comfortably off, the Dunstons positively rich.

Margot chewed on the end of her pencil, then added Sophie's name to her list. The girl might cast off her excessive shyness in time. And if she stopped squinting behind those spectacles, might even become less plain.

Which left poor dumpy Dora, the girl's only claim to charm, and therefore inclusion on this exclusive list, being her parentage. The Ferguson-Walshes were one of the richest families in the district.

Margot had missed out on an alliance with the Lindens for poor dear Selene, but the Ferguson-Walshes would make a very good alternative for darling Bertie. If she could but bring him to the point. Margot sighed. She had rather hoped that Bertie and Dora would have taken to each other by now, and if young people today were not half so pernickety they would certainly have done so. Yet it remained Margot's all-consuming dream to bring the marriage about. She hadn't yet given up hope, and enjoyed Edith Ferguson-Walshes full support in her campaign. If the two women had their way, the young couple would be married by Christmas.

The September picnic to Kelda Bay was Margot's chance to bring this desired state of affairs to fruition. This would be the crowning glory of her year. If she couldn't bring Bertie to a decision at the picnic, then she would eat her best hat!

Chapter Six

The golden September sun burned through the wreaths of mist floating over the lake. Flat calm, it was a perfect day for a sail. The mountains basked in the sunshine. Even the becks were running quietly, as if reluctant to disturb that quiet autumnal magic.

From the moment she arrived at the small stone jetty, Lily knew she was not welcome. Margot and Selene ushered their guests aboard, fussing over where everyone else should sit, ignoring her completely. Edward Clermont-Read scarcely glanced in Lily's direction as he poured water into a copper vessel rather like a small tea urn.

'It's called a Windermere kettle,' Bertie whispered in her ear. 'Since that's where it was first invented. Contains a coil of pipe through which high pressure steam from the boiler passes. Boils water in ten seconds, once we've got up full steam.'

Lily said, 'I see,' though really she didn't, and Bertie grinned at her, as pleased as if he'd invented it himself.

'Like her? The boat, I mean. Built on the lines of a real steamship, only in miniature.'

As the *Faith* set sail for Kelda Bay Lily told him she thought the boat looked perfect, sleek and gleaming from hours of loving care. Despite her more prosaic motives for wanting this invitation, she'd experienced an unexpected feeling of happiness simply climbing aboard. It had been like stepping into another world: refined, leisurely, gracious. A world where everyday cares and worries did not exist.

A white funnel shone in the September sunshine and the engineer opened up two glass doors through which he began to tinker with the engine.

'Be laying her up for winter soon, eh, George?'

'Aye, Mr Albert. Clean the boiler tubes, and give her a scrape and varnish.'

Not a soul addressed Lily as Bertie led her through the panelled saloon and found her a seat on one of the blue leather couches. 'You'll be comfortable here,' he told her. 'While I go and help Pa up front.'

Lily thanked him, and after dutifully smiling at one or two people who pretended they hadn't noticed, perched resolutely on the edge of her seat, gloved hands clasped tightly together, trying not to regret her decision to come.

Her new blue print dress with its braid trim had seemed perfectly wonderful when she'd first altered it, and even when she'd put it on this morning. Now, it felt drab and second-hand. For all she'd trimmed her new straw hat with a fresh pink rose and a length of baby blue ribbon, it too felt somehow cheap and tawdry.

At the far end of the boat, sitting in the stern, she could see Selene talking earnestly to her mother. The two of them kept looking daggers in Lily's direction. Would Bertie suffer a dressing-down for daring to bring her? She rather thought so.

She glanced in the opposite direction, to where Bertie stood at the brass wheel so he could be in charge of steering the steam-yacht as he clearly loved to do. He caught her eye, lifted a hand and waved. Upon the instant Lily felt better. She drew in a deep breath and slid back more comfortably upon the seat, deciding that cruising was really rather pleasant, and she fully intended to enjoy the day. Even the smell of the hot steam and Welsh sea coal was intoxicating.

And if no one had welcomed her with open arms, what of it? She was here at Bertie's invitation, which had nothing to do with Margot Clermont-Read. He was of age, after all, and could surely choose his own friends?

Deep inside, Lily knew this to be asking a great deal. No one in their right mind could consider her friendship with Bertie suitable. But so far as she was concerned, that was the whole point, wasn't it? She hadn't agreed to attend this picnic in order to have Bertie fall in love with her, but to find the opportunity to speak her mind to the Clermont-Reads.

Having reminded herself of her motives, some of her pleasure in the day faded. To find herself seated in the very vessel which had ploughed down and killed her darling Dick was suddenly almost more than she could bear, and she'd waste no time in telling them so. Lily tightened her small fists, longing to jump to her feet and embarrass these people with her accusations before all their fine friends. What sweet revenge that would be!

Managing to restrain herself, she lifted her chin to the sun where it streamed through the window, and turned her attention to the beauties of the passing scenery. Perhaps they might calm her shredded nerves. Lily certainly meant not to be overwhelmed.

They steamed along the eastern shoreline of Carreckwater past Blengarth Hall, a Gothic mansion built during the last century by a Liverpool shipping magnate. Woodlands of birch, oak and alder crowded the shoreline, interspersed at intervals by the precipitous face of craggy rock dropping sheer to the water. Finally the upper reaches of the lake brought a long stretch of shingle, known locally as Kelda Bay, and the *Faith* steamed silently closer to shore.

'Nice, ain't it?' Bertie enquired at her elbow, as if he had invented the spot especially for her.

Lily smiled up at him. 'It's lovely.'

'Kelda is the old Norse word for spring,' he told her. 'I'll show it to you after tea. The water is lovely, very fresh and clear. It'll give us a few moments' peace away from the family.'

She had to ask. 'Did they mind your inviting me?'

'I didn't ask their permission.'

This should have pleased her, but instead a tremor of apprehension ran through her as Bertie handed her down on to the tiny wooden jetty. As she turned to thank him, Lily thought how handsome he looked. His sandy halo of hair, bleached to a new fairness by the summer sun, seemed backlit by the glorious sweep of the Langdales and Bowfell behind him.

'I'd best go back and help Mama, mustn't neglect the old thing. Are you all right?'

Lily smiled up at him. 'I'm grand.' And she would have been, except that Selene chose that very moment to push hurriedly past, causing Lily to lose her balance. One foot slid into the water, soaking her in seconds.

Selene looked disdainfully down at her predicament. 'Oh, dear, how very clumsy of you.'

'It were your fault, not mine,' Lily protested, too annoyed to consider her words more carefully.

'It *were*? What sort of language is that?' Selene let out a trill of laughter. 'How very quaint.'

Lily winced at her own mistake. She'd been taking such care to do everything right and speak properly, but next to Selene's well-bred tones, her own voice sounded vulgar and broad. 'You know what I meant.'

Selene quickly checked that Bertie was still engaged in attending to Mama and then stepped closer to Lily. 'Don't think we aren't aware what you're up to. It won't work. We'll see you never get your thieving hands on our darling Bertie. We know how to deal with money-grubbers like you.'

'I don't know what you're talking about.'

'Don't you?' laughed Selene, cruelly mimicking Lily's accent. Then shot up her parasol and swung it above her head. 'Suit yourself. You'll find us fearsome adversaries.' Erupting into fresh peals of laughter, she turned up her elegant nose and flounced off.

If the sail across the lake had been silent and difficult, tea was a nightmare. Not a soul except Bertie acknowledged Lily's presence.

For once Margot had chosen to dispense with servants and ordered Selene to lay the white damask cloth and set out the silver and glass with her best china – though not without incessant instructions as to each correct placement.

'Much more fun this way, don't you think?' she trilled, moving a glass half an inch to the right. 'Perfect, though I do say so myself.'

Plates of sandwiches were passed around, cakes offered at such a distance from herself that Lily soon began to suspect a calculated design in the fact that barely a morsel of food reached her plate. It wouldn't have been so bad if Bertie hadn't been so engrossed in lighting a bonfire, or if she hadn't been so hungry.

She tried to concentrate upon a family of coots swimming merrily by, but from the corner of her eye she could see Edward Clermont-Read approaching and her heart gave a little flutter. Would this give her the opportunity she sought?

Lily intended to ask if he'd visited The Cobbles recently, and when he denied it, as he surely must, she'd demand to know why, since he owned so much of it. Did he not care about the people forced to live in his poor miserable dwellings? Of course he didn't care, she would go on to say. Didn't you kill my own sweet love without a word of apology? The words were already forming on her tongue when he leaned closer.

'I fear we are neglecting you, Miss Thorpe. Would you care for a slice of Madeira?'

And to her very great amazement he slid a slice of cake from his own plate on to hers. Even more alarming, when she met his calm grey gaze, he closed one eye in a slow and solemn wink. For one head-spinning moment Lily thought she might actually laugh out loud, despite her better judgement. But then Margot's commanding tones reached them loud and clear. 'Edward, what are you about?'

He turned on his heel and strolled away, as if nothing untoward had occurred. But every word Lily had been about to utter had quite gone from her head. What had it all meant? Thrown into confusion, she frowned at the offending item on her plate and fell into a deep study. Oh, dear, why had she come? Rose was right. What could she hope to achieve? The Clermont-Reads were far too clever for her.

It startled her that this man whom she'd been about to accuse of gross negligence and an act little short of murder should take the trouble to share his tea with her. Was he genuinely sympathetic or merely trying to make her think so?

'Pray pay attention, Miss Thorpe, when you are being spoken to.

Stricken, Lily glanced up to find herself the centre of attention. 'I was saying that you hold exceedingly egalitarian views upon matrimony,' Margot stated pompously, and Lily looked even more confused.

'Egalitarian?'

Selene giggled. 'I doubt she understands the meaning of the word, Mama.'

Margot rolled her eyes, begging the assembled company to pity her for what she was forced to suffer, while Edith Ferguson-Walsh hid a smile behind her napkin. The more foolish this little hussy appeared, the more perfect a bride her own darling Dora would seem for dear Bertie.

Bertie must have sensed her thoughts for he came strolling over, blazer flying open, hands in the pockets of his white bags, a blue silk cravat knotted carelessly about his neck. He looked what he was: a dashing, carefree young man with plenty of money, and not a care in the world.

'Egalitarian means that you believe anyone should be allowed to do as they wish, Lily, without disapproval. No matter how poor, foolish, or unwise they may be.'

Edith Ferguson-Walsh felt moved to comment. 'Marriage is so very important. I always think a gel shines best in her own home.'

Margot sniffed into her lavender-scented handkerchief, as if something close by had offended her. 'So long as she is the right sort of gel.'

'But of course, I do so agree.' Edith eagerly followed Margot's lead and simpered a half smile up at Bertie, wishing Dora would say something on her own account. She tried to bring her daughter into the conversation. 'Didn't you remark only the other day, Dora dear, that you believe the salvation of the starving poor must lie in education?'

'Tinkering with education is what has got this country into the mess it's in,' Margot retorted, instantly destroying her friend's plan.

'All this money wasted on Working Men's Institutes gives the masses ideas they are not equipped to handle. There are certain matters, and matrimony is one, for which they are quite unfitted.'

'I say, Mama, leave off,' Bertie chuckled. 'This is beginning to sound like a sermon.'

'If the status of family life, and society with it, is not to be eroded, adequate funds must be found.'

Bertie laughed. 'You're surely not suggesting that marriage should be the prerogative of the rich? That a chap should buy himself a bride, like he buys a motor or a steam-yacht? Bit hard on everyone else, what?'

'Don't be foolish, Bertie,' she snapped. 'I never said the poor could not be blessed with the sanctity of marriage.' Manufacturing a laugh, as if the very idea were preposterous. 'Heaven forbid! I am simply suggesting that when matrimony is contemplated, proper provision should be made. A few years of careful saving before people embark upon it might save us all a good deal of trouble in the long run.'

'That shows how much you know,' Lily burst out, unable to keep quiet any longer. 'My parents would never have been wed at all in that case, which wouldn't have been quite fair on me, now would it?

'Upon my word.' Margot fanned herself furiously, overcome by the vulgarity of Lily's reckless interruption. But Lily did not even notice, too busy ploughing heedlessly on.

'They've barely scraped a living all their lives. And whose fault is that? Not their own, I can tell you. They've striven to keep a roof over their heads, in one o' them pig sties you dare to call houses. I've wondered at times why they bothered. Even a pig would turn up its nose.' She was on her feet, tears spilling out as fast as the words, heedless of how far she had breached the bounds of good manners. But then, this was what she had come for, wasn't it? Too late now to turn back.

'They saved what they could, and I'm damned if I'll let my family be blamed for daring to marry, just because they're poor. Or for living in a stinking hole like The Cobbles that your husband, as landlord, should have sorted out long since!'

A gasp from the assembled company met this reckless remark and Lily held her breath. Edward Clermont-Read's face bore an expression of shock, as if he'd never considered the matter before. As if the idea he might in any way be negligent was entirely new to him. But then, what possible excuse could he give? Lily had taken her revenge at last.

He stepped forward, eyes blazing with anger. 'Are you implying that I'm to blame for the state of The Cobbles?'

Lily pulled herself up to her full five feet four inches. 'Aye, that's exactly what I'm saying.'

'You don't perhaps think the folk who live there bear some responsibility for the mess?'

'No, I don't, as a matter of fact.'

'I've spent a small fortune repairing roofs and walls that are as quickly broken again. I once put in an experimental water system with a tap at the end of one street, only to find someone stole the damned thing! Certain youths in the district actually seem to take pleasure in destruction.'

Lily knew this to be true, but not for the world would she admit it. This man would never understand the sense of defeat that permeated the place, nor how one tap in one street could cause such outrage and envy in the rest that they'd sooner see it destroyed.

'We're not all like that. Our house is as clean as my mam can make it, make no mistake,' pride compelled her to explain. 'And you've done naught about our running damp, nor the cockroaches, nor ...'

'*Enough!* We have ladies present,' Edward coldly stated, his tone making her shiver even in the heat of her argument.

Selene pointedly added, 'Which you, of course, are not.'

An outbreak of giggles started, growing into a chorus of bubbling delight, and Lily stood as if struck, her heart sinking with dismay. This wasn't at all the affect she had meant to achieve. The object had been for these toffee-nosed friends of his to be disgusted with Edward, not herself.

Desperately she attempted to rectify her slip with a spirited defence. 'So what if I'm not a lady? I've naught to be ashamed of. My mam and dad are decent folks who've every right to wed if they wants to, and have children. Six to be exact. And if I were born afore they'd quite tied the knot, what of it? They had problems over religion, and needed to find a house to live in. It makes no odds to me,' she finished on a fine note of defiance, realising too late how far her temper had taken her. Cheeks pink, Lily's voice faded into silence. What could she do now to rectify her blunder? Oh, dear Lord, save me, she prayed. Didn't Rose say I'd hurt meself more than them? And I have.

'Dear me,' said Margot at last into the ensuing silence, making a great show of being shocked even as she dabbed tears of amusement from her eyes. 'What a dramatic life you must have led.'

How splendid, she thought, that she'd succeeded in showing the girl up for what she truly was: a common slut. A good thing too that Bertie should be witness to her shame. Now she. addressed her son with gentle regret, tinged very slightly with reproof. 'You see what a tangle you have put us all into, Bertie.'

'Tangle?'

'By bringing poor Miss Thorpe upon our picnic, you have succeeded only in embarrassing her, and ourselves, by her revelations. I can't imagine what you were thinking of.' Margot smiled wearily upon her guests, seeking their sympathetic support.

To Lily's great surprise, a red stain swept up Bertie's neck. 'Steady on, that's going it a bit strong, old thing. Lily has the right to speak up for her family, if she wants to.' The sound of his voice, as much as his valiant defence of her, brought Lily's head round for this was not the conciliatory tone he usually adopted when addressing his mother. He was clearly very angry on Lily's behalf and meant Margot to recognise that fact.

'Bertie, it's all right,' said Lily, laying a hand upon his arm.

Edward too stepped forward to drop a hand on his son's shoulder. 'I believe enough has been said. Too much, Bertie. I suggest you leave it there.'

But he shook the hand away. 'Lily hasn't embarrassed anyone. It's no fault of hers what her parents did. That was damned near an insult. Take it back, Mama. Lily's my friend.'

'No one needs a friend like Lily Thorpe.'

'*I* do.'

'Stop being naughty, Bertie.'

'Dammit, I'm not a *child!*' He clenched and unclenched the hands held stiffly at his sides, cheeks fiery, while Margot continued to speak condescendingly.

'Darling boy, you know full well that I have your best interests at heart.'

'So long as I do as you say.'

'Run along and talk to Dora, there's a dear. Your father will see poor little Miss Thorpe back home to where she belongs.'

'What if I refuse to run along, or let you take Lily home?'

Margot's eyes flashed. 'We want none of your temper tantrums this afternoon, Bertie. You've brought shame enough upon your family. There are girls whom one marries, and those one dallies with. We all know which sort of girl Lily Thorpe is. She's practically confessed it from her own lips.'

An awed silence fell upon the assembled company, the only sound that of a wood pigeon cooing in the woods behind them, and the crackle of Bertie's long-forgotten fire where he'd meant to toast muffins.

Now he met his mother's gaze unflinchingly. 'Lily can't be blamed for her own birth.' He lifted his chin in a gesture of defiance. 'I've told you, she's my friend. My very dear friend. Lily's a good sport and dashed good fun to have around. Not always making jibes at a chap, or wanting to put him down. Dammit, I might even marry her.'

Margot's face went white then bright red. 'You'll do no such thing!'

Bertie put his arm about Lily and pulled her close to his side. 'I just might.'

The opportunity for revenge was simply too tantalising for Lily to resist. 'And I might just accept,' she said. Whereupon, for once in her life, Margot Clermont-Read actually fainted.

Lily stood on the Persian carpet in the 'little' drawing room, facing Margot Clermont-Read with head held high. The gloomy landscapes seemed to oppress her, adding to her depression. The heat of the small fire in the grate suffocated her, so that Lily could scarcely breathe. What have you done? a voice asked, somewhere inside her head.

'What d'you think you are about?' asked Margot, echoing the

thought. 'Have you no compassion? Are you so out for revenge you would heartlessly ruin my poor boy's life?'

What followed was the most difficult hour Lily had ever spent in her life. Margot spoke at length about Bertie. How he was a foolish boy who had taken temporary leave of his senses.

'Fascinated, no doubt, by your cheap feminine allure. What sort of person does that make you, Thorpe?'

Lily couldn't bring herself even to consider the question. Revenge or no, she'd gone too far, and knew it. It made her tremble to think how she'd dared to stand up to Margot Clermont-Read in the first place. What her mam would say if she knew she'd revealed all the family secrets in that shameful way, Lily didn't care to consider. Really she'd no idea how to extricate herself from this mess without losing even more face.

Yet even as these thoughts raced through her head, Margot's switch to the use of her surname, as if Lily were a servant and of no account, infuriated her afresh. If the woman imagined this tactic would intimidate her, then she'd badly misjudged her adversary. As this thought took hold, laughter welled in Lily's throat. By heck, you had to keep your sense of humour in all of this! What a laugh that Margot Clermont-Read should be in fear and trembling because Lily Thorpe, a girl from The Cobbles, had said she might marry her precious son. Lily pursed her lips tightly together, to keep the laughter in check.

'Since you refuse to speak, I'll tell you what kind of person you are – a common whore!'

Lily flinched. What was the woman suggesting now? 'I beg your pardon, I'm no such thing.'

'You've been seen going in and out of a certain notorious house in Fossburn Street,' Margot informed her.

Lily gasped. "Oo told you that?'

Margot's eyes gleamed. 'Never mind who told me. Is it true?'

'It's true I visit, right enough. Rose is my friend. Surely you don't imagine…'

'Oh, but I do. And if Bertie were to hear of it, he would think so too.'

What could she say? How could she defend herself without condemning Rose and Nan? Only a blind man or a fool wouldn't know what went on in that house. But Margot would never believe Lily wasn't involved. Tarred with the same brush, that would be her opinion.

'Think what you like, Bertie'll never believe it.' Lily could only hope this was true. Then in a calm and reasonable voice, 'All I ask is justice. You never even came to Dick's funeral, just sent a few flowers and washed your hands of him. Mr Clermont-Read thought he could buy off my grief, as if it were a business transaction. Neither one of you thought to apologise to, or help, his poor widowed mother.'

Margot wasn't listening. She drummed her fingers upon the arm of her chair, barely waiting until Lily had finished speaking before continuing with her own line of argument. 'I would've thought that even a woman of your low morals would stop short of such wickedness. Bertie is a sweet sensitive boy who wouldn't hurt a fly. If you care for him in the smallest degree, as you claim to do, you must release him. Would you make him a laughing stock, a pariah among his friends?'

'Happen my revenge is in seeing you sweat.' Lily almost smiled, though inside she felt cold and numb, as if this were some other person attacking Margot Clermont-Read and not herself at all.

Margot leaned back in her seat, folding plump, ringed hands upon a stiffly corseted stomach. 'Ah, of course. In that case, I suspect the matter can be settled quite quickly. Sweating is not something I approve of. We'll accept, for the sake of argument, that you have won, that you have gained your revenge, or justice, whatever you care to call it. Will that do?' She reached for her purse and drew out a tightly rolled bundle of notes. 'There's twenty pounds. More than you usually get paid for your services, I warrant. Certainly more than your Godforsaken family have ever seen in their entire pathetic lives. Take it and go. But leave my boy alone!'

Lily stared at the banknote as if so much as to touch it would scald her fingers. Then she lifted her furious gaze to Margot's.

'Keep your money. If you want to know, I'd no intention of ever going through with it. Bertie only said it to annoy you. I backed him for the same reason.' She stepped closer and wagged a finger in Margot's furious face. 'But I've had enough of being treated like dirt. If he asks me again, happen I will marry him. D'you hear me? And spend the rest of my life making you regret you ever clapped eyes on Lily Thorpe.'

Bertie, apparently, had suffered a similar painful interview with his father. They'd rarely seen eye to eye, and this did not help matters one bit. To Lily's great surprise and almost, it had to be said, her triumph, Bertie stuck steadfastly by her. He claimed that after these months they'd enjoyed together, he'd quite fallen for her and no one, not even his snobbish parents, could alter his feelings. Edward was furious.

Lily told him that her own family would see things differently. But in this, she was to be disappointed. They agreed to meet Bertie because Lily asked them to, but their reaction was muted. Clearly uncomfortable in his presence they kept glancing at each other, a bemused expression on each anxious face.

Hannah took the opportunity to speak on the subject to her daughter as Lily helped brew a fresh pot of tea. 'What are you thinking of, lass? He's the landlord's son. One of the nobs.'

'What of it?'

It was true that Bertie looked incongruous in their shabby kitchen, sitting on a hard stool instead of a brocade-covered sofa, drinking tea from a mug instead of bone china. But not for the world would Lily admit as much.

'I thought you hated that family, 'cause of what they did to Dick?'

'I do hate them.'

'Then you shouldn't think to wed their son.'

Even Rose was unsympathetic. 'You're mad,' she said, when Lily spoke of her intentions. 'He's a lovely man but weak and foolish. He'll drive you up the bleedin' wall in no time. The Berties of this world aren't made for marriage.'

No one, it seemed, was prepared to see her point of view. Lily persuaded herself that her motive for going through with it was not simply revenge. She liked Bertie as much as she could like any man, now that she'd lost Dick. She'd given up on love, hadn't she? Much too painful. Bertie was fun, they enjoyed each other's company, and he'd take her out of The Cobbles. She presented this argument to each and every one of her family and friends, but they were unimpressed.

'Think again,' they said.

'Don't do it.'

'You'll rue the day.'

'It's too high a price to pay.'

'They'll eat you alive.'

But Lily wasn't listening.

Nathan Monroe, watching events closely, had the audacity to tell her that she'd be better off with him. He deliberately waylaid her on her way home from the fish market. 'If it's marriage you're desperate for, I might consider asking you meself.'

Lily stared at him, utterly shocked. 'You can't be serious?'

'At least I'd be man enough for you. Not a broken reed wanting to get even with a snobby mother who's anxious to marry her son off to any horse-faced female who crosses his path, simply because she's rich.'

'Bertie isn't a broken reed. He's kind and amusing and very generous. And he isn't marrying me to get even with his mother.'

'You are. Why not him too? In one fell swoop he can get his own back on an over-critical father, and foil his ambitious mother's plans.'

Lily firmly rejected the suggestion. It was far too uncomfortable. 'Bertie adores me. He's said he loves me a dozen times. Not that you would understand the meaning of the word.'

'At least we'd be of a type, you and me. Two cups from the same pot, eh?'

'Marry you, a bully and a jail bird?' Contempt etched every line of her young face as Lily glared up at him, resolutely recalling every trick Nathan Monroe had ever played on her. Successfully managing to ignore the attractive way his eyebrows flared, how the corners of his mouth twitched constantly into that provocative smile. 'Live for ever in The Cobbles?' She glanced about the street with disdain. 'You must think I've no brains in me head.'

'We could climb out of this hole together.'

Lily laughed, the sound loud and strident, even in a street bustling with activity. 'You'll never get out of The Cobbles, Nathan Monroe. This is where you deserve to be. Like a rat in a sewer.'

He stepped back from her, bright blue gaze shrewdly assessing, and for some reason she shivered. Foreboding perhaps? Or regret? A fanciful notion, she told herself crossly.

'I never said for certain that I would ask you,' he quietly reminded her. 'I only said I might. That if I did, you'd be better suited to me than to that duck-head.'

'Thanks again for the generous offer,' she cockily told him. 'But I'll not be so desperate till I'm ninety, blind and senile. Not even with me dying breath would I contemplate marriage with the likes of you.'

Perhaps it was this last confrontation which finally decided her. The very next day, when Bertie again begged her to elope with him, Lily accepted like a shot. No one but Nathan saw them go.

Chapter Seven

Edward Clermont-Read faced Captain Swinbourne in the Steamship Company office and felt closer to hatred for his own son than was right and proper in any father, even one as sorely tried as himself.

He understood only too well that if you failed to achieve status through birth in this world, you needed wealth and influence in order to command any degree of respect and obedience. Ferguson-Walsh had been about to invite him on to the town council, recommend him for a magistracy, Edward was certain of it. He wouldn't now. In one night Bertie had undermined a lifetime of striving. Men like Swinbourne could look upon him with near contempt.

If this was putting it rather strong, it didn't seem so from Edward's point of view. Life was treating him badly at the moment. There was little comfort to be found at home. Margot had almost thrown an apoplectic fit when she'd discovered Bertie's note saying he'd borrowed the gig to take them to Gretna Green, where he and Lily meant to marry.

'You do see, Mr Clermont-Read, how appreciated your assistance would be,' the Captain was saying. 'In addition, the price of everything – provisions, wood, coal – is rising.'

'Then put up the damned ticket prices!'

The Captain winced as if struck. 'I'm afraid I've already put them up as much as I dare. Any more and we'd lose customers. Besides which, I'm offering you the chance to increase your investment. The *Lucy Ann is* a fine ship but out of date and too small to make real money. We've packed on as many as six hundred on occasions but with a larger vessel, say one hundred and fifty feet long instead of a hundred, and five feet wider, we could take a couple of hundred more passengers at a push. Which would naturally increase our profits.'

'And your overheads.'

'We need to progress, Mr Clermont-Read.'

Edward had seen the overloaded Public Steamers, packed with factory girls from the mill towns and families out on a day trip, far too often to be troubled by any fears about safety. Why should he worry if the ship was too small? Though it was tempting to consider ways of increasing his profits, ready cash was in short supply. A fact which added to his ill humour.

'Progress? Pah! I've spent my life on such a quest.' He returned to a gloomy contemplation of his personal problems. He'd left Margot in bed this morning, as usual, bemoaning her lot and still refusing to rise because her life was in ruins. She'd been there for nigh on two months. Even Selene was beginning to lose patience with her mother.

Meanwhile the recalcitrant pair had settled in The Cobbles, instructed never to darken Margot's door again, and all that rot. His *son* living in The Cobbles, for God's sake! Yet he had made no protest when Margot had turned the boy out, had he?

From all accounts the Thorpe family were no more enamoured of the situation than they were. Though, by God, they should be, Edward thought. He heard the Captain noisily clear his throat and forced himself to concentrate upon the matter in hand.

'I'm afraid you've caught me at a bad time, Swinbourne. Manufacturing is going through a sticky patch at present. Outclassed and out-priced by the damned Germans. Even the Americans. It's almost as if the Empire stands for nothing any more. Imports are increasing, which does me no good at all, don't you know? Exports are bad, which leaves me a bit stretched. God knows where it'll all end.'

Captain Swinbourne was not in the least interested in Clermont-Read's problems. All he cared about was that the man was well-to-do and his largest shareholder, therefore his best bet to touch for a loan at a reasonable rate of interest. So far he was meeting with little success, mainly because of the man's irascible temper, caused no doubt by the madcap behaviour of that young son of his.

'It'll all change when war comes. Iron and steel are the markets to go for, Mr Clermont-Read. And shipbuilding.'

Edward gave the man a sour look. 'You would say that, of course. There'll be no war, dammit! Lot of speechifying and posturing, I'll admit, but it won't happen. I should've invested my money overseas instead of in textiles. Stick with the staples, I told myself. Cotton is safe, always safe. I ship it to half the world, don't you know? But it isn't what it was. The future lies with the dominions, or so they tell me, only I'm too old to emigrate and start again.'

Swinbourne laughed as if this were a joke. 'We both are, but not quite done yet, eh?'

'I've certainly no spare cash to waste any more in playboy entertainments such as this tin bucket. Those days are over. Might ask for me shares back rather than putting more in.'

Captain Swinbourne went white to the lips. This was the last thing he wanted. If Clermont-Read withdrew his goodwill, then he might as well scuttle the *Lucy Ann*, never mind build a new craft. He'd be finished. 'Let's not be hasty,' he soothed. 'Perhaps you'll take a glass of port with me and we'll see if we can't come up with a solution.'

But even after two glasses of excellent port and a sizeable slab of Stilton, Clermont-Read still departed without making any promises whatsoever. Captain Swinbourne sank his head in his hands on a wave of despair, so engrossed in his own misery he did not hear the door open or the click of boots on the rough wooden flooring.

'Excuse me, sir. Wondered if I could have a word?'

A polite cough stirred him. 'What is it now, Monroe? I'm not in the mood for any more problems. Get back to your ticket office where you belong.'

But Nathan was already closing the office door, even having the gall to take the very seat so recently vacated by Edward Clermont-Read.

Swinbourne lifted his head, incensed by the cheek of the young man. 'Who said you could sit down?'

Nathan folded his arms and relaxed into the leather chair. 'I reckon you'll be happy enough to offer me a seat when you hear what I have to say.'

Starting married life in The Cobbles was not at all what Lily had planned. It was clear her family were far from comfortable at being forced to take into their home the son of their landlord, despite their protestations to the contrary. They'd much rather have kept Nathan Monroe, who'd been forced to move out to accommodate this change in circumstance, for until Bertie could find a job there was no alternative.

'I respect all, but bow the knee to no man,' Arnie told him. 'So long as you appreciate that, young man, we'll get along fine. Gentleman of the road or lord of the manor, you're welcome in my house.'

Lily did not feel truly welcome but surprisingly Bertie accepted the situation as if, in his own words, it were all some merry jape.

'It's no joke, lad,' Arnie sternly warned him. 'You'll not be laughing long when your belly starts to wonder where the next meal's coming from. That'll wipe the smile from your face.'

Bertie simply said, 'I won't be a nuisance. We'll be out of here in two shakes. Soon as Mama gets over the sulks.' Then grinned broadly at everyone, winning a giggle from little Kitty.

The sleeping arrangements were far from ideal, with no space for a married couple to sleep together in the overcrowded cottage. Not that Lily minded too much, since she wasn't too sure how she would feel about doing 'It' with Bertie. She'd managed to avoid it so far, and was happy enough to continue to sleep with her sisters while he bunked down with Matt and Jacob. The only thing that really troubled her was that she was right back where she'd started from.

Mama apparently did not get over her sulks that first difficult week, nor even the first month. No word came from Barwick House. It was as if Bertie had ceased to exist. For his part he made no effort to find work. Lily continued to help her mother on the fish stall, although Bertie constantly assured her that he could afford the weekly sum for their keep from his allowance and she'd really no need to work. Lily, however, had every intention of maintaining her occupation which, as winter approached, in any case proved necessary for once again Hannah suffered numerous chills. Discomfort mounted as the small cottage began to reek of camphorated oil and mustard poultices, and space became even more limited with the constant supply of washing steaming before the small peat fire.

Bertie insisted that if Margot did not come round within the next week or two, he would find them a place of their own.

'Don't worry about it.' Hannah said. She liked the young man and the regular income he brought in was desperately needed at this time. 'We can manage if you can.'

'We might be poor,' Arnie told him, pride in his voice, 'but we're better off than many. We have three grand beds between us, a stool or chair each to sit on, and enough food on our table for growing child and working man alike. I've allus kept a roof over our heads and paid our way, for all it's been a struggle at times to find the rent. We don't believe in moonlight flits at this house. Honest but poor, that's what we are, and we want for naught.'

'I can see that,' Bertie assured him. 'You have a fine family, Mr Thorpe.'

'Aye, well, my bairns thrive because we tek good care of 'em. We keeps 'em clean so they don't sicken. Lot o' sickness in these parts. The fever ambulance comes round all the time. But not to our house.' Arnie cast an anxious glance at his wife, as if he were tempting fate by such a proud declaration.

Bertie made suitably sympathetic noises.

'But we're not stupid, don't think we are. I've seen to it that all my bairns can read. I keep abreast of world events, see what Lloyd George and his parliament are up to. What the unions are doing. All this unrest, strikes and such in Liverpool and Manchester – I'm not a union man meself but they have my sympathies – make no bones about that. They're right to fight. Power should be shared a bit more fairly.'

'You've a right to your principles, Mr Thorpe. Applaud that in a chap, I do,' Bertie agreed. 'The working man should indeed be heard.'

Arnie generously offered his newspaper for this new son-in-law to read, should he have a mind to check out world events himself.

Bertie declined.

Lily listened to this conversation which took place in some form or other every evening before the pair of them toddled off for a half of bitter at the Cobbles Inn, and struggled with her own contradictory feelings. She was glad that Bertie liked her parents, and that they had accepted him, yet felt a strange disquiet, as if life were no longer quite real. Could she really be *married* to Bertie Clermont-Read?

And still living in The Cobbles!

Why had she done it? For revenge? Now that the angry impulse was passing, Lily wondered what on earth she had let herself in for. What had she hoped to achieve? Did she love him enough to spend the rest of her life with him? Did she heck as like! She must have been barmy. Driven by that wicked temper of hers.

If nothing else brought home the reality of her situation, it was made clear enough that very first Sunday when the Thorpe family went, as usual, to the Parish Church.

Arnie and Hannah, followed by their children, took their usual seats at the back, Bertie along with them. A flurry of whispers rippled along the pew as everyone shuffled up a little to make space for him, and a score of glares followed his every move. Lily and Hannah exchanged glances.

Where should Bertie sit? With his wife and the common folk on the back pews? Or up by the altar, with his family and the rest of the well-to-do who paid for private pews? It was a well-established system instituted in order to reinforce the hierarchy of class. In the middle of the church sat the artisans, shopkeepers and other skilled men, who thought themselves above those in the back and were anxious to emulate, as best they could, those in the front.

Hannah didn't know where to put herself. Though she

preferred her own private visits to Benthwaite Methodist, she came to St Margaret's as often as she could to please her husband, for all she never felt entirely comfortable in its stiff, hushed atmosphere. Now she fully expected to be struck dead on the spot for daring to bring this young man into the wrong pew.

There was Edward Clermont-Read glowering across the church at Bertie, as if he'd like to drag him from the back pew by the scruff of his neck. Selene was doing her utmost to seem entirely unconcerned even as her face flushed hotly with embarrassment. There was no sign of Margot, for which Lily was thankful. Bertie gave her hand a little squeeze as if to say, Don't worry, it's all right.

But worse was to come. As they left the church by the side entrance as usual, leaving the centre front door for the Clermont-Reads and Ferguson-Walshes, the vicar took a quick side-step towards them. For one second Lily thought he was about to congratulate them on their recent marriage, but ignoring her completely, he took hold of Bertie's hand, shaking it firmly.

'Good to see you here, sir. A fine morning.'

'Indeed.'

Then he scurried back to his duty of seeing out those others of the congregation who were worthy of his personal attention, without so much as a glance in Lily's direction. The Thorpe family, along with the others from the back pews, went home unacknowledged as usual. Even marriage to one of the elect, it seemed, couldn't alter the rules of class.

No word came from Barwick House and eventually Lily found a small cottage for them in Mallard Street, too close to the lake to be quite healthy but at a rent they could afford. Now, at last, they could begin married life proper. She wasn't sure whether it was nervousness, fear or excitement that she experienced as she faced her first night alone with Bertie. Once, she'd been filled with curiosity about such matters, but that had been when she still had Dick. Her life now seemed to be rapidly spinning out of her control.

'I don't know what to do,' she told him, sitting up in bed in her best white nightgown with the crochet collar, and thinking how cold her feet were.

Bertie stood in his long drawers and nightshirt and gave the matter some thought. 'Not had much experience with gels meself. Boys' school and all that. And the milk-sops Mama paraded in front of me would never do anything so rude.'

This brought forth a giggle. 'You really are naughty, Bertie.'

'Am I?' He came close to the bed, taking in the small pert breasts rising and falling beneath the thin cotton lawn of her gown.

'Have you – ' Lily flushed – 'never done it before either then?'

'Wouldn't say that, old thing.' He manfully puffed out his chest. 'A chap has to practise. The odd maid was willing, don't you know?'

'Oh, Bertie.' Lily regarded him from wide sad eyes. 'You're not one of those rogues who get girls in trouble, are you?'

'Dash it, no. I'm a gentleman. Wouldn't be so unsporting.'

Lily was beginning to feel more relaxed, and risked a shy glance in Bertie's direction as he stripped off the under-drawers. His legs weren't bad. Quite straight and firm, not at all knobbly. She imagined them wrapped around her and didn't find the idea alarming. Seeing her interest, he grinned at her and recklessly threw off his nightshirt, whereupon Lily's heart quickened in alarm as her eyes fastened on that previously unseen part of a man's anatomy.

'Don't worry. I won't hurt you.' If he didn't get on with it, he'd find his gun cocked and ready miles before he could take aim. He drew back the sheets, pushing her back against the pillows and drawing Lily's nightgown up over the sprightly firmness of her breasts. Then he straddled her rather as he might his favourite horse. 'We'll work it out together, eh? What d'you say?'

They managed, in fact, to work it out quite well.

The mysteries of womanhood were at last revealed to Lily, and after it was all over and they lay hot and sticky with their efforts, she really didn't feel inclined to complain. Bertie was a vigorous, enthusiastic lover, eager to please and clearly enjoyed every minute of it. And if his whooping shouts of pleasure as he thrust into her sounded more like a hunting call than romantic wooing, Lily found she didn't mind, not really. It all seemed like good fun and she was done with romance, wasn't she?

Lily's first baby was born some nine months later, and beautiful though she undoubtedly was, little Amy's birth seemed to Lily like the final closing of the trap. She'd end up like her mother for sure now. What was to stop another and another? Lily certainly had no idea.

Hannah's health unfortunately continued to cause concern. She suffered one cold after another and should have seen a doctor, had the Thorpe family been able to afford one.

Instead, Lily visited a herbalist's shop on the corner of Drake Road. Dusty and filled with an odd odour, it was nevertheless well-stocked with powders in screws of paper fastened by elastic to cards, sold three for a penny. Even more mysterious potions were secreted in a myriad range of tiny drawers. The herbalist claimed to be a marvellous diagnostic with the power to cure any sickness, without even seeing the patient.

Lily plucked up the courage to ask him for something for herself too.

'I d-don't want no more bairns just now, you see,' she stammered. 'So I wondered if happen you knew of some way to stop 'em?' The herbalist regarded her for a long silent moment from above his glasses before fumbling beneath the counter and handing her a packet.

'Mix a teaspoonful with water and use on a sponge,' were his instructions, and for a mad moment Lily almost told him she used a face flannel and soap, but then his meaning dawned and, blushing hotly, she paid her money and fled.

So they struggled on as best they could, with Emma and Liza now carrying the burden of the housework at home, and though Lily called in on her mother every day and it broke her heart to see how thin she got, both of them despaired over what more could be done.

'You've enough to worry over,' Hannah would say. 'See to your own problems.'

Bertie was proving to be something of a disappointment. He seemed quite incapable of supporting his new family. And Margot had now cut off his allowance.

'Dash it, Lily,' he'd protest whenever she suggested he look for a job. 'What could I do?'

She did succeed once in gently bullying him into taking a job as potman at the Cobbles Inn. But he drunk most of his meagre wages in whisky, and gambled the rest away at black jack before the first week was up.

'Sorry old thing, couldn't resist it. Not my fault if they pay a chap a pittance, is it?'

Bertie, Lily realised, had no sense of the value of money. What a family could live on for a week, he could gamble on a single throw of the cards. Whatever he'd wanted previously had always been provided for him. He couldn't seem to adjust to the fact that life was different now.

She'd taken over the job herself in the end. Afternoons and some evenings, Liza worked alongside Lily now on the fish stall in place of Hannah, which was a help in a way, for most of the time Lily had the bairn with her. Bertie complained that he knew nothing about nappies and feeding bottles so if she left little Amy at home, how could she be sure she'd be properly looked after? At least Liza was happy to play with the child while Lily worked.

Bertie spent his day on his 'inventions'. These consisted of endless drawings done on any scrap of paper he could find or buy with money they could ill afford. He drew planes and boats and motor-cars, without hope of ever being able to bring one of his designs to fruition. But if Lily ever said as much, he would vigorously protest.

'Have faith, Lily. I'll find the money one day, then you'll see.'

But this life was far removed from the one he'd enjoyed at Barwick House, his family home. There were no servants in The Cobbles. No cook to make delicious dinners or prepare cream teas. No pretty housemaid to fetch hot coffee and rolls to his room for breakfast in bed. Here in Mallard Street, what you couldn't provide for yourself, you did without.

Lily made a huge pot of broth every Monday, hoping that would last them for most of the week. On Sunday afternoons she went mushrooming, raspberry or blackberry picking, seeking whatever was in season. Even nettles could make a tasty soup if you found them fresh and young enough.

She baked two large loaves every Tuesday evening, marked them with her initials and took them down to the communal bakehouse where she paid a penny-farthing to get them baked. The first time she'd done this, she'd come home the next day to find Bertie had eaten an entire loaf, all by himself. She'd nearly gone demented.

'That should've lasted us till Friday. D'you think we're made of brass?'

But he'd looked at her with such soulful eyes and told her how hungry he'd been, and how sorry he was, that she felt bound to forgive him. 'Don't be cross, Lily. I won't do it again,' he promised.

But of course he had. Used to plenty, how could he adjust to poverty rations? Yet how could she scold him? He would touch her cheek with his soft lips, slide his smooth hands along her neck and over the curve of her breast, and all protests would die to a whisper within her. He'd tell her how silky was her skin, how soft and curling her hair, how sweet she tasted. Lily would ache to put Amy quickly to bed so she could lie in his arms and have him kiss her all over and do things to her that made her blush with shame the next morning.

For all she'd found less satisfaction from her act of revenge upon his family than she'd expected or hoped, and despite all their hardships and worries, surprisingly, Lily didn't regret marrying Bertie Clermont-Read, not for a minute. Being married had opened up a whole new world to her, and Lily couldn't say she didn't enjoy it.

Margot rose from her couch, where she'd progressed from her bed, the day Selene put on her best lambswool jacket and announced she would go and bring Bertie back from The Cobbles that instant, even if she had to drag him by the scruff of his neck.

'Will you truly?'

'I can't bear this situation another moment.'

'Tell him that all this trauma has made me quite ill,' his mother declared. 'Tell him that if he does not return, I shall cut him off without a penny.'

Selene gave a wry smile. 'I doubt he'd believe you. Haven't you always given him everything he asked for, and more? Besides, you know full well, Mama, that Bertie has a poor grip on life. He thinks no further than his next meal or entertainment.' Selene wanted him home for her own reasons. If her chances of marriage had been slim before, owing to the naturally high standards she set herself, they were almost nil now. Who would wish to be allied with a family who harboured a madman living in The Cobbles?

On this occasion she deigned to allow George to accompany her, since no lady in her right mind would tread the streets of The Cobbles alone. It was just as well she did. The moment she climbed down from the gig, a tramp approached with his cap held out. When she would have brushed past him, he made a grab for her arm. Horror-struck, Selene thrust him off, almost kicking him into the gutter, then strode unheeding away.

'How very unpleasant to see beggars littering the street. It really spoils the pleasure of a drive, don't you think?'

George made no comment.

Having ascertained the whereabouts of number two Mallard Street, Selene wrapped a scarf about her hat and face, pressed a rose-scented handkerchief to her nose and regarded the house with a shudder of repulsion.

'I'll come with you,' George said, eyeing a group of youths who hovered close by.

'And risk losing the horse? Don't be stupid, man. Pray wait for me here. I'll not be more than ten minutes.'

'I'll come looking for you after fifteen, horse or no, miss.'

Such gallantry, she thought. Nor was George at all bad-looking. Tall and straight-limbed, with black curly hair and a ready smile, she'd often considered the possibility of a little dalliance with him, but rejected it. It didn't do to put oneself in debt to a servant. And she must save herself for the right man. Pity, though, that such attributes could rarely be found with a sizeable bank balance attached.

Selene found Bertie seated in the midst of unimaginable squalor. Still in his nightwear, though it was gone eleven in the morning, he sat bleary-eyed, a mug of tea at his elbow, looking pathetically sorry for himself with a screaming infant on his lap. She almost found it in her heart to pity him. But then Selene recalled the misery of these last months; how all invitations to parties, balls and the like had completely dried up. The recollection soon hardened her heart.

There were some matters which simply could not be forgiven. Betrayal of family was one.

He was flatteringly pleased to see her. 'I say, Selene old thing, what're you doing in this neck of the woods? Don't tell me Mama is rolling out the crimson carpet of forgiveness?'

Selene looked about the shabby room with dismay, her kid-gloved hands keeping the hem of her pink voile dress several inches from the ground in case it should become soiled. A pan of milk had boiled over on the hob, leaving a trail of sticky yellow fluid all down the brass fretwork. A basket of ironing stood on a stool, waiting for attention. Upon the kitchen table lay scattered a half loaf of bread and a dish of some indistinguishable mush. She wrinkled her nose in distaste. 'What on earth is that appalling smell?'

Bertie jerked his head at the ceiling. 'Smoked herring.' Strung high across the room was a wire upon which hung flat fish, split open and smoking above the fire. Selene shuddered.

'Makes your eyes water, eh? You get used to it though. Taste delicious when they're done.' He grinned.

His pleasure infuriated her all the more. 'You're to come home this instant, Bertie. Get your coat. You've made Mama quite ill with all of this, and she'll stand no more of it.'

His face tightened. 'Is that what she told you to say?'

'She's concerned. This is no life for you.'

The child let out another wail, stiffening her tiny body in fury.

Sighing, Bertie got up and started to stir the glutinous mess in the dish. He offered a spoonful. The baby opened her mouth and bawled all the louder. Bertie seemed entirely unperturbed and simply raised his voice above the din. 'Sorry we're in a bit of a mess today. Overslept. Amy had a bad night. Poor thing's teething, don't you know? Kept us all awake.'

Selene could hardly believe her eyes. Could this truly be her own brother in this appalling dung-heap of a kitchen, feeding a raucous infant as if it were the most natural thing in the world? 'Bertie, what are you thinking or You must get out of this place. Mama really is ill. She needs you.'

'Rightio. Soon as I've finished feeding Amy, I'll go and pack.'

'You mean you'll come?'

'You don't think I want to stay here, do you? Though I must say I find the people more friendly than I expected. Always ready to enjoy a tankard of ale with me.'

'So long as you're buying, I suppose?'

Bertie gave a shame-faced grin. 'That was the way of it, at first. Temporarily out of funds now, old girl. Don't suppose Mama would ... No, course not.'

Selene pressed home her advantage. 'She might. Once you're back in the fold, you'll be her darling boy again. She'll give you anything you ask.'

Surprisingly Bertie frowned, indicating with a jerk of his chin the scatter of papers that littered the rug. 'I have plans. I could survive without Mama. I really don't mind a bit of squalor, Selene. It's pomposity I can't stomach.'

She recognised the sincerity in his soft brown eyes, but Selene was rapidly losing patience. 'Oh, Bertie, do come along. I haven't all day. You've made your point. If you come home now, Mama will be quite different, I promise. Don't you want to get out?'

'I'd leave tomorrow, this minute – given half a chance. Lily would too.'

'Lily?'

'Course. She hates this place even more than I do.'

'I dare say she does. We all know that's one of the reasons she

101

married you – to escape.' Selene picked up an enamel dish of goose grease between finger and thumb and dropped it back upon the table with a shudder. 'We're not talking about Lily. We're talking about you. She'll survive as she did before.'

Bertie looked puzzled for a moment, and then as her meaning became clear, utterly stunned. 'I couldn't leave without Lily. She's my wife. And this little monster here is my darling daughter.' He lifted the baby high in his arms and gently shook her. For a second Amy stopped crying and almost smiled at him.

'There, did you see that? Love your papa?' He jiggled the baby some more.

'Don't be ridiculous. Small babies don't have emotions.'

'Amy does.'

Selene watched in horror as a dribble started at the child's nose and Bertie wiped it away with his thumb, then tucked the infant back upon his lap, whereupon she wailed all the louder. 'I say, you don't know anything about making porridge, do you, Selene old thing? Lily left Amy with me because she's teething, but she won't eat the stuff I've made, and won't stop crying for a second.'

His words were spoken to the empty air. Selene had gone.

Chapter Eight

Nathan felt pleased with his progress. Captain Swinbourne had been shaken at first by his offer to invest in the Steamship Company but had accepted all the same. As well he might. True, Nathan didn't have the funds which Clermont-Read might have offered, which meant the new ship must be put on hold, but Swinbourne was a desperate man. He'd spent one too many afternoons at the card table to refuse help, even from someone who'd only risen from ticket collector to booking clerk. By the time Nathan had outlined his plans for increasing trade Swinbourne was willing, if not exactly eager, to clinch the deal.

Improving the waiting room came high on Nathan's list, dingy and depressing place that it was. Many local people used the steamer to get about, as it was quicker and more convenient than travelling by horse and cart on the poor country roads. But they needed to be encouraged, particularly with the threat of the coming motor-cars. For now these were currently a pleasure confined to the very rich, though Nathan believed things might change. A man had to look to the future. Besides which, if the Carreckwater Steamship Company was to survive, it should look as if it were thriving.

The refurbishment of the fore-saloon for first-class passengers on *Lucy Ann* was another essential, and they should also provide refreshments. Nathan remarked that it wasn't enough to be full on Bank Holidays with mill workers and half empty the rest of the time. There had to be other ways of increasing profits.

Quickly promoted to Business Manager, and now a shareholder, a good deal of his time was now spent writing letters to railway and charabanc companies, hoteliers and the like, offering special deals for outings on Carreckwater. By summer he hoped these efforts would start to pay off.

He didn't intend to stay Business Manager for long, nor a small shareholder. Nathan knew himself to be ambitious. He meant to go all the way to the top. He'd started from just about as low as you could get, with a lot to put behind him, so what did he have to lose?

Now he strode happily home through The Cobbles, heedless of the dirty streets for he could scent the tang of autumn in the breeze: wood smoke and peat fires and soft brown earth. It was a scent which reminded him of days out mushrooming with his mother. She'd always told him it was magical, unique to her beloved Lake country. The best place on God's earth, she'd called it. He'd believed her then, and still had no reason to dispute it. But then he'd been in places since where all you could smell was the next man's vomit.

Nathan felt privileged to spend his days by the lake; to watch the glitter of leaves, topaz, gold and saffron, as they drifted down on to water that glowed like molten honey in the autumn light.

He loved the friendly cluster of green mountains, drawing their cloaks of autumn rust about them, and the invigorating crispness of the northern air, something he'd missed on those miserable journeys south. He loved this whole damned country, and now that he'd managed at last to return to it, meant to stay. One day he would build himself a house by the lake. Why not? All it took was money.

For now he had the use of two rooms and a tiny kitchen on the first floor of a house on the corner of Drake Road where it crossed with Mallard Street. His landlady was not the interfering sort, but Nathan looked upon the arrangement as temporary. He'd find somewhere better soon, a whole house to himself, one that he owned, not rented. He hated to be beholden to anybody.

He heard the noise the minute he turned the corner. Jeering laughter, the sound of bricks being thrown and glass breaking. What now? There was always some trouble or other in this place.

A gang of youths had evidently set upon some poor fool. He was making a valiant fight of it, whoever he was, fists and feet flying every which way. Not an uncommon sight in The Cobbles. Nathan had learned early on in life not to interfere with other folk's problems. Hadn't he enough of his own? So he skirted the group, ready to hurry by, but then realised the man had gone down. Nathan caught a brief glimpse of a blood-splattered head being hammered into the dirt. There was no mistaking that sandy hair.

'Hit the toff!' someone shouted. 'Let 'im have it.'

Nathan didn't hesitate. He launched himself into the melee with a terrifying roar, grasping collars, cuffing chins, flinging bodies to left and right.

'Here, who the hell are you to interfere?'

Nathan peeled the flailing bodies off the heap one by one until he reached the last. Hands came up to grasp his throat and he only just managed to thrust them away.

'Leave off. I'm on your side, you daft idiot!' Then he pulled Bertie to his feet. Even when he'd succeeded the man wasn't for standing still. Knocking Nathan's supporting arm away, Bertie set off after the now rapidly retreating youths at a hobbling run.

'Let them go,' Nathan shouted.

'No, dammit. I'll knock their heads together when I catch them, see if I don't.'

'Are you mad?' Nathan charged after him and dragged Bertie to a halt, though he continued to struggle furiously to be released.

'Let me go, dammit! The blighters broke our window. Could've hit Amy. And they ruined my new hat. Finest felt, Russian leather band with a silk lining. Cost a damned fortune. I'll show the brutes what's what.'

Nathan gave a shout of laughter. 'I believe you would.'

'I'd've killed the bastards if you hadn't interfered.'

Nathan tightened his grip on the furious Bertie and flattened him against the wall. 'There are six of them at least. More likely they'd kill you.'

Bertie stopped fighting instantly and began to shake. In a more subdued voice he said, 'I'd kill for a whisky.'

Nathan chuckled. 'That's more like it. After a fight with the Mackenzie and Adams boys, you deserve one. Come on. I admire your spunk for taking 'em on. A whisky it shall be.'

With Amy parked in her pram beside them, the two men stood at the bar enjoying a tot or two of whisky, generously provided by

Nathan. They exchanged a few fighting anecdotes, examined various scars resulting from these valiant confrontations, and generally warmed to each other's company.

Nathan told Bertie his spunk would make anyone think twice about tackling him in future, and Bertie told Nathan something of his plight and of Selene's visit.

'You mean, you had the chance to leave and you turned it down?'

'I couldn't leave Lily, could I?' Bertie sounded affronted at the very idea. 'Pa would only start on at me the minute I walked in, and Mama would weep and wail. I'm not sure I'm quite up to all of that sort of tosh.'

Nathan laughed. 'You're an odd fish and no mistake.'

After an hour or two Amy started to grizzle and Bertie thought she might be getting hungry. Nathan suggested they should mend the window.

'Wouldn't know how.'

'I know someone. Dab hand with glass he is.'

'Can't pay the blighter. Clean pockets, old chap,' Bertie said, ruefully smiling as if it were of no consequence.

'You can pay me back later.'

'Jolly decent of you. Won't forget.' But of course he would, and they both knew it.

Laughing, Nathan shook his head, unable to understand a man who could have everything and settled for nothing. But then, he didn't have quite nothing, did he? He had Lily.

Winter was not the best time to work on a fish stall. As the cold deepened Lily cut up an old pair of ribbed stockings. Two halves she pulled over the tops of her clogs to help keep her feet dry, the other two were for her hands, leaving the fingers free to gut and fillet the fish. Sometimes they were that cold she felt sure they'd drop off.

She wore a pinafore over her jumper and skirt, and a cardigan and thick coat over that. Finally she draped a sack over her shoulders to keep the worst of the rain off. Even so she was often wet and frozen to the bone.

Working behind the bar in the Cobbles Inn, for all the stink of old straw on the floor and thick pipe smoke in the fetid air, was almost a pleasure after that, if only for its warmth. Though what her mother-in-law would think if she knew, Lily didn't care to imagine. Women rarely set foot in a public house, let alone worked in one. Not decent women. Nor would she even have considered it if Jim the landlord weren't a friend, Bertie useless, and herself near desperate.

She ate her sandwiches and drank her bottle of cold tea at dinnertime, listening to Rose chattering away as usual about Nan's 'friends'.

'She gets worse. Stands at the doorway beckoning 'em in now, she does. Still, we have to eat, I suppose.'

'Has she ever – well, you know?'

Rose frowned, and then her small face cleared as she laughed. 'What, asked me to join in? No fear. She knows I've more sense. I'll have to move out if she doesn't stop. Anyroad, it's ages since you came to visit us in Fossburn Street.'

Lily admitted this to be true. 'When I'm not working, Bertie likes me at home with him.'

'That's a bit of a rum do.'

'He hates to be left alone too much.'

'Not ashamed of us, are you?' Head tilted, Rose challenged her to deny it.

'Don't be silly.' But the accusation had made Lily feel uncomfortable. 'I'll come over one evening next week, all right?'

'Fetch Bertie an' all. Me mam'll keep him company while we have a natter.' They both giggled, amused by the thought of Nan with Bertie. Lily thought she should be glad really, that Rose had asked her. She found it oddly lonely, being married.

By four o'clock they'd thankfully sold the last of the fish and vegetables. It was dark even then, and they were all shivering with cold. Rose went off home to Fossburn Street. Lily wiped down the stall while Liza swept all around, then gathering up the empty baskets, they set off for home. Lily had managed to buy a few cracked eggs cheap, and meant to take them to her mother on the way. Hannah needed them more than she did at present.

They'd not had a bad day though. With Christmas coming up folk were prepared to spend. But profits were still down. When she could, Lily bought fish from Flookburgh and Whitehaven to add to what her father caught, in order to make a decent income. Even then it was cutting it fine. Arnie did his best, of course, with what bit of boatbuilding he could find. And at least he no longer had the boys to worry about. Jacob had gone to work for a shipbuilder in Liverpool, and Matt was in Fleetwood where the fishing was better. But there were still the three girls to feed and Hannah to care for.

Lily found her mother in bed, as usual these days, one or two old coats piled on top of the thin crocheted blankets in an effort to keep her warm.

The curtained portion of the room once occupied by her two brothers seemed oddly bare without them, and Lily felt a pang of regret for their robust strength. Yet she was glad they were out of this Godforsaken place, glad they at least had a chance in life.

Emma was trying to coax Hannah to try a taste of watery soup, but she kept pausing to cough up blood into a rag that should long since have been put in the wash. Lily found her a fresh one, her heart clenching with pain at the sight of more ominously soiled rags on the bedside table. 'Never mind that soup, Mam. See what I've fetched you.' She kissed the pale face. 'I'll whip you up a nice egg custard. How about that?'

'I'm sorry about all of this, our Lily.'

'What's to be sorry for? T'isn't your fault.'

'Feel's like it is. How's the bairn? I haven't seen her for ages.'

'She's at home with Bertie. Teething, and too cold out. I'll fetch her when you're better.'

Hannah nodded, the bleak knowledge in her eyes that she might never get better, nor see her precious grandchild ever again. 'Did you do well on the stall today?'

Hannah's voice seemed to Lily more frail and weak with each passing day. It didn't take a herbalist or doctor now to diagnose what was wrong.

'Don't talk. It'll only make you cough more.'

'I've felt better today,' Hannah fiercely declared, as if she could make this true through sheer will-power, 'I might get up tomorrow.' Which, as Lily had predicted, set off a fit of coughing which took some time to ease.

While Emma tended to her mother, Lily put the rags to soak in salt water and tore up some fresh ones from an old flour sack. Back in the kitchen she faced her father. 'Mam needs a doctor.'

Arnie grunted.

'Have you been paying into the club like I told you?'

'I paid what I could, when I could. It's all used up.'

'What d'you mean, it's all used up?'

'Our credit. We've none left.'

'Surely you could manage a penny a week? Mam needs a doctor.'

Arnie gazed upon his daughter with bleak eyes and Lily felt sick, guessing what was to come. 'I've not even a penny to buy a twist of tea. I've been laid off from the boatyard. Boss says I'm never there when he needs me. Allus out on t'fishing or taking care of Hannah.' He sat down like a man exhausted, gazing up at the ceiling as if he could see his wife through it. 'I don't know what else to do, our Lily. I'm at me wit's end. I love yer mam, you know I do. I don't seem to have the energy to go on wi'out her.'

'Oh, Dad.' She went to him and held him close while he sobbed on to her shoulder. It was the most painful experience of her life. How could her father have come to this? Arnie Thorpe was strong, always had been. A good and kindly man. And here he was, a pitiful wreck, his heart broken with grief. 'Have you enquired about the sanatorium?' She felt his body stiffen.

'She'll die if she goes there.'

Lily knew her mother would die if she didn't go, but couldn't find it in her heart to say so.

'No, she won't. She'd get the care she needs. I'll see what I can find out.' Again she held her father close, fighting the tears blocking her own throat. It wouldn't do for them both to break down. 'If The Cobbles wasn't such a filthy place, happen fewer people would get consumption. And we know who to blame for that, now don't we?'

'Aw, Lily, don't start on that caper now,' Arnie chided, blowing his nose and trying to regain his composure. 'There's naught we can do.'

Oh, but there should be, she thought.

Lily did the best she could to make Hannah comfortable, though she managed little of the egg custard, then brewed Arnie a mug of sweet tea and cuddled her distressed sisters, offering what advice and comfort she could.

'I'll have to go. I've me own family to see to.'

Emma's face was pinched and frightened. She it was who carried the burden of caring for Hannah, taking more time off school than she should. 'You'll come tomorrow as usual, Lily?'

'Course I will. Do I ever miss? I'll bring you summat good to eat.' How she would manage to keep such a reckless promise Lily couldn't at the moment imagine. But she meant to, come what may.

'Will you fetch me a bull's eye, our Lily?'

'I will, Kitty. If I have to catch the animal meself.'

Kitty giggled. 'I meant a toffee ball.'

'Oh!' Lily pretended surprise. 'That's different. We'll have to see if I'm passing Mrs Robbins's shop then, won't we?'

'You pass it every day.'

'Aye, usually with an empty pocket. Still, we'll see what tomorrow brings. Now keep your peckers up, the lot of you. You do Mam no good pulling long faces.'

But as she hurried away, Lily's own heart was heavy. Hannah had devoted her life to caring for her family. Nothing had ever been too good for them. Not for her children the bad teeth and bare feet so common among the chronically poor. She'd toiled to provide the best food she could manage, even if it was too often only stinking fish. There was no better food for the brain, she'd told them.

The rain started again as Lily strode down Carter Street. She pulled the sacking close about her neck, less vigour than usual in her stride. Her body felt bone weary, a hundred years old.

As she turned the corner into Mallard Street, she was surprised to see a group of men outside her own cottage, then recognised one of them. Nathan Monroe. What was he up to?

When Lily reached the men and took in what had happened, the smashed window with glass everywhere, rain pouring in all over her table top, Amy screaming like a banshee, life was suddenly too much. A bolt of fury shot through her and she lashed out at Nathan Monroe without stopping to think.

'What the bleedin' hell have you done now, you wicked bully?' Her arms flailed, hands slapping whatever bare flesh she could reach while Nathan defended himself as best he could. Then hands were gripping her, Nathan's hands, hard on her arms, and Bertie's voice high with panic.

'Leave him be, Lily. He's *helping*, not attacking us.'

But instead of simply stopping, she broke down in tears, and for a while it seemed as if she would never stop.

When Lily heard the whole sorry story she was forced to offer an apology to Nathan, for all she did so with bad grace. In her eyes he would never be anything but trouble. Lily hated everything about him: his broad handsome face, untidy brown hair and fierce brows. And the deep grooves etched between nose and wide mouth, even if that mouth did smile at her with disturbing good humour whenever she happened to glance his way. Most of all she hated his brooding blue eyes, which she didn't care even to think about.

'Bertie was managing to stand up for himself very well, as a matter of fact,' Nathan was saying. 'But he was a touch outnumbered.'

'Though not outclassed. What a lark!' Bertie agreed with a grin. 'The way you ploughed into them, tossing them aside like bobbins! And I bloodied at least one nose, I can tell you. Rather like being back at school.'

Lily stared at her young husband and wondered if he'd the least idea what he was saying. Those youths, unlike his public school chums, would have thought nothing of beating him to a pulp. For that reason alone she should be grateful to Nathan Monroe for intervening. 'What was it all about, anyroad?'

'I don't think they cared for my new hat,' Bertie remarked, with his usual air of unconcern.

'Hat? What new hat?'

He held up the battered item. 'No good now, old thing. Have to chuck it.'

For a whole half minute Lily couldn't speak. Then she flew to the cupboard and pulled out the battered tea caddy where she hid her savings. She gave it a quick rattle and breathed a sigh of relief.

Utterly shocked, he said, 'I wouldn't take your money, Lily,' while Nathan studiously kept a blank face. A fact which infuriated Lily all the more.

'How did you pay for it then?'

'On Mama's account, old thing. She'll never notice. Had to have one. Winter coming and all that.'

Lily stared helplessly at him, letting the anger drain from her body. What was the use? Their child needed food in her belly. Rent had to be paid. Her own mother might die of consumption but Bertie bought a new hat. The right clothes for the right occasion was too much a part of his life-style for him ever to understand hers. It was a wonder he didn't still change for dinner.

Lily slapped jam on a few thin slices of bread and made a great show of carefully scraping off the excess, while grudgingly issuing an invitation for Nathan to stay to tea, fully expecting him to refuse.

'Glad to,' he said, lifting the soup pan on to the hob when he saw it was too heavy for her to manage. 'I could do with a bite after this afternoon's adventures.' The two men exchanged a look of silent agreement that no mention should be made of the whisky drinking session.

Lily doled out sparse portions of hot soup, wanting to save some for her family the next day, as promised. She followed it with the jam and bread and a mug of tea each. The meal may have been poor, but while Lily sat silent was nonetheless merry so far as the two men were concerned, as they recounted the joys of the afternoon.

'Did you see that rascal's face when you popped him one?' Bertie chortled. 'He wondered where on earth you'd sprung from.'

'You nearly popped one on me,' Nathan laughed, and his

descriptions became so wildly extravagant and yet so sharply funny that even Lily found herself smiling, eyes dancing, momentarily catching Nathan's laughing glance and moving as quickly away again.

'Have you had enough?' she asked at last, taking away his plate.

'The soup was tasty. Thanks.' She could tell by the doubt in his voice that the food fell short of what he was used to. He was no doubt still hungry.

'D'you have much trouble getting meat?' he casually enquired, and while Lily bridled with indignation at the implied criticism, Bertie sighed and happily closed his eyes, content before the warm fire.

'We get by,' was all she was prepared to admit. Not that she could remember the last time she'd tasted a bit of pork, or even liver. 'Bertie shot us a rabbit the other week, didn't you?' She forbore to mention that there'd been little meat left on it, since he'd blasted most of it away.

'I could get you a pig's head. Make lovely brawn with that.'

Lily stiffened, even as her mouth watered. 'We need no charity, thanks very much. We can manage well enough on us own.'

'Sometimes a bit of venison comes my way.'

'I'm sure it does,' she responded, a dryness to her tone which left them all in no doubt how she believed he came by it.

A short silence fell and every part of Lily seemed to prickle with a new awareness. Why did he watch her so closely? Why did Nathan Monroe go to so much trouble to help Bertie? They weren't in the least bit alike. They came from quite opposite backgrounds, a world apart in fact. Yet they chattered away like old friends.

Silence fell, disturbed only by the shifting of hot ashes in the grate and Bertie's gentle snores. Why did Nathan linger? Why didn't he have the grace to offer his thanks and go?

Attempting to ignore him, Lily turned her attention to sewing buttons on one of Bertie's shirts, but couldn't resist surreptitiously studying Nathan from beneath her lashes. He'd bought a new coat by the look of it. Navy blue, in a fine cloth. And he'd shaved. Looked almost respectable for once, despite his hair being as wild as ever and far too long. Lily recalled Rose's words and almost smiled, forced to concede that no one could deny his good looks. To her horror she found his blue eyes resting upon her, studying her with amused interest. She drove her needle into a finger and, giving a little yelp, jumped to her feet, blood spurting on to the clean shirt.

'You've hurt yourself.' He leaned towards her and Lily flinched quickly away, wrapping the finger in her pinny.

'It's nothing. I'm tired, that's all. I'm off to bed now, Bertie. It's been a day and a half.' She made no mention of her visit to Hannah, not feeling able to cope with his sympathy. Yet now she glared at her husband, wanting him to ask, needing his interest and willing him to look up and say he'd come to bed too. Then this odious man would be forced to leave. But Bertie slept blissfully on, tired as a result of all the unusual excitement. As Lily went to the door at the foot of the stairs, Nathan followed her.

'I've no wish to offend, Lily. I thought you'd mebbe like a bit of something tasty for your mam. I know she's ill.'

He seemed even bigger close to, his head almost touching the low ceiling. Tight-faced, Lily took a step back, unwilling to meet his gaze again, and found herself up against the door post. She couldn't quite co-ordinate her hands to do her bidding and open the door. Hadn't it always been so when he was around? Hadn't he always taken pleasure in making her tremble with nerves? Hovering so close to her she could smell the musky maleness of him, see every hair on the back of the hand which rested on the door jamb beside her. Why did he put on this show of understanding? Why did he pretend to care, when quite clearly he wanted only to frighten and humiliate her?

'Bertie can provide whatever we need,' she sharply informed her. It was a bare-faced lie and they both knew it.

'The offer stands if you change your mind.' Then he lifted his hand and let the back of his fingers drift lightly over her cheek. Lily recoiled as if he'd scalded her.

'I've told you, we can manage. Thanks all the same.' She felt pride in the firmness of her voice and, stiff-backed, pulled open the door and went upstairs to bed. But unfortunately not to sleep. From below drifted the low hum of voices, interspersed with soft laughter.

Long after Bertie had slipped into bed, quietly, so as not to disturb her, Lily still gazed wide-eyed into the darkness, sleep held at bay by the memory of a smile, by a touch as smooth as silk and the fact that her body seemed to hum with newly awakened desire for a man who was not her husband. A man whom she claimed to despise.

Bertie did not agree with Lily's poor opinion of Nathan Monroe. The two became such fast friends they were rarely seen apart. It riled her to watch the friendship develop yet know herself powerless to prevent it. Too often when she came home from work she would find them both sitting at the table, playing dominoes or cards, or simply chatting and laughing. Or the pair of them would go off some place, not telling her where. What they were up to half the time Lily did not care to consider. Was Nathan teaching Bertie his wicked ways? she worried, alarmed and frustrated.

And if a part of her felt jealous of the new friendship, or trembled a little when Nathan brushed by or even glanced in her direction, not for a moment would she acknowledge it. She had her family, and her lovely Amy. Nathan Monroe was trouble. The last thing she needed was to become involved with such a man.

Yet despite her best efforts he occupied Lily's thoughts waking and sleeping. Her skin yearned to feel again the promise of his caress, her eyes followed his every move. She knew he was aware of her interest, yet was quite unable to prevent herself. Knowledge of his power over her was clear in the amused light in his eyes, the twist of his mouth. He held her spellbound, like a mouse facing a snake. Yet much as Lily longed to force Bertie to banish him from their home, she didn't have the energy to protest.

Her only salvation was to fill her days with work. To become so tired she did not have the energy to think. With so many people to care for, so many people depending on her, money became a constant worry.

Lily was determined Amy shouldn't suffer or be deprived of anything she needed. The child would soon be needing shoes. Her baby toes were kept warm in knitted bootees, but in a few months Lily knew she would be walking, and by next winter would need something far more substantial. She was growing at a rapid rate.

'She's a credit to you,' Rose would say as she jiggled the infant on her lap. 'So she should be, the way you coddle the little blighter.'

Lily half starved herself in order to buy fresh vegetables for the child. Hannah had passed on many of Kitty's old clothes, but Lily longed to make Amy something new, something of her own, that no other child had worn.

Each week she'd put aside what she could to that end. A farthing here, a halfpenny there. Little enough, but over the months she had meant it to accumulate enough to enable her to buy proper shoes, and material which she could sew into a new frock and coat and bonnet. Hand-me-down rags weren't good enough for her child. Not for Bertie's lovely daughter.

The money was there in the tea caddy, safe, untouched even by Bertie's extravagance. Now she weighed these plans against the reality of her mother's illness. What price a child's pair of shoes against a woman's life, a family's needs?

Facing up to reality, Lily took the few coppers she'd managed to save thus far and bought more eggs and milk for her mother. She'd make Amy a little custard of her own, as a treat. There were months yet before the shoes would be needed.

She also bought liver and bacon and made both families a delicious and tasty meal for once. With the last penny she bought a fresh bottle of medicine from the herbalist. It contained tincture of opium which he assured her would ease the spasms. The sacrifice was worth it for it did indeed make Hannah better. The coughing eased and her mother got some rest at last.

And Kitty got her bull's eye.

But it wasn't enough. Days later the bleeding grew frighteningly worse. Arnie pawned the kitchen table, two of their three chairs which he'd carved himself, and the clock he'd bought Hannah on their wedding day. Then he brought the doctor. Thus Hannah was taken at last to the sanatorium.

Chapter Nine

Purple dusk was darkening to blue-grey as Nathan and Bertie pushed off from the small jetty. Sharp spires of spruce and larch stood sentinel against the fading light, and beyond lay the backdrop of bronzed hills that circled the lake, which all too soon would melt into a forbidding black. There was no sound but the crunch of shingle as the boat slipped into the water, the oars shifting in the rowlocks, and a faint swish as they dipped deep.

Midnight was the best time for trout, Nathan explained, and just before dawn, when the fish come up to feed. 'I know of holes and haunts where the trout lie between the islands, good for night-trolling.' He hoped Bertie would keep quiet. He couldn't do with a fisherman who prattled. 'It's important we don't frighten away all the fish,' he warned.

'Absolutely.'

Bertie was keen to prove his worth. Lily's scathing tones when he'd told her his plan still rankled. She'd looked at him as if he were a complete idiot.

'Fishing? Why fishing, for heaven's sake? It's a dying trade on this lake. You won't make any money out of it. Dad makes little enough.'

'Nathan says he knows a good place. You could sell them on the stall.' He was beaming at her like a small boy, eager to please.

Lily had lifted her eyes to the ceiling and sighed. She very nearly asked him why he didn't go out with her father, if he was so keen. But Arnie was working all hours on odd jobs, struggling to recoup his possessions – in between visiting Hannah at the sanatorium, so had no time for the idle fancies of his daft son-in-law.

'I want to prove that I'm not the toffee-nosed idiot he thinks me, Lily. At least fishing is something I've tried before, as a boy.'

'Hardly the same.'

'Nathan says it's a start.'

She'd lost her temper then, shouting at him that all she ever heard these days was Nathan this, Nathan that. Couldn't he find other friends besides Nathan? Bertie couldn't understand why she hated the man so much.

'I'll make my own sandwiches, clean my own boots. I just want you to be proud of me, Lily. I have the right clothes already.'

'Oh, well then, if you have the right clothes.' And she'd started to laugh, the fierceness in her hazel eyes melting to honey as she told him she was proud of him already.

He smiled now, remembering Lily's laughter, as Nathan handed him the fourteen-foot trolling rods from which the baits would be trailed astern, and instructed him how to splay out the thirty-five yards of line. Bertie struggled to take it all in.

'The trace has three swivels and is made up of stout round gut. The seven-hook pattern flight serves the purpose and all the parts should be of the best material. We'll use minnows as bait, since they're plentiful at the moment.'

'Haven't the first idea what you're talking about, old boy, but tell me what to do, and I'll do it,' said Bertie, equably enough.

Nathan rowed the boat slowly, picking out landmarks with ease as his eyes adjusted to the gathering gloom. They tried first the shallow grounds by the beck mouths where the trout were often found, then they moved across the lake to the opposite shore, drifting the boat at just the right speed for trolling. They came beneath a group of overhanging trees where the fall of insects and caterpillars might tempt the fish to rise.

'We have to catch 'em while they're actually feeding,' Nathan whispered. 'Sometimes the waters go crazy when they all come up at once. Once they've finished, they'll go down to the depths to digest the food, and we've had it.'

Nathan always enjoyed the silence of the night, the long shadows, the way the light never quite went on a cloudless night like this. The very loneliness of the sport excited him. It gave him time to think. About his past troubles, those that lingered, and the loneliness that still filled his life.

All those years dreaming of this return. Amazing really that here, in his boat, was the man who'd robbed him of what he most wanted: Lily.

Why had he imagined he could come back out of nowhere, and have her?

Why should she fall into his arms after the tricks he used to play on her? He'd done it simply to gain her attention, of course, and out of anger at the state his life had been in at that time. A stepfather knocking him and his mam about. Too afraid to leave the brute, or displease him in any way. His mother had faded into a poor frightened shadow and though she'd done her best to protect her son, the effort had cost her her life in the end and left him with nothing but bitterness.

It was then that he'd run away to sea. The old escape. If such an action had solved any of his problems, Nathan was not aware of it. Added to them more like. Oh, he'd seen the world right enough, and more misery and inhumanity than he cared to recall. He'd saved every penny he earned, gambled recklessly to double it, taken crazy risks with only one object in mind: to get back to the Lake Country where he belonged. And to Lily.

He'd meant to explain all of this to her. How he'd always loved her as a child, and always would love her now as the beautiful woman she had become. Somehow there had been neither the time nor the opportunity. Lily's animosity towards him had made that abundantly clear from the start.

Now she'd married, so it was too late for apologies, too late to achieve his long-cherished dream. His chance of restoring his character and winning her approval was gone for all time.

The worst of it was that Nathan doubted she even loved this idiot she'd tied herself to. Too busy playing the vengeful child to plan her life as she should. Though lately, little by little, he could see it dawning on her that marriage was for life. That, once embarked upon, it couldn't be lightly set aside.

'There's a whole shoal running,' Bertie cried.

Nathan glanced across at Lily's husband, leaning over the edge of the boat as he squinted at the floats, watching for a tug on one of them.

'Take care, you'll fall in if you lean too far.'

'Just look at them all! We're in luck.'

One small push and he could topple the fool head first into the water. Wouldn't that satisfy Lily's need for sweet revenge against the Clermont-Reads, if they lost their one and only son? Just as poor old Mrs Rawlins had lost hers. There were more bodies in the depths of this lake than would ever be recovered. Who would know?

'Here,' he said, reaching forward. 'Let me help you.'

Margot picked up her plate of poached salmon and threw it at the maid. Since the girl had the sense to duck, it hit the silk brocade-covered wall instead.

'Now look what you've done! Wasted perfectly good food which you know is an abhorrence to me, and ruined my dining-room wall into the bargain.'

Betty dabbed at the marks on the wall with a napkin and considered packing her bags. She'd have left this house long since if it hadn't been for George Potter, the handsomest chauffeur she'd ever set eyes on in a long day's march. The only man she knew who didn't make fun of Betty's country plainness, or her aching feet. It would take more than Margot Clermont-Read's wrath to drive her away.

'Yes, ma'am,' she said, trying to sound suitably contrite while hanging on to the last shreds of her pride. 'Happen you're right. It were a touch overcooked. I'll speak to Cook.'

'Was. *Was* overcooked. Oh, what's the point? Ignorant fool! Pick up the plate and clear up that mess this instant. Then bring me a very small portion of asparagus soup instead.'

'Yes, ma'am.' Betty could feel the veins in her legs start to throb even now. Hadn't Cook herself finished off the soup at luncheon? Happen if she hurried with the next course, the mistress might forget she'd asked for it.

'Really, Mama,' Selene intervened. 'It isn't anyone else's fault that Bertie is being so stubborn. Certainly not mine, nor Pa's, nor even poor Betty's here. Far be it for me to cosset a servant, but it is time you either accepted the situation or did something about it.'

'So say all of us,' Edward growled.

'Why aren't you fetching my soup, drat you?' Margot demanded, turning upon the hapless maid again. 'We can't sit waiting all day, girl. Clear that up later.'

When Betty staggered back beneath the weight of a huge dish of roast lamb, she placed it before her master without a glance in Margot's direction. 'Soup's off, ma'am. Cook says she's very sorry.' Spoken in her smallest voice, leavening the bad news with a bob of a curtsey directed at no one in particular.

Edward, his mind on the state of his shares which appeared to have fallen yet again, according to today's *Financial Times,* paid no heed and set about attacking the crisp layer of charred fat. He growled his displeasure.

'Cook will be even sorrier if this lamb tastes as tough as it cuts. Why cannot we get decent produce these days, Margot? I swear this is mutton. Stringy as old leather it is. What are we coming to when we cannot even trust our own servants?'

Weak with fear, yet desperate to defend Mrs Greenholme, since the cook's temper was every bit as unpredictable as her master's and mistress's put together, Betty recklessly offered a reason.

'It's the butcher, sir. Says he's not sending another item of good food into this house until his bill is paid.'

A terrible silence met this offering, and Betty, sensing a deterioration in the atmosphere, hastily begged leave to retire. She scurried away vowing never to return at peril of her life, and carefully closed the dining-room door.

'Pay his bill indeed,' Edward stormed. 'I settle the damned thing once a year, don't I? What more does the fellow want? Never satisfied some of these shopkeepers. Who do they think they are?'

'I'm sure I don't know, dear,' Margot sourly replied, still peeved at the loss of her salmon. 'But I shall die of starvation if you don't hand me food of some sort or other, tough or no.'

'I don't work every hour God sends to eat burned leather,' Edward loudly complained. 'The woman will have to go.'

'If you'd ever paid the same attention to your son as you do to what's on your plate, he might not have run away from home,' Margot asserted, reaching for her handkerchief as the ready tears spurted.

'Oh, for goodness' sake, not that old saw again. Now listen here, Margot.' Edward waved the carving knife at wife and daughter, making them both sit up very straight, eyes wide with sudden alarm. 'I've heard enough moans and groans about that young idiot to last me a lifetime. Is that quite clear? Either he comes home or he doesn't. And if the latter, so be it. The choice is his, not ours. There will be no more stopping in bed all day. No more languishing on your couch. No more weeping and wailing, or indulging in tantrums. The boy is not dead, for God's sake. He has left home. Admittedly not for a home we approve of, but there isn't a damned thing we can do about it. Do you understand?'

'It is simply that this girl...'

'Margot!'

Even Margot understood the limits of her husband's patience and finally subsided. Besides which, she was excessively bored with staying in bed or on a couch all day, and had long been wondering how to end her protest without losing face. It was doing no good at all to her figure. Nevertheless Edward's outburst had alarmed her. He was normally such a passive man.

The very next morning she rose at eight o'clock precisely, and sailing into the morning room, attended her husband at his breakfast for the first time in months.

'Good morning, Edward. Kedgeree, my dear? Your favourite.' Lifting each lid she found sausage, bacon, coddled eggs, but no kedgeree. 'Heavens, above, has Cook no sense? Even the toast is burned. And this coffee is quite cold. Ring the bell this instant. I'll have words.'

Edward folded his newspaper with a sigh, secretly regretting the loss of his quiet morning peace as it vanished like mist in the sun.

'I shall take breakfast on the *Faith* on my way to the station, my dear. Fothergill will attend me.' He aimed a kiss some inches above her head. 'I will see you on Friday, m'dear, as usual.'

'Of course, my darling.' And fondly they bid each other goodbye, Edward pondering, not for the first time, that the secret of their happy marriage might well lie in his long-distance working life.

When he had gone Margot whirled through the house like a dervish, telling the servants standards had slipped during her 'illness'. Now she was going to 'knock their heads together' and 'tighten the reins'.

'No more slipshod behaviour. Do you hear?'

Not a soul could miss her strident voice, or avoid being harangued, shaken or lectured in the following days. And not a soul amongst them didn't wish her back on her invalid's couch!

By Friday, when the master returned home, as usual, Betty again approached the dining room in fear and trembling, her face paste white, knees shaking.

'There's an urchin at the door, ma'am.'

'An *urchin*?' Margot spoke the word as if to say 'rat' or 'sewer'.

'Yes, ma'am. Says could you fetch a doctor to Mallard Street, right quick?'

'What are you talking of, girl?'

Betty struggled, her mouth gone dry with fear, and continued, pitifully slowly, 'Close – to – death, he says. Beggin' your pardon ma'am. So will you come – right quick?'

'Who dares order me to do anything, quickly or otherwise?'

'The urchin, ma'am. The messenger. Though what does he know about a person being close to death? Him no more'n a boy.' Betty turned to go, as if she would personally shoo him off the doorstep and box his ears for daring to sully it with his presence.

'Who is close to death?'

'Oh, ma'am, didn't I say?'

'No, you did not.'

"Tis Mr Albert, ma'am,' Betty suddenly wailed, and waited for death to strike her, as it surely must, for bringing such dreadful news to her mistress.

Lily and Bertie moved into Barwick House that very evening. The Clermont-Reads would naturally have preferred to take him in without the encumbrance of a wife but, in his delirium, he'd stubbornly clung to Lily's hand with such strength no one dared deny him.

Edward put the blame for his son's illness squarely on Bertie's own foolish shoulders. Margot blamed Lily. And having now got her son back under her control, meant to keep him that way.

For Lily it was all too much. First her mother, now Bertie.

She'd actually laughed when the two of them had returned from their fishing trip to stand wringing wet on her doorstep, complaining Bertie had fallen in and Nathan had gone to his rescue. They'd looked pleased as two young lads might on baiting their first fish as they held a creel of fat trout between them.

'Fish aren't my favourite food,' she'd told them, hands on hips. 'Don't you dare drip dirty water on my rugs.'

'You'll love the way I cook them,' Nathan had replied, blue eyes glinting.

Towels had been brought, and clean clothes found. Then Nathan had fried three fat trout, each wrapped in a sliver of crisp bacon. A right merry and satisfying breakfast it had been too. Lily had gone off to work with a full stomach for once.

She never learned quite how the accident had come about but absolved Nathan of any blame, not simply because of the fried breakfast but also because somehow he'd managed to repossess all her father's belongings. Even the clock. Lily assumed it was by some foul means or other, but thought it best not to enquire too closely.

Two days later she'd come home from work to find Bertie burning up with fever, his clothes again wet through – this time with sweat. His voice croaked ominously too. Never had Lily known such fear. Without hesitation, she'd sent at once for his family's help.

Now she could only marvel at Margot's iron control in what must, for her, be a terrifying situation.

Bertie was quickly installed in his old bedroom where the doctor carried out a full examination, listening to his heart, peering short-sightedly down Bertie's throat and finally declaring him to be suffering from diphtheria, a dangerous and contagious disease with an uncertain prognosis.

'See he doesn't talk. He'll need careful nursing. Someone will have to sit with him at all times.'

Lily stepped forward, anxious to help.

'I'll see to him, Doctor,' Margot declared, before she had time to speak.

'Give him lemon juice and honey to soothe the throat, bring down the fever with ice, and steam kettles are good for the congestion. If we can get him through the next few days, the chances are he'll make a full recovery.'

No one dared consider the alternative. Above all, the doctor informed them, it was vital the contagion did not spread.

His instructions were carried out to the letter. Blankets were soaked in disinfectant and hung at every door. Ice was brought from the ice house for Bertie to suck, and no one but his mother allowed near him. True to her word, Margot herself sat with him throughout the night.

As the fever continued to rage, all Lily's offers to share the nursing were bluntly refused. She was shown to separate quarters and largely ignored, permitted only to stand behind the shielding blanket from time to time and speak a few loving words. She liked to think that her voice soothed Bertie.

It was the morning of the third day before the fever abated. Even as everyone sighed with relief the doctor issued fresh warnings, saying this was a critical period, that recovery could be halted by unexpected heart failure or paralysis of the throat or limbs.

'Not in this case, Doctor,' Margot stoutly declared. 'I will not permit it.'

'Indeed, young Bertie is fit and strong. He should do well, particularly in view of the excellent care he has received.' A warning tone was still strong in his voice. 'But that care must be maintained for some considerable time yet. Complications can appear up to seven weeks from the onset of the disease. You're tired, Margot. You must rest or we'll have two patients on our hands.'

'I've offered to help,' Lily daringly put in, only to be frozen by her mother-in-law's glare.

'I consider that you have done enough already. He would not be in this state at all were it not for you, miss. I assure you, I am perfectly capable of caring for my own son.'

Knowing this to be true, Lily stumbled over her words. 'I – I could at least sit with him. I'm his wife, after all. He'd want me by him.'

To her relief the doctor supported her. 'Of course he would. The girl's right, m'dear. Keep up with the steam kettles, watch for the congestion getting worse, and call me if you are at all worried. Now, Margot, no need to be too protective of the boy. I'm sure you can safely leave him in the hands of your daughter-in-law for a few hours. Bertie will like to see her there when he wakes.'

As Margot opened her mouth to protest, the old doctor raised his eyebrows, fixed her with his very sternest expression above the rims of his spectacles, and, to Lily's astonishment, Margot instantly subsided. He was, after all, an old friend. She walked from the room, meek as a lamb, took the two sleeping tablets he prescribed, and slept right through till the next day.

Lily sat by Bertie's side and silently wept. Was this all her fault?

She considered Hannah's illness to be the work of providence. Few people remained healthy in The Cobbles. But to inflict disease on poor Bertie, simply because she'd been set on vengeance against his family, was another matter altogether. If the unthinkable happened, how could she ever make up to the Clermont-Reads for the loss of their beloved son? She'd never wanted Bertie to suffer. He was her husband and a kind, generous man against whom she had no complaints.

Admittedly, if she hadn't been so set on justice for Dick she would never have married him, and he would never have come to live in The Cobbles. Margot was quite right. It was her fault, for he would never then have caught diphtheria.

But as Bertie's fever broke, Selene's began.

More blankets and disinfectant were prepared, yet more kettles boiled. Garlic was rubbed upon Selene's throat, lemon juice and honey dribbled down it, but she went from bad to worse. Her neck was horribly swollen, her face white and blotched with yellow sores, voice so husky she could barely speak. Even her breathing rasped like an old woman's.

Bertie began to sit up in bed and feed upon boiled onions, considered excellent for purifying the blood, or soft bread and milk served to him on a spoon by his fond mama, while Selene was left largely to the ministrations of the servants.

Guilt drove Lily to flit between the two Clermont-Read women, doing what she could for both and receiving thanks from neither.

It was on the second night of Selene's fever, when Lily was sitting with her, that the nightmare began. Half nodding in her chair and near to exhaustion, Lily was jerked awake by a terrible choking sound. It vibrated in the back of Selene's throat like a death rattle. Lily went quite cold with fear.

Running out on to the landing, she shouted for help through the silent, sleeping house. 'For God's sake, fetch the doctor!'

There was a moment of total silence then pandemonium broke out as feet came running from every direction, including Margot's from Bertie's room.

'What have you done to her?' she screamed. 'Would you kill my daughter too?'

The accusation was so cruelly unexpected, Lily fell back gasping. By the time the doctor arrived Selene was clearly in serious difficulties with her breathing.

'I'll have to slit her throat,' he said, and in his calmest voice launched into an explanation of how he needed to open the windpipe through Selene's neck to enable him to insert a tube which would permit her to breathe.

'You'll take no knife to my daughter's neck,' Margot stormed, rearing at him with clenched fists.

'It's called a tracheotomy, and is perfectly safe. I don't have time to argue with you, Margot. She'll die if I don't do it.' He was already unpacking his bag while Margot railed and sobbed.

It took both the housekeeper's and Lily's combined strength to drag the demented woman from her daughter's bedside. Only when she was firmly locked in her room did Lily feel she could leave her.

Moments later she was back at the doctor's side, ready to obey his every instruction. What followed was the most terrifying time of her life. The minutes stretched out like hours, though it must have been no more than seconds. The doctor was amazingly quick and efficient and Lily marvelled at the steady sureness of his hands, particularly in view of Margot's screams of rage still reverberating through the house.

When the tube was safely in place and Selene's breathing normal again, they both gave a sigh of relief, able to breathe again themselves. Lily shuddered to think what might have happened if the doctor had not been so quick.

'Will she be all right now?'

'Thanks to you, young woman, yes, she will. But she'll need careful nursing. See the tube is not disturbed. We don't want infection setting in.' As the doctor washed his instruments in the hot soapy water she provided, he spoke kindly to Lily. 'Had you not spotted the difficulty and called me at once we would most certainly have lost her.' He glanced back at his death-pale patient, carefully dried and put away his instruments, then snapped shut his bag. 'Don't fret about Mrs Clermont-Read. Many women suffer hysteria when their children are threatened. It's not uncommon.'

'Thank you, Doctor.'

He nodded, satisfied Selene was in good hands. 'I'll call again in the morning.' And almost fainting from exhaustion, Lily made no protest as he called a maid to sit with the patient for a while, insisting she needed rest herself.

Returning, exhausted, to her room, Lily would have liked to take her own sleeping child into bed with her, and breathe in the sweet baby smell of her. But she'd left her safely in Betty's care. And just as well.

When Edward returned home the following Friday he sent at once for Lily.

'I cannot tell you how much in your debt I am. My wife too.' Lily said nothing to this, for Margot had certainly given no indication of gratitude during the whole week since the frightening occurrence. But looking into Edward's face, Lily saw that he at least was sincere. Perhaps she had underestimated her father-in-law.

Both patients made a slow but steady recovery. But while Bertie regained his lively spirits and was soon joking with the maids and Lily, Selene took quite the opposite course. She blamed her sister-in-law entirely for the illness, a fact which Lily found hard to deny.

'Were it not for your vindictiveness in marrying Bertie, I would not now be permanently scarred,' was the accusation she repeated daily.

As the invalids settled in for a long convalescence, Lily's time in the sickroom became ever more restricted. She was permitted to sit with her husband for half an hour a day only, almost sure that Margot stood outside the room with her pocket watch, checking off the minutes.

Though she found such behaviour unsurprising, even understandable, Lily found it hard to have all her offers to be of service refused. She spent hours in her room playing with her adored Amy, who seemed the only sane thing in this mad house. Then one day Margot came to see her there. The rustle of her satin gown and the creak of her corsets warned Lily of her mother-in-law's approach so that she was standing waiting when Margot flung open the door.

'I thought you might be skulking in here.'

Lily could think of no polite response to this unfair accusation, so waited for whatever might come next.

'I've been considering your position.'

'I would've thought my position was quite clear.' Lily had long ago resolved not to be dominated by this unpleasant woman. Though her heart might be hammering in her chest like a trapped pigeon, she meant to stand by that pledge.

Margot folded her hands at her waist and fixed Lily with a narrow glare. 'I've spoken with my son about you, and Bertie has no wish for you to leave him.' More's the pity, her expression clearly stated.

'Leave Bertie?' Lily snatched Amy up from where she sat on the carpet and held her close. Though whether it was the baby or herself she was attempting to protect, wasn't quite clear. 'Why on earth should I leave him? He's my husband, the father of my child, your grandchild.'

Margot's lip curled with contempt. 'So you say. We've only your word for that.'

Lily gasped. 'Bertie knows that she is. And odd though it may sound to you, we're happy as bugs in a rug together.'

Margot shuddered. 'Such common expressions! Wife or not it is time you earned your keep.'

'My keep?' What was the woman suggesting? Lily possessed nothing but the clothes on her back. How could she pay for her keep? 'I haven't worked on the fish stall for weeks. I've no money to give you for my keep.' She wanted to add, Even if you needed it, which you surely don't.

'Quite.' Margot's dark eyes gleamed. 'You are, however, accustomed to work. Therefore, I have decided that you can pay your debt in kind.'

'What sort of debt?'

'For the damage you've done to my darling children. Don't pretend to deny it.'

Lily remained silent.

'I'm sure you'll agree that class is the bedrock of civilised society. The class you are born in is quite unalterable. It would be cruel to attempt it. Quite against nature.'

'D'you reckon you can pretend our marriage never took place? Bertie'll never permit it.'

'Bertie will do as he's told.' The words sounded like the crack of a whip. 'As he always has. Marriages can be ended, my dear, quite as easily as they are begun. It may take me a little time to persuade him, but I'm quite sure he will agree in the end.' She almost smiled at Lily. 'He may, perhaps, wish you to continue to occupy his bed. You will not find me too censorious on that score. It is not uncommon for a gentleman to take a mistress from among the serving classes, so long as she doesn't harbour ambitions above her station or get herself into trouble.

'Mrs Greenholme, our cook-housekeeper, will instruct you in your duties. Pray report to the kitchen along with the other servants at five-thirty.' Margot swirled away in a bustle of skirts, her task complete.

'What are you talking about? Servants?'

'Pray do not be late. Unpunctuality is considered bad form in this household. Good day to you.' And Lily watched her go in stunned silence.

Chapter Ten

Barwick House was a solid, lime-stoned mansion, well furnished with Corinthian pillars, porches, conservatories, and bay windows whence could be viewed the magnificence of the lake. The elegant gardens, stocked with rhododendron, laurel, azalea and similar trouble-free plants, stretched for a good hundred yards down to the shore where from a small stone jetty could be launched the steam yacht, *Faith*.

From her pink and white bedchamber, Margot could sit and enjoy the beauties of Coniston Old Man, Crinkle Crags and Bowfell, rimed with morning sunlight or hazy with the afternoon heat, without ever setting foot upon any of them. She learned these and other mountain names like a litany so that later she could impress her guests with her knowledge as they took luncheon or tea in the fine drawing rooms, panelled library or elegant dining room.

Her current obsession was not, however, the mountains, but a life devoted to the care and nurture of her two darling invalids. Not for a moment would she admit to it but Margot felt perfectly satisfied with the way things had turned out.

Dear Bertie's illness, from which he showed no lasting ill effects beyond a natural weakness, had in her eyes proved most propitious. Though he still insisted on having Lily sit with him each afternoon for an hour, Margot used every excuse she could think of to have these sessions curtailed, or even cancelled altogether.

Fortunately, Lily showed some degree of common sense in the matter and made no mention of her new status to him. Clearly she was too proud. As for his part Bertie showed little concern for what his wife did with the rest of her time – a happy state of affairs which Margot meant to encourage until she had succeeded in ousting Lily from his life altogether.

If she had to tie her son to his bed, she simply would not permit him to return to *that* woman.

Selene was a different matter entirely.

'The poor girl has suffered terribly,' Margot mourned to her guests. 'But then, I only just managed to snatch her from the jaws of death.' Embroidering the truth so she could feed upon their ready sympathy, as if she personally were responsible for Selene's miraculous recovery.

'Her dear papa is purchasing an entire new wardrobe for her, naturally. Guaranteed to bring a gel out of the doldrums, eh?'

She forbore to mention how carefully it must be designed in order to conceal the unsightly scar upon the once perfect white throat. Despite the good doctor's assurances that it would fade to nothing, given time, Selene had become prone to daily hysterics on the subject. Margot resolved that not a soul must know of the disfigurement, in case it should further jeopardise her increasingly slim chances of matrimony.

If Lily had expected or hoped for Bertie to notice her changed circumstances, she was not at all surprised when he did not. She could well understand Margot's complete domination over him. The woman was fearsome.

'Since I'm to act like a servant, then I'll live like one,' Lily announced, and despite Margot's half-hearted protests that she might stay in the blue room, she moved in with Betty. The girl seemed friendly enough for all she complained constantly of bad legs and chilblains on her feet, due largely, Lily guessed, to the unheated attic room.

Apart from their initial surprise, none of the servants remarked upon the strangeness of the set-up. Or certainly not to Lily, even if privately they whispered behind their hands. She supposed this was partly due to their having long since grown used to the eccentricities of their mistress and the class she represented. They were also far too anxious about their own jobs to dare comment upon a situation which was really none of their concern. Lily was friendly and a hard worker, one of their own sort in fact. So they accepted her without comment.

Not even Edward seemed to notice Lily's plight, which again did not surprise her in the slightest.

On that first night she made up a make-shift bed for baby Amy in a bottom drawer and settled herself into the hard truckle bed beneath cold, unforgiving sheets knotted with scratchy darns. Silence fell upon her like a heavy blanket, cold and dark and lonely.

As she lay freezing in the bed, a lump came to Lily's throat at the thought of Bertie. She might well have married in haste, and for all the wrong reasons, but she was fond of her young husband and missed his cheerful presence in her life. Not to mention the warm comfort of his body beside her in bed.

Where did he imagine she was sleeping? In splendid comfort, no doubt. Did he think she strolled with his dear mama about the park, took tea with her in the little parlour and meals with his family, bare-armed and fancy-frocked, in the freezing dining room? A giggle of near hysteria rose in her throat at the very idea which Lily quickly stifled by stuffing the sheet in her mouth. It was a relief really that this was not the case, the servants' hall being much warmer and a sight more friendly.

Mrs Greenholme, the cook, had taken quite a shine to little Amy, making a point of providing suitable meals for a growing infant, even delectable titbits now and then.

'Though not too much spoiling, my precious,' she would say, as she handed Amy a gingerbread man she'd baked specially.

A small voice came to her now out of the darkness. 'I made her mad once. Locked me in the cellar for a week, she did.'

Lily was appalled. 'Didn't your parents complain, Betty?'

She heard a throaty chuckle. 'God knows who they are – I don't. Will yours help you?'

Lily thought of explaining all of this to her own family and gave up. 'No.'

'There you are then.' And that was the end of the matter so far as Betty was concerned. A new friendship had been forged. Lily curled herself up like a mouse, tucking her nightdress round her frozen feet. The nights were bitterly cold up here in the attic where no sun ever reached. Tomorrow she'd ask for a hot water bottle. Surely that would be allowed? Though she'd slept in worse conditions, oh, yes. And it was only temporary.

Margot would come out of her temper in the end. Bertie would get well, and in the meantime at least they'd be well fed. No, life wasn't all bad. Reaching out a hand, Lily stroked the curls of her sleeping child. What a blessing she had in Amy, who was the most loving and placid of children. Lily adored her, and so long as she was fine and healthy, which she certainly would be in a grand house like this, what else mattered?

Her last thought as sleep claimed her was of her small cottage in Mallard Street and that wonderful trout breakfast. And the curving smile of Nathan Monroe.

On Sunday afternoons the invalids were permitted to rise for an hour and sit in the little drawing room to take tea with Margot and Edward. This was on the strictest understanding that they were not in any way to be alarmed, excited or disturbed, which somehow meant that Lily was rarely invited.

Margot got around this problem by telling Bertie that Lily chose to visit her family each Sunday. It was proving to be a bitter winter, the diphtheria lingered on, and Lily was concerned for them.

'The poor do not have our sense in staying within doors and keeping properly warm,' Margot explained.

Bertie predictably responded by insisting food should be sent, coals, blankets, and whatever else the Thorpe family should need.

Margot hushed him and smoothed his brow, assuring her son that all was well. Hadn't she dispatched a beef jelly only this afternoon? Unfortunately Arnie was out of work again, but Hannah was holding her own at the sanatorium. Really, they didn't know how well off they were and Bertie mustn't excite himself. Privately, she considered a little food and coal a small price to pay to be rid of Lily Thorpe for a whole afternoon.

What she did not tell Bertie was the fact that Sunday was Lily's only free time, for she was now confined entirely below stairs. Nor did she tell him that his wife left Amy, or 'the brat', as Margot privately dubbed the child, with Betty. If she had, he'd want her brought to the little drawing room, which would never do.

These steps taken towards ridding them of Lily would not be her last.

She was also actively engaged in discussions with their man of affairs, seeking advice on the legal position. After all, the harlot may well have foisted someone else's brat upon her poor darling Bertie.

Margot had once briefly touched upon the subject to Edward, though as usual he had made no comment, hardly seeming to notice or care what was going on since he only came home at weekends. Half the time Margot felt his mind was a million miles from Barwick House, if not with his dratted business then with his boats. She did not trouble him with these domestic trifles again, since she felt well able to take care of them herself.

Lily's duties appeared to be of a general and somewhat inconsistent nature. She accurately assumed they were the ones no one else wished to do, and were changed daily, entirely at the whim of her mistress.

She might be asked to clean away the ashes and light fires in all the rooms, sand the wooden floor boards, shake out rugs, dust plaster cornices, or scour out the pantry with hot water and soda crystals, then scrub the back steps. Another day might be taken up entirely with shoe cleaning, as if she were the boot boy. Or she'd be set to black-leading the boot scraper and kitchen range, and buffing up the fire irons.

Peeling vegetables with Betty for hours on end was the most hated job. But of one thing Lily could be certain, the tasks would be as unpleasant and as difficult as Margot could make them.

Her mother-in-law also had a nasty habit of changing her mind at the very worst moment. One morning Lily spent an hour or more in the little drawing room, taking down all the pictures in preparation for wiping the frames, as instructed. They were heavy and dusty, necessitating a precarious climb up a ladder to reach them. She'd finally got them stacked ready, those she could actually lift down anyway, when the double doors were flung open and Margot swept in.

'What are you doing with those pictures, girl? Making off with them, I shouldn't wonder.'

Lily bit her lip and, acutely aware that any other maid thus addressed by her mistress would bob a curtsey, pointedly did not. She didn't even get down off the ladder. But then, she wasn't an ordinary maid.

'I'm doing the job you asked me to do, Mother-in-law,' she calmly responded, tilting her chin. The two women's eyes met and held, and in that look a challenge was issued of which both were aware. Not simply a fight over Bertie, but a bid for power.

'Put them back this instant. I'm expecting guests to arrive at any moment.'

Lily's heart sank but she managed to smile, determined not to rise to Margot's provocation. The woman had planned this strategy deliberately, of course, in order to instil a sense of insecurity. 'You could entertain your guests in another room, of which there are any number.'

'I dare say I may be allowed to choose which room I use in my own home. I will certainly not be dictated to by you, conniving little madam that you are! You belong in those kitchens, Lily Thorpe and...'

'Clermont-Read,' Lily interrupted.

'What?'

'My name is Mrs Clermont-Read. Like yours,' Lily said, quiet but firm.

'*Thorpe* is still your name so far as I am concerned, and if I have my way, it'll be Thorpe again.'

'Bertie might disagree.'

'Then Bertie will need to have the facts of life explained to him a bit more carefully.' Margot folded her arms and smiled, though there was not a scrap of warmth in it. 'You realise you put his life in danger each time you take one of your frequent trips back to your odious Cobbles?'

For a moment Lily was quite taken aback. Then she rallied. 'I would never endanger Bertie's life. I go only to visit my family, who aren't sick. I thought you were glad to see the back of me for a day?'

'I half hoped you might stay there. But your toing and froing is dangerous for my darling invalids. You might pick up some other dire infection and pass it on. If you mean to stay at Barwick House, for the present, such visits are not at all in keeping with your new status as Bertie's wife.'

'New status? That's a laugh.' She descended at last from the ladder and made no further pretence of working.

'Therefore,' Margot continued, as if she had not been interrupted, 'you will desist.'

Lily might clench her fists, burning with furious frustration, yet she knew she must hold fast to her resolve never to rise to these vindictive assaults. Becoming embroiled in an argument with Margot only reduced her to the woman's own petty level. In any case, what more could she say? Margot was as slippery as an eel, changing her mind, and her line of argument with the unpredictability of a serpent.

Lily picked up her duster and departed, leaving Margot gasping with rage amidst the dark and dusty landscapes that littered her best Persian rug.

Despite everything, without fail, at three o'clock each afternoon Lily put on her best print frock with the blue braid trim, and brushed her hair till it glowed a rich chestnut colour. Then she would pin it neatly on top of her head, letting a few stray tendrils escape about her ears and brow. She'd rub pork dripping into her hands each and every night in an effort to keep them smooth. Now she buffed them to a new silkiness. She liked to look good for Bertie. Lily pinched her cheeks and bit on her lips to bring some colour to them. Lastly, she would wash Amy's hands and face then present herself and their child at Bertie's room, for what was the only enjoyable part of her day. Once, as she passed by an open door, she was spotted by Selene.

'Lily.'

She stopped and waited quietly, gently rocking the bairn in her arms, resting her chin against Amy's sweet-smelling cheek. 'Yes?'

Selene picked at the lace collar of her bed jacket with pale fluttering hands. 'You do realise that I blame you for this?'

Lily sighed. 'I rather think you've mentioned it before, once or twice.'

'Oh, you rather do, do you? Trying to speak properly, are you? Trying to ape your betters?'

Lily flushed, saying nothing, for perhaps there was some truth in the accusation. She was indeed struggling to improve herself, for Bertie's sake. Yet she felt ashamed now for trying to speak more carefully whenever Margot or Selene was around, as if in some way she were denying her true self.

Selene was glaring at her low-cut neckline, at the smooth white column of Lily's throat. 'Where are you going, dressed like that?'

'To take tea with my husband.'

'Did Mama buy you that gown?'

'I made it myself. You've seen it before.'

A small silence, then Selene gave a trilling laugh. 'Of course. Dear heaven, you people think you can be as well dressed as we are.'

Lily made no mention of these trials to Bertie. She felt she owed him that much at least. It was enough to see him smile again, well on the road to recovery, for all he still looked deathly pale and fragile. Not for the world would she jeopardise his health. If he told her how pretty she looked and they passed a pleasant hour together, then Lily was content.

Today he was seated on the chaise-longue at the foot of his bed. 'Dash it, but I miss you, Lily,' he told her, reaching out to kiss her the minute she sat beside him.

'By heck, we are feeling better then?' Laughing softly, she kissed him back. 'I miss you too, you great soft lump. But you have to get well, don't you? No excitement, that's what your ma says.'

'Hang Mama.' His velvet brown eyes shone with need, which set them both giggling like naughty school-children, Amy chortling with glee between them, demanding her share of the kisses.

'Let's sneak into bed, Lily. Have some fun, eh?'

She pretended to appear quite shocked. 'With Amy here? The very idea. Not to mention your ma arriving unexpected like.'

'She'll come on the dot of four-thirty. Always does.' Which was true, and when Margot did come to end the little tete-a-tete, Lily again placed a kiss upon Bertie's cheek. As she did so, she whispered in his ear, 'I'll happen have summat special for you tomorrow, in view of this new need of yours.'

'Oh, Lily,' he breathed, 'will you?'

'We'll see.'

They sat side by side on the chaise-longue, only on this occasion Lily had left little Amy with Mrs Greenholme. Politely they waited, neither daring to glance at the other, while Betty served tea as she always did. The moment the door closed, Bertie grasped Lily's hand and kissed it. 'Oh, golly, it's dashed lonely without you, Lily.'

They made love, fast and furiously, on the bedside rug, both of them panting like steam engines by the time they'd done.

'Let's get into bed and do it again, more slowly,' he urged.

Lily sat up to adjust her clothing, glancing anxiously at the door. 'What if Betty should come back?'

'She never does.'

'Or your mam? Oh, heck, where are all my hair pins?' Lily began to search the rug, hampered by Bertie's attempts to kiss her neck, her ear, her mouth.

'There's lots of time. Mama will be fully occupied with her own affairs for half an hour exactly,' Bertie said, busy at Lily's dress buttons as she searched on all fours for the means to restore order to her tousled hair. 'You have such lovely soft skin, Lily. And you're a real sport.'

'I have to be wi' the likes of you around, don't I?' she said, gasping as his fingers finally found the nub of her breast and slid it into his mouth. On the instant her limbs turned to liquid fire and she flung back her head, shamefully wanting more.

'Happen I really am a wanton,' she gasped, her own hands pushing weakly at his dressing gown, quite of their own volition.

Bertie was annoyed by this suggestion. 'The hell you are.

Anyone would think we didn't have the right. You're my wife, dammit.'

Lily giggled. 'Course I am. Fancy me forgetting that.'

In seconds he had lifted her into the great bed and Lily had forgotten all about the pins, the maid or even Margot. It took less than a moment to peel off every layer of clothing, each of them keenly aware of the shortness of the time they had together. Bertie made love to her with a slow deliberation that left them both shuddering at the climax. Afterwards they lay together between the soft linen sheets, Bertie with his head on her breasts, caressing her thigh with one lazy hand.

'I know you didn't love me when I married you, old thing. But it ain't been too bad between us, would you say?'

Lily kissed him on the top of his head. 'You're grand, as me mam would say. I'm very fond of you, Bertie. No one could have a better husband. What's love, anyroad?'

Love was what she had felt for Dick. But she'd lost him, hadn't she, and the pain had near sliced her in two. No, best to do without love, and Bertie was a good second best. Unexpectedly, a vision came into her head of Nathan Monroe, all smart and clean-shaven, enjoying supper at her table, smiling at her from those crystal blue eyes. A shiver rippled up her spine as she remembered again the silky smoothness of his fingers brushing against her cheek. How dare the man come unbidden into her thoughts? And when she was making love to her husband.

'Take me again,' she said, putting his hands to her breasts, wanting to banish the waking dream. 'Would you believe it, me, Lily Thorpe, in bed with the toff of The Cobbles? A man who can see off a gang of louts with one hand tied behind his back.' They were off again, Bertie tickling and caressing her most vulnerable places with those teasing hands of his, till Lily was begging for mercy even as she wriggled beneath the sheets in a pretend effort to escape him.

Neither heard the footsteps approach, nor the sound of the door opening.

Only when the bed covers were flung back and Margot's eyes

scanned every inch of their naked flesh, did either become aware they were no longer alone. Unfortunately, they were both far too involved in the heat of the moment to care.

'Drat it, Mama,' Bertie said, as equable as ever for all he was panting for breath between each thrust. 'Don't you ever think to knock? A chap must have some privacy, don't you know?'

As the door slammed shut they both collapsed into fresh peals of laughter.

Bertie decided that he was perfectly well. There would be no further confinement to his room, no more invalid meals of milk sops, nor freezing salt baths. He was young and fit, possessed a beautiful wife, and meant to enjoy life to the full.

Lily and Amy moved out of Betty's room and into Bertie's. Margot might grind her teeth with fury but she knew there wasn't a thing she could do about it. Her plan, thus far, had failed. The girl even occupied a place at dinner each evening, and Bertie seemed to delight in instructing his young and undeniably common wife in the intricacies of handling cutlery and wine glasses. Thankfully she had the good sense to keep her mouth shut on these occasions.

Worse, the woman's brat was established in the nursery suite with a nursemaid to attend her. Margot had attempted to point out to her son the error of this arrangement, but he'd only laughed.

'She's *my* daughter too, Mama. Know you wanted a boy, son and heir and all that, but mebbe next time, eh?' Then he'd winked at her in a most vulgar fashion. Margot shuddered each time she recalled it.

Catching them in bed together had not surprised her in the least. Hadn't she said all along that the girl was a harlot? But she dreaded to think of the outcome. That a son of this trollop might one day occupy Barwick House as its master was surely more than she could be expected to stomach?

'Over my dead body,' she kept telling Edward.

Yet Margot knew that if she objected too strongly, or too soon, as she had already attempted to do, Bertie could turn exceeding stubborn. Might even take it into his silly head to return to The

Cobbles. He'd said as much, quite bluntly. Really, he was the most vexatious boy imaginable.

She even found herself being forced to supply Lily Thorpe, as she still thought of her daughter-in-law, with a wardrobe of respectable clothes to wear, at Bertie's insistence.

'Dashed well deserves it, poor thing. Can't have my wife looking like a damned servant, now can I?'

With a strength of will Margot hadn't thought she possessed, she ordered the carriage and sent Lily off with a protesting Selene to the mantle-maker. It was the most humiliating defeat to date, but in her eyes a mere skirmish. The battle may have been lost, but not the war.

The residents of The Cobbles were not so fortunate as those of Barwick House. Diphtheria raged through the overcrowded streets like an inferno, and it soon became clear to Lily that Margot's advice to cease calling there had been entirely correct. The last thing she wanted was to spread the disease still further, perhaps even endanger the life of her own child. She watched Amy with anxious eyes but the child seemed as healthy as ever, baby cheeks glowing with health, hair already showing signs of her father's sandy curls. Lily smiled to see her. Margot wouldn't be able to deny her parentage for much longer.

A letter arrived in her father's careful handwriting, saying the family was quite well, considering, and he was keeping them within doors as much as possible. Hadn't she known they would be? Never ailed a thing, Hannah's merry band. Not long afterwards a second letter came, brought by a boy whom nobody wished to touch. He left the note under a stone and ran off. By the time it had been thoroughly wiped with disinfectant Lily's heart was pounding. She knew it must be bad news, else why would her father write again so soon? The ink had run and was hard to read, even so the words jumped out at her, blunt and stark.

'Our little Emma died last night,' Lily read, and felt the life drain from her own body. 'We're burying her tomorrow. But don't you come home, lass. The sickness is everywhere.'

Not attend her own sister's funeral? Somehow it seemed obscene. But she knew Arnie was right. Lily shut herself in her room and gave herself up to helpless grief. How could her lovely Emma be dead? She was a child still, ten years old and full of fun. Why, only a few Sundays back they'd taken a picnic out into the words, playing hunt the acorn, Emma skipping and giggling as any child should. How could she be gone? It wasn't possible.

What of the others? Kitty and Liza? Were they safe? And Arnie himself? At least Hannah was out of that dreadful place now, slowly recovering in the sanatorium.

In the days following Lily felt as if she would go mad in the isolation of her grief. But much as she ached to run to Arnie's side, she followed his advice and stayed away.

When finally the quarantine period was over, the first thing the Clermont-Reads wished to do was give thanks, along with the rest of the community. Once again they attended St Margaret's Parish Church, glad to meet up with old friends. Lily breathed a sigh of relief to be out in the late April sunshine, to hear a cuckoo deep in the woods, see the green spears of daffodil shoots turning yellow in the sun, smell the wild hyacinth and garlic flowers. She felt as if she'd been down a long dark tunnel, and had at last been let out into the light. Even so, watching a swan take off across the lake, wide wings beating in the warm air currents, again brought Emma to mind and how she'd used to save her jammy crusts for the birds. A lump came to her throat and the ache in her heart swelled to a greater pain. How could the family go on without Emma's cheerful face about the place?

It didn't feel right to be sitting with Bertie in the front pews when her own family were in their usual places at the back. By rights she should be with them, helping them nurse their grief if nothing else.

Lily could see her father sitting stiff-backed, looking as if he'd shrunk, cheeks hollow and gaunt. He was no longer the brawny well-set up chap he had once been. The loss of a beloved daughter so soon after his wife's sickness had clearly taken its toll.

Lily tried to catch his eye, but he stubbornly refused to meet her gaze or heed her frantic signals. It was as if he wished to make a point of not fraternising with those in the best pews. He had never fully understood Lily's marriage, nor quite approved of her 'getting above herself', as he called it. Much as he might have believed the alliance with Bertie to be a mistake, moving into Barwick House was worse in his eyes. So, smothering her distress, she waved instead to Liza and Kitty, and the two girls waved eagerly back, small faces bright with happiness to see her.

She'd go round to the side entrance when the service was over and talk to her dad, no matter what Margot said. Lily needed that even if he didn't, as well as to offer comfort to her sisters.

But by the time she had escaped from the Clermont-Reads and pushed her way through the crowd, there was no sign of her family anywhere. Lily very nearly ran after them but Margot called to her, insisting they were due for coffee at the Dunstons' before going on home for lunch at one. Bertie too urged her to hurry. Only Edward seemed to understand how she felt.

'Are you all right, Lily?' he asked as she fell silently into step beside the Clermont-Read party.

'Why shouldn't I be?'

'I saw you waving to your father, and him turning away.'

'He's a proud man, suffering more than he can rightly cope with at present.'

'You too, I shouldn't wonder, losing your young sister in that dreadful way.'

Unable to respond to the unexpected kindness in his voice, Lily looked up into Edward's face and saw it to be genuine. She'd always imagined her father-in-law to be hard and merciless, caring only for profits and bank accounts. And his own family, of course. It shook her deeply to see his concern for her, and made her wonder if she knew him at all.

Lily remained thoughtful throughout the ensuing visit, and as they walked home an idea started to form in the back of her mind.

After a lengthy Sunday lunch of roast beef and Yorkshire pudding, followed by a substantial apple pie, eaten in a silence broken only by the ticking of the clock, Edward was the first to leave the table.

'I'm off down to the jetty. See how *Faith* has weathered the winter. Got to get her ready for the Easter cruise.'

'Tea at four, dear,' Margot said as he strode out of the door, as if civilisation would cease if this tradition were not adhered to. Lily was on her feet. 'May I be excused too?'

'With pleasure.' Spoken in the sweetly acerbic tone Margot usually adopted when addressing Lily in front of her son.

Bertie departed with her, wanting to know if she was all right. Out in the hall Lily turned to him with a smile, anxious to put his mind at rest. 'Of course. I have to be for you and Amy, don't I? Now you go and have your afternoon nap. I want a quiet word with your father.'

'What about?' Bertie put his arms round her waist, pulling her close. 'I'd enjoy my nap much more if you came with me.' Laughing, she tapped him playfully on the nose. 'You still need your rest. Run along now and be a good boy.'

'What secrets have you got with Pa?'

'No secrets. I'll tell you after I've seen him.'

He kissed her cheek. 'All right, Lily. Adore you, don't you know?' And off he went, whistling, as blithely happy as always.

'Dear God, you do an' all,' she said, and wondered why it made her feel so bleak.

Chapter Eleven

May was the start of the cruising season, though a preliminary cruise at Easter had become a tradition. In readiness, all about the lake, steam-launch owners were checking their craft. They'd spent the winter scraping and varnishing, cleaning and oiling tubes and boilers and pistons. No coal or wood could be left in over winter so these had to be replenished, and the engine fired to make sure it hadn't seized up. The bilge pumps were set working and lastly all the brasses cleaned and polished till every part shone like gold.

This was the job Edward loved best. With his sleeves rolled up and his hands a mess of grease and dirt, he was a happy man. There were times he wondered why he'd ever bothered moving from blue overalls to white collar. Yet as he stood up to ease his aching back and run his eye over his beloved boat and elegant home, he couldn't help but feel a tug of pride. Aye, he'd done all right. He had that. Who'd have thought a simple, hard-working Lancashire lad could do so well for himself' But then Lancashire folk had never been afraid of hard graft. Not in his experience.

If only it was as easy to hold on to money as it was to make it in the first place, he worried. Where it went, he didn't rightly know. Slipped through Margot's fingers like water it did. And as for that son of his ...

George said, 'Will you be building a new boat this year, Mr Clermont-Read?'

Edward almost snapped his reply. 'Isn't the *Faith* good enough for you then?'

The chauffeur-engineer's usually placid face looked stricken and he rubbed his hands on his overalls in an agitated fashion. 'Oh, yes, of course, sir. I wasn't meaning to imply she wasn't. It's only that Master Bertie said something to me the other day about a design he'd been working on.'

'Bertie's a dreamer.'

'Looked quite good to me, as a matter of fact, sir,' George said, keeping his tone conciliatory, all too clearly showing his awareness that he needed to tread softly over this father-and-son issue. 'Has an end fire boiler, so it would be easier to shovel. I've seen others like that, gives the boat a better turn of speed.' He gave an indulgent smile. 'Course, Master Bertie is more interested in the idea of a petrol-driven engine. Very forward-thinking, he is. Give me steam any day though, I told him.'

'He's a useless lump who only knows how to spend money without working for it!'

George wished, not for the first time, that he'd kept his mouth shut.

'Mr Clermont-Read?'

'What is it, dammit?' Edward swung round, surprised to find Lily at his elbow.

'I wondered if I could have a word?'

'Now?'

'In private.'

Edward looked as his filthy hands, at his boat, and at the way George so carefully avoided eye contact, and sighed. 'Aye, well, happen we could do with a rest.' He reached for a rag and started to clean the oil off his hands. 'Go and get yourself a cup of tea, man.'

George wasted no time in snatching the opportunity to enjoy a bit of warmth in the kitchen, and a crack with Mrs Greenholme. She might have made some of her delicious scones, if he was lucky.

When the man had gone, Edward turned to Lily, his voice still tetchy. 'Well, what is it? I haven't all day, as you can see.'

She cleared her throat, not quite knowing where to begin now she was standing before him. 'It's about The Cobbles. I've been thinking a lot about it lately.'

'Oh? Wanting to go back there, are you?'

'Heavens, no, never that. My parents weren't always so poor,' she burst out, anxious suddenly to have this made plain. 'Once upon a time me dad did well with the fishing. We had money to spend, and The Cobbles wasn't such a bad place to be then. Dad didn't have to work all the time in those days. He used to tek us bairns out in t'country. We'd make daisy chains, and dam streams and have picnics.' She smiled at the memory. 'He was allus a kindly, caring man. But then the fishing started to die and everything changed. Things started to go downhill and The Cobbles with them. My family weren't the only ones to suffer.'

'Well, I can't be responsible for putting more fish in the lake.' Irritated, Edward picked up his varnish brush and turned back to his beloved boat. He really had neither the time nor patience to listen to Lily's moans. Hadn't he enough with Margot these days?

'We used to buy new clothes and have plenty of good food on our table,' Lily persisted. 'Now there are few jobs, a poor future and The Cobbles is a mess. It's no wonder it's rife with disease.'

Edward gazed at her, scowling in fury. 'Are you trying to put the blame for Bertie's diphtheria and your sister's death on my shoulders? Is that what this is all about?'

Lily very nearly quailed before the fury in his gaze. Yet this was the man whose boat had run Dick down. Who'd refused to help repair their cottage and a dozen others like it, then sent his ferret of an agent round fast enough when they were behind with the rent. Therefore this was the man on whom she needed to take her revenge, not Bertie, not even Margot, for all the woman drove her mad. And she meant to do it, no matter what it cost her. Lily picked up a cloth and applied a dab of varnish to the boat's scuffed woodwork. Edward watched her, surprise on his face. He didn't interrupt when she started to speak.

'I warrant you haven't set foot in The Cobbles for years. If ever. I reckon it's long past time you did.'

You'd have thought she'd asked him to visit the moon, judging by the expression of shock on his face. 'You wish me to visit The Cobbles?'

'I reckon it's your duty.'

For a long, awe-filled moment silence stretched between them and Lily wanted very much to turn tail and run from his furious gaze. But she held her ground, turning all her attention to applying the varnish, even if it was going all over her hands.

Then, to her complete surprise, Edward threw down his own brush and let out a shout of laughter.

'By Gad, you're a rare one, Lily Thorpe. Never give up, do you?'

Lily suppressed a smile. 'Not that I've noticed.'

'You've not managed to get our Bertie working though, have you?'

'Not yet.'

'Happen that's not your fault. I know you tried. You've at least managed to make him a touch more human.' There was a pause while he nibbled at his moustache. 'All right, you're on. I'll visit your damned Cobbles, and prove to you that I am not responsible for its state. That lies squarely with its inhabitants.'

On the day they'd chosen for the visit, it was raining. The rain came down from the grey mountains, swept across the lake in a thick cloud, hammered against the old boathouses, rushed up Fisher's Brow and battered every roof in the district known as The Cobbles as sharply as stair-rods, which was what the locals dubbed this heavy and relentless type of rain. They knew too that it would continue all day long, soaking people and houses with impunity, flooding gutters and leaving no part of the area dry. It was the worst possible day for Lily to prove her case, as it provided Edward with the perfect excuse to blame everything wrong in The Cobbles upon the weather.

Yet for all the damp discomfort the streets were still full of people, hurrying to their work or to the shops, going about their business as best they may. Washing still hung from lines, and would remain there for days since there was nowhere else to put it. Bare-footed children splashed in puddles and, as the two of them made their way down Drake Road, a man came out of a back kitchen and urinated against the wall of his cottage.

'There you are. Doesn't that prove my point?' Edward stormed, appalled by such vulgar behaviour.

Lily pushed a lock of wet hair back from her brow. 'Do you own all the houses in this street?'

'I do.'

'Do they all have privies?' She smiled when she saw Edward scowl. 'Quite. So if the single privy shared between six, ten, or more houses is usually occupied, can you blame him?'

Edward only glowered in silence. As they walked up and down the various streets and alleys, Lily pointed out other problems. The missing slates on roofs, the lack of proper guttering, the fact that many of the streets were little more than dirt tracks. 'Where children play, mind, despite what you saw that man do.'

Edward again protested his innocence but as Lily marched him in through the back door of one hovel after another, leading him through insanitary sculleries, grim kitchens, bedrooms where black fungi grew upon the walls and ceilings hung broken and untended, his protests faded away and he grew increasingly horrified. Why had he not been informed of the true state of this place? Wasn't this the responsibility of his agent, Percy Wright? What was the man doing? Yet in his heart Edward knew the responsibility lay with himself, and himself alone. He'd never checked, had he?

Lily was saying, 'As I understand it, The Cobbles formed the original Carreckwater. Once the rest of the village was built, given a new name and later developed, this area became more and more neglected.'

The very reason why, of course, Edward had managed to buy it so cheaply. As an investment, he'd thought. Now he could see it was very far from that.

'Me dad says that them who has the vote, has the power. So things should start to change now Asquith has brought in the Franchise Bill. With votes for all men over twenty-one, the landlords won't have the power they once had. Which everyone knows was too much.'

Edward's face grew tight. He'd been against such liberal open-mindedness and hated now to be put in the wrong, though this girl was making a fine job of cornering him nicely in his own mess. He adopted his most pompous tone. 'Allow me to explain that that is the way of the world, the way it is meant to be. Certainly the way life has developed over the centuries. There are those who rule and those who serve.'

151

'Happen it shouldn't be that way,' Lily replied with spirit. 'For one set of folk to look down upon another set just because they have more money, happen that's wrong. And equally wrong that the poor are considered unimportant, that other folk believe nothing need be done to make their lives better, just because they don't vote.'

Struggling to hold on to his patience, Edward attempted to explain. 'We English, unlike the Scots, Welsh and Irish, have little in the way of folk customs and the like. Therefore we make more of class. Quite rightly, in my opinion, since it's folk like me, wi' a bit of class like, who drive the engine of this country, like a big boat on the lake. But it's open to all to change their lot in life. If you're not born with it, you must work hard to raise the means to purchase it, as I did, else sink into squalor as your family have.'

Lily flinched, and, sidetracked by some warped logic in his argument, began to doubt for the first time her ability to succeed in her quest. Why should he help them? He must know she wanted to make his life difficult simply out of revenge. He could just as easily burn The Cobbles to the ground and make his money elsewhere. She could think of no reply.

'It's good to see you care, Lily,' he said, magnanimous in his victory. 'But if these people don't like it here, they can always move out.'

'You mean, they can either stay and die of disease, or leave and be homeless and die of starvation?' Lily watched with interest as his discomfort returned and with it a pronounced tetchiness.

'It's important to be successful. To have an aim in life.' Edward was desperately struggling to hold on to his theory of economics, rather than dwell on the scene before his eyes. Better that than observe a small toddler crawling through the filth of this rain-soaked back yard, following its mother who'd run to fetch a bucket or two of water from a tap at the end of the street. Edward shuddered with revulsion at the prospect of living such a life.

Lily captured the wailing infant and carried it safely back into the house.

'It's all right Lucy,' she told the worried mother who quickly returned, splashing water recklessly from her two buckets in her haste. 'I've put him safe under the table.'

'Thanks, Lil.'

Edward refused to meet her eyes as they left the yard. He took refuge in lighting a cigar, clamping it furiously in his mouth and visibly relaxing as he drew in the welcome fragrance of it. 'We landlords, the well-to-do if you like, must be in control, because we have the power and the money. We're the ones with the education, the intelligence, and the skills.'

'Have you never considered that the poor might just have a touch of intelligence themselves?' Lily mildly enquired. 'Might even welcome a bit more schooling, given the chance. Particularly in a lovely spot like the Lakes with its growing tourism. Why should poor folk put up with squalor? Why can't their skills be improved?'

'You can't blame all the ills of the country on me,' Edward barked, hating the feel of the rain running down his neck, soaking him through. Hating being put in the wrong and wanting only to get this dreadful visit over with and return to his warm, dry, pleasant home. 'It's my duty to take my place in running the country, and the Empire, at whatever cost. But I can't be responsible for every miserable soul who lives in it.'

Lily stopped and looked up at him. 'Can you not?'

'No. But there's no shame in ruling, or in trying to improve oneself and move up in the world, Lily. It gives a man pride.'

'You mean a self-righteous sense of superiority?'

He made a noise of derision, deep in his throat. 'Margot's right. You're far too egalitarian for comfort, lass.'

'Aye,' she said stoutly, this time unconcerned by the word. 'Happen I am. Praise the Lord. Or, worse, a Liberal, eh?' She laughed. 'I remember celebrating Empire Day in school along with the rest of 'em. Dressed up in a sari, or pretending to be a native in a grass skirt.'

She stood facing him in the back street, close by the very ash-pit roof where she and Dick had kissed and dreamed of escape, of building a good future together, of doing exactly as Edward Clermont-Read now suggested – going up in the world. Would they then have become leaders and rulers as heartless and uncaring as he? She sincerely hoped not, even if they had managed to reach such dizzy heights. Lily felt annoyed by Edward's arrogance, his assumption that he must always be in the right. She drew in a deep breath and fought on as never before. He owed her, didn't he?

'I know naught about the rights and wrongs of such things as Empire. Happen folk don't want to be ruled, nor told what to do all the time, while naught is done to improve their lot.'

Her voice was growing more fervent as she warmed to her argument. 'Mebbe they just want a bit of a start like, to help themselves. A bit of consideration. Then they can make their own decisions, their own mistakes, and be independent. The folk *here* need consideration,' Lily flung an arm out, indicating the miserable scene, 'a bit of help to improve their lives, not be blamed all the time because they're poor.'

Edward was staring at her, nonplussed, admiration for her spirited defence of The Cobbles dwellers growing despite himself. At last he asked more quietly, 'So, what is all this talk of politics about, Lily? What is it you want from me?'

Had she gone too far? She hadn't meant to get embroiled in all this Empire stuff. What did she know about it anyway? Nothing except what her teacher, Mrs Jepson, had told them all those years ago. But Edward had riled her with his pomposity and talk of class. She was fair sick of such talk, she was really. Lily couldn't stop now. She shook back her wet hair and continued undaunted, 'I want you to do summat for this place. You spend enough money on your fancy house, on dinners and posh frocks, not to mention your steam yacht. It's time you spent a bit on the houses you expect your tenants to live in and pay good money for.'

Edward looked affronted. 'There are worse places, Lily. In Manchester, for instance, which I see every day. The people of Salford might think the folk here well off by comparison.'

'I dare say they might, but that's no reason to stand by and do naught about the mess we've got on our own doorstep, is it? We'd mebbe have less misery and disease in this world if we all did a bit more.' She jabbed a finger at him, hazel eyes glittering with heartfelt passion. 'I read in Margot's paper the other day how half a million children are ill fed and diseased. We ought to be ashamed,' she finished stoutly, refusing to be put off by the way he bit down hard on his well-chewed cigar. 'But you landlords are all the same. You do naught because t'other chap does naught either.'

This was, of course, quite unanswerable. Edward, being a fair-minded, if blinkered, man could recognise when he'd been neatly cornered. 'You have spirit, Lily, I'll give you that. You're not afraid to make a stand for what you believe to be right. I like that in a person, particularly in a woman.'

She gave a half smile. 'That compliment sounds a bit back-handed to me. I say I'm as good as the next man, woman or no. I'm certainly as good as you, Mr Clermont-Read, any day of the week.' And to her amazement, Edward chuckled.

'By heck, lass, you may well be right. You're a woman and a half, you really are. Does nothing frighten you?'

Now her smile widened to a grin, and with the flat of both hands she wiped the rain from her face, pushing back the tendrils of hair that stuck to her rosy cheeks. The gesture seemed sharply to delineate the sculpted beauty of her face. 'As a matter of fact, there is. I fear for my child – your grandchild – growing up in a hole like this. Becoming one of the half million who die, like my sister Emma.

'If I'm a fighter, it's for them, for our Emma and others like her.' Her throat became constricted with sudden pain. Lily glared at the muddy hem of her dress, taking several minutes to bring herself back under control.

Their silence lasted the whole length of Carter Street as they swished in and out of puddles, then Edward said, 'If I agree to help you, what would you do for me in return?'

Nonplussed, Lily stopped to face him, causing a woman walking with her head down against the rain, to bump into her and curse. 'Like what? What could *I* do for *you*?'

'You haven't exactly been a cooperative daughter-in-law, now have you? You must be well aware you drive Margot to distraction.'

'Is that my fault? She was against me from the start.'

'Do you wonder at it, in view of your elopement?'

'That weren't my idea,' Lily said heatedly.

'Wasn't.'

Lily flushed at his reminder of her poor grammar while Edward drew deeply on his cigar and blew out two smoke rings. They both watched as the smoke rose slowly in the damp air to be battered apart by raindrops. Then their collective gaze moved on to the sight of a small, half-naked child seated on a doorstep, bare feet splashing in a puddle murky with unknown horrors.

Edward sighed. 'I'm not sure how I'm going to find it, but you can have some money to improve your precious Cobbles. Only it'll be a waste of time. It'll be as bad as ever the week after you've done, see if it isn't. In return you must make every effort to fit into life at Barwick House, as Bertie's wife. Do you understand what I'm saying?'

'I've not been given a chance to fit in.'

'I'm giving you one now. I'll speak to Margot, as I'm speaking to you. No more dissension. You're Bertie's wife and we must accept that. If I'm to do something about this -' he glanced about him in unconcealed disgust, 'you will make every effort – *every* effort,' he emphasised with a wag of his cigar, 'to get along with Margot and fit into your new life. Is that agreed?'

It was amazing, Lily thought, how all her efforts at vengeance always backfired on herself.

Lily's first task was to recruit assistance. Bertie readily volunteered, though even at her most courageous Lily dared not defy Margot by taking her recently recovered son back into the den of iniquity whence he had caught his fever, particularly in view of the bargain she'd struck with Edward.

Dora Ferguson-Walsh, however, was only too ready to stand in his stead, bringing along a group of equally worthy friends to help. Lily also went in search of Rose.

'Aye, I'll help, but what we can do I can't imagine. Making any improvement to this place seems bleedin' well impossible!'

'You'll be surprised,' Lily said, with the kind of resolution in her eye that no one could withstand.

The first thing they did was to issue everyone with carbolic soap, derbac for nits and lice powder. Then there was a medicine, known as 'the mixture', which claimed to be a cure-all. Lily and her team administered it to every willing mouth, old and young alike, for whatever conceivable ailment they complained of, from a bad back and sleeplessness, to coughs and colds, sore throats, ring worm and measles. Any suspicious symptoms were reported to the doctor who sent along the fever ambulance. The diphtheria epidemic had largely run its course, but no one was taking any chances.

Limewash was issued for cleaning walls, disinfectant by the bucketload, something vicious called Klenzit Kleener and yards of sticky fly-papers in an effort to stem the growing invasion of bluebottles.

'You're right, Rose, it seems little enough, but it's a start,' Lily told her friends.

Each evening she would go back to Barwick House where she'd wear one of her new gowns and sit at table eating beautifully cooked food from best china plates. Her heart wasn't in it but Lily knew she'd little choice in the matter. She became two people, living in two worlds. Lily Thorpe of The Cobbles, and Lily Clermont-Read of the fancy lakeside mansion. There was a strange unreality about it all, yet she couldn't deny that her life with Bertie was pleasant. They would walk in the garden together of an evening, enjoy the delectable food at Margot's tea-parties, picnics and dinners. And make love in the big brass bed. Best of all Lily played with her darling daughter, watching her grow safe and strong, and beautiful. The ease and comfort of it all grew upon Lily, little by little; insidious, seductive, adding to her sense of guilt.

Each morning as she returned to The Cobbles, she knew that half her eagerness to get there early derived from a desire to catch a glimpse of a certain figure. Nathan Monroe had volunteered his services from the start, but, tipping her nose in the air, Lily had stubbornly told him that his assistance would not be needed.

'I'm sure you've far important matters to attend to,' she'd told him. 'Like bullying your way to the top on the backs of the poor you so outrageously overcharge on that steamship of yours.'

'It's not my steamship. Yet.'

'There you are then. Exactly my point,' she said, rather confused, and flounced off, cursing herself for becoming embroiled in yet another dispute with him, for didn't it only unsettle her?

Lily really had no wish for Nathan Monroe to help her at all. That would mean seeing him every day, working alongside him, feeling his closeness. No, that was the last thing she needed. Yet still she looked for him, felt nothing but misery if he didn't appear for a few days. She pretended that this was because he irritated her so much, refusing to recognise the way her cheeks bloomed whenever he came near, the way her breathing grew shallow and her heartbeat quickened at the mere sound of his voice.

To compensate for these inconsistencies in herself, Lily stepped up her quest and squeezed yet more money out of Edward. He scowled and protested but finally agreed to make more funds available.

'Don't forget our agreement,' he reminded her. 'You'll be expected to attend Margot's ball at the end of the season. I've spoken to her about it and she's agreed to have you fitted for a new gown.'

It almost burned Lily's throat to agree, but fortunately Margot chose not to be present at the dress-fitting session, though Selene enjoyed the experience enormously.

'Dear heaven, it's like turning a mule into a mare. What sensible square hands you do have, Lily, and quite ruined by all this work you do, of course.'

'All in a good cause,' she said in a tight little voice, struggling to hold on to her temper, as promised.

If she was not the socially acceptable wife for Bertie that Margot would have wished, what did it matter? Lily had the extra money she needed for her plan for The Cobbles. She didn't care a jot about Margot's ball, or her agreement with Edward. Her aim was to take him for every penny he was worth, wasn't it? In payment for Dick, for Emma, and for her poor mother who still fought for her every breath in the sanatorium.

Throughout that summer Lily made regular visits to Hannah, though she was only permitted to wave to her from a distance. She lay in a high iron bed that, like a dozen or so others, stood in a regimented line along a veranda that had one glass wall which could be thrown open to the weather. Though freezing cold much of the year it was considered health-giving, the only palliative for consumption. It seemed to do Hannah no harm. Lily was delighted to find her making progress.

She sorely missed her mother's companionship, and when the work got too tough one day, turned away from The Cobbles and all its associated problems and walked instead up the steep hill to the sanatorium. At last acknowledging her obsession with Nathan Monroe, Lily decided that she was in dire need of Hannah's counsel. She needed to get her life in order, to subdue all thoughts and desires for a man not her own husband. Lily wondered what her mother's reaction would be if she dared ask for such help?

For once she was actually allowed into the day ward, and found Hannah seated in a cane chair, smiling and looking almost her old self. Lily would have liked to run to her but this was not permitted. Instead, mother and daughter both wept, at last able to share the grief that still haunted them both. Thankful to be together again.

They could have talked for hours instead of the permitted twenty minutes, Lily telling Hannah about her efforts to clean up The Cobbles, Hannah more interested in family. She asked after Arnie, Liza and Kitty. 'And your own wee bairn?'

'Oh, Amy's fine. She's walking now, and into everything.' Lily was happy enough to talk about her lovely daughter, how she was growing out of babyhood and into a proper little person of her own now, and with her father's colouring and her mother's hazel eyes. But when Hannah enquired if she was being a good wife to Bertie, Lily grew confused with feelings of guilt over the thoughts which filled her head day and night. Memories of cosy suppers with Nathan and Bertie; of Nathan's touch upon her skin; of the intimate way he used to smile at her, as if they were two people sharing a secret her husband knew nothing of. How just to be aware of being in the same street as him set her nerves jangling.

Her decision to ask for advice set aside in this confusion, Lily changed the subject back to her work in The Cobbles. 'Everyone's pitching in. It's wonderful what's being achieved. And it's costing Edward a small fortune.'

'It'll not last. He'll grow bored and refuse any more, as others have done before him,' Hannah said. 'Anyway, I thought you wanted out of that place?'

'I am out.'

'So why go begging folk for help?'

Lily felt a surge of irritation with her mother. Why couldn't she see? Why couldn't she understand that you had to fight for what you wanted in this world? 'I did. I do. But why shouldn't we ask for help? The Clermont-Reads owe it to us, owe it to everyone who lives there. They make enough profit out of us. You should see the money they spend on their tea-parties and picnics. One such would keep all of Mallard Street in grub for a week. Anyroad, I'm not doing this for their benefit, or mine for that matter.'

'Aren't you? This isn't about that accident then? About Dick?' The blunt question silenced Lily. Hannah had always been too sharp when it came to reading her daughter's mind. As always it made her feel vulnerable to be understood so well. Lily fixed her gaze on her hands as she clasped and unclasped them in her lap, in case Hannah should read other thoughts in her eyes.

'What if you lose that lovely husband of yours through spending too much time worrying over the state of summat you can't do aught to change?'

'But we are changing it, and Bertie's in favour.'

'And Edward Clermont-Read?'

Lily couldn't help but smile. 'Growing poorer by the minute.'

Hannah, ever wise, raised her eyebrows in an unspoken query. 'He's not a bad man. Thoughtless happen. A bit put upon by that wife of his, and too trusting with his agent, but he means well. The Clermont-Reads won't thank you for wasting their money in this way.'

160

'If The Cobbles had been a decent place, happen our Emma would still be alive today.'

'That was God's will. If she was called, what could we do to save her?'

'We can at least make The Cobbles a clean place for her sisters to live in, then they won't be called too.'

Seeing her mother's wince of pain, Lily wanted to offer comfort but Hannah had as quickly gone all tight-lipped again. In her opinion bemoaning one's lot was a sign of weakness and only made matters worse.

Lily made her excuses and left fairly soon after that, but as she swung down the hill away from the sanatorium she harboured no regrets for her campaign. Nor could she feel any sympathy for Hannah's grim acceptance of whatever life brought. To see the Clermont-Reads suffer as Dick, Emma and everyone else in The Cobbles had suffered, and, yes, as Hannah herself had suffered as a result of poverty, wasn't that what she wanted? Sweet revenge? Justice? Surely it was worth any price?

The price, however, proved more than even Lily had bargained for.

Chapter Twelve

Mrs Greenholme met her at the door. This was so unusual that Lily knew at once something was wrong. Had Bertie suffered the much-dreaded relapse? She broke into a run and flew up the steps. 'What is it?' Tell me.'

The kindly cook took hold of Lily's hands and led her with tender care, not to Bertie's room as expected, but to Amy's.

Lily gazed with dawning horror upon the tiny figure of her daughter lying so still in bed, a maid sponging the frail body with cool water. 'She took sick this morning, just after you'd gone.'

'Why didn't you send for me?' There seemed to be a roaring in her ears and Lily fell to her knees beside the bed, her world collapsing about her.

Mrs Greenholme's voice seemed to come from some far distant place, hushed and respectful, filled with the same fear that held Lily now in its cruel grip. 'Betty was the only one willing to go to The Cobbles, but she couldn't find you. We sent for the doctor. He says we're to get down the fever, fast as we can. That's what we've been about all day. He says the epidemic might be largely over, but there are still one or two outbreaks.'

Lily struggled to take in the woman's words, as if they came from a long way off. One thought dominated all else in her brain. *Why did Amy have to be one?* She hadn't even been near the place. *But I have,* the relentless voice continued.

The roaring came again, seeming to paralyse every part of her body. Lily could not move a muscle, could barely speak or think. Dear God, what had she done? Had her crusade for revenge led her to put her own child in danger?

She must make Amy better, that was the answer. Not stand here doing nothing. Amy didn't live in The Cobbles, did she? She lived

162

here, safe and warm in a rich man's house. As a strange unearthly calm descended upon her, Lily called for ice, and blankets to be brought up, though this had already been done. She took the cold cloths from Betty and started work on her precious child. But her efforts were to no avail. The nightmare was over frighteningly quickly. By midnight Amy's temperature soared. By dawn she was dead and Lily inconsolable.

She did not weep or shed a single tear. The tears she'd wept for Emma, and for Dick could not help her now. They failed to break through the pain that held her heart like an iron vice.

How could she go on living without her child? It wasn't possible. What right had the sun to shine, the world to keep on turning? Lily walked to her room and carefully closed the door. She washed her face and cleaned her teeth, put on her cotton nightdress and climbed into bed as if everything were perfectly normal.

She would wake tomorrow and find Amy asleep as usual in the make-shift cradle at the foot of her bed, soft pink mouth puffed out gently in sleep. But in the night when she woke, disturbed as she often was by Amy's cry, she found the cradle empty, a silent rebuke to her failure as a mother to protect her child. Then, giving a terrible guttural cry, she smashed it to pieces and with her bare hands ripped the fine linen sheets to shreds.

Lily sat in her room for days, emerging only to walk behind the tiny coffin and see her child put to her final rest. Still no tears fell. Even in the depths of her devastation, Lily took sanctuary in anger, not sorrow. It was the only emotion that could keep her free from the emotional abyss waiting to swallow her up. She did not seek sympathy or pity. She wanted none, knowing they would unhinge her.

Not that either was offered to her at Barwick House.

Margot considered it inappropriate to mourn for a child who might or might not have been her granddaughter. She told her grieving son quite bluntly where he should lay the blame: with the child's mother.

He believed Margot when she told him Lily had taken Amy to

The Cobbles, and for the first time in their married life Bertie turned away from her.

He wept, a man broken by grief. Lily could hardly bear to watch him, for how could she deny her responsibility? Neither Bertie nor Selene would ever have set foot in The Cobbles if it hadn't been for her, nor been ill as a result.

Her penance now was that she'd lost the person who'd mattered most to her in all the world. Amy had paid the ultimate price for Lily's own folly.

And all because of her quest for revenge.

Days after the funeral, grim-faced and against all advice, Lily returned to The Cobbles. Proving, in Margot's eyes, that she was indeed an unfeeling mother.

Builders, joiners and plumbers had been sent in by the dozen and Lily worked beside them like a mad woman. She mixed cement, installed guttering, laid water pipes and sewers for the taps and lavatories that sprang up in every back yard, even carried blocks of stone. No one dared deny her the right to help or she would turn on them in spitting fury, fierce as a tiger. Nor did she allow the men much time to rest.

'Why are you taking a tea break? Work harder. It must be finished by winter,' she stormed every time they stopped for a breather. Rose steadfastly struggled to keep everyone's spirits high. 'Give 'em a chance. They're only human, for God's sake. At least now we won't have to trek miles in search of a privy, with our legs crossed and our bums frozen stiff.'

Once, Lily might have giggled at the crude but wondrous picture this conjured up. Now she had lost any ability to smile. Amy would never laugh again, so how could she?

The task was enormous, could take months, and they didn't have months. Other babies might fall sick and die. Even Edward no longer protested that she was leading him to the brink of bankruptcy but silently handed over whatever money she demanded.

Lily resolved to finish the work, no matter what the cost, so that

Amy would not have died in vain. She no longer found any pleasure in it. Bitterness and cynicism now clouded any sense of achievement. But everyone else was beginning to appreciate the miracle she had wrought.

'The Cobbles'll be the best part of Carreckwater before we're done,' Rose told Edward. 'The nobs'll be queuing up to buy houses here. And Edward Clermont-Read will be its greatest benefactor.'

This seemed to please him, but to Lily, her arms still aching for want of her child, it seemed yet another bitter irony, proving once more the folly of her quest.

Surprisingly, Dora Ferguson-Walsh proved to be a tower of strength. Knowing Lily could not bear to work with the children, she set up a fund to collect money for clothing and shoes then lined up scores of urchins in the street, dosed them with medicine, shaved off their lice-ridden hair, and sent them away reeking of disinfectant and happily sucking on a mint ball.

'It'll only grow again and the lice come back,' Lily bluntly told her, and Dora's plump face broke into a smile.

'Then we'll have to come and do it all over again, won't we?'

Lily didn't say she was grateful for Dora's efforts, she couldn't. Instead, she demanded to know why she was bothering to help. 'Don't say because I asked you to.'

'For Bertie. Who else?'

The sense of guilt which pierced Lily's heart at this simple statement added still further to her pain. Dora should have married Bertie, not herself. She would have made him a better wife.

Lily grew thin and pale and both Rose and Dora urged her to take more rest, which only made her strive all the harder. Lily wanted to put right everything she had made wrong, but couldn't. It was far too late.

The only answer to her pain was work.

She was attempting to lift a huge block of limestone one morning when a harsh voice rang out.

'That isn't your job, Lily Thorpe. You're making a grand effort here, but leave that for the men.'

Staggering beneath the weight of the stone, Lily stubbornly

clung on. 'I can manage. It's no business of yours what I do.' Without even glancing up she knew it to be Nathan. In her mind she could see him before her, standing so straight and tall, arms folded, face dark and condemning. She dragged the stone inch by inch, sweat pouring down her face, soaking her cotton frock, as with gritted teeth she stubbornly held on. She might have succeeded too, she decided, if she hadn't come over all peculiar. The top of her head seemed to lift off as pain shot up her arms and gripped her by the back of her neck, even as her shoulders seemed to be dragged from their sockets by the weight of it.

Then her knees buckled and Nathan caught her as she fell, pushing aside the offending piece of masonry to grasp her tightly in his arms. He whispered her name, laid his cheek against hers. It was smoothly shaven, like cool silk against her burning skin. The familiar scent of him enveloped her as surely as his arms enfolded her, and Lily gave herself up to the bliss of it. No one else had held her so throughout the terrible weeks of her grieving. Now, suddenly, it was too much to bear.

All her carefully built defences collapsed.

Tears welled up from a place deep inside that Lily hadn't known existed. At first they came in great dry racking sobs, breaking from her like shards of broken glass. Then despair overwhelmed her in great gulps of anguish. She wept, she sobbed, she railed, she raged. The pain was indescribable, like nothing she had ever known, nothing she would ever wish to know again. She wanted to lash out and destroy everything, as if in that way she could dispel the pain. Nathan held her fast, preventing her.

When the storm finally subsided into heartbreaking but sorely needed tears, he wiped them away with the palm of his hand, cradling her close on his lap as if she were a child – or his very dear love. And in that instant, Lily wished that she were.

From the day Lily finally broke down and wept on Nathan Monroe's shoulder she kept away from The Cobbles. The hard work, even the anger, had been an essential part of her grief. Now she couldn't bear to go near. It was up to others to carry on without her.

All very right and proper, according to Margot. 'Life must go on, and it was a doomed enterprise from the start.'

'It's not doomed. I just need a rest.'

If Lily was as concerned with avoiding Nathan as The Cobbles, she made no mention of that fact. She recalled her bargain with Edward and used this as an excuse to stay away, expressing herself willing to carry out Margot's bidding. 'I want to be a good wife to Bertie. Show me how.'

'Well, well. So we may make a human being of you yet.'

With more resignation than she had ever intended, Lily submitted to Margot's tutoring with gritted teeth. As expected, Margot rose to the challenge with an almost sadistic pleasure. Day after day she had Lily walking up and down stairs and passageways with huge volumes upon her head.

'The proper deportment is essential to straighten your back.' In Lily's opinion it wasn't crooked.

She lectured and hectored her daughter-in-law upon the gentility of a lady's existence, the protocol of paying social calls, working for charity, acquiring social chit-chat, and of course such niceties as the correct method of pouring tea, lifting a cup and saucer without spilling it, and filling hours of each day with perfect cross-stitch.

'You must pay a call upon all the young wives in the district.'

'Why?' Lily was driven to ask, and Margot's eyes widened.

'In order that they will call upon you, of course. My dear, if you do not pay calls when they are due, you will be cold-shouldered, even cast out, by society.'

Lily longed to ask how she could be cast out from a society which still did not recognise her existence, but Margot was still talking.

'If you wish to be included in all the many entertainments next season, you must do your duty. For Bertie's sake, if not your own. Hasn't he sacrificed enough?'

Lily's heart sank as, too late, she recognised the trap. Bertie was a sweet and kind husband and she had brought him nothing but unhappiness with her ill-fated quest for revenge. She'd given him sickness, poverty, and the death of their only child. Nothing else must be allowed to spoil his life. Certainly not Nathan Monroe. She vowed to be the wife Bertie needed.

Lily's very first dinner party was a disaster. She had taken particular care with her gown, a beige-pink with burgundy trim, and Betty had piled her soft brown hair into a most becoming chignon. Lily was standing before the long mirror in her room, going over all Margot's complex instructions in her head, when her mother-in-law walked in.

'I've decided it would be best if you did not attend dinner tonight. One of the young men has cried off so our numbers are uneven, and you really are not ready for society yet, my dear.'

Lily was shocked. Days of acquiring the necessary etiquette, hours getting ready, and all for nothing? 'But I must.'

Margot smiled and patted the air an inch from Lily's hand. 'I shall explain you've been ill. That you are not quite up to the mark.' Which was true, for once the tears had started, they'd barely stopped. Lily had sobbed herself to sleep night after night, misery hanging about her like a shroud. Each morning she woke to a dark depression, wishing she needn't rise from the safety of her bed to face the world. Only her wish to recompense Bertie for the terrible damage she had done him got her through the day.

'Bertie will expect me to be there.'

'He will understand perfectly that you cannot be.'

'Yes, but...'

Margot was halfway to the door. 'Help Mrs Greenholme in the kitchen, there's a dear. I'm sure you wish to be useful, and all the maids will be fully occupied serving.' A final frosty smile and she was gone, the door clicking firmly closed behind her.

And so Lily's first dinner party was spent in the kitchen. Rivers of tears fell into the greasy water as she washed up at the big pot sink with a huge apron wrapped about her fine party gown. Mrs Greenholme studiously kept her opinions on the matter to herself.

The ban continued for two whole weeks.

'How can I ever learn if I am not permitted to try?' Lily persisted.

Bertie, still numb with grief, chose not to intervene and for once she felt like hitting him. At last Lily persuaded Margot to allow her to join them for a dinner party – a decision she was soon to regret. Lily used the wrong knife for the fish course, dropped a spoon from sheer nervousness, and earned herself a reproving glare by declining the oyster patties. Then, as Selene pointedly leaned over to adjust Lily's napkin to the correct position on her lap, somehow a glass of red wine got knocked all over the white damask tablecloth.

Afterwards she was called to the little parlour for her sins to be listed. 'You see, my dear. As I said, you are not ready.'

She wanted to protest that if Selene hadn't interfered at exactly the moment she'd reached for her wine ... But what was the use? Even Bertie seemed bent on seeing her in the worst light.

'Most embarrassing for Mama. For all of us, actually.'

Lily swallowed her misery and sense of failure. 'I was nervous. I need more practice.'

'Exactly. Mama has told me how you resent her offering advice – which is for your own good, don't you know? You can't go on sulking in your room, forever being difficult and refusing to cooperate. Life goes on and you've got to face up to your responsibilities, old thing.'

Lily's mouth dropped open. She longed to protest. Margot had entirely twisted the truth, making out it was she who had refused to attend the dinner parties, rather than Margot refusing to allow her to come.

Lily wanted to say that she had never willingly spent time in her room. Someone, kind-hearted Betty perhaps, had removed the broken fragments of cradle. Now the room seemed emptier than ever, and she could scarce bear to stay in it for a moment longer than necessary. But what was the point? Why make matters worse than they already were?

The 'lessons' were redoubled and Lily dutifully, if somewhat reluctantly, accompanied her mother-in-law on a relentless programme which, as well as the recognised social events such as Grasmere Sports, Rydal Sheep Dog Trials and Yacht Club events, included soirees, picnics, tea-parties and balls which took place almost every week in one or other of the fine houses around Carreckwater.

Strangely, it was Bertie who was the one most likely to cry off these days. He spent less and less time at home, claiming he preferred to take long walks over Benthwaite Crag or up to Glebe Woods. He'd often disappear for the entire day on the surrounding fells, carrying his lunch in a pack on his back. He'd walk over Hollin Fell, or as far as Little Langdale. He never asked Lily to go with him on these rambles, nor did she offer, assuming them to be a necessary part of his healing process. Sometimes he'd disappear for days on end and tell no one where he'd been.

But he never missed one of Margot's steamer picnics. The steam yacht would sail, silently and majestically, out to one of the many islands with only a passing moorhen to disturb the peace.

A huge table would be spread with the finest china and glass upon pristine white cloths. Should the weather appear uncertain this would take place aboard the yacht beneath the striped canopy; otherwise in the open at the selected spot.

Several bounteous hampers would be unpacked, the quality of the food being beyond description. There would be the finest game pies and roast duck, smoked salmon and potted char, and a choice selection of desserts to tempt the most jaded palate.

Fothergill the butler would serve champagne from a silver bucket marked with the *Faith's* crest, and two maids in frilly aprons likewise decorated, so no one was in any doubt about the wealth of the boat's owner, would serve tea to the ladies and offer delicacies to tempt fragile appetites.

And while the food was consumed, Margot would instruct her guests upon the scenic beauty around them or launch into a well-rehearsed history of the chosen island.

'A hermit monk once inhabited this place,' she informed them as they disembarked upon Martinholme. 'He spent his entire time planting trees, when he wasn't on his knees praying, poor man.'

At another she might give details of the Civil War, and how the island had been defended against capture by the opposing forces.

Or how a man once held an auction to rid himself of a wife who had become a trial to him.

'Darling Edward would never do such a thing, would you, my dear?' she simpered, and he harrumphed and lit another cigar.

No one could say that Margot Clermont-Read was not the perfect hostess, always prepared to entertain and educate her guests. She made very certain that her elegant party was not inconvenienced by sailing too close to the Public Steamers with their unsightly cargo of trippers and mill girls.

'Heavens, at times there are as many as a thousand people milling about the bandstand, tennis courts, and steamer terminal. Why do they clutter up the lake so? They quite ruin its tranquillity.'

'It's a pity they have nothing better do,' Edith Ferguson-Walsh agreed.

Edward's favourite occupation was, of course, steering, while George tinkered with the engine or fed it chips of wood from the two barrowloads he'd put on board for the afternoon's sail.

Lily sat with a frozen smile on her face, hoping her wide flowered hat would not blow off in the breeze, while she strove to remember everyone's name and all she had been taught. Once more she could feel the trap closing around her. It was no comfort at all to realise she had created it for herself.

Lily felt quite unable to take her troubles to Arnie. In any case, she guessed what her father's reaction would be. She'd made her bed and must lie on it. That would be his view.

In any case, he had enough problems of his own to worry over with a sick wife, work to find, and the girls to bring up.

Her main source of friendship came from an unexpected quarter. Her regular visits to The Cobbles necessitated her using the ferry to cross from Barwick House, which lay on the western shore of the lake, to Carreckwater on the east.

The ferry was largely responsible for bringing the outside world to Barwick House. The butcher and grocer's boys brought their deliveries on it, the postman the letters and even a telegram once in a while. Coal and wood came the long way, by road, but milk was delivered in huge metal churns, right to Mrs Greenholme's kitchen door.

Passengers used the ferry to go to town and back for shopping or to visit a friend further down the lake. There were various small jetties used as pick-up points, all marked with a bell or whistle to call the boat over.

Lily would make her way along the shingled shoreline to where a small folly stood some hundred yards from the perimeter of the gardens. Here a bell was sited, the sound of which would carry across the lake, alerting the ferryman, Bob Leyton.

Then she would sit, arms curled about her knees while she waited for the old man to set down his mug of tea or leave his fishing line safely secured then ease the small boat from the stone jetty and row across the lake to fetch her.

Sometimes he would have several customers: walkers, climbers, couples on holiday, children wanting a special treat. At others there would be only herself. Lily liked it best when she was alone.

Ferryman Bob would take his time then. She'd sit on a log, suck one of his mints, and listen to his stories of his adventures at sea, or the day the Windermere ferry sank with a load of quarrymen aboard. Forty men had perished, Bob's uncle among them.

'Not my father, he ran the ferry here. My family has held the licence for the Carreckwater ferry for three generations, and I'm to be the last,' he would tell her, shaking his head over what he termed his sad bachelor fate.

Lily would only laugh and call him an old sea dog with a woman in every port.

'Just as well I never did wed,' he'd finally admit. 'Would've made the poor woman's life a misery.'

Since then she'd taken to ringing the bell whenever loneliness or the ever-present pangs of her loss threatened to overwhelm her. It seemed to Lily at times that she had no one else to turn to.

On this day in late September, when the woods all about glowed with bright colour, she knew she should feel glad to be alive. But her heart lay cold as stone, heavy and still in her breast, as if there were no longer any point in its functioning. She'd tucked a shawl about her shoulders and walked for miles. Finally she reached the small folly and rang the bell. The sound of it echoed over the water, splintering the golden silence with its silvery notes.

A cormorant flew across the lake, skimming the water, sharp as a black dart. She could see the familiar thread of smoke coming from Ferryman Bob's cottage chimney. It comforted her just to see it.

She sat on a handy log, prepared to wait.

Ferryman Bob was a round little man with a shining bald head, usually kept covered with a knitted cap into which were stuck a selection of fishing flies and old badges from his navy days. From somewhere within its folds he could produce a stub of a cigarette, a match, safety pin, or even a boiled sweet. He claimed his pockets were too full of string and important tools to find any space for such delicate objects.

When he wasn't attending a call for the ferry, or warming his stockinged feet by the fire in his tiny cottage, he was usually to be found on the end of the jetty or sitting on a rock with a line out in the water. There was nothing he enjoyed more than gazing silently upon the broad expanse of water, gemmed with emerald islets. This was his world, and he loved it.

'You're lucky I bothered to come,' he said now, tying up the small rowing boat. 'I could see the water creaming wi' trout. I've probably lost me only chance of catching one now.'

Lily only smiled, well used to his taciturn manner and knowing he meant none of it.

'I felt like a bit of crack.'

'Talk away,' he said, joining her on the log. 'I'm all yours till the next bell rings.' He pulled out a crumpled cigarette stub and, cupping it between yellowed fingers in the palm of his hand, sucked it into life with the flare of a match. 'What d'you want to talk about then?'

Lily shrugged. 'Anything.' Anything but Margot, or Edward, The Cobbles, or Bertie's endless sulks, she added silently. As usual it was Ferryman Bob who did most of the talking.

He told her of the ghost who rang the bell on cold winter

evenings, when there was no one wanting a ride. Lily laughed at his solemn expression, refusing to believe such a tale.

'It must be the wind.'

'Not on a cold, starry night.'

'Have you ever seen a ghost?'

'I have. A poor woman whose bairn drownded in a storm. She keeps looking for it, poor mite, calling the ferry to help her.'

Lily shivered, thoughts of her own lost child piercing her sharply. She reflected on this sad tale with wide, believing eyes then saw the crinkles about his own. 'You're having me on.'

'Every word is true as I'm sitting 'ere.'

'Well, I'll not believe it.'

'I see your chap sometimes, out and about.'

'Do you?'

'Don't say much, do he?'

'Not a lot.'

'I takes him to the steamer pier quite a bit.'

'Oh?' Lily didn't want to talk about Bertie but wondered, fleetingly, what purpose he could have in Carreckwater. She rarely saw him these days, and whenever she did the glazed hardness in his once soft brown gaze troubled her more than she could say. 'No doubt he meets up with Nathan Monroe and they go off fishing, or more likely on a drinking spree together.'

Bob cast her a sideways glance, sucked the last out of the cigarette and sent the butt spinning into the lake where it fizzed and sank. 'I wouldn't know, and since I'm not his wife, I don't ask.'

Lily smiled, for there was little old Bob didn't know. Despite being well past eighty he was no fool and possessed all his faculties, as he proudly informed every one of the passengers he rowed across the lake each day with nothing but his own strength.

His clothes were serviceable and nondescript, well covered with oil, and he wore a waistcoat beneath his disreputable tweed jacket so that he could have a pocket for his gold watch. This was of great importance to him, as he'd told Lily at some length on numerous occasions. It had been presented to him by his work colleagues when he retired from the quarry and took over the ferry from his father.

He took it out now and examined it with care, as if he had an urgent appointment somewhere.

Most of the time this evidence of brisk efficiency served his customers well. When they called for the ferry from across the lake, or rang the bell he provided for the purpose, they could say with certainty that Old Bob would not take long to arrive. Nor did he. He knew that folk were more often than not in a hurry to get wherever they were going, and he'd little patience himself with dawdlers.

'Hurry along there.' he would say, sounding like a conductor on the horse-omnibus. 'You'd best look sharp. We tow the islands in come nightfall.'

This tale often confused the tourists and some had been known to believe him, which only added to his enjoyment. He loved to express his waggish sense of humour, almost as much as he enjoyed running the ferry. It gave him a sense of his own importance.

As for Master Bertie, well, it was no wonder he was always in a tearing hurry. Not that it was any business of his, nor his place to say where he hurried to. There were some matters best not talked about. Certainly not to this nice little lass, who'd suffered enough.

Chapter Thirteen

1913

A lone yacht tacked across the ruffled waters of Carreckwater as everyone gathered on the shore. Wild duck and greylag geese protested noisily at the unexpected intrusion, exercising their territorial rights over a lake which had changed little since the Ice Age. 'Carrec' was the old Celtic word for rock and the lake lived up to its name. Cut by glaciers, its steep sides rose precipitously out of the water, climbing into what must appear to be towering mountains to the wildlife surviving here.

The September breeze was warm and mellow, even at this early hour, and Bertie threw a crust or two of bread on to the water. Instantly it was stirred into a frenzy by a family of mallard squabbling furiously over who should have the largest piece. A black-necked grebe won the prize, swimming hastily away into the reeds, looking very pleased with itself. Even Lily laughed, and there was little in her life to amuse her at present.

She felt nothing but gratitude to Bertie for his offer to hold this picnic for all of her stalwart helpers. The season was drawing to a close and work on The Cobbles was largely complete, so he'd decided they should celebrate with a day-long picnic, starting as soon after dawn as people could manage.

Lily had been the first to arrive, sitting on a rock watching the sky blush pink as the sun slid into place. She'd always loved the dawn and watched with pleasure now as a few wispy strands of mist still clung to the tops of the trees and rolled down the mountains to settle upon the water.

Later, Rose arrived with her mother Nan, who always enjoyed a party. Dora and her team of worthies came accompanied by their young men. Even Selene had agreed to join them. A dozen or more young people were ready for a good time.

Only one person was missing, and Lily became aware of his presence the moment he walked across the shingle, looking fresh and handsome and immaculately dressed, very much a man of means. This would be the first time she had seen Nathan Monroe since she'd cried on his shoulder. How could she have been so foolish as to let him see her weakness? She should have kept her grief private, safe, as she had learned to do. Embarrassment flooded through her as she worried over what he would say to her.

He nodded as he walked by, but didn't approach or pause even to wish her good morning. Feeling affronted and oddly rebuffed, Lily turned her face quickly away, not wishing to have it appear she was watching him.

The group sat about in the growing warmth, enjoying their picnic, giggling at silly jokes and singing 'Coming Thru' the Rye' and 'D'ye Ken John Peel' at the tops of their voices. It was far more relaxed than any of Margot's formal affairs.

The food may not have been as sumptuous but they nibbled happily enough on chicken legs and cold Cumberland sausages. Bertie lit one of his famous bonfires, and started to toast muffins, joking and laughing with everyone, telling them what a relief it was not to have to eat milk pobbies any more, as if having diphtheria were the funniest thing in the world.

To watch him, Lily thought, you might believe him a brainless idiot with not a scrap of feeling or strength in him. But you'd be wrong. He'd stood up valiantly to the young thugs in The Cobbles, showing remarkable courage. Lily had witnessed his grief over Amy which had been as keen as her own, along with his brave determination to carry on with life, because that was the correct thing to do. Despite their current difficulties, largely caused by his family, the memory of their loss alone would keep her by his side.

She caught his eye and smiled at him with real affection, and he beamed cheerfully back.

'Feeling better, old thing?'

'Yes, thanks.'

'That's the ticket.'

He was a good husband to her. She really had no reason to complain.

Most importantly, this party proved that at least some good had come out of it all. The people of The Cobbles would benefit even if Edward was complaining that she'd made a pauper of him. Which Lily didn't believe for a moment.

'You must be feeling pretty pleased with yourself.' Nathan was suddenly at her side, and Lily's heart gave an uncomfortable thud. But it was no more than surprise, she told herself.

'You shouldn't creep up on people like that,' she said, sounding cross, but he only smiled.

'It's quite an achievement.'

Filled with panic, Lily glanced over at Bertie for assistance, but he was deeply involved in a seemingly hilarious conversation with Nan. She wondered if this should concern her, if she should go to him, yet felt oddly reluctant to move.

Acutely aware of the man now sitting at her feet, Lily wished fervently that Bertie had not invited him. She'd done her utmost to keep Nathan Monroe's involvement with her project to the minimum, but she'd failed. He'd stubbornly insisted on helping whenever he could, whether she liked it or not.

Now she moved a fraction away from him, stirring up a little self-protective anger. How dare he patronise her and ingratiate himself with their party as if by right?

'The residents of The Cobbles are certainly feeling pleased,' she said, rather pompously.

'At your playing Lady Bountiful, you mean? But you didn't do it for them, did you?'

Anger flared, bringing Lily to her feet in an instant. 'How dare you? Of course I did it for them, and for my father, my mother and sisters. My child!'

The challenge in his blue eyes instantly died. 'Of course, Lily. I'm sorry.' He grasped her wrist, as if afraid she might walk away from him if he didn't keep a hold on her. Lily thought that might very well be the case. 'Can we walk for a moment?'

Unable to protest, she allowed him to lead her along the

shoreline, away from the crowd. They walked in what might be termed companionable silence for some minutes as Lily waited, almost breathlessly, for him to speak. What was it he needed to say to her? Why had he singled her out in this way? She suffered a tumult of emotion whenever she felt him near. What in God's name was happening to her?

When he spoke, his voice was no more than that of a polite stranger. 'You look lovely by the way.'

'Thank you.' Was he teasing her? Lily couldn't be sure. 'Lavender silk. You've come up in the world, Lily.'

She gritted her teeth, saying nothing. Why must he always remind her of her origins?

They walked for a while more in silence. 'Perhaps you'd care to hear my bit of good news?'

'Which is?' Her tone was meant to be refined and controlled, as Margot had taught her, but it came out sounding only pettish, as if indicating she really had little interest in his affairs.

'I've been promoted.'

'Again?'

'To General Manager.'

'Heavens, you'll be running the company next.'

'My intention exactly.'

Lily glanced at him from beneath the brim of her straw hat, intrigued, despite herself. 'You've changed,' she said, the words popping out before she could stop them.

'Because I'm no longer a spotty youth who plagues young girls?'

'Something of the sort.'

'You've changed too. Though not necessarily for the better, Lily. You're quite the little opportunist now.'

'Damn you to hell,' she said, and turning on her heel, strode away, stiff-backed.

The young men took part in sailing races, very nearly overturning one yacht in the fickle breeze, yet finding the danger amusing rather than alarming. The girls put on their knee-length bathing costumes and daringly splashed in the shallows, shrieking and giggling like schoolchildren at the icy bite of the water against their warm skin.

Then they lay about on the shingle putting the world to rights, as young people love to do.

Dora, rather surprisingly, caused a flurry of argument as she expressed admiration for the suffragette Emily Davison who had died after throwing herself beneath a horse at the Derby in June. The others seemed to feel more sympathy for the jockey.

Selene entertained one bored young man with titbits from her *Woman at Home* magazine, as if he might be interested in dress patterns and household hints. Lily almost giggled to see the expression of feigned interest on the poor man's face.

Bertie was more concerned with rattling on about the speed boat he would build one day, while the other young men earnestly exchanged opinions upon the war in Bulgaria and whether the Balkan States ever would sort out their squabbles. It was, of course, all too far away to be taken seriously on a lovely, sunny autumn day in Lakeland. And they were having far too much fun.

Later, Bertie suggested they go out in the *Faith* and have lunch on board. 'Pa won't mind, though she's a mite slow. When I build my own boat it'll be petrol, naturally. A four-stroke engine.'

Selene issued a heavy sigh. 'Oh, do sit on him, someone, before he launches into a technical description. What a yawn he is!'

And poor Bertie was attacked on all sides until, laughing, he and a couple of Dora's friends went off to fetch the *Faith,* the shriek of its whistle announcing its arrival some time later.

'No swimming from the boat,' Bertie told them firmly. 'Too dangerous. Water too bally deep, and damned cold out there, don't you know? Not to mention weeds, hidden rocks and deep gullies.' But they did tow one of the sailing dinghies behind them, just in case there was enough wind for another sail later in the day.

The afternoon became unexpectedly hazy with heat and they all grew deliciously lazy. With the sun beating down the steam-yacht plied silently up and down the lake, visiting Bertie's favourite haunts while he sat quite happily in the stern, one hand on the steering wheel, a mug of tea at his elbow.

'Perfect bliss,' he said, gazing out across the shimmering water, sheltered by the steep-flanked hills all about. 'Though she definitely needs a touch more speed, wouldn't you say?'

'Oh, do shut up, Bertie,' Dora said, in such a surprisingly bossy voice that everybody laughed.

'An Indian Summer, what a joy,' Selene said, hooking her arm through Nathan's and smiling up into his face.

Lily had been sitting on the engine roof, arms wrapped about her knees in her favourite position as she enjoyed the warmth of the sun and the laughter of her friends. Now she found herself looking directly into a pair of piercing blue eyes.

Relaxed and confident as ever, Nathan Monroe smiled his intimate smile, challenging her to break his hold upon her. Then, quite casually, he turned and let his gaze rest thoughtfully upon Selene. In that moment Lily saw her best opportunity for revenge yet. But for some reason the taste for it had turned sour in her mouth.

Nathan Monroe would be the last man the Clermont-Reads would want for their daughter. Entirely unsuitable. And, strangely enough, if for very different reasons, Lily couldn't help but agree.

The shore seemed a dozen miles away. Matchstick yachts bobbed up and down at their moorings, a few late tourists milled about the band stand, empty now that the summer crowds had gone. No crack of ball on racquet echoed from the tennis courts at the end of the bay, no children in summer hats fished off the pier – though the boat-hire company still seemed to be doing a brisk trade. From here, in the centre of the lake, it seemed like another world, green with bright moving dots of colour, while on the steam-yacht all was calm and silent.

People had drifted away to sleep off an excellent luncheon, not to mention a huge pot of tea boiled in the Windermere steam kettle. Lily prepared to do the same, the sun warm on her neck. She settled herself in a comfortable wicker chair on deck, trying not to notice that Nathan was still engrossed in close conversation with Selene. Even the line of their bodies, sitting so close together, made her feel all hot and prickly. She closed her eyes so she couldn't watch.

It must have been an hour later that she woke and knew at once that something was wrong.

Lily could see nothing at all. Where once had been the lake, green woodlands and craggy rocks, there now lay a blank whiteness. Fog! An autumn mist had settled on the water, blotting out everything in sight. Ignorant as she was of these matters, even Lily understood its dangers. A boat could drift for hours in such conditions, its passengers growing steadily colder and more confused.

She sensed Nathan's presence beside her even before he gently touched her arm, almost as if she had silently begged him to come to her and he had obeyed. 'What are we to do?' she asked him. 'Where's Bertie?'

'Doing his best to steer in a straight line by keeping an eye on his wash. Far from ideal. I've come to tell you to go below.'

'No, I want to help. What can I do?'

'I've told you,' Nathan said, his voice calm but firm. 'Go into the saloon with the other ladies.'

From the depths of the fog, the steam-yacht's whistle shrieked and a small cry escaped her throat. Lily hastily began to do as she was bid but Nathan's hold on her arm tightened, easily preventing her from moving, though he had just told her to do so. He jerked his head in Bertie's direction, invisible even the short length of the boat, swallowed up by the fog. It was as if she and Nathan were alone in a silent white world.

'Has it been a success then, this marriage?'

'Of course.'

'Does he make you happy?'

'We're perfectly matched, thank you very much. Bertie is a dear. Though his mother and sister are less so, admittedly.'

He grinned. 'Don't let them interfere. If you were my wife, I'd protect you against all comers. Were I a marrying sort of man, that is, and the girl I wanted was still available,' he added, rather more quietly.

Lily stared as the meaning behind his words slowly penetrated. She longed suddenly to lean her head against those broad shoulders as she had done once before and pour out the confusion she felt at being a part of two worlds and belonging to neither. Every bit of her cried out for him to stroke her brow, her cheek, her throat, as she so clearly recalled him doing as she had wept upon his shoulder. And to caress her in less discreet ways, to help her unleash the passion she felt battened down deep inside, if only to prove that she, at least, was still alive. But she must never, never permit such a thing to happen. What was she thinking of? She must concentrate on Bertie.

'We're very content.' She pulled her arm free and stepped quickly away, so hastily in fact that she half stumbled as she came up against the deck rope looped along the side of the boat.

Instinctively, Nathan reached for her. 'Are you sure?'

With immense strength of will, Lily shook him off as she straightened her spine, thankful in that moment for Margot's strict training. 'I've told you, we're perfectly content.'

'Content? Ah, yes, of course. Safe and unemotional. But is it enough?'

'Of course it is enough,' Lily sharply responded, pricked once more into irritation by his calm.

'Wouldn't you prefer passion?' Then before she guessed what he was about he had pulled her hard against him and covered her mouth with his own. Warm, moist and dangerously exciting, it was the most outrageous, most cataclysmic, moment of Lily's entire life. As the kiss deepened she felt as if her whole body had spun out of control, held in a soft limbo by the mist. Her fingers clung to him, grasping his neck for support she drank in the taste of him as if her very life depended upon it. Then quite abruptly he let her go, leaving her bruised and wounded, knowing she would never recover.

'That wasn't the kiss of a happily married woman.'

On impulse Lily lifted one hand and struck him. Nathan didn't even flinch.

From a great distance the steam whistle shrieked and from close by came the sound of Bertie's voice, calling for Nathan. He and Lily stepped apart.

'Ah, there you are, old chap. Thought you'd slipped overboard. What are you up to? Trying to steal off with my wife, eh?'

'Would you blame me?'

'Not at all, you old rogue. But the elopement will have to wait,' joked Bertie. 'Got to get out of this pickle first. Stand up on the cabin roof, will you? You might be able to see over the mist and direct me, old sport.'

Bertie was instantly swallowed up again by the white fog as he hurried back to his post.

For a moment neither of them moved, then Lily turned away, anxious now to seek the company of the others. But she could not escape Nathan's last words, for all they were barely above a whisper.

'I'll make you mine, Lily. Make no mistake about it, you belong to me. Always have and always will. And one day I mean to collect.'

Lily's whole life had changed. What could she have been thinking of? Had she completely lost her reason?

She felt cold and shivery and strangely light-headed. Yet the warmth of Bertie's body beside her in the big double bed offered no comfort that night. If Lily slept, she was not aware of it. Her heart pounded, she felt ill and sick, and her eyes stared up into the darkness till they were gritty and sore, yet still she could not rest.

What would one kiss mean to him? A great deal. Hadn't he told her so?

She knew in her heart that these feelings had already been there between them, unacknowledged.

Perhaps, because of Nathan's outrageous behaviour to her as a boy, she'd refused to admit that he might have had good reason for being such a rebel: problems at home perhaps, or some other unhappiness. Nor had she accepted that he might have changed now that he was a man.

Could the reaction she'd felt each time she looked into those blue eyes have been simple attraction then and not fear at all?

Lily put her head under the pillow and tried to bury her thoughts. Yet she could not banish from her mind the memory of the pent-up desire that had trembled through his body as he had held her close, or the matching excitement that had burst within herself like sunrise after a dank day.

How could you? she scolded herself. You're married to Bertie, a fine gentleman, and don't you ever forget it. But she wanted to forget – oh, she did indeed.

His voice had followed her even as she'd run from him. 'Come to me when you're ready, Lily. I'll be waiting.'

Shocked and indignant at her own reaction as much as his effrontery, Lily made a vow that she would never go to him, no matter what her own weakness might crave. She would never see him again, if she could avoid it.

Bertie snuggled down beside her, his curly head deep in the soft pillows. He gave a gentle snore and Lily groaned. Who was she fooling? She longed even now for this to be Nathan in bed with her. To have him take off her clothes and make love to her with a fierce, all-consuming passion. She knew by that intimate smile, by the way his fingers had lingered upon her arm, and the heat that had flared between them when he'd kissed her, that he wanted it too.

Yet had he wanted Selene as well? Now the sickness inside her grew worse. If she'd still hated him, still been seeking revenge against the Clermont-Reads, what better way than to encourage their precious daughter to become involved with a ne'er-do-well like Nathan Monroe?

But it was long past time to let the dead rest, to forget her quest for revenge and concentrate on the living. Time to build a new life. What kind of a life that could be when she was married to one man and loved another whom she had always professed to hate, was quite unanswerable.

At the end of October came the Autumn Ball, the highlight of Margot's social calendar. It was very much a country affair, with dowagers smiling proudly upon their lively offspring while they sat and contentedly chatted about the state of their gardens, the hunt, or who had won the Yacht Club Trophies this year.

A three-piece orchestra played the dances of the season: the waltz, polka, quadrille and lancers. Margot stood proudly at the door welcoming every guest personally, as if she were Queen Mary herself.

Lily, with little heart for such delights, was on her very best behaviour, saying little and eating less. She curtseyed, smiled, nodded to all and sundry, while Bertie remarked how beautiful she looked.

She wore a blue silk gown trimmed with cream roses about the hem and sleeves, its décolletage low and daring. Yet she did not feel beautiful. Lily felt like a waxwork with a painted smile upon her face, and a manufactured heart in her breast.

How she longed to feel happy again. She'd longed to escape from The Cobbles, move out of one world into another. Now, glancing about at the pretty young girls in their pale frocks, Lily knew that she was an outsider still, would always be so. She'd also failed to protect her own precious child in this clean, scented world from being tainted by the one she had left. Entirely her own fault.

Tears filled her eyes on a sudden rush of guilt and sadness, and Bertie was beside her on the instant. 'Don't cry, Lily. We both miss our little Amy, I know, but life must go on. Not forget exactly, but carry on, for her sake.' He slipped an arm about Lily's waist. 'Maybe start another baby soon, eh? When you're ready.'

She felt a surge of gratitude for his kindness. 'It's just that on top of everything I find these events rather overwhelming.'

'All a bit strange, eh? Miss the old Cobbles?'

'That would be silly.'

'Course not. I miss it too. You were different there.'

'Was I?'

'We both were,' he said, an echo of sadness in his voice. 'I only want you to be happy, Lily. You've been so down lately.'

'I am happy.' And she danced a waltz with him to prove that it was true.

Lily couldn't bring herself to think of having another child. Not just yet. The long cold months of winter seemed endless but she continued her valiant struggle to make Bertie a good wife in every other respect. She wrote down and memorised Margot's instructions. She accepted every invitation, practised her grammar, her curtseys and deportment. Her punctiliousness in manners and grasp of current affairs were entirely suitable to her place in genteel society, and no one could fault her smiles.

Most importantly, she never permitted herself to think of Nathan Monroe. Not for more than the odd unguarded moment anyway.

Nor did she visit The Cobbles, not even to admire the new improvements or see her family. Lily decided that the only way for her to settle to her new life, was to put the old one firmly behind her for good. She confined her contact with them to a regular weekly letter, filled with news of her new activities and entertainments. It was meant to explain why she was too busy to call.

She thought herself very brave and noble, but none of her endeavours quite worked. Lily could see it in Bertie's eyes whenever he looked at her. In the way he paused, as if thinking twice before speaking to her, often changing his mind and saying nothing at all. And the times he spent away from home grew ever longer.

It was Selene who supplied the reason.

Lily was sitting in the summer house struggling to understand world affairs by reading a newspaper article in preparation for a dinner party that evening with the local Member of Parliament.

She was, for once, quite pleased to be interrupted by her sister-in-law. 'Heavens, Selene, I can make nothing of this. It appears to applaud Britain's diplomacy as the way forward to peace, yet to me it seems riddled with complacency.'

Selene draped herself comfortably upon a wrought-iron garden seat, smiling with a charm which should have set alarm bells ringing. Lily was too engrossed in the newspaper's views on a possible war to notice.

'As if Britain alone knows what's best for the world, and can solve all of its problems with a sound scolding.'

'I haven't seen my brother around much lately?'

'It says here that the Balkan States need a good talking to. Perhaps we should loan them Margot?' Lily giggled, expecting

Selene to join in her little joke. Instead she fidgeted with the bobble-trim on her peach linen gown and emitted a heavy sigh.

'Is Bertie home today?' When Lily said nothing, she continued, 'You know where he goes, don't you?'

Lily, still frowning over the article which she was following with the tip of one finger, smiled abstractedly. 'I'm sure you are going to enjoy telling me.'

Selene did so love to make trouble, Lily thought. No doubt she was jealous, if Nathan Monroe was out fishing with Bertie, it meant he wasn't with her. Lily knew the friendship existed, certainly on Selene's part, because she'd seen her taking detours to the pier to watch for him.

'Of course, it's perfectly fashionable for a man to have a mistress. Kings and princes do it all the time. And Bertie does like to be fashionable.'

The print blurred before her eyes and Lily was finally driven to redirect her gaze to Selene's smirking face. 'What did you say?'

'My darling brother. He's taken quite a fancy to a certain house on Fossburn Street. Bertie always did love to slum it.'

It was as though Selene had hit her full in the face. Nan. A mistress was one thing but *Nan?* Dear God, no. Bertie as a customer of Rose's mother seemed somehow beyond endurance. With commendable control, Lily got to her feet, folded the newspaper with excessive care, and without even a glance in Selene's direction, walked from the summer house across the garden and into the house.

Later, when she tackled Bertie on the subject, he did not trouble to deny it.

'You ain't the fun you were, old thing,' he said with genuine regret in his voice. 'Doesn't signify that I love you any the less. But a chap needs his fun. Absolutely essential. You're wrong about one thing though.' He laughed then, as if it were all some merry schoolboy jape. 'T'aint Nan I call on, but Rose. Dashed fine gel she is too.'

Somehow it was the final straw.

That night Lily moved out of his bedroom, and the very next day she went in search of Nathan.

Chapter Fourteen

For the remainder of that cold winter and well into spring, Lily experienced love as she had never known it before. Pride was of no consequence. It mattered only that she was with the man she loved.

Nathan had welcomed her without any sign of triumph, or even surprise. When she'd appeared on his doorstep that first evening, he'd simply held open the door and without a word from either of them, she'd stepped inside.

For a long moment he'd looked at her, then put his hands to either side of her face and kissed her brow: so chaste, so innocent, and yet the very softness of his touch had ignited her passion. The intensity of his expression had made her knees shake so that Lily thought she might crumple.

His love-making had been everything she desired – slow and tender, swiftly rising to a tide of passion that left them both exhausted. It was as if she had waited her whole life for this moment.

Later, as Lily lay with her cheek against his bare chest, there was no guilt, only complete harmony and deep satisfaction. She told herself that she'd never claimed to love Bertie, sweet and kind though he'd always been to her, and as enthusiastic and generous a lover as a wife could wish for. Yet their coupling had been nothing in comparison with this. She had never yearned for Bertie, never shivered with desire at the merest butterfly kiss on her brow. Loving Nathan was entirely different. It consumed her.

Yet she learned that embarking upon a passionate affair was not a comfortable experience. Constantly looking over her shoulder, she took risks, once even borrowing the gig without permission. She left it standing in the street, and someone came knocking on Nathan's door to tease him about his newly acquired wealth. That taught her to be more discreet. But as winter clung fast to the hills and valleys of Lakeland, where else could they go to be alone?

After that she went on foot. She would call for the ferry, trying to avoid the curiosity in old Bob's eyes as he transported her twice-weekly without a single question asked.

Nathan gave her a key to his house on the corner of Drake Road. He'd bought the property from his landlady and, save for a housekeeper who came and went like a ghost, lived in it alone. Which was exactly as he liked it. No prying neighbours, no one to tell him when to eat, or get up, or go to bed. So long as Lily took care to enter unobserved, preferably under cover of darkness, it offered complete privacy for their meetings.

Sometimes she would tell herself that she wouldn't go again. But as the appointed hour drew near, she'd shake with nerves, desperate to escape her responsibilities at Barwick House. Sometimes she'd cry off with a headache from whatever function Margot was planning and hurry to Nathan's side. But there were times when this was impossible, and she'd have to wait till the guests had departed before daring to sneak across the shingle and ring the bell.

On these occasions Ferryman Bob's efficiency seemed to vanish and he would cross the lake as slowly as a snail, complaining his working days grew longer and more tiring the older he got.

Lily would sit in the prow of the boat and speak not a word. What could she say? Her nerves were too tightly strung with worrying whether Nathan would have had the patience to wait for her.

He always did, if sometimes he grumbled at her lateness. Lily would try to explain how difficult it was for her to get away, the risks she took for him and the way Margot watched her with eagle eyes. Nathan would shrug those massive shoulders of his and smile, as if he were perfectly certain she would come to him at whatever cost.

When once Lily dared to ask him what they were about, and where this would all lead, he said, 'Don't think of the future. Be happy as we are. You know that I'm not a man who likes commitment.'

'Selene seems to think you are. She imagines you are well worth pursuing as a husband.'

He cast her a sideways look which said everything, and told her nothing. 'Jealous?'

Somehow this made her feel cheap and tawdry, but her twice-weekly visits continued. Nothing would keep her away. His love healed her, brought her back to life, though were it not for the very real and shuddering passion that consumed him when he made love to her, Lily might have believed Nathan didn't care for her at all. But he did, she knew it. A man of independence, ambition and pride, he didn't care to admit quite how much.

And throughout it all, Lily and Bertie continued to be perfect friends.

Margot's social calendar continued as usual and Lily played her part in it with increased assurance. If she bloomed with a more brilliant radiance, wore her gowns with a more bewitching grace, nobody questioned it. They imagined she had finally overcome the worst of her grief and homesickness for a life long gone; that she'd finally settled to her new responsibilities.

'How that girl has blossomed,' they would say.

'Not a girl any more but a beautiful, elegant woman.'

'A lady.'

Lily laughed when she heard them, remembering how she'd once quarrelled with the Clermont-Reads over this very point. Perhaps she had got her revenge, after all, in a most unexpected way.

Only once did Bertie suggest she return to his bed. 'I'll give Rose up if you want me to, Lily?'

She made no comment. She certainly had no wish to restore marital relations, so what Bertie did with his time was of no concern to her now.

If she stopped to think on it the wound was still raw. But perhaps that was only hurt pride. She'd not seen Rose from the moment she'd learned of the liaison. Not so naïve as the child she had once been when they'd first met, Lily now fully understood the nature of Rose's 'friendship' with Dick, as well as with Bertie.

Perhaps their dual misfortune was that while Rose seemed set to follow in the path of her mother, Lily had no hope of emulating hers, with not even one child to love.

At one time that might not have troubled her. Now Lily viewed Hannah from a different perspective. She saw that her mother had been, and still was, loved by a good and faithful man, had enjoyed the fulfilment of being loved and respected by a brood of healthy children. What more could a woman ask for? Lily, childless and torn between two men and two worlds, who once had set little store by such things, would have given anything now for such riches.

Lily told herself she couldn't expect to have everything in life. Nor must she ask for it. She had Nathan, didn't she? At least as much of him as he was prepared to give. Lily marvelled now at how she could ever have hated him, ever have thought him a cruel bully.

Oh, but he was no angel. He gambled furiously, often all night. On these occasions he'd go straight into his office at the Steamship Company, without troubling to go to bed at all. But he never allowed these sessions to clash with Lily's visits so she happily accepted them as a part of his nature, no real threat to their relationship.

The cold uncertain days of spring gave way to the warmth of early-summer. The rhododendrons and azaleas came into bloom, and the clumps of yellow globe flowers, wild hyacinth and garlic flowers that clustered all along the shoreline. The sun brought colour to Lily's winter-pale cheeks, her hair glowed with a rich chestnut sheen, and her hazel eyes positively danced with delight at the slightest provocation. She looked as she felt, shiny with love. It seemed a miracle that no one ever commented upon it.

Despite all her insecurities, the pain she had suffered, and the subterfuge she was forced to endure, Lily was happier than she had ever been. So long as she could be with Nathan, what more did she need? She had learned to be discreet. The least she could do for Bertie was to ensure that she did not embarrass him, and he extended the same courtesy to her. They lived separate lives while remaining the best of friends. It was an arrangement which worked well enough and Lily couldn't see why it shouldn't continue.

Then three things happened in quick succession, and everything changed.

It began innocently enough, on a warm day in June like any other. Lily had woken with a feeling of suppressed excitement that she really oughtn't to feel. Yet it fizzed inside her, nudging away all sense of what was right and proper.

She ran downstairs on light feet, humming softly to herself. This evening she and Nathan would meet secretly, as arranged, in Carreck Woods. It didn't get dark till quite late at this time of year, and they'd taken to meeting there whenever he could get away from his duties at the Steamship Company.

Not that she'd seen much of him recently, and Lily had frequently complained that his boss worked him too hard.

'I've my living to earn, my life to lead, as have you, Lily,' he'd replied, and she'd learned to be satisfied with that. She daren't quarrel with him too much or he would punish her by staying away for nights on end, leaving her pacing back and forth in the empty wood, railing silently at her own folly.

'It's only that I love you so much,' she would say, and then he would kiss her, as he always did, pushing her down into the green undergrowth and making love to her till her fears were silenced, until the next time.

This morning Lily's fears and dreams seemed suddenly of no account as Edward's newspaper told of the assassination of Archduke Franz Ferdinand. Having survived one attempt on his life, he now lay dead in Sarajevo and the spectre of war loomed large.

In the little parlour later that day, Margot seemed more concerned with whether her guests preferred China or Earl Grey tea. The tea was poured, delicate pastries handed round, and the room positively hummed – though more with social tittle-tattle than talk of foreign affairs.

Lily sat with Dora, the pair sitting in a private corner where they shared a plate of smoked salmon sandwiches and exchanged nostalgic memories of their time in The Cobbles.

'I do miss it in an odd way, you know,' Dora said. 'The challenge of getting all those children clean very nearly defeated me. Mind you, I learned to bathe three at a time – that way they could help each other with all the scrubbing.'

Both girls laughed. Lily liked Dora. Their friendship had blossomed during those hard months, and she now saw her earlier dismissal of her erstwhile rival as another middle-class female seeking a husband as incorrect. Or rather, Bertie's assessment of her, which she'd accepted, had proved to be entirely wrong. Dora wasn't simply a well-meaning do-gooder. She had hidden depths. In addition, she possessed a surprisingly strong stomach, unflappable good sense and a wry sense of humour.

Her homely face grew quite serious as she reached for a second sandwich. 'It opened my eyes, I don't mind telling you, Lily. There were children there actually stitched into their clothes, would you believe? For warmth, they told me. Yet how were they ever to be washed, I asked them? They simply looked at me with those blank accepting stares, as if I were speaking a foreign language.'

'It's another world,' Lily softly reminded her. 'One of survival, where cold is more likely to kill you than a bit of muck. Or so they think.'

Dora brushed her hands together, sending a shower of crumbs from her skirt all over the Persian rug and cast an anxious glance in Margot's direction to check if she'd been noticed. 'It's changed me, Lily. I can't go back to being a simpering miss after something as *real* as that. Mama wants me to marry, of course.' She pulled a face. 'But this war will put paid to that idea.'

Lily laughed. 'Of course you will marry. No talk of war, I forbid it.'

There was a pause as Betty refilled their cups. 'I shall do something terribly useful. Certainly not sit at home and sip tea.' She scowled at one of Margot's best Dresden cups and saucers on the small table before her, as if it were demanding she did exactly that.

'War.' Lily spoke in a voice hushed with fear. 'I can't bear to think of it.' Would Bertie join up? Would Nathan?

'You'll have to think of it. It's going to come. Nothing's more certain. Pops was saying only the other day that there are probably some funds left over from the South African War Comforts Appeal. The committee who managed it are planning to reform and provide medical care for the wives and children of those called up. I shall present myself as a volunteer at their very first meeting.' She nodded her head so vigorously that a hair pin fell on to the plate on her lap. Dora left it there. 'Why don't you come too?'

'You've thought it all through.'

'Of course. Mind, if I have my way that will only be temporary. I'd much rather join the Red Cross, train to be a nurse. Something truly splendid.'

'What could *I* do? If it happens. Which I'm sure it won't.'

Dora gave her what Lily could only describe as an old-fashioned look. 'Heaps of things. Roll bandages, collect woollens, raise funds to buy sheets for the hospital. I'll let you know after our inaugural meeting, shall I?' She leaned closer, sensible grey eyes grown oddly bleak. 'Believe me, Lily, there's going to be a war, and all our young men will be in it.'

The splintering of china, and Margot's surprisingly calm voice instructing the unfortunate miscreant to 'run along and fetch a dustpan', interrupted their conversation. Both girls raised their eyebrows at each other, for the anticipated explosion had not come.

'Poor Betty,' Lily said. 'She's taken quite a shine to George. She probably heard what you were saying and no doubt fears he too will join up.'

'Drivers and engineers will be greatly needed.'

But there was no sign of the little maid. 'Sobbing her heart out in the kitchen, I shouldn't wonder. It's most unlike Margot to take the loss of one of her best china cups so quietly.'

Always uncomfortable with servants, Margot generally took the view that the louder you berated them, the more in charge you were. But though she'd chivvied more than usual today, her patience had remained exemplary. Suppressed excitement fizzed from her like the froth from a bottle of champagne. She could hardly contain it.

'What's wrong with her?' Dora whispered. 'Not at all her usual carping self.'

Lily shook her head, stifling a giggle as she reached for a meringue. 'Haven't the faintest idea. You'll have to ask Selene when she arrives. Mama-in-law confides nothing to me.'

And why should she worry when in less than three hours she would be in Nathan's arms?

Seconds later, all was made clear when Fothergill appeared at the door and Selene herself swept in. She wore a fragile gown of coffee silk and cream lace, her blonde hair swept up into a wickedly clever chignon. Her eyes at once turned to meet Lily's, and in that moment her pale beauty was compelling. The reason soon became all too apparent: she was not alone. By her side was a man, and instantly the matrons burst into a frenzy of tutting and twittering as he strode confidently into their midst.

Dora was busily relating some amusing anecdote and took no notice at all, until she saw the change come over Lily's face. 'What is it, Lily? What…'

It was Nathan who stood by Selene's side. There was something in the way he remained there, so quiet and expectant which brought a blast of cold fear to Lily's heart, as if a hand were wringing every drop of life from it.

Margot clapped her hands delicately together in an effort to gain the attention of the chattering company. 'Ladies, ladies, may I present to you Mr Nathan Monroe, the new owner of the Public Steamship Company, and my darling daughter's intended husband.'

That night, too unbearably miserable to sleep or to tolerate her own company, Lily went to her husband's room. She stood by his bed in her peignoir, weeping like a child. 'Are you asleep, Bertie? I feel in need of some company tonight. Do you mind?'

'Course not, old thing. Come in here and cuddle up with me.' Generous as ever, he pushed back the covers and Lily crept into his arms to sob out her anguish on his shoulder.

Why hadn't she taken Selene's infatuation seriously? Why hadn't Nathan been open with her?

Because he didn't wish to hurt her? Or because he didn't care what she thought? Or because he was entirely pig-headed and independent? More likely ambitious, Lily realised. What better way forward than to ally himself with the richest family on the lake. Hadn't she done exactly the same thing.

Dear God, he would be her brother-in-law!

In that terrible moment when Lily had forced herself to go to the 'happy couple' and offer her congratulations, kissing each cheek, shaking hands, she'd come as close to hating him as ever in her life before.

His eyes had focused tellingly upon her and he'd whispered in her ear, 'Don't be hurt. I'd much rather it was you.'

She didn't believe him. Why had she ever believed him?

Bertie did not ask why she wept and she did not tell him. When there were no more tears left, Lily at last slept, cradled in her husband's arms where she felt safe and secure, cherished as a child.

She hadn't intended anything to happen between them, of course, needing only his warmth for solace. But perhaps waking to find his familiar body beside her recalled the happier, early days of their marriage. Or perhaps she simply needed to prove that she was still a woman capable of being loved, wanting to obliterate the deep sense of betrayal. Whatever the reason, when he kissed her, Lily made no protest. When he lifted her nightdress she welcomed him as readily as she had ever done.

Afterwards she cried again, but not with joy as she would after a night with Nathan. Lily cried for what she had lost. Everything.

In the first week of August, as Dora had predicted, war was declared. The 4th Border Regiment, having gone off to their annual camp in Caernarvon, returned the very next day to their headquarters to await further orders. The St John Ambulance put out a call for volunteers; the banks closed for several days while they worked out how best to deal with the situation. Even food prices soared as people rushed to stock their larders.

'Which just goes to show how very disorganised some folk were in the first place,' pronounced Mrs Greenholme, from the comfort of her well-stocked kitchen.

Kendal Drill Hall became a hive of activity, serving out one hundred rounds of ammunition to each man who enlisted, preparing the Territorials for departure amidst a chorus of enthusiastic cheering and the weeping of wives and sweethearts.

Nathan and Bertie were two of the first to volunteer.

And last but not least of this trio of disasters, Lily discovered that she was pregnant. Though which man was the father she had no idea.

Chapter Fifteen

1915-1917

The war was not, as so frequently predicted, over by Christmas. Lily found work was the best way to dampen the painful desires which came unbidden at any time of the day or night, triggered perhaps by the sight of her beloved child.

Thomas Albert Clermont-Read made his appearance in March, 1915, providing the family at last with a much longed for son and heir. Certainly Bertie welcomed him as such. If Lily had any thoughts to the contrary, she kept them to herself.

It had proved to be a difficult pregnancy. Lily seemed to be sick the whole time. The very idea of Nathan's marrying Selene was almost more than she could bear. She felt used and more isolated than ever.

There had been many occasions during those long months when she had longed for Hannah's rough commonsense and blunt good humour and, despite a very real sense of betrayal, she'd even missed Rose.

But Margot wouldn't hear of Lily's visiting her old friend. 'A visit to The Cobbles? Are you mad? Haven't you already lost one child?'

This so filled her with fear that Lily gave up all hope of seeing her family ever again. They, like The Cobbles, were a part of her past now, where it was best to leave them.

Lily wrote to Bertie twice a week, and he insisted she write to Nathan also.

'Every chap needs as many letters as he can get in this hell hole,' his letter instructed her, patriotic fervour in every page. 'See you write to us both. Selene too.'

How could she argue with such a plea? For all Selene believed her own daily letters to her fiancé were surely enough.

'He's an old friend,' Lily patiently and inaccurately explained. 'We owe it to them both to keep in touch while they're living through this horror.'

But she wished, almost as fervently as Selene that she could escape the task, while waiting eagerly each day for a reply.

Lily longed for, and dreaded, like a breathless young girl, Nathan's first leave home. A dozen questions buzzed in her head, thoughts and feelings she needed to express. Sometimes she felt herself to be almost going mad with the fear that she might never see him again.

Then one day, unbelievably, he sat before them in the little parlour with a cup of Earl Grey tea balanced upon one knee, swallowing tiny sandwiches whole. Margot, for once, was not present, but Selene had taken great pleasure in inviting Lily to this little tea-party, in order to show off her intended.

He looked so fine and handsome in his khaki uniform Lily wanted simply to sit and drink in the sight of him, etch every line of his face and figure into her memory to make sure she would never forget them. He too, it seemed, above Selene's chattering, was bent on doing the same. It felt at times as though they were the only two people in the room. Lily wished, with all her heart, that they were.

Only once, just before he'd joined up, had she confronted him on the subject of his coming marriage, reminding him that he'd claimed not to be a marrying sort of man. He'd kissed her softly then, saying he would miss her. 'A man has to look to his future, Lily, and you aren't free, are you? You never were.'

Now, watching him smile patiently at Selene's remorseless chatter, Lily told herself that if Bertie hadn't been unfaithful she might never have got involved with Nathan Monroe. But no, she couldn't blame Bertie. The fault was entirely hers. She'd wanted Nathan, there was no denying that fact.

What a fool she'd been! What a mess she'd made of her life. But she must look upon it more objectively. If she'd read more into their time together than he had, the fault surely lay in her own foolish sentimentality? Nathan had never actually said he loved her, never used the word. And he certainly had every right to marry, if he wished.

If only he hadn't chosen Selene, who was preening herself even now, as sleek as a cat devouring cream.

Lily sipped at her tea, praying no one, in particular her ill-tempered sister-in-law, would see how her hand trembled as she replaced the cup in her saucer. Nor did she dare lift her eyes to Nathan's one more time for fear she might betray herself by blushing. Or by running into his arms.

It was amazing the way Selene could chatter on, oblivious of their mutual absorption in one other. She was busily recounting the trouble she'd experienced in purchasing her latest gown. To listen to her, you would have thought that Britain had become involved in the greatest war mankind had ever known simply to vex her. So like her mother.

'Would you believe, they told me I simply could not have the material I wanted?' she complained. 'The very idea!'

Nathan turned to his bride-to-be, smiling his most devastating smile. 'It must be most annoying for you, my dear, that supplies are so difficult to obtain. Nevertheless, I have to say that you would look perfectly charming whatever you wore.'

Selene flushed with delight, making a half-hearted protest, while Nathan, with a swift but provocative glance in Lily's direction, which no one but herself could interpret, leaned closer and placed a kiss upon Selene's uptilted nose, and then upon the softness of her mouth, making her blush deepen.

Lily jumped up, depositing her cup and saucer with a clatter on the tea tray. Making hasty excuses that she must see to baby Thomas, she almost ran from the room.

Lily grew ever more thankful for her war work which kept her fully occupied. But hard as she strove to do her bit, it never seemed good enough so far as her mother-in-law was concerned. Margot had risen to the occasion by chairing several committees. Always in her element when giving orders and handing out work for others to do, she managed to give the appearance of being rushed off her feet without actually doing a stroke.

The war was a nuisance to Margot in one respect. It meant she must associate with the kind of people with whom she would not normally exchange the time of day – a situation which quietly amused Lily but which meant that whenever Margot felt bored or tired, which was frequently, she put the blame squarely upon her daughter-in-law, often using little Thomas as a bargaining tool.

If Lily should attend too many meetings, show herself to be working hard or raising more money than herself for the poor or the hospitals, Margot accused her of neglecting her son.

If Lily stayed in and devoted herself to her child, Margot claimed she was deliberately avoiding hard work and refusing to face up to the reality of life in wartime.

Selene declared herself too weak to do anything. Ever since the diphtheria, she had taken to playing the invalid whenever it suited her to do so. She sat about dreaming of her wedding, collecting her trousseau and planning the house she believed Nathan, or Edward, would build for her.

Life at Barwick House became increasingly difficult: three women playing out their own small war, with poor Edward gloomily returning home each weekend to spend his free time acting as a kind of reluctant referee.

And behind all the histrionics and sulks hung an ever present fear: for Bertie, for Nathan, for Dora Ferguson-Walsh, now driving an ambulance somewhere in France, and for all the other young people who had joined up on a wave of patriotism. For this reason alone Lily held her patience better than she would otherwise have done, and continued to play the dutiful daughter-in-law. But it was going to be a long war.

The front line was one long hell hole. The flare of lights and the flashes of tracers would from time to time reveal its stark outlines. The skeletal shape of a tree; a coil of barbed wire with an effigy hung upon it like a rag doll. The humped figures of men lying about – as if playing some boyish game. It seemed as if they would all get up and dance when the music started. Yet these boys who had become men overnight would never dance again. Gazing upon them, Nathan knew they were dead.

Even as the thought passed through his mind a shell exploded and the body flew into the air with balletic grace to fall to earth with a sickening crunch. The noise filled his own body as if it had a life of its own: a screaming, roaring, explosive crescendo of sound. Nathan aimed his gun and fired in furious retaliation into the blanketing darkness. Seeing nothing, he pressed himself into the mud, wanting it to swallow him and make him invisible even as he gave his all to survive.

That's all he had to do, really, stay alive, so he could see Lily again. Was that too much to ask?

He and Bertie had joined the same regiment together, a common thing for blokes, or pals as they called them, to do. They'd been sent to the front almost right away, rapidly discovering that war was not the lark Bertie had so enthusiastically imagined it would be. It could not be played out as if by gentlemen in a football match, or lads in some good punch up, and be over by Christmas. It was an endless, indescribable, unmitigated horror.

Nathan had stayed with the foot slogging. Bertie had taken the first opportunity to join the Flying Corps.

'Still mad about your matchstick aeroplanes?' Nathan teased, and Bertie had simply laughed, madcap as ever.

'More fun, soaring high in the sky. Nothing to beat it.'

'Well, good luck.'

'And to you.'

Nathan hadn't seen him since.

He remembered clearly that first leave. Merely to watch Lily move about the room had been solace to his soul. The swaying of her hips, the sheen of her chestnut hair, the way her gaze had fixed on his so entreatingly. And the way her teeth had chattered against her cup as if, like him, she was hard put not to beg him to make love to her there and then. His body ached still with the pain of his need.

If Selene hadn't been so wrapped up in her own affairs, she'd have noticed for sure.

He'd wondered since what had ever possessed him to get involved with the woman. A twisted sort of ambition, perhaps? The idea that since he could never have Lily, he might as well have money and position instead. Was that it? Yet it was much more challenging and exciting to make his own fortune, which he was well able to do. So why? And why had she accepted him? Because Selene rather enjoyed the idea of marrying the local bad boy turned good?

It was some time now since he'd been on leave, and he was tired. Everyone was tired. The fighting had gone on too long. Even the Boche were losing heart, while the British guns pounded ever harder against enemy lines. Yet if we're winning, Nathan wondered, how come the casualty lists lengthen daily?

He wondered again how Bertie was. Did he too lie in some field, a bloody bundle of rags amongst the splinters of his precious aircraft?

Again an explosion rent the air. Another man screamed and Nathan flinched.

In the next bright flare he saw a sight that must have come directly from hell. In a sea of mud pitted with shell holes and strewn with bodies, the carcase of a horse, its rider still attached, lay before him. Beyond that rats scurried, dipping in and out of a pool which daylight would no doubt show to be red with blood. Pockets of creeping yellow mist hung everywhere, hampering the efforts of those few who, like himself, were still left alive and searching for their comrades. The stench was unbearable yet Nathan did not gag on it.

The regular shots and explosions from behind the German lines made little impression upon him now. Nathan was beyond fear. You still had to believe in hope and life and the future to feel afraid. He had long since given up on those. Real fear, the cold stomach-churning stuff of sick nightmares, came afterwards, when the battle was done. It was always so.

'Dear God, Rose, you scared me half to death! What in God's name are you doing lurking about here?' Lily could have kicked herself for being caught sneaking out of Nathan's house on the comer of Drake Road. She'd called to see if his housekeeper had heard any word from him. She hadn't.

'Waiting for you.'

'For me?'

'It's been a long time, Lily.'

'Yes.'

'You've been busy of course.' But the smile said she knew of a different reason for their failing friendship. 'Can you spare a minute now, d'you reckon?'

'Of course.'

Reluctantly Lily followed her one-time friend down Drake Road and along Fossburn Street. As Rose pushed open her own front door and ushered Lily inside the small house, the familiar over-sweet cheap perfume hit her, bringing with it the memory of copious tears and, strangely, a picture of Dick's handsome face.

Mingled with the scent of violets was an all-pervading smell of stale cooking, dust, and an acrid scent she'd much rather not name. Lily screwed up her nose in distaste, and wished instantly she'd managed to be more composed as Rose gave a grunt of amusement at her expression.

'Quite the lady now, eh? I'll keep you no more'n a minute. Five at most.'

'So long as I'm not late for…'

'Dinner?' Rose peeled off her coat, the very same one that Hannah had made for her all those years before, looking even more frayed and faded now. She began to riddle the ashes in the half-dead fire with a rusty poker. 'Oh, aye, we wouldn't want you to miss your grand dinner, now would we?' Rose put down the poker and Lily watched in silence as she added a few screws of paper and chips of wood to the cinders, then carefully set three pieces of coal upon them.

'I'll not ask you to sit down. Bit mucky round here. Wouldn't want you to mark that nice blue coat. New is it?'

Lily sat. 'Rose, don't be like this. I've done nothing to deserve it.'

'Oh, you haven't, have you?'

'No. If this is about you and Bertie, there's really no need. When I found out – well, I made no attempt to stop him coming. Not once. Not when I realised it was you and not – not your mam.' She tried a tiny laugh, to recapture the way they'd once both declared they'd no wish to end up like their mothers. But it failed to lighten the grim atmosphere. For she would have been lying to say Bertie's defection hadn't upset her. 'Bertie and I...'

'I don't want to know. It's naught to do wi' me how you and Bertie go on.'

Lily saw Rose bite on her lower lip before turning her head away to reach for a taper from the mantel-shelf and hunt through papers and accumulated rubbish for a box of matches. Lily wished desperately that she had not come.

'What is it you want? I must get back to Thomas, and we've...'

'Naught to say to each other? No, happen not. You stopped calling long since, didn't you? Too grand now for the likes of us. When's the last time you set foot in your own mam's house, let alone mine? Wouldn't know whether they were alive or dead, would you? Nor even care, I shouldn't wonder.'

Stung by these remarks, Lily felt sick. 'That's not true. Life isn't all that easy for me either, if you want to know.' She felt a sudden jolt of fear. 'Are Mam and Dad in trouble? Is that what this is all about? Tell me.'

'They're getting older and sadder, like the rest of this Godforsaken world.' Rose regarded Lily with eyes that might have been laughing were it not for the cynical twist of her mouth. 'It's a poor do, though, that you have to ask me how your own parents are. I reckon you should know, don't you?'

Rose applied a flame to the paper and wood, then stepped back, brushed off her hands and held them out to the growing warmth while Lily searched her mind for the right words to explain her situation. But what made sense sitting in Barwick House no longer seemed appropriate. She feared for her child, of course. But was that the only reason?

'It'll soon get going, the ash is still warm,' Rose said. 'Then I'll put t'kettle on.'

'I really haven't time. Thomas will want his tea.'

'I heard about the bairn.' Rose halted in the process of filling the kettle long enough to nod at Lily, the faintest gleam of kindness now warming her dark eyes. 'I'm glad for you.'

'Thank you.'

'Bertie was – must've been delighted.'

'Yes.'

'Aye.' Softly. 'He missed little Amy.'

A small silence as Lily struggled with a rush of emotion that rose swiftly to block her throat and prick the backs of her eyes. She stood up rather abruptly. 'If there's nothing else? Thank you for your concern over my family. I'd best be going.' She half turned, anxious to quit the claustrophobic room with its memories of men tramping up and down the wooden stairs. Bertie apparently one of them.

'Oh, I forgot. You mustn't miss your dinner.'

Something in her tone got to Lily. She whirled about to face her one-time friend. 'Don't criticise me for being neglectful. You didn't adopt this holier-than-thou attitude when you pinched my husband, did you? Or Dick, for that matter. Why don't you find a man of your own for once?' Then she strode down the small passage to snatch open the front door.

'How is he?'

There was a plaintive note in Rose's voice, revealing at last the purpose behind her waylaying of Lily. But she didn't stop to answer. It was only much later that she wondered how it was Rose knew where to find her.

A favourite part of Lily's day was when she walked little Thomas out each afternoon. She would point out a cheeky robin, a busy moorhen, or pluck a buttercup to hold under the baby's chin to see if he liked butter.

The lake was quiet now. The big Public Steamers had stopped running, partly because of lack of fuel, and partly because most of the men who worked on them had joined up. Lily thought this rather sad, and it certainly created problems for the folk who lived about the lake, war or no war.

On one such expedition she ventured round a grassy peninsula and, lifting weeping willow branches to allow her to pass, encountered Edward working on his beloved *Faith* up a quiet backwater.

'So this is where you get to. There'll be no pipes left if you rub much harder,' she teased.

'Lily.' Edward turned to her with pleasure. He'd grown fond of this daughter-in-law of his. Rough diamond though she may be, Lily had spunk. She was the only person he'd ever known to stand up to his wife.

For Lily's part, she'd warmed to him since his efforts over The Cobbles.

He let her kiss his cheek, beaming at her as she did so.

Thomas took the opportunity to grasp a bunch of Edward's hair with the tenacity known only to a robust two year old.

'What a scamp. Come to Grandpa then. May I take him?'

'Of course.'

For the next ten minutes Edward was fully absorbed in playing with his grandson while Lily smiled and enjoyed the sun. But when the toddler began to grow restless, Edward asked if he could take him into the boat.

'I won't drop him into the water or anything. I'll take great care of him.'

'I know you will. You can show me your precious boat too while you're at it.' With a plump little hand held in each of theirs, Edward and Lily climbed aboard the *Faith*.

As he talked, Edward found his polishing cloth and went back to his polishing. 'Here you are, laddie, help your grandpa.' The child immediately tried to copy the old man, making them all laugh. 'Real chip off the old block, eh? He'll make a good boatman one day.'

Lily agreed that he probably would, not wishing to consider exactly which block he was a chip from. Then she was rolling up her own sleeves, picking up a rag and dipping it into the metal polish. Edward watched her in amusement.

'You wouldn't catch our Selene or Margot cleaning a boat. Cleaning anything, in fact.

Lily cast him a sly grin, hazel eyes sparkling. 'I'm not Selene or Margot, am I? Bertie loves this steam-yacht. He was always happiest when he was out in her.'

'Bertie likes wearing fancy clothes and driving up and down the lake, but ask him to do aught involving work and he'll be conspicuous by his absence. You'll never see him roll his sleeves up.'

'Oh, I'm sure he would,' Lily protested.

D'you know what it is exactly that you're cleaning, Lily?'

She laughed. 'No.'

Edward proceeded to describe the mysteries of the many pipes and tubes and pistons, Lily understanding about one word in five. But by the end of the morning, the *Faith* had benefited from their efforts and Lily found she'd thoroughly enjoyed herself. Baby Thomas was black from snub nose to chubby knees, but it would do him no harm, she decided. His grandfather had enjoyed the experience most of all.

It came to be a regular weekend activity for them all, and Edward in particular made the most of it. For Lily it was a welcome relief from being in a household of women and she found she enjoyed learning more about her father-in-law's hobby and the two became easy in each other's company.

'You've fitted in well with us, Lily, I'll grant you that. I know it was difficult at first, but you've made a lot of effort and I, for one, appreciate that. But don't neglect your own. Family is important, lass. If you neglect something, it tends to die. Never forget that.'

On the day she heard that Bertie had been wounded and was in an army hospital at the front, Lily finally took her child to visit Hannah. Perhaps it was some primitive instinct to run to her mother at this time, even a mother she hadn't seen since before he was born.

It had taken all her courage to open the much-dreaded telegram. She'd quickly scanned the few words then closed her eyes in relief, handing it over to a near-hysterical Margot before going at once to the nursery. There she bundled her son into his best blue sailor coat, stuck a hat on his head and carried him quickly downstairs, shaking with emotion. It seemed imperative she should get out of the house.

Margot stopped screaming long enough to confront Lily in the hall, demanding to know where she was going.

'Out.'

'Out? My son lies dying somewhere in France and you are going *out?*'

'I need fresh air.'

'You should go to him. Be the good wife he deserves.'

Lily barely paused as she hastily made up the big pram. Thomas was far too old for it now but it was quicker than letting him walk on his short chubby legs. At the door she said only, 'We don't know that he's dying. But if he is, then his son will need all the family support he can get. Including those members he hasn't yet met.'

As she set off down the drive at a brisk pace, Margot's cries turned to fury. 'You're not taking my grandson to The Cobbles!'

Heart thumping, Lily didn't even glance back, only pushed the pram steadfastly before her. At the folly she rang the bell and waited impatiently for the ferry to come. Bob was adept at manhandling the pram into the boat, and was all concern over Bertie.

'Don't you fret now. He's a fine healthy young chap. He'll be right as ninepence. Mind, too many of our young men are going missing.' He sadly shook his head, making the fishing flies on his hat cavort in a mad dance. 'That Nathan Monroe might've got hissel killed. Did you hear?'

Lily couldn't find her voice to reply to this and shivered as if a goose had stalked over her grave. It was six weeks since she'd received any letter from Nathan. What madness was the world coming to?

It was hard to imagine death could come so near when here in Lakeland a late-summer sun still shone and a few half-hearted tourists wandered the woodland paths, no doubt feeling guilty at taking a few days away in the middle of war. A young boy stood knee-deep in water where a beck flowed into the lake, happily guddling for trout. Bertie had told her it had been a favourite sport of his as a child. Now he was a man with his life torn apart by an endless war.

Bertie must live. He must come back to her. Nathan too.

Oh, for those blissful days of steaming out in the *Faith,* and lovely picnics by the lake. Days of youth and hope, now long gone.

Old Bob set her down at the Fisherman's Inn, and Lily walked past the fine terraced villas along The Parade, through Fairfield Park with its empty band stand and along the promenade. If she came this way she could avoid Fossburn Street, which would suit her very well. She had no wish to see Rose today.

At the old boathouses she paused, remembering another summer's day when Bertie had kissed her properly for the first time. She'd teased him into it, of course, wanting him to fall hopelessly in love with her so she could get close to his family and take her revenge on them. How young and intense she had been, full of fire and fury. To her surprise she'd grown truly fond of Bertie, and in the end lost all taste for the fight.

Giving the pram a hefty push she turned left into Fisher's Brow, feeling as if she were stepping back in time as she struggled up the hill. Lily had constantly assured herself that Margot was right to insist she keep her son away from The Cobbles. It was a dangerous place, filled with dirt and poverty and disease. This was the first time in years that she'd actually walked these streets in broad daylight. Her recent visit to Nathan's housekeeper at the corner of Drake Road on the very edge of the district, had been a furtive affair in late-evening. Even the enforced visit to Rose's house afterwards had been hasty.

Yet today when she walked along Mallard Street, where she and Bertie had first lived, she was surprised by how remarkably clean it appeared. Every house had net curtains prettily looped or frilled, an aspidistra or pot dog reclining on the window sill.

Turning into Carter Street she was instantly struck by the fact no filthy water ran along it. There was no mud, no rats, no men urinating, or bare-bottomed children sitting in muck. Where once it had been little more than a dirt track, deeply rutted and filled with puddles, the whole area was now a sound metalled road. A horse-bus came along, stopped to allow several chattering women to disembark before clanging its bell and starting off again. Lily could hardly believe her eyes, so entirely different was it from The Cobbles she had once known and hated. Even the children playing with hoops in the street looked better fed and clothed than in her day.

Hot with guilt, and the long walk, she jiggled the pram to keep her son happy as she tapped on the door of number four, pausing a moment while she waited to take note of the changes here too. The door had been painted a sensible dark green, the flagstones in the back yard gleamed from much scrubbing and white stoning, and there were pots of geraniums now on the ash-pit roof.

All was peaceful and quiet, not even a sound from the Adamses next door. But then both boys were away in the war, so how could there be?

Lily waited with growing trepidation. What would she say to her mother? How could she explain these years of neglect? She must somehow get it across how she'd striven to be a good wife to Bertie, to keep her bargain with Edward. How she'd owed it to the Clermont-Reads to put her past behind her because of little Amy, and her regrets over her own ill-fated quest for revenge. As Lily considered the weakness of her argument, she armoured herself with a shell of defiance. She vowed not to let Arnie bully her, or her mother make her feel guilty. They didn't have to live with Margot after all.

Lily flinched when she heard the click of the sneck and then she was looking into her mother's face. In that moment all her defiance melted away like snow in the sun.

'Mam? Oh, Mam,' she cried, and falling in her mother's arms, began to weep.

Chapter Sixteen

Hannah sat rocking the child on her knee. Thomas contentedly chewed on a gingerbread biscuit, far too young to understand the undercurrent of emotion, or the questions not being asked amongst the idle comments made above his head.

'He's a fine strong bairn. Big for his age.'

'Yes.'

'And Bertie such a neat chap.'

'Not exactly small though.'

'Not got his father's sandy hair then.' She was fluffing up the cap of dark curls on the child's round head.

'Takes more after me, I suppose.' Clearly a lie, Lily thought, since Thomas was so much darker.

'No doubt it'll change as he grows, as will his eyes.'

There followed an achingly long pause in which Hannah smoothed the dark locks and smiled into her grandson's surprisingly blue gaze while she considered her daughter. Not that this smart young woman in the fashionable double-breasted jacket and wrap-over skirt, button boots and fancy wide-brimmed hat, bore any resemblance to the ragamuffin child she'd given birth to twenty-three years before.

'We're hoping Bertie will be sent home soon,' Lily burst out, anxious to deflect attention from her son's looks.

'Where is he then?'

'They don't say. He tried to work out a secret code in his letters and postcards home, but I know nothing about France so could never understand them. Dora would know but she's in France too, driving an ambulance. Asked me to go with her. Did I tell you?'

Hannah shook her head, gaze steady upon her daughter's bright face, not saying, How could you have told me when I haven't seen hide nor hair of you in years? Yet Lily sensed it in the bleakness of her mother's eyes, and the deep grooves drawn between nose and mouth. Hannah had recovered well from the consumption, but perhaps less so from her daughter's neglect.

Lily talked on, filling the silence, assuaging her own guilt. 'I was pregnant at the time, so how could I go? Now I'm stuck at home with Margot's committees.' She laughed as if it were the funniest thing in the world.

'I'm sure they must keep you very busy.'

'We have to supply sheets, bed socks, pyjamas and the like for the soldiers who come to convalesce at the hospital. Roll miles and miles of bandages.'

'And you have the bairn to care for.'

'Yes, I have this little monster.' Lily leaned forward and tweaked the boy's nose, making him shout with laughter.

Hannah's face was thoughtful and again the silence grew awkward between them. Lily struggled to find something to say. 'How are the boys?'

'Doing well in the Navy. They visit whenever they can get leave.' Again the implied criticism.

'And our Liza and Kitty?'

'Kitty's ten. Liza's sixteen, and courting young Joe Broadley.'

'Oh, lord, that makes me feel old.'

They talked of the war, of campaigns lost and won, of which family in the street had suffered a casualty or the ultimate tragedy. Lily longed to ask if Hannah ever heard any news of Nathan, but daren't risk it. At last the words burst out. 'I would've come sooner only...'

Hannah stiffened. 'No need to explain. I'm sure you had your reasons. Though I would've enjoyed being there when this little chappie came into the world. A mother likes to be with her daughter at such times.'

'Oh, Mam, I wish you could have been too. Margot wouldn't ... I didn't like to...'

'Nay, don't tell me she's got the better of you at last? Who'd've thought me own daughter would ever admit such a thing.'

Lily might have taken this as jest, were it not for the condemnation on her mother's face.

'I wasn't in a position to argue.' She gave a sheepish smile. 'Margot was very much in charge.'

'I dare say she was.' Hannah didn't ask why Lily hadn't brought her newborn son to see her as soon as she was recovered, or at any other time in the two long years since. She didn't need to. The question hung between them, held by that deafening silence. When she could bear it no more, Lily fell on her knees before Hannah and gathered her mother's work-worn hands in her own.

'Mam, I'm so sorry. I didn't meant to hurt you. Can't we be friends, like we used to be? With Bertie gone, I can't bear to think of us like this.'

Hannah stiffened. 'That's what this visit is all about, is it? You might be about to lose a husband so thought you'd best make it up wi' your mam, eh?'

Lily's face paled. 'No, that's not true. I've hurt you, I know I have. But I feared for my child, after Amy… I was only thinking of Thomas … Of disease and…'

'Plenty of babies survive here now.'

'I hadn't realised how much it had improved.'

'You never came to find out.'

Again the guilt bit deep. She'd needed to live entirely in her new world and abandon the old. But how could she explain this without its sounding as if she were ashamed of her own parents? And she'd been afraid to risk her mother guessing of her affair with Nathan.

There was a moment in which Hannah considered her daughter's very real distress, seeing there were secrets held back and wondering at them, yet trying to put herself in Lily's place, stuck in a fancy house with Margot Clermont-Read and that superior daughter of hers – Selene, wasn't it? Criticising Lily at every turn, no doubt, making her feel inferior because she'd been born the wrong side of the blanket and the wrong end of town. Drat the pair of them for driving this wedge between Lily and her family!

But this was her lass and she loved her, so she would forgive her. Hannah opened her arms and gathered Lily close, holding her lovingly as she used to do when she was a child.

'You're here now, that's all that matters. Let's put the past behind us, eh? We'll set the bairn down for a nap while us'll have a cup of tea and a bit o' crack. What d'you say?'

'Oh, Mam. That'd be grand.' Lily's face was awash with fresh tears and Hannah smoothed them away with the blunt tips of her rough fingers. Kissed her daughter's cheek.

'Five minutes in your old home and you're talking as bad as ever. What happened to the elegant Mrs Clermont-Read?'

Lily shook her head. 'She's still your Lily underneath.'

For the first time, Hannah smiled. 'Well, I'm right glad about that, lass. Right glad. And he's a bonny wee bairn.' No matter who his father is, her eyes said.

When it was time to leave, Hannah rested a hand upon Lily's arm, her eyes on the child. 'You'll come again soon? When your dad's in next time. He's missed you.'

Lily nodded, her eyes again filling with tears. 'I will, don't worry. I don't care what the Clermont-Reads say, I'll not stay away.'

'Aye, see you don't. We all have to stick together these days.' She helped Lily tuck Thomas into the big black pram and stood at the yard gate to wave to him.

Then before Lily set off she asked the question that had burned in her head all afternoon, as casually as she could. 'Do you ever hear anything of Nathan Monroe? You remember, your old lodger?'

A pause before Hannah answered. 'Aye, I remember. No, I've heard naught. Is it true that he's to marry Margot's daughter?'

Lily swallowed, her throat gone suddenly dry. 'Yes, it's true.'

'Well, fancy that. Rumours have been flying for years about one thing or t'other. Not that I let on to your father what I hear. He sets great store by a person's good name.'

Lily looked into her mother's knowing eyes. 'Yes, I suppose he does.'

Hannah said, 'I couldn't quite tek it in though. What a pair they'll make! Chalk and cheese, eh?'

Lily kept her voice carefully neutral. 'Margot would've preferred him to be richer, but she was so worn out by Selene's fussing that she soon agreed. Anyway,' she said, looking anywhere but into Hannah's eyes, 'he's doing well for himself – or at least he was before the war – and afterwards no doubt he'll carry on where he left off before...' Her voice faltered as she wondered if that was quite true, if he'd even return.

'He was a good friend to your Bertie.'

'He was, still is.'

'Does he write to you?'

'He used to.'

'Not heard from him lately then?'

'No.' Struggling to keep her voice normal.

Hannah sadly shook her head. 'These are terrible times we live in, lass. His housekeeper used to hear from him regular, but she was telling me she'd heard naught for weeks. I hope he's all right.'

'Yes,' said Lily politely. 'So do I.'

By Christmas 1917, war weariness was rife. In Margot's opinion the government had no right at all to ration food or restrict any facet of civilised life. Wasn't it difficult enough with one's servants having joined up out of patriotic fervour, leaving her with only one young housemaid and Betty to run Barwick House? Unthinkable before the war. The sooner it was over the better. Even the King had asked them to eat less bread. The very idea! Margot chose to ignore this particular request as hysterical nonsense. Would it put any more food in the mouths of the so-called poor, or hasten the end of this ridiculous war if she half starved herself? And no one could accuse her of being selfish. Hadn't she worked unstintingly for the hospital committee since the war began? At great sacrifice to her own social life.

Fortunately Betty was proving to be a most capable girl. With the advantage that she was no oil painting so unlikely to catch a beau, even if there were one around. Margot had instructed her in cooking and personally dispatched several Christmas puddings to Bertie, determined that at least one of them should reach him.

So in view of the difficulties, she saw no reason why Edward shouldn't take his three womenfolk to the Marina Hotel to celebrate the festive season. At least that establishment would not be short of local produce.

They dined in fine style on turbot and roast duck, followed by a raspberry and redcurrant tart, and, as luck would have it, met up with the Kirkbys. Margot had been reliably informed of the couple's recent move into the area and had been dying for exactly this opportunity.

'Who are they when they're at home?' Edward mumbled, as she prepared to make herself known to them.

'Mr Marcus Kirkby has taken that big new white house by the golf club – Rosedale Lodge. Quite charming. He owns a munitions factory in Liverpool, I believe.'

Edward sat up a little straighter, even took the cigar he'd been about to light from his mouth. He'd taken a few too many losses recently. Exports were almost at a standstill and he wondered sometimes where his next shipload would come from. A new contact might be useful. Lily had persuaded him to run the *Faith* as an extra ferry for people, at weekends at least, when he was home. Not that Edward ever minded an excuse to go out in his lovely boat but Lily wouldn't hear of taking much money off the locals who used her, so more often than not he was out of pocket after he'd bought the coal. As always with one of Lily's deals. But she often came along too, happy to stoke for him since George had been called up. Not minding when she got her cheeky face all smutty. Though how much longer he could continue to be so generous was a worry. 'He'll be comfortably off then?'

Mother and daughter exchanged a speaking glance. 'We should welcome them into the locality, do you not think?'

Margot hurried over the introduction of Lily, calling her 'my poor little daughter-in-law', thereby stamping her firmly with the appropriate credentials. Selene she kept to last, delighted to see how Marcus Kirkby lingered over her hand. When the introductions had been completed to everyone's satisfaction he suggested they all adjourn to the lounge, for coffee.

Lily, to Margot's very great relief, excused herself on the grounds that she must hurry home to care for Thomas.

The fact that Kirkby possessed a wife already was undoubtedly a disappointment. She would not have been against finding a better match for her darling Serene. However, Margot decided the woman must have connections, for all she looked as if she dined on cold gruel. Margot settled her increasingly corpulent frame into an easy chair and prepared to be agreeable. These were not people to offend.

The ladies were soon exchanging the usual pleasantries while Edward and Marcus fell into deep conversation about who was winning the propaganda war, what would be the outcome of revolution in Russia, and the many difficulties Marcus experienced in getting his supplies delivered. 'You're in transport, aren't you?' he asked. 'So you'll understand.'

Edward, well warmed by brandy, concentrated hard. 'Freight. I own a modest fleet of merchant ships. Move stuff from A to B, don't you know?' He wished now that he hadn't taken that third glass as he became suddenly aware of an opportunity he really shouldn't overlook. He sat up straighter. 'Perhaps I can be of service? If you need supplies fetching, I'm your man.'

Marcus looked doubtful, even embarrassed at finding himself cornered. 'You misunderstand me. I am the supplier. I manufacture arms for which I have my own transport. It would be far too risky to use anyone else.'

'Of course, of course.' Edward's disappointment was all too evident and Marcus, considerably sharper at the best of times, and having been far more abstemious with the alcohol at luncheon, wondered at it. Edward Clermont-Read might be a bumbling old fool but he was not without substance. A fine house together with the usual accoutrements of the well-to-do, warehouses in both Manchester and Liverpool, plus his merchant ships.

And a daughter.

He glanced again at Selene, now quietly engaged in conversation with Catherine, her whole body poised in a way which revealed her awareness of him. His interest quickened. Who knew what the future might hold, or when an acquaintance or friend might prove useful? Selene Clermont-Read, for one, showed undoubted promise.

Clearing his throat Marcus Kirkby directed a polite smile at her father. 'I shall remember your offer, though. I like a man of enthusiasm and, should I find myself hard pressed or in need of transport, it might be useful to know of a service I can trust.'

Edward, who had slumped back in his chair, hastily searched for his cigars and offered one to Kirkby. 'Just say the word, old chap.'

As Edward went through the ritual of clipping and lighting the two Havanas, describing the many attributes of his fine ships, Marcus shifted his gaze to find Selene openly considering him across the table. A half smile played about her lips and then, quite provocatively and infinitely slowly, she slid out a pointed pink tongue and licked them. He almost burst from his chair in excitement. He could have taken her there and then, amongst the coffee and petits fours.

Selene turned to Catherine and casually remarked upon the exquisite style of her gown. With very little more flattery, she had elicited an invitation to come to dinner at their charming home the very next Saturday.

'I thought three of my bridesmaids should wear pink, and the other two a deep burgundy velvet.'

'Dear heaven,' replied Edward, brow furrowing deeply. 'Five bridesmaids? There is a war on, drat it.'

Selene paused briefly to kiss the top of his head as she flounced past him to stand before the oval mirror above the fireplace and tease her curls into place. 'Don't be such a spoilsport, Pa. You know that my fiancé and I have decided not to marry until the war is over. So you have plenty of time to prepare.'

She never called Nathan by his name, only ever by his status in her life, as if he should have it emblazoned on his hat badge like a military honour. Or perhaps she saw him as a prize she'd won for her trophy shelf. Selene had heard no word from him for months, but refused to give credence to rumours he was dead. She was quite certain that he would be at her side when required. For the moment it was pleasant to enjoy the kudos of being engaged without suffering the irritation of having to do anyone's bidding but her own.

She tugged at the bell pull and when the maid answered, instructed her to fetch her best beige coat and scarf.

'Where are you off to now?' Edward snapped.

Margot, comfortably ensconced in the window seat where she could work on her accounts and keep an eye on the comings and goings of boats on the lake, thereby discovering who was visiting whom, directed a knowing smile upon her offspring, and a less beneficent one upon her husband. 'I reminded you at breakfast, dear, Selene is invited to dine with Marcus Kirkby this evening.'

'Ah, forgot.' Edward frowned, not quite easy in his mind as he recalled how attentive the man had been to her. Didn't seem quite proper somehow, yet he hadn't liked to object when he hoped for the fellow to put some business his way.

'He's sending his motor.'

Edward scowled all the more. 'Motor? Humph. You'll not be late home I trust?'

'I really wouldn't know,' Selene said, buttoning the glass bead buttons on her wrist-length gloves. 'We'll have to come back the long way, around the lake by road. Now I must hurry. Mrs Kirkby likes her guests to be punctual.'

'And I'll check the state of my shares, to make sure I can afford this damned wedding of yours. If it ever happens,' said Edward sourly.

'Oh, it will happen, darling Papa. Do not fear.' Popping another kiss on her father's frowning brow, she flounced off to her dinner party.

When she had gone he turned the glower upon his wife. 'What's this all about? What's she doing spending time with Kirkby? He's married, for God's sake, and she's engaged to wed that Nathan Monroe.'

Margot managed to give every impression of innocence. 'It's all perfectly proper and above board. You did hear her say that his wife would be present?'

'Aye.'

'Well there you are then. Though I agree he does seem quite smitten with our darling daughter.' Margot sniffed, implying she could say more had she a mind to but, showing unusual fortitude, confined herself to facts rather than speculation. 'The wife is not at all well, poor creature.' A significant pause. 'And he is exceedingly rich.'

Edward had opened his mouth to protest as a good father should. Then closed it again. Money talks, as they always said. And who knew what could happen, in a war?

The dinner party, so far as Selene was concerned, proved to be an outstanding success.

There were two other couples present, both of whom were known to her. The vicar, the Reverend John Warcop, and his wife, and the Gowdrys, accompanied by their daughter Millicent who, in Selene's opinion, grew more and more like the horses she apparently doted upon.

'Poor Millicent's last hope of matrimony was lost in the trenches,' her fond mama whispered to Selene as they sipped their sherry. 'Such a tragedy. But at least she did have the pleasure of being engaged. Better to have loved and lost, as they say.'

A sop to sad womanhood, if ever there was one. Selene managed to offer appropriate words of condolence and while Mrs Gowdry bumbled on about how at least they would not now be denied the pleasure of their darling daughter's company, Selene compared poor Millicent's dilemma with her own situation. Finding it uncomfortably similar rather took the edge off her own contentment. To devote her life to spinsterhood? To live forever as a daughter? A *chaste* daughter? Could that be the fate in store for her?

If Nathan Monroe did not survive the trenches, she too would be spoken of as a woman who had loved and lost. She too would be the recipient of pitying glances. The very idea was intolerable. All that trouble to catch herself a rich husband only to be robbed of him by war! It simply wasn't fair. There must surely be other compensations, ways of achieving the same goal. A rich man to shower her with the attention she deserved.

Selene cast her glance around the assembled company and let it rest thoughtfully upon her host. Marcus Kirkby was some years older than herself, of course, perhaps in his late-thirties, but what did that signify?

If he no longer had the charismatic energy of youth, at least he possessed the essential attributes of middle age. He was not unhandsome. Some might even call him a fine-looking man. Straight-backed, firm of stomach, a neat head of hair only slightly receding, and clearly with access to a first-class tailor. She had never seen him anything but impeccably dressed. The double-breasted grey suit he wore this evening must be of the finest wool, the trousers sharply creased. His navy silk neck tie was the very last word in elegant understatement beneath a very proper stiff collar.

As if sensing her interest he raised his glance above the head of the vicar's wife who was busily explaining her war work to him, and smiled at Selene across the room. There was everything she could have wished for in that glance. A shiver of anticipation ran through her as she returned the smile with a coquettish tilt of her head.

The highlight of Selene's evening was when Catherine Kirkby, a whey-faced creature who found life generally, and her husband in particular, somewhat overwhelming, sat her next to Marcus during dinner.

'You can entertain him with your youthful chatter, my dear. He has heard all of my tales a dozen times over.'

Which perfectly suited Selene's plan. She spent the entire meal being utterly attentive to her charming host. She quite surprised herself, in fact, by her own generosity. A suitably modest air of complete absorption and gentle encouragement brought forth his entire life story, exactly as the best magazines decreed. Certainly the most pertinent details.

'I made my first fortune in shipping and am now seeking my second in munitions.'

'How terribly clever you must be,' she purred. 'I do so admire a man who knows what he wants in life and makes sure he gets it.'

Marcus Kirkby's grey eyes rested upon her flushed face with interest. Selene Clermont-Read was an enigma. The pouting sulkiness of her pale face only added to her beauty, in his opinion. But while she sent him languishing looks, she wore her dresses buttoned to the chin. It was a most delightful chin, but he rather regretted missing the delights of a firm throat and breast, such as only a young woman possesses.

He leaned closer, his breath lightly brushing her ear. 'What do you think I am wanting right now?'

It was perfectly outrageous of him to make such a remark to any young woman, let alone one seated at his own wife's dinner table. But such niceties had never troubled Marcus Kirkby. He hadn't become rich by worrying over what other people might think of him. Quite the reverse. While others dithered, hindered by morality, Marcus took what he wanted without hesitation.

To his great delight Selene did not gasp or faint or reach for her sal volatile as many young ladies might have done. She rested her eyes upon her folded hands and smiled, very quietly and secretly, to herself. It was the most sensual reply he could have hoped for, bringing the throb of his desire to a delicious hardness.

Beneath the drape of his wife's very best damask cloth he gently squeezed her hand, and then her knee, and watched with delight how the flush deepened.

Selene did not let him have what he clearly wanted that evening. It was far too soon, and he too much the gentleman to ask. But she readily accepted his offer to drive her home in place of the chauffeur, and as he kissed her hand at her door, left him with the distinct promise of more. In fact, Selene was so aroused by the whole episode that she didn't even trouble to call her maid to help her prepare for bed that night. She tore off her clothes herself and lay shivering with excitement in her cold bed, visualising how she could put an end to this depressing state of chastity.

The following Sunday Lily took Thomas to lunch with Hannah and Arnie. It was a much more modest repast than the one at the Marina Hotel but Lily had brought a plate of mince tarts which Betty had made specially.

'You didn't make them yourself then?' Hannah instantly asked, and Lily was forced to admit that she had not.

Arnie said, 'Different world, eh?'

'Yes,' Lily agreed. 'Different world.' Hoping her mother wasn't going to start on her. Not now they were friends again.

The family spent a delightful afternoon together before Lily left at three o'clock, anxious to have Thomas home before dusk. The ferry wasn't running because of the uncertain weather so she took the omnibus as far along the lane as she could. After that there was nothing for it but to walk the last mile. Almost at once, soft thick flakes of snow began to fall. Lily loved snow, but chiefly on a Christmas card, and not when she was wheeling her baby out in it. Thomas at first played with the flakes, trying to catch them and sucking them noisily on to his lips, but then, as his cheeks grew wet and the cold penetrated, he began to cry.

'Oh, lordy, I shouldn't have brought you out today. Margot will have my guts for garters.' Then came the clip-clop of hoofbeats and the unmistakable roll of the gig's wheels. 'Selene! Oh, thank goodness.'

She was, as usual, driving at a cracking pace but Lily didn't hesitate to step into the road and flag her down, for all she was heading in the opposite direction.

'Stop, please!' Lily's breath made puffs of steam in the cold air as the snow swirled about her, casting a cape of white over the shoulders of her Christmas red coat. 'Where on earth are you off to in such weather?'

'Out to tea, if it's any concern of yours.'

'You'll never make it. It's coming down thick and fast. Turn round, Selene, and take us home please? We're frozen to the skin.'

Selene shrugged. 'It's hardly my fault, sister dear. Really, you should be more responsible with that child.' And with a flick of the reins she put the horse to a trot and left Lily with her crying baby in the empty road.

'Drat you!' Lily shouted after her. Her words were instantly lost in the swirl of snow, but it made her feel much better to have said them.

No one was surprised when Selene did not return home that night. It would have been quite irresponsible for her to even attempt it, since all the lanes were rapidly filling up with snow. Edward grumbled it had been foolish of her to set off in the first place, while Margot vigorously defended her daughter, saying she'd behaved with perfect good sense.

'One does not risk offending people like the Kirkbys by simply not turning up when invited. It was perfectly proper for them to put her up. Lily should have done likewise and stayed at home with her parents instead of risking Thomas catching cold. Besides, it could prove most propitious. With their connections who knows where it might lead?'

'Where can it lead?' Edward wanted to know, feeling peevish and slightly bilious after a large lunch, and because nothing had yet come of this new business acquaintance. 'One fiancé is surely enough for anyone, I would've thought. Even for our Selene. By heck, my stomach's bad. I reckon that duck must've been off.'

'Oh, do stop being so common,' Margot chided him. 'Take a powder and go to bed.'

When he had willingly obeyed her instructions, Margot sat on in the window seat and watched the swirling of the snow in the darkness, a small smile upon her face. Darling child, a daughter after her own heart. Nathan Monroe had been well enough at the time. The man had money and charm, was undoubtedly attractive and on his way up. But Selene deserved a better husband. By which Margot meant richer. If Catherine Kirkby could introduce her to the right circles, she might very well discover one. So, all in all, the snow had proved to be a Godsend, for once.

Chapter Seventeen

Tea had passed pleasantly enough, and when the state of the weather had been noted and remarked upon, the decision was made that Selene should stay and a room prepared for her. After dinner the three enjoyed a game of bridge with a dummy hand in place of the fourth, though this proved less than satisfactory and finally Marcus called an end to the game and offered the ladies a glass of Madeira by way of a nightcap.

'If you will excuse me,' Catherine said, 'I shall decline, but do please pour a glass for Selene.' She explained how she liked to retire early whenever possible. 'I have had three miscarriages, I'm afraid, and never quite been myself since.'

Marcus, very much the solicitous husband, escorted his wife to the foot of the stairs and remained there until she reached the landing. 'I shall be no more than half an hour, my dear.'

Catherine smiled. 'No need to hurry. Entertain our guest. I shall read for a little, until I am sleepy.'

They had drunk two glasses of Madeira and talked in a companionable if desultory fashion when Selene judged it time to make her move. She stretched delicately, stifled a pretend yawn and rose. 'Thank you so much for your kind hospitality, Marcus. I shall sleep like a top tonight.'

He was sprawled in a wing-back chair, one foot propped on the brass fender, clearly warm and mellow and with no inclination to move. Yet Selene hoped he would do so. Her head felt muzzy with the wine, her chest tight with anticipation and excitement. If he didn't take this opportunity she felt sure she would die.

When he still made no move to rise, she tried again.

'I'd best go.' As she brushed past his chair, as near as she dared, he put out a hand and caught her wrist. Selene looked down into his eyes, in shadow from the lamp behind him.

'My wife will be asleep by now.'

'Very sensible of her. I should be too.'

'You don't look tired.'

'Don't I?'

'You look – quite beautiful.'

Selene could scarcely breathe. She stood as if paralysed while every part of her pulsated with this new and dangerous desire.

Marcus said, 'I would like to touch you.'

She'd planned this scene a thousand times. She would be in the guest bedchamber with her hair loose and spread over her shoulders. Marcus would come to her by candlelight and, enraptured by her beauty, would stroke her pale hair and delicately kiss her before slowly removing her garments. Then he would initiate her gently into the art of love-making, and she would learn what every woman longed for. What her harlot of a sister-in-law enjoyed through the dull respectability of marriage. Only this would be far more salacious.

Selene waited. She yearned for this man with every fibre of her being, curiosity making her almost want to screech at him to get on with it.

She closed her eyes in ecstasy as his fingers smoothed her cheek and traced the line of her lips. The heat from the dying fire as the logs fell into clouds of hot ash made her feel warm and languorous with desire. His hand slid down the column of her throat, unbuttoning as he went. Selene put up one hand as if in protest, and gently he removed it.

'What is it? Are you afraid?'

Would the crescent-shaped scar repel him? Hesitantly she allowed him to inspect it. Then, smiling, he leaned closer and gently licked the scar with his tongue. Fire shot through her and with her own hands Selene ripped the remaining buttons apart, revealing the twin peaks of her breasts beneath the chiffon frills.

'You are a temptress.'

'Am I?' She wanted to be. Oh, indeed she did.

His hands slid over the silky skin, fingers probing every soft curve, hardening the buds to a painful sensitivity Selene could barely tolerate. Then they moved on to her hips, and he was lifting the layered skirts of her sensible afternoon costume. Selene could feel the roughness of his wool trousers against her silk-stockings as he cupped one hand on the cushioned warmth of her. Her eyes shot open, looking straight into his as riotous shafts of desire ran through places she had never revealed to anyone, even herself.

'Marcus?' She whispered his name in surprise, wanting him to know that it was all right, that anything he wished her to do, she would do it, and gladly. He saw the promise in her eyes and, smiling, removed his hand, brushed down her skirts, pulled her bodice closed and stepped away from her.

'Dear, dear, what am I thinking of? And me a happily married man. You are young and far too tempting. I trust you will forgive my weakness? I am a mere male, after all, with needs unquenched by an invalid wife.'

'O-Of course.' She was disappointed, shaking with emotion, the pain in her belly so unbearable that she could hardly bring herself to speak. 'Really, there's nothing to forgive.'

'I would hate it if you were angry with me.'

'I'm not.'

'Good.' The backs of his fingers caressed her bare throat through which no breath moved. 'I've an idea you and I could be good friends. Friends are so important, do you not think?'

'Marcus?' Selene felt giddy, so utterly out of control that she swayed, almost fell.

A breathless pause and then words no longer seemed necessary. In seconds she was lying beneath him on the rug, and in the wake of gentility came savage demand. An animal need that must be sated. When he entered her, the fierceness of his thrusts robbed her of her innocence as well as her maidenhead. Selene had to bite down hard on her lip, in order to stop herself from crying out against the pain of it. But as he too quickly reached a grunting climax, she was already begging him to do it again.

So far as Edward was concerned the ill winds of war were at last blowing him some good. He'd never felt more grateful than for the business put his way by Marcus Kirkby. The man certainly hadn't proved easy to deal with, driving a hard bargain on price. Germany had invaded Russia, turning it red with politics and blood as the Tsar and his family were slaughtered. The war might last for another three years. Edward was expanding fast, had leased another warehouse, ordered the building of a new ship, even told Margot she could have the new curtains she'd been asking for. Things were looking up. And he had every reason to believe that when the war did eventually end, his arrangement with Kirkby would go from strength to strength.

For once his family seemed content. Bertie had fully recovered from his injuries, even managed to get himself cited for a medal apparently by capturing a group of Germans and taking them prisoner. This had put Margot in a good frame of mind and he had to confess to a touch of pride in the boy himself. At last.

Lily visited her parents regularly, devoting every moment she could spare from baby Thomas to her war work and growing far more adept at juggling her two worlds. Edward felt as proud of her as if she were his own daughter. He also considered her a better daughter-in-law than his wife deserved. Selene too seemed happier, strangely enough, and had forged quite a friendship with Catherine Kirkby.

The year progressed pleasantly enough, war or no war. Life was being kind to him at last.

Then came the breakthrough everyone had longed for. In France the German forces, boosted by troops released from the Eastern Front, pushed the allies hard, taking back Soisson and Rheims. The 'Big Bertha' gun prevented them from taking Paris, however, and this gave the allies fresh courage to finish them off.

By the end of September Bulgaria had surrendered. In October peace talks began. And on 9 November the Kaiser abdicated, followed on the 11th by complete surrender.

And that was it. Everyone could heave a sigh of relief. The guns fell silent all across Europe as the Armistice was finally signed.

No one had believed the Great War would last more than a few months. They'd laughed when Kitchener had predicted it would take three years and the lives of a million men. In fact it had taken four, and more than twice that number dead or wounded in Britain and the Empire alone. 'The Lost Generation' was the phrase now on everyone's lips. Those who had escaped the bullet, trench fever, being gassed or losing parts of their body or their lives in some awful way or other, were now dying of Spanish Influenza. It was a stinking world all right, Bertie reflected. He supposed he should consider himself lucky to have escaped largely unscathed, give or take the odd shrapnel wound.

He got up from the bench and handed the unsmoked half of his cigarette to the chap still huddled in the corner of it, nodding at his, 'Ta, mate, good on you,' and walked away across Green Park, hands deep in his pockets, chin sunk on to his chest.

Where he was going he had no idea. Home, he supposed. To Carreckwater, Lily and Mama. He should make his way to Paddington, or was it Euston? His mind wasn't as sharp as it used to be. He couldn't quite remember where the northern trains went from.

What a pantomime the last few days had been! And what a let down. Just like the damned war. Bertie still marvelled at how swiftly four years of torment could be resolved.

The map of Europe had been redrawn, the tyrants put in their place, where he sincerely hoped they would remain. The war to end all wars was over, and he had survived.

Everyone had gone mad at first, not surprisingly. But there'd been no enthusiastic crowds cheering them as the weary troops had disembarked, the novelty of flag waving having long since worn off. Empty quays and silence had been their welcome after four long and bloody years in France. Medicals consisted of no more than a quick tap on the chest and a bath to delouse them of God knows what. Then a few restful nights on a soft mattress, for which he'd been grateful, and this morning fine speeches from their commanding officer, a parcel of rations, chocolate, cigarettes and a few quid in his pocket.

What had it all been for? They'd be sure to ask him back home. Peace? Democracy? Freedom?

He could almost hear Margot's strident voice in his ear. 'This is my son, the hero, home from the war.'

He shuddered. Some hero. They'd tried putting him in requisitions, because they'd thought he might have some residual weakness after the diphtheria. He'd soon put paid to that idea, reminding them that officers weren't supposed to suffer the same physical ills as other ranks.

He'd gone on to spend most of the war with the Royal Flying Corps, spotting where the enemy were so our boys would know where to attack. He'd enjoyed the flying which was right up his street, but as one of a mere handful of planes about the same business, the powers-that-be had refused them permission to bomb German cities. While he and the other pilots railed against the frustration of not being able to go in and finish the job properly, the politicians held them back with smart words and endless arguments. Until the end, when the support of tanks and aeroplanes had finally won the day.

Bertie had missed out on that particular shindig, in hospital again having a bit of a plane dug out of his leg. Bloody frustrating, though he supposed he should be grateful it had left him with no more than a slight limp.

So now he was a free man. Free to go on with his life – whatever that might be.

He'd eaten the chocolate, smoked most of the cigarettes, now he jingled the coins in his pocket and rubbed his eyes wearily. God, he was tired. He'd go to his club. Hadn't been to London in an age. If being demobbed didn't deserve a bottle of champers, he didn't know what did. Maybe he'd stay overnight, set off back to the Lakes tomorrow. Where was the rush?

The one bottle turned into two when he met up with a few chums, and the one night into three as the celebrations continued. Some of them had been out for six months or more without a sniff of a peacetime occupation. An officer friend of his had lost all his money to some conman who'd sold him shares in a company that didn't exist. Another had found his wife had left him, run off with the chap who'd used to look after his damned horses, would you believe?

'The world's changing, old chap,' the man mourned. 'Ain't going to be the same. 'S'all right for you. Back to the family business. Little wife waiting.'

Bertie winced, said nothing and ordered another bottle. It would all have to go on his father's account but he deserved a bit of relaxation after that hell, and before he faced Edward with the knowledge that his son wasn't the hero he expected.

After a hearty breakfast the next morning everyone drifted away, and Bertie was forced to do likewise. He strolled along the Embankment, breathing in the fresh morning air as he struggled to sober up and think clearly. The place was full of soldiers wandering aimlessly like him. No doubt many had been walking all night, trying to get away from their thoughts.

A thin drizzle started and he hunched deeper into his greatcoat. He'd never been one for ambition, never had the urge to make his father proud, much to Edward's disgust. He'd been content to take life as it came, happy to enjoy himself with his drawings and dreams. Life had always seemed fun, filled with youthful promise. A lark. Now he knew different.

Strangely, having no real purpose no longer appealed. He'd seen the mess in the trenches, his chums screaming in the last throes of death, even if he hadn't shared that final horror. He'd been privileged to survive. Now to idle away that life which had cost others so dear seemed somehow obscene. Yet what could he do? He still had no skills. There was little point in pretending he wished to join his father in the family firm. Shifting paper around an office all day long while being ordered about by Edward held little appeal.

He'd survived the worst war in history with his life intact, and hadn't the first idea what he was going to do with it.

A passing boat sounded its hooter out on the Thames and for a moment Bertie thought of home, of the lake at Carreckwater, of the dear old *Faith* and the jolly picnics they'd had. It'd all been ripping good fun.

How much did a ticket to the Lakes cost these days? Maybe he had enough if he didn't eat much on the way. I can't put a railway meal on Father's account, he thought, with a wry smile. Might run to a packet of limp cheese sandwiches, if such a thing still exists.

'Buy a box of matches, guv'nor?'

Bertie focused with difficulty upon the man on the pavement before him. He was filthy and unshaven with one leg, the khaki greatcoat and the tray hung about his neck telling its own story. What a bloody waste! This chap had probably survived Gallipoli or the Somme practically to die of starvation on the streets of London.

Bertie emptied his pockets into the man's tray. There was exactly three pound notes, one half crown and a fistful of coppers. More than he'd thought. The man gasped.

'Thanks, guv. Keep my family from starvation that will.'

'Go and find a proper job with it,' he said. 'One worthy of a bloody hero, one leg or no.' Then he wandered off, wondering how he would now pay for the train. But he couldn't face going back, not just yet.

Bertie began to check through a list of chums in his mind for any likely to offer him the loan of a bed, a pound or two, even a job. He couldn't push Pa's debts at the club too high. Anyway, he'd be too easily discovered there. Maybe he could get rid of this sense of shame and frustration if he made something of himself before he faced the family. Was that what he was suffering from? Was that the reason for the sour taste in his mouth, the bitterness in his throat?

Bertie hunched his shoulders and turned left, then right, wandering indecisively, bumping unseeing into people until he reached Trafalgar Square. The place seemed full of pigeons and yet more soldiers, nobody paying them a blind bit of notice. Was there no escape? He found a bench and collapsed on to it, breathing deeply.

Piggy Fielding. The name came to him out of his past. They'd been in the same dorm for years, and Bertie had been made welcome more times than he could remember by Piggy and his family. His people had owned a cottage in Sedbergh where they'd both attended school, and a house over in Hampstead. He'd call on the old sport before he made any firm decisions.

Edward could wait a bit longer with the plans he'd no doubt drawn up for the return of his only son. Margot would be busy with her charities, doing her bit, as she called it. Who'd have thought it of her?

There was his lovely Lily to consider, of course. He'd never regretted marrying her. Very easy to live with, was Lily. She'd not minded a bit about his little bit of hanky-panky with Rose, so far as he could tell. Though why should she? What chap didn't have a mistress these days? He'd thanked his lucky stars that she wasn't the prudish sort, if a bit blow hot, blow cold as to whether she let him into her own bed.

He missed Rose too. Warm and responsive, she'd always been good for a cuddle. But he'd felt compelled to give her up after young Thomas was born. Daft, really. What difference did it make? Anyway, the world was full of girls called Rose. Particularly here, in the capital. Plenty ready to be kind to heroes, or even to those who, like him, only gave the appearance of one.

A soldier asked him for a cigarette. Bertie handed him the packet then wandered off down Cockspur Street. Still befuddled with the after-effects of too much alcohol, though mercifully free from headache, he walked for what seemed like hours and found himself by Piccadilly Station. Drat it! Had he been walking in circles? Now what?

Then he saw Rose, or someone very like her, leaning against the newspaper kiosk and it came to him how long it had been since he'd shared a bed with anyone, let alone his wife. Not since that French girl on his last leave in Paris. Heavens, that must be nearly eighteen months since.

Bertie felt a not unpleasant ache begin somewhere low down as he considered the comfort this girl could offer. She fancied the look of him too, he could see it in the way she caught his eye and tilted her chin so cheekily at him. Her dress was a dull blue satin that had seen better days, but it outlined a pair of exceedingly shapely legs.

What was the hurry after all? Lily could wait a bit longer.

He brushed his fingers through sandy curls, straightened his jacket, pushed back his shoulders and sauntered over. Maybe she'd accept an IOU.

Lily stood on Windermere station watching the people about her crying and laughing, some desperately seeking loved ones, others fainting when they didn't come or even, sometimes, when they did. People kissing each other, often complete strangers. Joy had become a common currency, freely exchanged.

It was a long time since people had been given the chance to feel happy. Emotions were running high. Her own stomach churned with excitement, and something very like fear. Now, at last, he was coming. But what would he be like? Just the same, or changed?

She'd made sure she was looking her best in a long jacket with a fur collar in a warm rust colour to set off her brown hair, together with a matching hat sporting a dashing feather. Bertie would like that. From beneath the coat peeped an ankle-length narrow skirt, buttoned right down the side of her hips to the hem. Rightly named a hobble skirt, it positively discouraged movement but Lily was fond of it.

A swirl of steam blanked out a whole group of people on the platform, leaving them laughing and choking and not minding at all as they walked blindly off with arms wrapped about their loved one. Lily watched them go with longing in her eyes.

She'd never expected Bertie to be romantic or particularly demonstrative in his affection. She knew he was fond of her and that had been as much as she could deal with, but she felt a pang of regret sometimes at the lack of love in her life.

The stench of soot and acrid smoke caught at her throat and set her coughing, eyes streaming. Lily pulled out a handkerchief to dab at them, then as quickly put it away again in case someone should think she'd been deserted and was crying.

As the platform cleared, there was still no sign of him. Surely he couldn't have let her down? For a moment she did indeed feel tearful as disappointment welled in her throat. All that anxious waiting and anticipation for nothing.

Perhaps he'd simply missed the train. He'd certainly promised to be on it. No great letter writer, yet he'd written to tell her of his imminent arrival. Lily curled her fingers around the crackling paper in her pocket, drawing it out to read it for the hundredth time. It was a typical Bertie-type note, written more than a week ago.

'Home next Saturday. Be on afternoon train. Wait for me. Love B.'

Lily folded it away again. She'd waited for four years. Another day or two wouldn't matter. Sighing, she turned away and bumped into a young couple, lips glued together, arms wrapped about each other in a passionate embrace. Her heart lurched. Then she dipped her head and hurried quickly from the platform. She really shouldn't feel jealous. Everyone had the right to love and be loved.

As have I, a voice in Lily's head reminded her. She was a healthy young woman, wasn't she?

What would be the state of her marriage when Bertie did come home? Would fond affection still be enough? Could they carry on as before, living their separate lives, with all that that implied? Or could she make the necessary effort to build a marriage that worked? Many questions but few answers.

Choking back tears, Lily felt oddly alone and abandoned.

She'd brought the gig to collect Bertie and his luggage, leaving it in the station yard. Now she skirted the horse-omnibus and the knot of people bustling each other in their eagerness to board, and set off in that direction as quickly as she could, mentally rehearsing the words she would need to prepare Margot for a disappointment.

At this very moment her mother-in-law was organising a feast of biblical proportions. The table had been laid with the finest silver and glass. The champagne was on ice. Every larder groaned with Bertie's favourite dishes, made in preparation for this great day. Except that the chief guest, the prodigal son, would not now be present.

Others too would be missing. Dora for one. She was lying in a French hospital somewhere. She'd written a long letter to Lily, declaring how terribly boring it all was, and how she couldn't wait to be up and about again instead of slowly recovering from pneumonia and exhaustion. Lily had written back instructing her to stay exactly where she was, or she would come and deal with her personally.

Then there was Nathan. Still with no word, the loss Lily felt had become a permanent ache in her heart. She'd learned to live with the silence. Many young men were missing after all, and some – a few anyway – did come home eventually. How could she possibly accept the idea that she might never see him again? It was too frighteningly final.

In the melee of the station yard Lily could make little progress towards the gig. Try as she might she kept being stopped by people who knew her, all anxious to share their news, good or bad. She learned a great deal about her old neighbours in that short distance.

Jim, the landlord of the Cobbles Inn, had survived but left one of his legs in France, Mrs Edgar of the cook shop informed her.

Mrs Robbins, who still supplied the choicest bull's eyes, stopped to tell Lily that Percy Wright, the agent who had once threatened them with eviction, had been officially declared missing, presumed dead, so there'd be no grave for his poor wife to visit and mourn by.

'He'll be one of the unknown warriors buried somewhere in France.'

Lily expressed her regrets, struggling to make them sound sincere for he had always seemed to her a most unpleasant man, for all she supposed he'd only been doing his job.

She paused to congratulate Mrs Adams on the return of her younger son. The elder had died at Gallipoli, quite early in the war, but young Josh, topping his tiny mother by a good foot and a half, stood beside her now, having survived against all the odds.

'And your own husband?'

'Been delayed, but he's on his way.'

'Oh, that's good.'

'Yes, isn't it?'

'Grand to hear a bit of good news for a change.' The woman proceeded to reel off such a litany of bad that Lily regretted having stopped to speak to her in the first place. But then from somewhere above her head came another voice, dearly familiar.

'Lily?'

She jumped as if she'd been scalded, for there he was. As if spirited somehow from the recesses of her mind into the wind-swept station yard.

'Oh, dear God…' Hand to her mouth she couldn't even say his name. He had lived in her mind for years. Now all she could think to do was stand and stare at him. Very tentatively she put out one hand to touch his cheek, as if fearful he might be a mirage or a puff of smoke left by the departing train which would disappear at her touch. 'Nathan?' She breathed the word like a caress, liquid gold on her tongue.

Without thinking of the wisdom of such an action, forgetting the open-mouthed Mrs Adams and her grinning son at her elbow, forgetting Mrs Edgar and Mrs Robbins, pausing as they were about to climb aboard the horse-omnibus, Lily fell into his arms. As he lifted her off her feet, swinging her round and sending her hat bowling across the station yard, she kissed him as though she would never stop.

'I should go,' Selene said, searching for her stockings. 'Mama will be having a small fit that I'm not home already.'

Marcus reached out one hand to smooth her bare back but made no attempt to get up from the couch. They were in his study, having sneaked her in via the French windows as usual. The door firmly locked, the servants ordered not to disturb him at his work, they were free to enjoy each other at their leisure. Upstairs Catherine took her afternoon nap, as usual. Later, she would come down and offer Selene tea and cakes, and the two would chat together, as the good friends they had become.

A scheme had been devised for every occasion. This was the procedure for a Saturday afternoon. Marcus approved of routine and discretion. Not that the latter was strictly necessary so far as his wife was concerned.

Catherine would not ask when Selene had arrived, or how she

had spent her time while her hostess slept. She never asked questions. It was one of the things Marcus liked most about her.

But today there would be no tea-party. Catherine would not even see Selene as she was expected home for the return of the warrior son. Marcus scowled his disappointment. He hated to have his plans upset.

'You'll come tomorrow?'

She shook her head. 'I can't, not with Bertie just home. It'll have to be next Saturday.' She leaned over to place a lingering kiss on his lips, allowing the soft warmth of her breasts to graze his chest. 'Will you miss me?'

'What do you think?'

'That you're a fortunate man to be so well served by adoring women.'

He chuckled, and, wrapping an arm about her, pulled her squealing back on to the couch. 'Perhaps I think you are both fortunate women.' He began to caress her with a new purposefulness and for a moment Selene sank against him with a sigh, the familiar excitement rising hot and sweet in her breast. Then she thought of Margot.

'No, I must go.'

'See what you do to me.' He indicated his arousal. 'How cruel to leave so soon.'

Selene slanted a glance up at him. 'I am not your wife, Marcus, so I must always leave, mustn't I?'

'There are times when I almost wish...' He didn't finish the sentence. He never did. 'But you're a damned sight more fun.'

Selene found that, after all, she could stay a few moments longer.

Much later, over a cup of weak tea in the station cafe, Lily saw that although Nathan had returned in one piece, with not a mark on him, he was not the same man who had gone away. He seemed in some way to have shrunk. No longer the big brawny chap he had once been, his face appeared gaunt and grey. His speech, when he spoke at all, was slow and halting and his eyes carried a haunting bleakness. She noticed too that he never moved his right arm. He left the hand resting on his lap while he drank his tea with his left. Lily had never seen him do this before.

But the sight of him across the table, near enough for her to touch, as she felt compelled to do every few minutes, was utter bliss. She had never felt so happy. As bubbly as a young girl, as if she had drunk a whole bottle of champagne. She could simply sit here and gaze at him all day, greedily drinking in every beloved feature. And he was gazing at her in exactly the same way.

'I-I can't tell you how glad I am to see you,' she said, for the hundredth time.

'Me too.' For a second his eyes lit up, telling her in more than words how he felt. 'B- Bertie?' he queried, and she pulled a wry face.

'Being perverse, as always.' She told him about the letter and the missed train. 'I shouldn't even be here. I should be hurrying back to Barwick House to give Margot the news that her chief guest has done a bunk.'

'I-Is he – all r-right?'

Lily could hardly bear to watch the agony it took for him to speak. Her head buzzed with questions. What had caused this disability? Gas? Or those terrible explosions? She'd heard talk of soldiers being too shocked to speak at all. But now was not the moment to pry.

'He's fine,' she said brightly, deciding the best thing was to behave normally. 'You know Bertie. He'll turn up tomorrow or the next day, bright as a button and with not one word of apology. "Got talking to this chap, old thing," he'll say.' She laughed at her own mimicry. 'And, no, I'm not being unkind.'

Nathan gave a lop-sided grin, one half of his face staying completely rigid. 'You're – right. Exactly – w-what he'll s-say.'

Lily's heart clenched with love for him and from then on she did most of the talking. She chattered on about her own war efforts. How she'd helped Edward clean the *Faith*, even run it as an extra ferry as transport was so short. He almost laughed at that, as if the idea of her working on a boat were too far-fetched to contemplate.

Lily grinned and went on to talk of her recent visits to her parents, and of Margot's committees. Should she mention Thomas? Discretion made her hold her tongue. She'd been about to mention Selene when she stopped abruptly.

'I've just had a wonderful idea!'

Nathan's brows lifted but he said nothing.

'*You* can be our special guest instead of Bertie. Back at Barwick House there's a Welcome Home feast of gargantuan proportions being prepared. Bertie isn't here to enjoy it, but you are.'

He shook his head, frowning fiercely, but Lily was in no mood for argument. Already reaching for her coat and hat, she urged him to leave his kit in the Left Luggage office until later.

'It'll be fun. When's the last time you tasted champagne? And you really ought to hurry straight to your bride-to-be.' Her words made them gaze thoughtfully upon each other. Here, in the station tea room, dreams were still a delightful possibility. Once they stepped outside, reality would intervene. Lily drew in a steadying breath and gave him a rueful smile. 'Ready?'

Nathan merely picked up his kit bag and stood patiently waiting for her to tell him what to do next.

As they walked towards the gig, a group of young soldiers were singing a chorus of '*Mademoiselle from Armentieres*'.

'At least,' she said, 'your presence will do me a great favour. It'll stop Margot from blaming me for not bringing home her darling son!'

Chapter Eighteen

Barwick House seemed to have been spring-cleaned especially for the occasion. The grey and white pillared facade glinted in the cool sunshine, long windows mirroring the blue of lake and sky. Along the shore clusters of hazel catkins hung like yellow candelabra from winter-bare branches, and beneath their shelter a carpet of purple crocuses and white snowdrops shyly flowered.

The ladies too were bright spots of colour against the pale green lawn in their unseasonably thin frocks, worn in honour of this special day – except for Millicent Gowdry, whose brown suit was so dull people walked past without even noticing her. Lily noticed Sophie Dunston with her spectacles sliding down her nose, and Felicia Morton-Cryer proclaiming loudly that her 'darling orphans' would now have to manage without her, since she really was perfectly worn out with all the work.

All these once likely candidates for Bertie's hand had come to welcome him home. But Bertie was not here. Even had he been, he was well and truly taken. Which sadly echoed the fact that with so many of their friends not returning from the front, the chances of matrimony for these girls had shrunk to almost nil.

Even the lively Heddington boys would never again fall out over who was to give up their chair for Selene, having been killed together on the Somme. Lily could hardly bear to think what the carnage must have been like out there. Thank God Nathan had come home safe and well, if not exactly sound. Hadn't she always believed he would? And with time and loving care, he'd improve, she was sure of it. Unfortunately, it would not be she who had the right to give him that care.

Lily linked her arm through his in a friendly fashion and smiled reassuringly up at him. 'You don't have to stay long. Just say hello.'

He nodded, eyes flashing a look of gratitude at her understanding.

They were stopped first by Clive and Edith Ferguson-Walsh, proudly relating the latest adventures of their brave daughter, though as Lily well knew, they'd done everything in their power to stop Dora going into the war. They were kind enough to shake Nathan's hand and congratulate him on his safe return.

Lucy and Philip Linden came next, showing off a bevy of children and a very flustered nanny. He'd managed to miss out on the action completely, he admitted, without explaining why. Seeing Nathan's mouth tighten, Lily made their excuses and led him quickly away.

'There's Margot. I can see her through the conservatory window with Selene. Do you want to go in on your own?' As panic filled his eyes, squeezed his hand. 'You don't have to.'

They set off across the lawn, feet sinking into the mossy turf, Nathan's hand closed tight on hers and he stammered out three words. 'D-don't – l-leave – me.'

Lily's heart swelled with love for him. Wouldn't she go with him anywhere? To hell and back if he asked, although that was silly. Hadn't he been there already? She couldn't bear to contemplate how it was that such a strong, forceful man had become so fragile.

'I'm so glad you're home.' Oh God, how she loved him, and yet she must somehow give him up!

Swallowing her pain, Lily couldn't help wondering what control, if any, she could exercise over Selene and Margot. She came to a swift decision and, glancing about to check they weren't overlooked, pulled Nathan into the azalea bushes.

'Perhaps it would be best if I were to go in and speak to them first. What do you think? I could explain about Bertie's not being here, and that I've got a surprise for them. Selene will be delighted.' She waited for Nathan to comment. When he didn't, merely continued to wait for her decision, Lily reached up and kissed him softly. 'It'll be all right, I promise. You stay here till I call.'

He nodded, indicating agreement, but his eyes were filled with anguish and he let her go reluctantly.

The pain in Lily's chest weighed heavy as she crossed the lawn.

They'd better be pleased or she'd give them what for! But then, he wasn't her man. She really should remember that.

Thankfully she achieved the house without being stopped, took a deep breath and entered the conservatory.

The sun streamed through the tall narrow windows and the cloying scent of gardenias, summoning memories of that long-ago graveyard, became almost overpowering, seeming to add to Lily's growing sense of unreality.

The tableau before her of two women in oyster silk pleated tea gowns and strings of beads, entertaining the elite members of the assembled company in the privacy of their conservatory, reminded Lily of some Impressionist painting. What was she doing living in this house with people she had vowed to hate? Why bring Nathan to Selene when she desperately wanted to keep him for herself'

But it was too late now to turn back.

Drawing in a deep breath, she began carefully to explain how Bertie had not been on the train after all. The few privileged guests hurriedly melted away, as if the artist had blotted them from his canvas.

Margot's outraged voice rang out, bouncing off the window panes like splinters of ice which refused to melt in the overheated room. 'Not here? How can he not be here? What have you said to my son to make him not want to come home?'

Lily sighed with resignation, her fears instantly being proved correct. As always Margot blamed her. Patiently she tried again, reassuring her that Bertie's missing the train had no doubt been an accident, a simple misjudgement of the time, or perhaps he'd been held up for some other reason in London.

'What other reason could there possibly be? He would certainly wish to see me, his own mother.'

Hastily Lily interrupted, in case this should turn into yet another of Margot's endless lectures. 'But I do have a lovely surprise for you both. Particularly for Selene.' And turning to her sister-in-law, Lily took both her hands in her own. 'There's someone waiting for you down in the garden. Someone very special.'

Selene merely looked blank.

'What on earth are you talking about?' Margot butted in, determined not to be ignored.

Lily smiled, struggling to dampen her own emotions and concentrate on the happiness of the woman before her. 'It's Nathan. After all these months of worry, he's come home safe and in one piece. How about that?'

'Nathan?' Selene whispered the name in wonder, as if she had never expected to hear it again.

Lily nodded, puzzled by her lack of reaction. Was the poor girl too stunned to take it in? 'Yes, Nathan. In person. Isn't it wonderful?' This was a girl so eager to be his wife she had spent the last four years endlessly planning and re-planning her wedding. Was the reality of seeing him in the flesh suddenly too much for her? These thoughts, racing through Lily's head in seconds, brought with them an echo of concern. Selene had never had occasion to handle sickness or show any kind of compassion. How would she cope with this new and different Nathan? 'Before you go to him, you ought to know that he is not quite perfectly well.'

'What do you mean?' Fear flickered briefly in brown eyes so like Bertie's, and Selene snatched her hands away.

'I'm certain it's nothing permanent. I believe they call it shell shock. God knows what the boys suffered out there. He'll need love and care, and plenty of patience to help him get well again. Now go to him. He's waiting for you by the azaleas.'

Selene half turned to Margot. 'Mama?'

Margot, who had remained silent through all of this, lowered her chin and clasped her hands upon a stomach grown plumper with the years. 'You must certainly go and see how dear Mr Monroe is. Then bring him up here for a glass of champagne and to meet our guests. We must all celebrate his safe return.'

But the smile on her face was stretched to an unnatural stiffness, and as Lily watched Selene weave her way slowly through the crush of guests, Lily feared she might have done entirely the wrong thing in bringing him here at all.

Over the next few days Nathan was to be a constant visitor to Barwick House. Margot surprised Lily by her apparent concern for him, dutifully inviting her future son-in-law to tea or dinner, urging him to call in for a chat or take a turn about the garden with Selene.

'So lovely at this time of year. Selene will require a garden nearly as pleasant when you are married, Mr Monroe. I trust you could manage that?'

Edward attempted to talk to him about his experiences but Nathan rarely responded, his silences seeming to grow longer as time went by.

Lily watched with growing concern.

With each visit Nathan seemed to shrink more and more into himself, his face tired and drawn. Sounds startled him alarmingly. It only needed Margot's pen to clatter upon the wooden floorboards and he would leap from his chair, ashen-faced and shaking. Lily guessed he slept little, and there was a constant tremor in his hand which caused the china cup to rattle against its saucer so fiercely that eventually Selene was driven to take it from him, emitting a deep sigh as she did so.

'I-I'm s-sorry,' he stammered.

Lily's heart went out to him. To watch Nathan daily strive to appear normal, desperately struggle to form his words, and so miserably and frequently to fail, brought her unbearable pain. His bride-to-be, unfortunately, was less charitable.

'He really makes no effort to converse,' she complained when he had finally, and silently, taken his leave one afternoon. 'Sits there saying nothing, not caring a jot how difficult it is for me.'

'I tried to explain that he's suffering from shell shock.'

In her cosy chair by the fire, Margot sniffed. 'There, didn't I say this would happen? We've given him ample opportunity to feel welcome in our family, no one can deny it. But as you say, my dear, he makes no effort. It's all sham, of course. "Swinging the lead", isn't that what they call it? Pretending to be suffering from some unknown disability, when really it is nothing but cowardice.'

Lily could hardly believe her ears. 'That simply isn't true. It's some kind of nerve damage.'

Edward said, 'I asked him what was wrong with his arm. Said he'd woken up one morning and found he couldn't move it. Wouldn't say why.'

'Perhaps he can't bear to remember,' Lily said.

'Seems to me that there's a lot about Mr Nathan Monroe that he can't bear to remember.'

Lily swallowed, not knowing what to say, for hadn't she once said exactly the same thing herself? 'He doesn't like to talk about himself, or seem to ask for pity.'

Margot clicked her tongue. 'If you ask me, he's a malingerer. Playacting to cover his cowardice. Not like my brave Bertie who single-handedly went behind enemy lines without any thought for his own safety.'

'And took a dozen prisoners while he was about it,' Edward finished. This was the closest he had ever come to expressing pride in his son, and his neck flushed slightly with the embarrassment of it.

'However,' Margot continued, warming to her theme, 'I really am having second thoughts about allowing our darling girl to rush into marriage. How will the man look, walking down the aisle with one useless arm hanging by his side? Not to mention that lop-sided leer. What will people think?'

The room seemed to grow perfectly still as Lily held her breath, waiting for Selene to tell her mother that what people thought of Nathan was unimportant. It mattered only that he was home, safe, and in reasonably good health. But she remained silent.

'Selene?' Lily gently prodded, at which she instantly burst into tears and ran from the room.

'Now look what you've done,' Margot said, and frowning at Lily, hurried off in the wake of her weeping daughter.

Each day Lily took the ferry and then the omnibus to Windermere station and dutifully waited for the afternoon train. Each day it arrived and unloaded its quota of passengers, a few less each time as the troops gradually came home but never the one she was waiting for. There was still no sign of her husband. Till one morning Betty brought her a letter, excitement in her voice.

'I think it's from Master Bertie. It has a London postmark.'

Lily recognised the handwriting instantly and longed to rip it right open, there and then. But, aware of the maid's curiosity, she laid it aside and continued to brush her hair. 'Thank you, Betty. Did Margot see it come?'

'No, ma'am.'

'Then leave it to me to tell her. Just in case it's bad news.'

Betty paled. 'Oh, yes, ma'am. Of course, ma'am.'

'Help Thomas get dressed, and give him his breakfast, will you?' Betty had quite taken to caring for the child. Margot had wanted him to have a nanny, but they weren't easy to come by during the war, many having gone into nursing, so Betty had played the role unofficially and enjoyed it.

When she'd carried the toddler away, cooing delightedly and promising him toast soldiers with his breakfast egg, Lily snatched up the envelope. At last the mystery would be resolved and an explanation given. But it was no more than another brief note.

'Can't come home just yet. Will write later. B.'

No explanation, no address, no indication of where he was staying or what he was doing. Lily screwed the paper up into a tight ball and flung it into the wastepaper bin in an unusual outburst of temper. What was he thinking of? Surely Bertie wasn't suffering from shell shock too? No, his last proper letter had told her he was fit and well, and couldn't wait to see her. What had got into him? How could they possibly rebuild their marriage while several hundred miles apart?

But then, once he was home for good, how would she cope feeling as she did about Nathan?

Irritated and confused Lily went to retrieve the letter and put it into her dressing-table drawer. She couldn't risk Margot's seeing it. Its very briefness would somehow be made to prove her own inadequacies as a wife. Lily would have to make up some story about his staying with friends he'd accidentally met up with. Which was very probably the case.

She stared at her own reflection in the mirror, smoothing her fingers over her clear skin. Time was passing. How much longer could she go on like this? Did she have any hope of happiness?

Lily forbore to mention the letter to Margot, and later that morning set off as if for the station as usual, in order that her mother-in-law should not grow suspicious.

However, instead of making her way to the folly and ringing for the ferry, Lily walked along the shore in the opposite direction, gazing out over the rippling waters. Such a beautiful day for early May, a soft breeze ruffling the silvered waters and fluffing up the feathered clouds that floated like swans in a wide blue sky.

Apart from a small boy and his father out fishing in a rowing boat, the lake lay empty and serene, with only the sound of a bubbling beck to disturb the peace.

No trippers crowded the piers and quay so early in the season, and there were still no Public Steamers in operation. Perhaps they would start again soon, now that Nathan was home. As soon as he was well enough, Lily thought.

Several of Edward's richer neighbours were saying the war had put an end to the era of steam. They were scuttling their old steam-launches and yachts by letting them sink into the mud at the bottom of the lake, since no one was interested in buying them any more. Edward had long since berthed the *Faith* up a backwater, where she was rusting quietly away, no longer taken out for ferry trips or jolly picnics on the lake. He seemed to have lost all interest in her.

In future, many of his richer friends meant to build themselves something power-driven and fast, as Bertie had once predicted. No more idling up and down the lake, they said. The days of leisurely serenity were a thing of the past. Lily thought it rather a shame. Not that it was any concern of hers what they did. Her own war work on the boat was done, which, in a way, she felt sorry about too. She'd quite enjoyed chatting with their customers, had loved the gentle glide through the waters and the sound of the steamer's farewell whistle as it departed from the jetty each time. She'd even enjoyed shovelling coal into the boiler.

Now she had to wear pretty frocks and smart costumes. Put her hair in a fetching chignon instead of scraped up beneath an engineer's cap. Her life had certainly been full of change and quite a few surprises. Lily had come a long way since the day she'd left The Cobbles for the last time, and for the most part she wasn't sorry.

She couldn't deny that it was much more comfortable living here at Barwick House than in Mallard Street, though she did have a few regrets, of course. The diphtheria taking her sister Emma and her own little Amy. Her mother-in-law, as sour and difficult as ever, and Selene as petulant. But Lily had little Thomas now, and a husband who was kind to her. When he was home. So why couldn't she be content?

The answer imprinted itself firmly upon her mind, and Lily wondered if she'd shouted it out loud as a moorhen suddenly launched itself into the water and set off in a great flurry to go nowhere in particular. When the ruffled waters had calmed to shimmering steel again, she spoke softly, not wishing to disturb the afternoon calm.

'Nathan, please don't marry Selene. How can I live without you?' Yet what right did she have to ask? She, a married woman?

Did that make her a harlot? A whore? The kind of woman Margot had accused her of being, whom even her own mother would cross the street to avoid?

'Oh, God, tell me what I am to do.' Lily closed her eyes but could not pray. Unlike her mother, she was not particularly religious and, much as she longed for help, it seemed like blasphemy to ask Him. 'You're right, God, it's my mess and I should sort it out,' she said sadly.

Lily was lingering in the wooded gardens, enjoying the dappled sunshine and picking a few daffodils to take to Hannah when she saw Selene come out of the house and hurry down the stony drive. But instead of taking the gig, as she usually did, she headed at a brisk pace along the shore path, in the direction Lily herself had first taken.

For no reason she could rightly explain, Lily found herself

251

stepping back out of sight behind a beech tree, curious to know where it was Selene was off to in such a hurry.

Selene pushed her way rapidly through the thick laurel and holly bushes that cloaked this part of the shore, crossed an open meadow, jumped a narrow beck and then, branching off at a tangent, let herself quickly out through a small gate in the top corner of the field. Lily knew now where she was going. The gate opened on to a path which led uphill through dense vegetation, before meandering for perhaps half a mile right to the door of Rosedale Lodge, the magnificent Gothic mansion occupied by Marcus Kirkby. And something about the way she walked told Lily that this little-used route was very familiar to Selene.

Lily remained where she was until Selene had quite vanished, letting the anger surge through her. Then she turned on her heel and flew through the woods on furious feet, kicking at broken branches that got in her way, swiping at branches, being clawed by brambles as she stormed heedlessly on.

How dare she?

Not for a minute did Lily imagine these visits to be innocent. It was all perfectly clear now. No wonder Selene hadn't looked too thrilled when Lily had brought Nathan home unexpectedly from the station. His return had really put a fly in her ointment. No wonder her mind always seemed to be elsewhere and she'd never been available to do any kind of war work or even simple chores.

After all the agonies Lily had suffered, worrying and depriving herself of Nathan's company. That little madam just upped and cheated on him, without thought or care. Who would Margot call the shameless hussy now?

Lily was so angry on Nathan's behalf that she'd almost reached the edge of the woods before she came to a skidding halt, panting for breath and quite red in the face.

Now what? And what did it have to do with her? How much, exactly, would Nathan mind?

Perhaps he wouldn't mind at all. He'd never actually claimed to be in love with Selene. Pretty as she undoubtedly was she was also spoiled and selfish. But of course, as the daughter of a wealthy businessman, she had other attributes. Nathan had never denied that he was an ambitious man who must look to his future. Weren't those his exact words? Lily would have liked to hate him for that fact alone, if only she had the will.

Because she had been expecting Bertie to arrive at any time, Lily had meant never to go to Nathan again, albeit every inch of her body longed to do so. But Bertie wasn't coming, and a reckless decision was already forming in the back of her mind, one she was helpless to control.

'Two wrongs don't make a right.' She could almost hear Hannah's voice giving one of her many Methodist sermons. 'If someone does summat wrong and hurts you, it don't mean you can do it too.'

But I need him, Lily thought. I need him now. She broke into a run, stumbling over stones and tree roots in her eagerness to get to him.

There was the question of whether she should even tell him of her suspicions. This sobered her so that she slithered to a halt to consider the matter more carefully.

He might not believe her.

He might accuse her of being jealous. Which she was, but that surely didn't alter the facts.

He might suggest Selene was visiting Catherine Kirkby, and not Marcus at all.

Lily recalled the time when even thick snow had not prevented the girl from going, though any sensible person would have turned back. She'd returned home the following day with the kind of perfect calm about her that only another woman, likewise in love, could interpret. Certainly it was plain enough now, looking back. Lily didn't feel it necessary to catch them together to prove her suspicions correct. But perhaps Nathan would, being a man.

Yet if she didn't tell him and he found out later, after he'd married Selene for instance, might he then blame Lily for keeping quiet? Say she could have saved him from humiliation?

Lily sank on to a log, put her face into her hands and silently wept. Whatever she did could turn out wrong. But, oh, how she loved him! How she longed to be with him day and night, to hear him say that he loved her.

Whatever her mam might say, no one else was playing fair so why should she? Bertie hadn't been honest with her, had he? Nor had Selene with Nathan. So for whose sake were they depriving themselves? Surely they had as much right to happiness as everyone else?

Lily paused only to check that Thomas was happily occupied playing with soap bubbles in the kitchen with Betty, a large towel wrapped about his neck. Then she offered up her lie.

'I thought I'd take a long walk over the fells this afternoon. Do me good to get some fresh air after this dismal winter. It's such a lovely spring day.'

'You do that, ma'am,' Betty cheerily agreed. 'Do you good. Master Thomas and me'll have us a nice wee tea-party. Don't you worry none about us.'

Betty insisted on packing a sizeable packet of sandwiches and bottle of lemonade, instructing Lily to wear her 'proper boots' and take a map and waterproof. 'Easy to get lost, and you never knows how the weather might turn. Be back afore dark or I'll have to set George off looking for you.'

Lily made the necessary promises and escaped, heart beating so loud she was certain Betty must hear her excitement or see it in her trembling hands.

She fed the sandwiches to the ducks as Ferryman Bob rowed her across, his knowing glances taking in those flushed cheeks, the unusual brightness in her hazel eyes. But he made no comment, confining himself to polite enquiries about her family.

'How's Arnie? Still at the fishing?'

'The fishing's not too good right now.'

'I did hear. How's he managing then?'

'I'm not sure. He doesn't say much.'

Ferryman Bob looked thoughtful. 'Aye, he's a proud man is Arnie.'

The moment they docked, she leaped from the boat and

hurried straight to the house on the corner of Drake Road, pushing the scribbled note she'd prepared through the letterbox. Now all she had to do was to hurry up the twisting path to Carreck Woods without seeing anyone she knew, and wait for him to come to her.

Chapter Nineteen

He came like a young giant, bursting through the thick undergrowth of hazel and laurel, tearing the clinging branches apart in his eagerness to reach her. In his ears was the roar of water from the beck as it tumbled down into the lake far below. Or it could have been the sound of hot blood pulsing in his head. Before him lay the ruins of an old bobbin mill which once had produced wooden bobbins for the Lancashire cotton mills in its prime, when cotton had been King. Now *he* felt like a King, rich with the power of his need.

But when Nathan came upon her in the clearing, lying back on the soft turf, her thick brown hair spread upon a pillow of lush green moss, he thought he had never seen anything more beautiful in all his life. He stopped, stricken by sudden uncertainty.

What rights could he ever have over her? She didn't belong to him. He had always believed that if he attempted to possess her, he would lose her. That she might vanish like some woodland sprite and be gone, as every other beautiful thing in his life had likewise vanished.

A shaft of sunlight caught her hair, firing it to a deep chestnut, then as quickly cooling as it moved on over her flushed cheeks and stroked the golden beauty of her throat.

His love for her was like a fire, one that would never cool, and one he could never properly express. For all his refusal to make an avowal, deep in his heart Nathan knew there was nothing he wouldn't give to make Lily his. Nothing he wouldn't do to possess her completely.

If that meant cuckolding his one-time best friend, so be it. He'd seen how short life could be, knew there might only be today. Why shouldn't he enjoy their love?

He saw that she watched him from beneath the crescents of her dark lashes, smiling a welcome. Somewhere high in the treetops a blackbird sang, and deep in the woods a pigeon softly cooed. At his feet a pair of voles rolled over each other in a clump of violets, then scampered off into the undergrowth. It seemed that every living creature thought of love this day.

She spoke his name softly. 'Nathan.'

How he had longed for this moment. Not since before the war had they last lain together. And he knew that for all the promises to himself over the years since, all the vows he had made, he still did not have the strength to resist her. Were they not predestined for each other?

He lay gently beside her, his fingers clumsy as he reached for the buttons on her gown. Sliding it from her shoulders he kissed her throat and the swell of a white breast, heart clenching as she instinctively arched her body against his.

Then he was fighting to get out of his own clothes with a wretched slowness, hating the uselessness of his frozen arm. He watched, mesmerised, as quickly she stripped off her own few garments with impatient hands. How her nipples leaped with life as a playful breeze teased them. But he would make them burn with a greater need.

She sat up, ripe and naked, her skin glowing pale as alabaster in the sun. 'Can you manage? Do you want me to help?' It was the wrong thing to say. Nathan flinched away from her, and Lily saw the expression on his face become defiant.

'I can manage.' The last thing he needed was her pity.

'I only asked because you look so tempting.' Though he wasn't the same young man who had gone off so eagerly to war, in her eyes he would always be attractive. 'And I'm nervous as a kitten.' She laughed.

He knelt before her then, glowering, afraid he might make a fool of himself. He'd heard of soldiers losing their manhood, of not being able to love their wives and sweethearts. 'If I-I revolt you, s-say so?'

Lily stared at him for a whole half second, then rolled those

257

glorious green and golden eyes as if he'd made the funniest remark imaginable. 'Why should you revolt me? Dear God, I can't keep my hands off you.' She lifted them to him, pushing her fingers through the crisp curls of his hair, as wild as ever, and when still he hesitated, 'For God's sake, will you come to me? I can't wait a minute longer. I can see you aren't missing the important parts, which look pretty healthy to me.'

For a moment she thought her deliberate bluntness had offended him, and this time he really would be angry. But after a stunned silence he put back his head and laughed, the sound deep and husky and highly sensual. 'Sh-shameless hussy.'

The word, so soon after she'd used it about herself and Selene, shook her, but then Lily tossed back her hair, and lifted one foot to curl her bare toes seductively against his chest. 'Don't think I shall spare you. It's every man for himself here. You've got one perfectly good arm, haven't you? And two legs. I'm not going to fight you off. If you can't take me with the resources you have available, you're not the man I thought you were.'

He grasped the foot and pulled her, giggling, beneath him. They came together at last, as Lily herself thought later, as sweetly as a knife into butter. He proved that he was still very much the man she thought him. Excitement mounted, as it always did between them, and they clung one to the other in a kind of desperate frenzy. Lily wondered how it was that after all these years this man could still turn her to liquid fire. Nothing could quench it, or separate them. Certainly not a marriage undertaken for any reason but love.

It was only later, as she rushed to be home before dusk, devising some fictitious route in her mind as if she really had walked over the fells, that Lily realised she'd forgotten to tell him about Selene. Or to ask him if he truly loved her.

Lily had never been happier. They met every week in the deepest, most secret parts of Carreck Woods. Sometimes by the ruins, sometimes higher on the fells behind a craggy outbreak of rock where there was nothing but a circling buzzard and a silence so complete that it hummed with a life of its own. If she ever recalled how she had watched Selene creep with equal furtiveness through a quiet garden to meet her own lover, then Lily put it from her mind. She might, after all, have been mistaken. Even if she wasn't, what could she do about it?

Best not to consider the long-term implications of her love for Nathan. Craving his presence as a flower might the sun, she lived only for the moment. Let the future take care of itself.

Once, Lily saw her parents' neighbour Mr Adams as he climbed down from the omnibus. She'd been forced to stop and exchange the time of day with him as politely as her impatience would allow, making all manner of excuses. But he hadn't been in the least suspicious about where she was bound in such a hurry.

She always ran when she was meeting Nathan.

They would lie within the shelter of the old stone ruins or beside the tumbling beck, and talk. They loved, they kissed, and loved again. The meetings became a compulsion which possessed them both, so that neither could concentrate upon any other aspect of life. Nathan neglected his business, Lily her child. It mattered only that they should be together.

But deep down Lily knew that when Bertie did come home, she would have to face up to reality. Could she end her marriage and still keep her beloved child? Or keep marriage, child and lover? Somehow, she rather doubted it.

No one could accuse Mr Adams of being a perspicacious man, but nor was he a fool. Seeing Lily run off into the woods had stirred a few memories of his own youth, which caused him to enquire of his wife later that day if she'd seen anything of the girl recently.

Mrs Adams, with her mind on a tasty bit of supper from Mrs Edgar's Cook Shop, paid him no heed as she hurried to buy a double portion of meat and potato pie.

The two women exchanged the time of day, commented on the weather, and proceeded to discuss the health of their respective families and how they were settling back to normal life after their various tribulations. It was quite by the way, and not at all meant as unkind gossip, that Mrs Adams remembered her husband's remark and the subject of Lily Thorpe as was came up.

'Waits many a long day at the station in vain for her husband, poor soul. I saw her that first time, crying her eyes out.'

'Aye.' Mrs Adams considered the matter. 'But that pal of his, Nathan Monroe, come home, didn't he? Devil's own luck he has. My word, that was a kiss and a half. Did you see it?'

Mrs Edgar felt compelled to agree that she had indeed witnessed the kiss with her own eyes. It had certainly been a li'le bit on the strong side. How many years in her distant past since she'd enjoyed such an amorous encounter. 'Her poor husband not coming home at all then? Got killed out there, did he?' Stating what she believed to be the obvious truth as she sliced a fair portion of pastry and placed it gently on Mrs Adams's warmed plate.

'Not that I know of. I'm sure Hannah would've mentioned it to me if her son-in-law had copped it.'

Mrs Edgar paused in the process of ladling out the meat and potato mixture with its succulent gravy, and the two women gazed at each other. 'Well, I never.'

'You never do know aught about folk really, do you?'

'I reckon we'd best make a few quiet enquiries after Mr Bertie. Wouldn't do to go imagining a chap dead if he's alive and kicking somewhere.'

Both ladies solemnly nodded.

Their 'quiet enquiries' involved Mrs Adams questioning her sister, whose husband's second cousin worked up at Barwick House. The cousin, a scullery maid in Mrs Greenholme's kitchen, asked the boot boy who said that he hadn't the first idea if Bertie would be returning home from war or not, and why did she want to know? When she explained, he was so taken with the shocking goings-on of his employers, that he made it his business to ask the groom who spoke to George the chauffeur, now safely returned to his old job and who, as luck would have it, was walking out with Lily's maid Betty at present.

The pair of them had quite a discussion upon the subject, and although Betty swore undying loyalty to Lily, as always, she confessed to noticing her mistress having taken a great fancy to rambling lately. 'And she comes back wi' not a speck of mud on her boots, and a wicked bright light in her eye.'

Privately she admitted to her own dear love that the rumours were very likely true.

Unfortunately this conversation took place during one of their secret trysts behind the rhododendron bushes, at a time in the afternoon when Selene liked to take the air.

'You only have to look at the pair of 'em when they're both in the same room together to know they want to eat each other up,' Betty continued, sighing at the romance of it all. 'But then he's always carried a torch for Lily apparently, since they were at school together all them years ago. Now she feels the same about him. Lovely, isn't it?'

George proved to be far more Puritan. 'It might be, if she weren't a married lady. I wouldn't want you carrying on in such a way, Betty Cotley.'

'Ooh, George. I never would. Not if I had a good chap like you coming home to me every night.'

A kiss followed, which took some time, while Selene, shocked into immobility by what she had heard thus far, felt herself grow hot with furious impotence. Betty and George wandered off into the woods, seeking greater privacy. Selene screamed her fury to the empty heavens. Then she stormed across the green lawns, marched right through the house, banging every door as she went, and proceeded to seek out her sister-in-law.

Selene confronted Lily in the conservatory, her beautiful face pale as the waxen lilies, and contorted with hatred. 'How dare you!'

So far as Selene was concerned, this dreadful girl had brought nothing but trouble to the family since the first day they'd clapped eyes on her, harlot that she was. She did not, of course, see her own behaviour in quite the same light, for all she was unknowingly repeating the very words Lily had privately used about her.

Lily made no attempt to pretend she did not understand. She guessed instantly that they had been discovered. The kiss at the station which everybody had witnessed, her visit to his house, and those foolish, reckless meetings in Carreck Woods. But, oh, such sweet times together that she couldn't regret them, even now, knowing she deserved every bit of her sister-in-law's fury. It was almost a relief in a way, that the truth was out.

'What can I say, Selene? It was wrong of us, we both knew it. But it's always been there, this feeling between us. I didn't realise at first, but then despite myself I couldn't deny it any longer.'

Selene's lip curled. 'Spare me the anguish. You have a husband already. Why steal *mine*? You're a *whore*! You always were. Bertie recognised that in you. Why d'you think he fancied you in the first place? You know full well how he has a taste for whores.'

Lily stood speechless, her mind numbed by the cruelty of Selene's words, half wondering if perhaps she could be right. About Bertie at least.

'I-I'm sorry.'

Selene brought her face within inches of Lily's, flecks of spittle flying in her fury. 'Being sorry isn't enough. I'll make you wish you'd never been born. Mark my words, Lily Thorpe, you'd best watch your back from now on.'

The engagement was off. Margot imperiously summoned Nathan to the house and informed him of this fact while he stood upon the Persian rug, eyes on the gloomy landscapes above her head. To her vast irritation he appeared as cool and enigmatic as ever, while she railed at him for destroying her precious daughter.

'You've lost a beautiful wife and the fortune which goes with her. For my part, Mr Monroe, I must say that I am vastly relieved the liaison is over.' There, that would show him! She folded hands clasped tight beneath her ample bosom. 'My daughter will learn to thank that heartless chit for saving her from a terrible mistake. You're not the man we took you for. Dear me, no.' Margot really couldn't imagine why she'd ever agreed to Nathan Monroe in the first place. Though she'd make Lily sorry, all the same.

As if reading her thoughts, Nathan graciously inclined his head. 'I'm sure you are correct in your assumption, Mrs Clermont-Read, but the fault was entirely mine. You must not blame Lily for this.'

'You forced her, did you?' Margot hated his coolness. She hated the calm indifference on his handsome face. She wanted to see him beg for Selene's hand, beg for forgiveness, for her charity, so she could enjoy the pleasure of refusing it.

'Perhaps pursued would be a more appropriate word.' He had the audacity to smile.

Margot fumed. 'How unutterly vulgar. My daughter can most certainly do better than a tin-pot lake steamer owner, mark my words, sir.' Catherine Kirkby would find Selene a husband from amongst her elite circle without the slightest difficulty, Margot was sure of it. 'Particularly one with such low morals.'

For some reason Nathan seemed to find this amusing and a surge of hot anger flooded through Margot again, setting her dumpling cheeks on fire. 'Besides which, Mr Monroe, I would never, *never* permit my daughter to marry a malingerer and a *cripple*.'

Now Nathan's half-smile truly did freeze, blue eyes glittering like ice. 'Not even a rich one?' he asked, whereupon Margot gathered her dignity and rose from her chair. Reaching for the bell pull, she managed a politely dismissive smile.

'Good day to you, Mr Monroe. I think there is no more to be said.'

'Pray don't trouble to call your servants, ma'am. I can show myself out.' He strode down the passage, flung open the front door and quit the house before the scurrying maid could reach him.

Lily's fate came hot on the heels of this interview, and was everything she had feared even if she did richly deserve it. She made no protest, offered no defence, meekly accepted every vile comment which Margot flung at her. Lily could have told her mother-in-law that Bertie had done worse, visiting the very house in Fossburn Street from which Margot had once accused Lily herself of offering salacious services. But what would be the point? Lily felt she did not have the right to risk damaging Margot's love for her son. In any case, Bertie wasn't here to defend himself. Wasn't her sense of guilt bad enough already?

She could have voiced her suspicions over Selene's own indiscretions, but Hannah's religious platitude still rang in her head: 'Do unto others as you would have them do unto you.' Not, unfortunately, a creed Lily could follow in all honesty, for she knew nothing could induce her to give Nathan up. She needed him, as he did her. And until Bertie came home she would continue to see him. But Margot's next words stunned her, left her open-mouthed and speechless.

'You'll pack your bags and leave this house within the hour, madam. Do you hear me?'

'B-but what about Bertie?'

'Perhaps my son will return home all the sooner once he knows that his errant wife has left. I always knew he had good reason for staying away. Now I realise what it is. And take your brat with you!'

Lily stood on the doorstep of number four Carter Street, bags by her side and child in her arms, staring with disbelief into her father's face.

'What do you mean, I can't come in?'

'What I say. You can't.'

'But this is my home.'

'No, Lily. It *was* your home. But it's not been your home for a good many years. You've even thought yourself too grand to visit us in it for much of the time.'

'I explained all of that to Mam.'

'Not to me.'

'I'm sorry, but...'

'If you've got problems with your husband's family, I'm sorry for it, but I can do naught to help.'

'You could offer me a roof over my head, for my child at least.'

'You should've thought of him before you started on this affair wi' Nathan Monroe, shouldn't you?'

So the gossips had done their work. Lily drew in a shaky breath. 'Can I speak to me mam?'

'No.' And he shut the door in her face.

Nathan was waiting for her in Carreck Woods, as she had known he would be. The hunched shoulders, the grim set of his mouth and the perpetual scowl were back. Every line of his body spoke of his displeasure. Perhaps he was angry with her for losing him Selene. He would accuse her of carelessness, of robbing him of his one chance to be rich. She must make him see that they were done with the Clermont-Reads now. Done with everyone, it seemed. They could go away together, start a new life. Hadn't she come to tell him so?

The old ferryman had promised to keep his eye on her things, and agreed to show the four year old a thing or two about ropes until she returned.

Thomas had looked confused, as well he might, when Lily had explained she was looking for a new home for them. Hadn't he already got a fine home? A big garden to play in, a swing, any number of toys, and people in abundance to wait upon his every need.

Lily wondered what sort of life she could take her son to, when even her own parents scorned her. But she had absolute faith in Nathan. He was the boy's true father, after all.

Now she stood before him, and without a word reached up on tip-toe silently to kiss his mouth. As her body melted against his, his arms came about her to swing her high and hold her tight as he always did. Then he laid her down, crushing the globe flowers and violets, and made love to her with a fierceness that melted his anger so that then he must love her again, with a tenderness that caused Lily to weep with joy.

Afterwards as they lay together, sun-dappled limbs heavy with their love-making, eyes closed as Lily lay against the warm curve of his wounded shoulder, Nathan idly stroked her hair. Not wishing to spoil the moment with talk of her plight, she dared at last to ask another question.

'Do you love me?'

There was a long, aching pause in which she listened to his heartbeat. A chaffinch flew close by. Landing on a branch, it puffed out its pink breast with self-importance and glanced cheekily about. The lovers watched in the silent stillness of the woods until the bird opened its wings and flew off again, envying its freedom.

'I've little trust in love, Lily. My mother loved my father so much she sacrificed everything for him, even me. Look where it got her. A beaten, sick, wreck of a woman, with a bitter young tearaway for a son. You must take me as I am, or not at all.'

'I want to hear you say it.'

Then he kissed the top of her head and whispered into her hair, 'I dare say I must feel summat strong for you, Lily Thorpe, or I wouldn't be here. Will that do?'

She lifted a face shining with love, lips parting for his kiss. 'Would you marry me, if I were free?'

The answer this time was even longer in coming as he studied her solemnly. 'Why does it matter, since you're not?'

'It matters.'

Very slowly, and with painstaking gentleness, he traced the shape of her blunt chin with one finger, outlined each flared nostril, the tilt of her eyebrows, the smooth pink of her cheeks, pushed back the heavy swathe of silky brown hair. One corner of his mouth lifted into that wicked smile she so loved. 'I seem to recall that I did ask you once, only you refused me.'

She laughed, all tension disappearing from her body.

As the kisses continued, now soft, now fierce and demanding, desire flared as it always would between them, and she opened herself to him, wrapping her legs about him so he could thrust deep inside her. He took her with a kind of desperate ferocity, almost as if this were their last time together, when really, Lily thought, it was a new beginning.

It was some time later, as they lay quietly together, the sunlight faded from the sky, that reality returned and Lily told him of her banishment. Shock and anger were reflected in his face.

'She's turned you out? The old witch. What would Bertie say to such behaviour?'

'He isn't here.'

'He will be soon. When he's ready to face the world again.'

'Do you want him to come back?'

'Don't ask me that, Lily.'

'I do ask you.'

'He's your husband.'

'I know.'

There was a small silence as Nathan felt his bravado fade away. Bertie had no doubt suffered in the war too. Might still be suffering. What right had he to inflict further hurt? 'What about Thomas? Doesn't Margot even care about her own grandson?'

Lily shook her head, voice hushed. 'She says I can't prove he's Bertie's son. It's true, I can't.'

For a long moment Nathan stared at her. 'What are you saying?'

'I think you know. I think you've always known.'

He closed his eyes. 'Dear God, Lily, what have I done to you?'

'Bit of a mess, eh? My own father has told me never to darken his door ever again.' She made her voice sound falsely dramatic. 'So I'm a poor abandoned orphan. I'll have to move in with you. Or we could go away together, start a new life.'

Cradling his frozen arm, Nathan hunched his shoulders and leaned back against a tree. Hadn't he enough to face, rebuilding a life that war had torn apart? He spoke softly, with regret. 'Trouble is, Lily, my life is here, with the steamer business. It was hard won, I don't want to lose it.'

She knew what he said was true. His business had been hard won. He deserved his success. Even so, she couldn't deny her disappointment. 'I thought you loved me?'

He gazed upon her trusting face, knew he had never wanted anything more than Lily beside him. He thought of Passchendaele, of the wounds the explosion had inflicted. But for all his arm was useless he was alive. Many others were not. If the war had changed him, perhaps it had damaged Bertie more, or he would be here too, with Lily. So how could Nathan run off with his best mate's wife? He simply couldn't do it. He'd acquired a conscience somewhere along the line. Something the old Nathan had never had.

He cupped Lily's face between his hands and kissed it with infinite gentleness. 'It wouldn't be right, Lily. You know it wouldn't. You're still married.'

'I don't care.'

'You must. Your reputation would never recover.'

'I don't care about my reputation.' She felt the beginnings of panic.

'Yes, you do. All those years turning yourself into a lady, to throw it away on a rapscallion like me? I'm no good for you, Lily. Never will be.'

The pain in her throat grew till it was almost impossible for her to swallow. 'I don't care about your past, about anything but being with you.'

His eyes were compelling and filled with a deep sadness. 'You care what they think about Thomas. Would you have them label your son a bastard? Go home, Lily. Make Margot believe you're sorry, that we'll never see each other again. And that Thomas is Bertie's son. It's the only way.'

She gazed at him then with eyes filled with fear. How could she do it? How could he ask her to give him up?

'I should have stayed away,' he told her. 'Instead, I've ruined your life.' Then, abruptly, he got up and walked away, and the silence of the woods washed over her – a silence so profound Lily dare not even break it with her tears.

Thomas was happily attempting to tie a double overhand and two half hitches when Lily reached the boat. He'd lost a button from his navy blue coat and a smear of oil streaked his small nose. She rubbed at the oil and kissed the nose, earning a squirm and a grimace for her trouble. Ferryman Bob glanced up and grinned.

'He'll make a good sailor, just like his grandpa.'

Lily struggled to find a smile. 'I dare say he will.'

But her mind was elsewhere, her heart strangely empty. She picked up her son and hugged him, feeling the need to hold him close in her arms. He was boy enough to hate this show of maternal affection in front of the old ferryman, and wriggled frantically till she set him down.

'Bob was telling me about the Kisel.'

'The Kaiser,' Bob gently corrected, nodding his head and making the flies on his hat dance as he launched into his yarn. 'I remember as if it were yesterday. Back end of last century that was. Around 1894 – no, '95. What a to-do! He lunched at the Old England, guest of Lord Lonsdale. Then he was taken up to Waterhead in the launch *Maroo*. His entourage followed in the *Elfin,* which had the cheek to overtake the Kaiser's boat.' He gave a cackling laugh at the memory. 'That didn't suit the Yellow Earl at all. All boatmen have their pride, you know, lad, just like your grandpa.' The old man continued with his tale but the words came to Lily as if from a long distance, for all she tried to show interest.

'Are we going home now, Mummy?'

Lily swallowed. She had no home. Turned from every door she had nowhere to take her child. Not even Nathan wanted her. Suddenly overwhelmed, Lily's legs started to wobble and before she could stop herself, she sank to her knees and burst into tears.

'By heck, what have I said now? I never realised my yarns were as bad as that.'

Ferryman Bob took her to the *Faith,* safe in her quiet backwater. It was the only place he could think of where there was a bed. He asked few questions, assuming there'd been some tiff with Margot that a good night's sleep would easily resolve. Lily did not disabuse him. He proved to be a kind friend, and set about organising her good and proper.

'You'll need provisions for tonight,' he said, and brought her pillows and blankets, a box full of bread and butter, bacon, eggs, and a pot of jam for the bairn. He lifted Thomas into the boat, and set the box by his feet. 'Stow this lot aboard for your mam. You're going to have to be a real sailor, lad.' As if it were all part of a game.

'Can I be a pirate?'

'Happen not. Pirates can get in a lot of bother. Now you do as your mam tells you, son. All right? You're the man of the house now.'

'Of the boat, you mean,' came the swift reply, followed by a giggle. Ferryman Bob shot Lily a wry grin.

'Sharp, that one.'

'Yes.'

Bob sounded the *Faith* for leaks, checked that the storm lantern was fuelled up and working. Then, satisfied she would neither sink, freeze nor starve, he helped Lily aboard. 'Will you be all right?'

Lily nodded. 'We'll be fine.' She didn't feel fine. She felt sick to the heart but Thomas was jumping up and down with excitement, and somehow she must find the strength to go on pretending it was all a game, for his sake.

'I'll come and see you tomorrow, lass. Keep your chin up.' Then she was alone with her son in the boat as a purple dusk crept about them, a stiff breeze rustling eerily through the branches overhead, seeming to emphasise her loneliness.

No one wanted her. Not Bertie who'd deliberately stayed away, not Margot who blamed her for everything, nor Selene who accused her of ruining her engagement. Not even Arnie, her own father.

Now Nathan had let her down. In his way he was doing the honourable thing. But it seemed to Lily as the sun sank behind the black mountains that she was quite alone in all the world.

Chapter Twenty

During the next few days alone with her child, Lily found a kind of peace. She woke each morning to a world of sun and silence, of soft green trees and the gentle lapping of water. It had rained quite hard during that first night, hammering on the roof of the saloon. But Lily and Thomas, cuddled up warmly together and deeply asleep, never heard a thing.

When Lily woke, surprisingly refreshed, the sun on the rain-washed new day lifted her spirits. Bathed in the pink and gold glory of early morning, the sight of the crisp clear mountains invigorated her. The familiar surroundings of the boat, which she'd grown fond of on their weekend ferry trips during the war, comforted her.

Urged on by Thomas's bubbling high spirits, Lily set about trying to recall the mysteries of the boiler which Edward had once so painstakingly explained to her. If only she had listened more carefully! Shovelling in coal was one thing, getting it started on her own another entirely. But Lily knew that the Windermere kettle could boil water in the twinkle of an eye, or any bucket of water set over the steam would likewise boil. Would it also fry bacon?

After half an hour, filthy and exhausted from her efforts, she gave up. The small failure had demoralised her completely and the tears that swelled in her heart finally overflowed. What reason was there to go on?

'Don't cry, Mummy. I might not be hungry.'

Lily rubbed her cheeks dry and smiled through her tears.

'I reckon we'll have to be pirates after all. Marooned on a desert island. Let's hunt for wood and light a fire.'

'Ooh, yes, yes!'

It was the best breakfast Lily had ever tasted. Thomas's high-spirited giggles, the bright comfort of a flickering fire, the smell of woodsmoke and frying bacon, all served to make her feel better.

Later, as Lily watched her son happily toss sticks of wood into the lake, delighted if one floated, moaning if it sank, she took stock.

Whatever she decided now could affect the rest of her life. Should she abandon her fine life at Barwick House, her carefully nurtured reputation, and go and live with Nathan Monroe despite the gossip and the censure of her own family? Wasn't this, deep in her heart, what she wanted most of all? And if it meant that she must bring her child up in The Cobbles, what of it? The place was much improved. She'd achieved that, at least.

But was it right to turn her son into an outcast, as he surely would be? The son of a fallen woman. It made her shudder to think of it.

Or should she, for his sake, beg Margot's forgiveness? Give Nathan up for good as he insisted, just when she had discovered the depth of his love.

Nathan or Bertie? Each represented a different part of her, a different world. Lily silently recalled her bright-faced, boyish husband and couldn't help but admit that she did worry over him. Had no wish to hurt him.

But she loved Nathan more.

The terrible dilemma of being a part of two worlds and belonging to neither made her feel, in that moment, physically sick. Here, on the *Faith,* was the only place she could create a world of her own. One where she could be her own person.

Lily lifted her face to the sun. 'It isn't too bad a world either,' she said to Thomas, before she had time to change her mind. 'Shall we stay here for a while? Have a real adventure?'

'You mean, not go home tonight either? Oh, yes. Please, Mummy.' Flinging his chubby arms about her neck, he smacked a wet kiss on her cheek.

Lily burst out laughing. 'But you must be good and promise not to fall in the lake?'

'Oh, I promise, I promise.'

'I might even teach you to swim.'

Another kiss till the two of them were rolling over in the grass, with the child stuck fast around her neck, both laughing as if they hadn't a care in the world. At least, Lily thought later, as she washed the greasy plates with difficulty in the cold waters of the lake, somebody loved her.

Ferryman Bob helped Lily clean the boat and get the boiler running. He brought her wood to burn, showed her how to operate the pumps and boil water in the kettle. Then on Friday afternoon Edward appeared, standing on the bank and grinning down on her. 'Well, would you believe it? Swiss Family Robinson. Permission to come aboard, Cap'n?'

'I'm a pirate, Grandpa, and Mummy is my slave.'

Lily laughed. 'I believe you've come to my rescue just in time, sir. This wicked pirate here was about to make me walk the plank.'

'Dear me, and before you've had your tea?'

Thomas giggled. 'Can I tie you up instead?'

'Why don't you do that, so long as I can have my tea at the same time. You've got the boiler going?'

'I reckon I've got its measure.'

'Put the kettle on then. I'm parched.'

Moments later they sat side by side, eyes on the blue-misted mountains, sipping mugs of scalding tea, which tasted so much better in the clean, spring air than in Margot's stuffy parlour, and ate scones with Ferryman Bob's pot of jam. Thomas practised his knots. The sun beat down on the fringed canopy while coot and mallard swam lazily by. They could have been any loving family out on a Sunday picnic, except for a certain formality between the adults, who carefully avoided eye contact above the boy's head. 'It's bonny here.'

'Mm.'

'We've neglected poor *Faith* recently, eh?'

'I suppose so.'

Seeing he could draw little from her, Edward said, 'I used to have a boat for freight too. Small-time, of course, and not as big as the Raven on Windermere, but I reckon folk found it useful for shifting the stone from the quarry or timber from the woods and such like.'

'Why don't you work her now?' It seemed easier to speak of other things.

Edward shook his head. 'Margot didn't care for messy boats passing her front door.' As if caught out in some minor disloyalty, 'Mind you, there was no money in it. The roads were getting better all the time and I was busy with my warehouse enterprise in Manchester, which subsidised the boat in her last season.'

'So where is she now?' Lily was interested, despite herself.

'Scuttled.'

Lily frowned. 'Scuttled? What on earth does that mean?'

'It means we decided she was neither use nor ornament, so we holed and sunk her.'

'Oh, but that's dreadful! What was her name?'

'*Kaspar*. Fancy name for a cargo boat, eh? It means treasure, and that's how I thought of her. She was a proper little beauty.' His sheepish smile grew sad. 'I might've made something of her if circumstances had been different, but we'd no real use for her any more so we scuttled her. Broke my heart, that did.' As if wishing to disguise this unwonted show of emotion, Edward briskly changed the subject, addressing his small grandson who was deeply engrossed in the tale.

'The *Raven's* still going on Windermere, though for how much longer we'll have to see. Fine cargo boat she is, built by T.B. Seath & Co. of Rutherglen on the Clyde. Made in sections and transported by rail to Penrith, then taken by horse-drawn dray to Pooley Bridge, put together and launched. Cost more than two thousand pounds. That firm sent boats in exactly the same fashion all the way to Africa. Marvellous, eh? Very inventive, the Victorians.'

'Golly,' said Thomas.

Lily said, 'Bertie is too, don't you think? He was always keen to design a really fast power boat.'

Edward's lips thinned. 'Power will never beat the grace of steam, not for me.' He stubbornly continued with his tale. 'They used to reward the crew of the *Raven* in kind for carrying large quantities of beer – which made the return journey a bit tricky.'

Edward roared with laughter, little Thomas enthusiastically joining in so that even Lily found herself smiling.

'You might not agree with everything Bertie does,' she persisted, 'but he would so like to make you proud of him.' She didn't really know if that were true but hoped to reconcile father to son, and perhaps lead on to her own problems. 'Can neither of you admit how alike you are? Each refusing to let the other see how they feel, yet both feeling rejected. It's proper daft.'

'You sound just like the old Lily.'

'Oh, she's still here,' Lily agreed with a wry tug at the grubby sleeves of her linen frock which had not benefited from her sojourn on the *Faith,* let alone the cleaning of the boiler.

'Aye, but tougher, eh?'

Lily frowned. 'Not necessarily. The old Lily was pretty tough, but she made a lot of mistakes that the new Lily would like to put right.'

Edward gave a wry smile. 'Story of my life.' He applied himself with vigour to polishing the boiler tubes with a rag, then quite casually remarked, 'Margot says you walked out.'

'Not exactly, but you could say it was for the best that I left.'

After a moment he halted in his labours and considered her too-bright eyes. 'She tends to go into a panic sometimes and say the first thing that comes into her daft head. Then afterwards she's sorry.'

Lily said nothing. Clearly she couldn't view Margot with the same benevolence as her husband did.

'We all make mistakes. Bertie too.' Edward cast her a sideways look which spoke volumes. 'Will you come home? She's calmed down a bit now.'

She sat in the sunshine, watching her father-in-law work on his beloved boat, enthusiastically assisted by the small boy. Never had Lily wished more than she did at that moment that little Thomas were truly Edward's grandson. 'Not just yet. We're having an adventure, aren't we, Thomas? We might sail away for a year and a day.'

Her son looked at her with solemn eyes. 'D'you mean in a proper boat, at sea?'

'Why not?'

The little boy considered. 'I don't think we could, Mummy. If we went away, like the Owl and the Pussycat, we might miss Daddy coming home.'

'Of course,' she said. 'How silly of me.' In her heart she knew that the trap she had built for herself all those years before might never open. Not now. Not even to let Nathan in.

The air was heavy with a humid heat broken only by the plip-plop of racquet on ball as Selene and her friends chased languidly up and down the tennis court. Lily was sitting with Thomas making daisy chains on the lawn while Margot dozed beneath her parasol, her soft snoring outdoing the noisy crickets. Out on the lake half a dozen small yachts lay becalmed in the still air, the only movement coming from the Public Steamer, at this moment gliding gently towards the distant pier where a blur of people waited in the heat haze. Only on the lake itself could any coolness be found and for once Lily rather envied the tourists their forthcoming cruise.

She closed her eyes and lay on the sweet-smelling grass, as always letting her mind drift back to Nathan, picturing him, loving him. Yet resolutely she'd kept away from him, for the sake of her child.

Lily had still not fully moved back into Barwick House, though Margot made no protest when she brought Thomas to visit. Strangely enough Selene seemed unperturbed by the whole business. She never once remarked upon her broken engagement. Almost as if it had never existed.

Thomas, thinking his mother's lying down was some kind of game, climbed all over her, dangling the daisy chain over her face, making her giggle and squirm.

'Look at the boats, mummy. They're stuck. There isn't enough wind.'

'Mmm,' she sleepily agreed.

'It would be all right in the steam-yacht. Can we take out the *Faith* this afternoon?'

'No, Ferryman Bob is working and Grandpa is away at his business.'

'Can't we ask George? Will we have another picnic? Can I have a go at driving it this time, if we do?'

'Oh, Thomas, do stop asking questions. You make me tired. We'll see.' She was drifting into sleep as the heat of the sun made her soporific.

A gentle snore vibrated softly through the summer air and the little boy giggled. 'Grandmama is asleep.'

'So should you be,' Lily murmured. 'Shall I take you upstairs?'

'No, no. I'm not tired,' he protested. Thomas hated keeping still. He had any lively four year old's boundless energy and inquisitive nature, being far more interested in the boats on the lake than sleeping or making silly daisy chains. Quickly growing bored with his uncooperative mama, and fearful she might keep her word and take him upstairs to his nursery, he set off across the grass at a great pace. Spotting a family of mallard he chased them right to the water's edge where, in his anxiety to catch them, he tripped over a stone and landed on his knees in the water.

'Whoops,' he said. But the water swished delightfully all over his shorts. He always enjoyed his bath each night when Betty splashed him or poured warm water over his head. Now he cupped his hands beneath the lake water and saw how white and funny-looking they went. Then he brought them up in a rush and splashed water over himself, giggling with delight.

The small flotilla swam tantalisingly beyond reach. Thomas lay on his tummy in the shallow water and waved his arms about as he had seen George do each morning in the lake. When he made no progress, he got to his feet and waded out a bit further. He heard a shout and half turned, laughing.

'Mummy, look at me! Look at me, Mummy! I'm swimming like you showed me.'

'Not without me to hold you.'

He could see her now, running towards him, but he wanted to prove how clever he was. Thomas lifted one foot which, unfortunately, was his undoing. Somehow his other foot rolled about on the slippy shingle in the lake and the next instant the water was over his head as he went down with a bump.

Then he was being lifted from the water, bright lights exploding in his head as he was held up high in the air, dripping like a fish on the end of a line. And, horror of horrors, he was crying.

'Mummy!' But it wasn't his mummy. It was a strange man who held him. His mother was there beside them in the water, and Thomas was instantly concerned. 'Mummy, Mummy, you're getting your pretty frock all wet.'

'It doesn't matter, darling. Nothing matters but you, my sweet.'

'You'd never think so, after what I've just witnessed. While you sleep, your son is drowning. *My* son was drowning.'

Lily looked up into her husband's furious face with a fast-sinking heart. For more reasons than one.

'It's all right, I'd seen him too. I would have got to him in time.'

'So you say.'

Lily sat on the edge of their bed, her face in her hands as she struggled to wipe away the tears. Thomas had been scolded, bathed and put to bed, but still she shook with shock. 'I would. He'd only been gone a minute. He was simply being naughty and running away because I'd told him it was time for his nap. Children are like that, up to mischief all the time. Sometimes I wish I had eyes in the back of my head. He's totally fearless, very much your son.' She'd said the right thing at last. Looking up, she saw the ghost of a smile. 'Don't be cross, Bertie. I'm so very glad to see you.'

She didn't say 'at last'. She didn't ask where he had been all these months, or mention that everyone else had long since returned. He put out one hand and awkwardly touched her cheek. 'You're right, old thing. It was only a few inches of water. I was probably over-reacting. Tend to these days, don't you know? Anyway, the little chap's come to no harm. I'd best teach him to swim, though, starting first thing tomorrow.'

'That would be an excellent idea, living as close to the lake as we do.' She put her hands to his face and kissed each cheek then his lips. There was no emotion in the kisses, only a friendly formality. 'I can't believe you're actually here.' She laughed. 'Listen to the pandemonium downstairs! Margot will be killing the fatted calf. She'll expect you down there for tea shortly, all spruced up and ready to answer her every question. You'd best hurry to bathe and change, or she might come up and do it for you!'

Bertie smiled. 'Mama wouldn't dare do such a thing. Not even when I had diphtheria.' But the jokes had eased the tension between them, established some kind of rapport, however shaky.

Lily stepped back from him. 'You look well.'

It was a lie. She looked into his frozen face, still handsome, still framed with a riot of sandy curls, to all outward appearances the very same man she had married years before. Yet not the same. Something had changed. Something indefinable had died within him.

'You too. I hear Nathan is home.'

She paused very slightly before asking as brightly as she could, 'Who told you?'

'Mama. She says the engagement to Selene is off. Why?'

Her smile had become stiff again, and a little forced. Lily walked to the door. 'I'll tell you about it later. There isn't time now.'

He nodded. 'I won't be long.'

Margot was a picture of solicitude and attention, bubbling over with happiness at the return of her darling boy. She fussed endlessly over him, fetching books and newspapers, cups of tea and cocoa, anticipating his every request so he never needed to stir from the chair opposite hers. And the questions poured out. 'Have you suffered terribly, my darling? Is that why you didn't come home right away? Or did you dread it for some other reason?' Casting a glance in Lily's direction.

'I'd some matters to sort out in my mind,' was all he would say on the subject, and Margot was punctilious in her understanding. 'Of course. How dreadful it must have been over there. I'm so proud of you. Your father too. Our very own hero.'

Bertie glared, then for no reason Margot could fathom, got up and walked out of the room. She turned instantly upon Lily, but even Margot could lay no blame on her on this occasion, for Lily had not said a word.

She wondered how much grace Margot would give her before revealing all her sins to Bertie.

They did not sleep together. That first night Lily tried to prepare herself, worrying over what her answer would be if he asked. He was her husband after all, and she was still fond of him. Yet she didn't feel quite prepared for taking up where they had left off. Nor was she ready to confront him with the facts of her love for Nathan. But he solved the problem for her.

'If it's all right with you, Lily, I'll sleep in my dressing room for a while. Need to get properly acquainted, don't you think? Used to each other again.'

'Of course. I agree.' Trying not to sound too relieved.

'Mama told me you've been living on the boat?'

Lily jumped as if pricked. 'Did she?'

'Something about Thomas playing pirates. He's a grand little chap, Lily.'

She released a quiet sigh. 'Yes, isn't he? Now go to bed, darling. You've had enough excitement for one day.'

The next day was spent quietly. Bertie pottered about the house and gardens. He walked in the woods and down to the lake, not venturing far. Sometimes Lily would catch sight of him standing on the sloping lawns, gazing out across the sweeping landscape of lake and green fields, neatly hedged in between pockets of woodland. And at the distant majesty of the hills beyond, as if reminding himself of their eternal beauty, making them a part of him again. But he made no move to take out the steam-yacht, nor even his own small dinghy.

Bertie did keep his promise to begin teaching his young son to swim. The two of them laughed and splashed together, Thomas seeming to blossom under his father's care and attention. Bertie too showed signs of the carefree, reckless young man he had once been. He became more relaxed, the lines of tiredness smoothing out of his old-young face, the haunted quality of his gaze warming to a new, if brittle, brightness. Lily watched them with pleasure.

He'd returned safe and well and so long as they were all three happy, what else could matter?

When Bertie came to her room on the fourth night and asked to get into her bed, Lily could not find it in her heart to refuse.

He lay beside her quietly at first, not touching her, not speaking. It was Lily who broke the silence.

'Do you want to talk about it?'

No reply. She could hear him breathing quietly in the darkness as she worried over what she should say, what she should do.

'We ought to talk, I suppose,' she said. 'About you and me. Thomas. Our future. There are things I need to say. How about you? Would you like to talk now?'

'No.'

Lily swallowed. 'As you wish. I'm so glad to have you home, Bertie. I've missed you.' Knowing that she genuinely meant it.

'Have you?' There seemed to be doubt in the question, a new insecurity. She searched for any indication in his voice that Margot had already been divulging secrets. Surely she would give her son time to settle in before tearing apart his marriage? Particularly since he was obviously still suffering from whatever had happened to him out there in France.

'Was it bad?' she asked now, very quietly. She wanted to tell him about Nathan's problems and about how, bit by bit, he had reacquired his power of speech, even regained a little movement in his useless hand. But she dare not, for that was dangerously close to the other matter which must not yet be discussed.

But she owed him something, didn't she? Some comfort at least. Lily quietly drew in a deep breath and slid an arm about his stiff shoulders.

'Would you like to make love to me then? Is that why you came to me tonight?' And to her amazement Bertie broke down into pitiful tears. He lay against her breast and sobbed out his anguish while she lay in stunned dismay, not daring to move as the sobs racked his too-thin body. She stroked his curly hair, kissed his cheek, and held him close as if he were a child.

'Poor Bertie. Darling Bertie. All that pent-up emotion. You're home now, my love. Quite safe. Smile for me and be happy.'

She steeled herself for the inevitable. She could love him. She must love him. Bertie needed to be loved. What would it cost her to show a little affection? Nothing. She owed him that much at least. He was still her husband, and they'd never stopped being friends.

Slowly he began to respond to her kisses. Lily took off her nightgown and encouraged him to slide his hands over her breasts and hips. 'Oh, Lily, I'd forgotten how very beautiful you are, how soft and silky your skin. You're as smooth and precious as a lily. I'm afraid I might bruise you if I press too hard.'

'Nay, lad, you'll not bruise me,' she teased, playing the old Lily. He lay on top of her and she slid her arms about his neck. 'Relax, Bertie. We always did get on well, didn't we? We're man and wife, remember, so how can it be wrong? Remember how you used to say that?' She chuckled at this old joke between them.

But he wasn't listening. He was making small grunting noises, kissing her face, her throat, her breasts, striving to recapture what they had once enjoyed. In his mind he saw other faces. Rose's, pretty and loving, which then changed into one with a gap-toothed grin, thin and hard, with life's experiences engraved in every line on the pallid dry skin. He could hear a laughing voice tease him.

'Come on, Bertie boy, don't be shy.' He'd hated it when she'd called him 'boy'. It reminded him of Edward, forever criticising, condemning.

'What game d'you want to play today, dearie?'

'Who's a naughty boy then?'

'Get on with the job in hand, boy, that's Florrie's motto.'

Boy? But he hadn't behaved like a boy, had he? The games he'd played these past months had been those of a man. A sick, disillusioned man.

Raucous laughter seemed suddenly to fill the room, fill his head, fill every part of him, and he put his hands to his ears to block out the sound. He could feel the sweat breaking out all over his body, the rigid stiffness in his legs, the flaccid warmth of his penis. Dear God, what was wrong with him? He couldn't do it. He couldn't defile Lily after what he'd done with those others. She had no idea exactly what he'd been up to during these months away. But *he* knew. Dear heaven, he could remember very well.

Lily kissed him again, trying to help him, but with a cry of anguish deep in his throat, Bertie thrust her aside and flung himself out of bed. The slam of his dressing-room door seemed to echo throughout the house.

The euphoria of homecoming had quite gone. Bertie became so highly strung that Lily could almost feel the energy emanating from him. He jumped at the slightest sound, complained of tiredness and lethargy yet could not sleep. He suffered constantly from headaches, argued with her over everything, and his naturally pale face seemed drawn with pain and worry.

'It doesn't matter,' she said. 'We're bound to feel odd together at first.' How could she tell him now, when he was suffering so? Yet how could they go on living this lie?

Was that the cause of this problem between them? Had Margot told him already? Or had Bertie heard rumours from the village gossips? Yet somehow Lily couldn't bring herself to confront the issue, in case he hadn't heard and the knowledge of his wife's betrayal only added to his difficulties.

As his irritability increased Lily strove to be patient. Sometimes in that first awful week, when it all became too much to bear, she would go and sit in the *Faith,* which was rather like visiting an old friend. Here, in the quiet backwater, lay a world far removed from either of the other two she struggled to occupy. A place she could call her own.

After that first terrible night Bertie refused, absolutely, to come to her bed.

'The war has made me impotent,' he told her.

'I won't believe it. You need only relax and you'll be fine.' Not that she wanted him to make love to her, but Lily felt she ought to try. Her heart ached for him, an emotional cripple, longing to help but not knowing how. Bertie surely deserved her support, even if she couldn't give him her love?

She would so like to have loved him, to have been a good and faithful wife, but knew she could not. Nor could she explain that while he'd been away she'd hurried twice a week, as eager as a young girl, to spend hours in another man's arms. In the woods, on the fells, wherever they could lie together away from prying eyes.

It no longer mattered that she'd dashed Selene's hopes of marriage, because she knew her sister-in-law was far too selfish to make Nathan happy. It hadn't really mattered that she'd been cast off by Margot, her parents, and the rest of society. All that mattered was her love for Nathan.

Living through the days without him had been the hard part. Purgatory in fact. Desperate for his hands upon her skin, his heart beating against hers, how could she have resisted him? He had been a part of her all her life. Lily wanted only to spend every moment she could with Nathan, and for all it shamed her to admit it, had no real regrets for her infidelity.

Her one regret was that somehow she must give him up. And for what? For a sick husband who was no longer a man.

Somehow, Lily knew, she must find the strength to face Bertie with the truth. Before he learned it elsewhere, and further damage was wrought.

Chapter Twenty-One

By the end of that first week, when Edward was due home from Manchester, Bertie scarcely spoke a word all day. Edward, on the other hand, had never seemed more lively as the entire family gathered about the long dining-room table. He insisted on opening a bottle of champagne.

'Or two perhaps. A man should celebrate the return of his hero son.'

Lily saw Bertie flinch but, her mind still busy with her own problems, only half listened to the discussion which ranged back and forth across the table during the long meal. Margot related gossip of past friends and how they had fared, who had married whom and how many children they now had. She talked of her own war work and how exhausting it had been.

'What a relief it is to be rid of it all. If I'd known the war was going to last so long, I would never have volunteered in the first place.' As if the Germans had deliberately prolonged the war simply to wear her out.

Selene, in cream and pink gauze, talked only of herself, as usual, and of the new friends she had found at Rosedale Lodge.

'Poor Catherine is quite the invalid. I've promised to go over more often. Marcus so appreciates my help.'

Bertie sat still as stone, appearing to listen to their chatter without taking in a word. She offered him a sympathetic smile, quietly whispering that perhaps he might like to retire early if he felt tired. But Edward was bringing out the port, instructing Margot to 'leave we men to it', and she was refusing, insisting he pour her a glass too.

'Very well, m'dear, we could break with convention on this special occasion. We shall drink a second toast to the return of our boy hero.'

'Will you stop that!' Bertie was on his feet, knocking his glass over as he shouted the words into the startled faces of his family. 'I'm not a *boy*. And I'm not a bloody hero! I did my job, that's all.'

'Of course you did your job. And of course you are a hero,' Edward said, surprise and a hint of annoyance in his voice. 'Why do you always put yourself down? Didn't you go behind enemy lines? Capture prisoners? Your commanding officer wrote and told us so when you were in hospital. I'm proud of you, boy. At last. Doesn't that please you?'

A hush seemed to descend on the assembled company while the words 'hero' and 'boy' sank deeper into Bertie's tortured mind. To his father he would always be a boy, a child who liked to play, who refused to grow up if it meant he must work hard. If playing the hero, as Edward so desperately wanted, would make everything right between them, he might just do it. But it could only work if it were true.

Bertie saw again a familiar, haggard face, the visions that haunted his sleep, appetites that could not be quenched. His wife's body, pure and white, that he dare not defile.

Somehow it all seemed to add up to the loss of his manhood. In that moment the failure became too great to bear. He pushed back his chair, rocking it on its back legs so that it almost fell over, put his hands to his head and began to keen softly, as if in great pain. Then as Margot put out a hand, he swung away from her to pace about the room, wanting to escape yet needing to stay and make them understand. Bertie knew that finally he must find the courage to face his father.

'All my life I've wanted you to be proud of me, yearned for it. I thought I might impress you with my boat designs, hoping you might find one you'd want to build. But, no. You mocked them as some kind of foolish game, not work at all.'

Bertie's eyes glistened with what Lily recognised to her horror as unshed tears. If he broke down in front of Edward it would finish him for good. 'But I never got my hands dirty, did I?' he was saying, lip curling. 'So it couldn't be proper man's work.

'Now, when at last you are proud of me, it's all false. I don't deserve your damned pride. I'm not who you think I am.'

Margot again tried to catch his hand as he strode by, but failed. 'Bertie dear, do calm yourself. Your father has every right to be proud of you. So am I. My son a...'

'Don't say it again. I'm no bloody hero! How could I be? Bertie Clermont-Read, the idle fool. Isn't that how you've always seen me?' He stopped his pacing, fury making him punch the table with his fists as he yelled into their startled faces. 'You're right. I am a useless fool. You want to know what happened? I'll tell you.'

He steadied his breathing, emptied his champagne glass in one swallow then turned to face them, eyes so cold and bleak that Lily's heart seemed to turn right over.

'I hopped that damned plane over the line so many times I went dizzy with it. My job was to check where our artillery was stationed, and where the enemy was. I rarely got involved personally with any fighting. A lonely war, that's what I had. So when I actually came down next to a German patrol, it stunned the life out of me. Would you believe it was my good fortune that it was Christmas, and they were all more in the mood for celebrating than for killing. Even greater good luck that I'd learned always to carry with me a few cigars. We have that in common at least, Father.'

Edward said nothing.

'I owe my life to those damned cigars.' Bertie almost smiled at the memory. 'They were all right, those chaps. Thought I was nuts to walk over to them with a cigar in my hand instead of a pistol. I shouted *"Joyeux Noel"*, since I don't know any German, and they burst out laughing. We shared their beer, my cigars and a few jokes, in French since it was the only common language between us. Afterwards they happily handed over their guns and surrendered without rancour. Jolly good sports, in fact. They were cold and hungry, I expect, and thought I might feed them.

'I led them to a nearby battalion dugout that I'd spotted when flying in. So there you have it. Some bloody hero!'

Margot's eyes shone with tears. 'But you were so brave to walk towards them.'

'They were singing Christmas carols, for God's sake. I knew I was in no danger.'

Margot turned to Edward. 'Tell him that he is a hero. It doesn't make any difference that it was Christmas and they surrendered.'

'They were still the enemy?' Selene asked, her pretty face the picture of puzzlement.

'They were drunk,' Bertie said bluntly.

Edward stared at his son for a long moment without speaking, an expression of disillusionment on his face. It was so dreadful to see, it made Lily shudder. 'You accepted a medal for that?'

Bertie shrugged. 'My commanding officer wouldn't hear otherwise. But it has blighted me, if you want to know. How could it not when more than half my mates have been blasted to bits or maimed?'

Edward ground out his own cigar in the remains of his strawberry meringue and stood up. Bertie watched with haunted eyes as he tossed aside his napkin and walked, head held high, from the room.

Margot got up too, all in a flurry, cast an angry glance upon all three of them, and seeking someone to blame, as usual focused her furious glare upon Lily.

'You should have warned me! You must have known what Bertie meant to do. You've allowed him to destroy his poor father.'

As she hurried after Edward, the three young people remained where they were, an unmoving tableau. Selene shocked into silence for once, Bertie frozen in his pacing, standing stock still the middle of the room, and Lily unable to think of a word to release them all.

But the silence did not last long. It was broken by an ear-splitting scream which brought them all from their paralysis and running out into the hall.

Margot stood at the foot of the wide staircase, face white as a ghost, swaying slightly as she put one shaking hand on the banister rail. Selene was the first to reach her.

'Mama? What is it?'

She didn't really need to ask. For there was Edward, halfway up the stairs. He lay crumpled like a rag doll, and it was perfectly clear to all of them that he was going nowhere, not ever again.

'My darling Edward is gone. What am I to do?' And the redoubtable Margot put her face in her hands and began to sob.

The funeral took place with all the pomp and circumstance that Margot, at least, considered necessary. A hearse drawn by no fewer than six horses with plumes in the grand old style bore her husband to the cemetery, and a marble monument to his memory was ordered to be placed on his grave with all speed.

Edward's friends and neighbours, together with members of his extended family, were invited to the house afterwards for one of Margot's famous luncheons. Salmon patties, Edward's favourite, were served together with chicken legs, game pies, potted char and anchovy butter. The finest Madeira was offered to the ladies, port for the gentlemen, and not a single person present could dispute the fact that no expense had been spared to give him a good send-off.

'Say what you like about her,' the gossips said, 'snobby and arrogant though she may be, there's no doubt she loved that soft-hearted husband of hers.'

'Aye, good pair they were, stuck together through the years. Worked hard and made a fortune.'

'He'll cut up pretty well, no doubt about that.'

Margot refused to have any truck with reading the will on the day she buried Edward, and gave the family solicitor short shrift for daring to suggest it.

'What with Selene locked in her room refusing to speak to anyone, Bertie in a sulk and the servants weeping all over the place, I really cannot permit it,' she said.

Margot did not mention Lily, to whom she had not spoken since the day of Edward's untimely demise. For wasn't she the one to blame for not warning them of Bertie's intentions?

'I shall call first thing in the morning then, Mrs Clermont-Read.'

'No.' Margot was wondering why solicitors were always so thin and sour-faced when they supposedly earned so much money. 'Not before two in the afternoon, if you please. I might have the strength by then.'

Arthur T. Groves, of Groves, Sutton & Barnfather, inclined his head and thankfully took his leave. He was in no hurry to face Mrs Clermont-Read. But the following day, at two o'clock precisely, he arrived as instructed, conducted his business and found no joy in the prospect.

When he had gone the family sat stunned, no sound but that of the doleful ticking of the grandfather clock.

It seemed that Edward had left nothing but debts.

There were a few shares in the Public Steamer Company, worth a very little, but his freight business was close to collapse and Mr Groves graciously but firmly explained that it could not be saved except by a further investment of capital, which they themselves did not possess. Not only were they no longer rich, they were in fact exceedingly poor. Could even lose the roof over their heads. It was Margot's nightmare come true.

'What nonsense,' she bravely riposted. 'Edward had recently expanded, rented extra premises, built a new ship – all on the strength of new business from Marcus Kirkby.'

'Indeed he had, and given time I'm sure the project would have proved a sound one. Unfortunately his borrowings were huge, far outstripping the profits at this stage in the venture. Your husband's name was well respected in business and banking circles. His word was his bond, you might say. Now that he is dead, that trust dies with him.'

Everyone tacitly understood him to mean that Bertie was not to be trusted with continuing the family business as soundly.

'All loans have been called in. A sad but frequent occurrence, Mrs Clermont-Read. I'm afraid Mr Clermont-Read's assets will not be sufficient to meet his debts.'

Now they sat and pondered on these words, letting the reality of their situation slowly sink in. After ten whole minutes of silence, during which time Lily could feel nothing but admiration for Margot's stoicism throughout the whole awful proceedings, Selene began to scream. She screamed so loudly and for so long that she had to be carried upstairs to her room and dosed liberally with Extract of Poppy.

Bertie announced he was going down to the Marina Hotel for a glass of something comforting. 'Perhaps even a whole bloody bottle of champers. Or a dozen strong whiskies.'

'How will that help exactly?' Margot sourly enquired, but he merely adjusted his hat to a rakish angle, collected his kid gloves and declared that it would at least make him feel a whole lot better.

The two women sat alone. Margot's eyes met Lily's, an accusing glare urging her to do the same. 'Go on,' she said at last. 'Leave the sinking ship, why don't you?'

Lily stood up, and calmly reached for the bell pull. 'I think we'll have another pot of tea, don't you? Then we'd best put our thinking caps on.'

Margot not only declined to follow this suggestion, but refused to discuss the matter at all. Nor, it seemed, had she any intention of economising. So far as she was concerned life must continue as normal, as if all the clocks had stopped on the day of Edward's demise.

'I will not believe it,' was her perpetual cry. 'I am perfectly sure that when the estate is properly settled, we shall find silly Mr Groves to be entirely wrong.'

It was the most miserable winter at Barwick House that Lily could ever remember. Glowering mountains blended seamlessly into clouded skies while rain battered the bay windows and ran down the soaking lawns into a slate grey lake. The cold was merciless, penetrating every room since fuel was in short supply and bedroom fires were banned. The coal merchant had apparently refused to deliver any more coal until his account was settled.

'The ingratitude of the man!' Margot stormed.

George was persuaded to cut logs for them, but most of the servants packed their bags and walked out, some of them with wages still owing.

Unperturbed, Margot ordered winter gowns for herself and Selene, looking askance when Lily refused even to consider one this year. 'There's nothing to be gained by turning into a drab,' was her immediate response.

'I'm not short of clothes to wear,' Lily pointed out. In fact she'd never been so well dressed in her life. 'I really think we should consider where our future income is to come from before we spend another penny. It isn't simply coal we're short of, Margot. How are we to pay the grocer or the butcher, for instance?'

'Or the candle-stick maker? Heavens, Lily, haven't you yet learned to set aside your working-class limitations? They shall wait, of course, as they have always done.'

'They won't wait forever.'

'How can I go to dinner in last season's gown?' Selene, still quietly harbouring a fierce resentment towards Lily, seemed to grow ever more sour and spinsterish, curling her once pretty mouth down into a perpetual line of discontent. Losing a fiancé had been unfortunate, but becoming poor was another matter entirely. 'It is utterly unbearable,' she declared in her pettish way. 'I refuse to tolerate it.'

She had, in fact, already entered into discussions with Marcus upon her dire dilemma. Selene had even asked him to leave his sickly wife, but held out little hope that he would do so.

'I really do not see how you have the right to tell us what to do, Lily. Our little difficulties need not concern you at all.'

Frustration bubbled up in her at the wanton way in which Selene was prepared to squander money, without a thought for where the next penny was to come from. 'Of course it concerns me. I have Thomas to think of, don't I? He needs food in his mouth, a home to live in. He is Bertie's *son*.'

Margot opened her mouth to make some acid comment along the lines that she only had Lily's word for that, but thought better of it. Thomas seemed to be the only heir to Barwick House she was likely to see in her lifetime, certainly the way things were at present.

If she lost him, she would have no one to inherit the house and the Clermont-Read fortune.

A voice inside her head reminded Margot that the latter had vanished and the former may not be hers much longer, but she paid it no heed. Moving out of her home was quite out of the question. 'It's too dreadfully common to be always discussing money. I will not permit it,' she said, closing the subject yet again.

The three women remained trapped in the winter-bound house with nothing resolved, and no hope of rescue.

Bertie spent his days in his room, or being waited upon hand and foot by his adoring mother. More often he was out of the house altogether, propping up the bar in some hostelry or other, if Lily was any judge. It was a worry to know how to persuade him to take their plight seriously. Perhaps, Lily decided, the answer lay with Rose. Certainly something had to be done. Bertie needed help, and Rose might just be the one to give it to him.

Lily found her still working her vegetable stall on the market. She timidly approached, not knowing what to expect.

'Well, well, look what the wind's blown in.' Rose stood, hands on hips, as the two of them took stock of each other. Time had not been kind to her. There were dark bruises beneath her eyes, her hair had lost its shine and the old coat which Hannah had made over for her lay in a crumpled heap on a pile of rotting cabbages.

Rose offered terse condolences over the loss of Edward then turned her attention to serving a couple of customers while Lily patiently waited.

When the customers had gone, she paid excessive attention to paring off the outer leaves of a red cabbage, letting a grim silence fall between them. At last she felt driven to ask, 'I hear Bertie's home?'

'Yes.' Lily glanced at her closed face, lips tightly pressed together like a young bud that refused to open. 'It's about him that I've come to see you.'

'He's not ill?' She glanced up then, the knife still in her hand. 'I heard he'd no injuries, no missing limbs, naught to worry over but a few old shrapnel wounds.' There was anxiety in her tone from which Lily took heart.

'He's well ... physically at least.'

'Thank God for that.'

'Yes.' Lily picked up a red apple, rubbed it against her sleeve, looked as if she might bite into it, then placed it back on the pile. 'I know we're not exactly friends any more, but I wondered ... Could we talk?'

'I'm listening.'

Lily glanced about at the crowd, all no doubt discreetly listening too. 'Somewhere a bit more private?'

'I'm due a ten-minute break. We could take a turn along the shore?'

They walked beneath the canopy of trees by the lake, as they had done on the day they'd first met so many years before, when Rose had explained the facts of life to Lily. Now it was her turn to relate her concern for Bertie, including a frank account of their failed attempt to resume marital relations. Rose directed all her attention on peeling a fat orange, the juice running over her fingers, while Lily kept her gaze upon a bank of clouds ganging up on Fairfield.

'He's got it into his head that he's impotent.' There, she'd said the word.

'Impotent? Bertie?' Rose almost choked on the orange. 'I wouldn't have believed such a thing possible.'

Lily had the grace to smile. 'Me neither.' Here she paused, afraid to go on, to explain what she needed. Unfortunately Rose was way ahead of her. She gobbled down the last of the orange, licked her fingers and, wiping her sticky hands on her apron, drew herself up, stiff and straight-backed.

'And you reckoned I might make him better, eh? Take up wi' your Bertie where we left off?' She gave a funny little laugh that sounded coarse and cold. When she folded her arms across her thin chest it might have been her mother Nan standing there. 'What sort of a request is that to make of an honest woman? Oh, aye, I'm honest. I haven't taken up me mam's profession, for all there's been plenty of opportunity. And, unlike you, I certainly could've done wi' the money.'

'I never suggested you had.'

'So what are you asking exactly?'

Lily sighed. 'I don't know. I came to you for help. Advice perhaps, from a friend.'

'You want me to give him back his manhood. Is that it? You must be mad!'

Confused, Lily acknowledged that the idea had been in her mind. 'I know it would be a lot to ask.'

'It's a bleeding cheek, that's what it is. And why? So you can carry on wi' your fancy man, undisturbed by conscience?'

Stung by this, Lily jerked up her chin but the words rushed out before she could stop them. 'How did you know? I mean – that's not the way of it at all.'

Rose's chuckle deepened. 'Oh, I reckon it is. Tell me I'm wrong then? Tell me you're innocent? Go on. I'll believe you where thousands wouldn't.'

A long silence, then Lily drew in a shaky breath. 'All right, it's true. How did you guess?'

'Nay, lass, it's common gossip. Did you really think they'd forget all about it, just because your husband has come home?'

'I must have him, Rose. I need him. He's in my thoughts day and night. Sometimes I can't eat I feel so sick with wanting him. I've tried to give him up, but I can't. I must see him again or I'll die!'

'By heck, you *have* got it bad.'

Lily looked at her one-time friend with pained eyes. 'But how can I leave Bertie with no money, no home, no child, and after all I've done to that family.' The tears that had been held back all winter finally flowed. Rose stood for a moment, nonplussed by such loss of control, then she gathered Lily close in her scrawny arms, tut-tutting and patting her shoulders as if they were girls again.

'Nay, don't tek on so.' When the tears had been mopped up by the dearly familiar red handkerchief, now more of a washed-out pink, Rose brought forth a bottle of cold tea from her capacious apron pocket and gave a sip to Lily. Well laced with gin, it warmed her stomach and steadied her nerves.

But for all her words of comfort, Rose held fast to her principles. 'You should be honest. Tell Bertie what you feel.'

'I can't.'

Rose wagged a finger reprovingly. 'I'll tell you why. Because you enjoy living in that fancy house, with the money and status that goes wi' it.'

'There isn't any money.' Lily spoke so quietly that Rose had to ask her to repeat it, more than once in fact, with long explanations in between, before she was finally convinced.

'By heck, that's a facer! 'Ow did it come about? And 'ow are you managing?'

The situation at Barwick House, Selene's sour sulks, Margot's refusal to face reality, was fully described. 'I must do something to help,' Lily finished. 'I feel responsible, you see.'

'I thought you hated the Clermont-Reads?'

'I do. I did. Though I never hated Bertie. Or Edward, in the end. He had his faults but we became good friends and I miss him. It was all my fault he went bankrupt. Everything is.'

'Nay, that's going it a bit strong. He must have made some mistakes to lose so much.'

But Lily wouldn't consider the idea, she was far too busy blaming herself. 'I must have spent thousands on The Cobbles. Now there's Thomas to think of. Bertie adores him. I couldn't take him away, let him think that...'

'Thomas weren't his, like?'

'Oh, Rose, don't ever say it.'

'You'll have to tell him, about Nathan at least.'

Lily shook her head. 'Not just now. When he's himself again. I don't think Margot has said anything yet, but I know she intends to. She's waiting for the moment when it'll do the most damage, I expect. Though the gossip-merchants might have got to him already and he's simply keeping it close to his chest.' She wiped away the last of her tears with the flat of her hands, an action more suited to the young Lily than the smart young woman in double-breasted blue costume and tilted hat that she now was. 'I know it seems silly that once I was out to damage them, to get my revenge, and now I feel I have to work to save them from disaster. But I set it all in motion. D'you see?'

'You mean, you didn't mind getting your revenge so long as it didn't affect you?' Rose's bluntness, as always, made Lily cringe with shame.

'I dare say that is what I mean. I wanted to teach them a lesson for being so heartless over Dick. Margot blames me for everything that goes wrong and she does have a point. It was all because of me that Bertie and Selene got diphtheria, and little Amy died. My determination to bleed Edward dry has left them all, my own son included, with a heap of debts and not even the money to buy a pound of sausages. It's all gone too far, and now I feel it's up to me to save them from disaster and Bertie from despair. Perhaps then he'll be a man again. Not that I want him to make love to me, you understand, but he does, so it hurts us both. I thought you might be able to talk to him, cheer him up. Oh, I don't know.' Her agitation was mounting, tears starting up again.

Rose, sobered by this sorry, if confusing tale, said, 'By heck, you are in a pretty pickle if you can't afford a pound of sausages!'

Lily met the teasing glance with a half smile. 'It sounds silly but it's true. We have grocery bills that would near bankrupt the Yellow Earl himself. I seem to be in a dreadful mess, with no one to turn to.'

'So what are you going to do about it?'

Lily chewed on her lip. 'I've one or two ideas, nothing definite. I'm not sure if I'm up to the job.'

'You're up to any job you put your mind to, Lily. Allus have been.' They were back in the market by this time, having walked full circle, and the two girls sat, almost contentedly, side by side upon a pile of old boxes and cabbage leaves as they once used to do.

After a pause Lily quietly continued, 'I'm sorry it came out all in a muddle. But you and I used to be good friends. I rather hoped we might be again.'

Rose rubbed at her nose, embarrassed by Lily's frankness. 'I reckon it were you what ruined our friendship, Lily, not the other way about. You got a bit above yourself and stopped calling on me.'

'You're right, I did, and I'm sorry. My father said much the same thing.'

'As for Bertie, well, if you married him for any reason but love that's your problem, lass. But it's a bit naive to think I could sort out his problems wi' talking. So I'll not take him on, if you don't mind. What his troubles are I couldn't rightly say but they're nowt to do wi' me.' Rose got up and started tidying her stall, quite unnecessarily.

After an even longer pause this time, she issued her final words on the subject, in short sharp sentences, as if she wanted to get them over with as quickly as possible.

'I don't reckon interfering between a man and his wife is a good idea. I've seen the black side of that. Got a mite too fond of him, I did. I'm not inclined to risk it again. Happen if you were to solve your other problem and let him go like, things'd be different. Till then, thanks but no thanks.'

Only when the remainder of the Clermont-Reads' ever-patient suppliers finally and shame-facedly refused any further credit, when the telephone company threatened to disconnect their fashionable telephone, and the electricity company to cut off their supply, did Margot finally concede that perhaps, after all, they might just have a serious problem.

Selene's solution was to throw yet another fit of hysterics then pack her bags and move out.

'I can't be expected to live in poverty,' she announced to her startled mother, as if it were a mortal sin. 'I've been offered a place as companion to Catherine Kirkby. Poor Marcus needs help. I intend to take it up forthwith. I suppose I may borrow the gig to remove my boxes and portmanteaux?' By the end of the day, with no word of protest from Margot, she had gone.

'What are we to do?' Lily asked Bertie.

'Thank my father for at least leaving us a well-stocked cellar.'

There seemed no help for it but to face the crazy idea that had been growing in her head all winter. Strangely, encouraged because of Rose's confidence in her, it now seemed the only solution. What Lily needed was to discuss the matter with someone before attempting to put it into effect. And the best person she could think of was Nathan.

Ferryman Bob told her she looked as if she'd swallowed the sun, her face was that lit up as she climbed aboard his boat. Lily sensed he would have liked to tease her further, but recognising the way she had her eyes fixed on the far shore as if willing it closer, he held his tongue and concentrated instead upon his rowing.

She almost ran from the jetty, past the boat yard and up Drake Road to hammer on Nathan's door without caring who saw her. But he wasn't in. Of course not. At this time in the morning he would be working. Turning, she ran up Mallard Street, and once out of The Cobbles headed straight for the pier and the Public Steamer office.

She'd kept away from him all winter, out of respect for Edward and to help Bertie cope with the trauma. Now she was desperate to see him again.

Chapter Twenty-Two

Lily attracted a few appreciative stares as she flew across the wooden pier and up the steps that led to Nathan's office. Dressed in a navy polka dot silk dress and wide straw hat on this bright spring day, she looked the picture of charming respectability, not at all the sort of girl to run after a man.

The sun glinted on the water and there was a queue forming already at the steamer terminus. A straggle of elderly couples wanting a leisurely cruise, a few families wishing to keep the children amused for an hour or two.

A breeze slapped against the lines of rowing boats, making them dance and jig about, and Lily could hear delighted squeals as girls and youths climbed gingerly aboard the rocking craft. For a moment she thought of Dick and his bright, eager young face gazing so adoringly into hers. She thought of her beloved baby and Lily's heart contracted, even now, at the loss of this most precious part of her. I'll make you proud of me, she silently vowed. See if I don't.

Nathan looked surprised to see her, but Lily saw the flare of excitement in his eyes. She'd never visited his place of business before, had almost been afraid to do so now.

'It's been a long time.'

'Yes.'

Nathan could think of no way to frame the hope that swelled and filled his heart in that moment. She'd come with good news, he could sense it, almost feel it bubbling out of her. Was she going to leave Bertie and come to him? He held his breath.

'I need your help, Nathan,' she said. She had to concentrate hard on her plan to stop herself from running into his arms. Hardly waiting for him to send away his clerk and chief engineer, she poured out her tale in garbled fashion, tripping over words in her enthusiasm. He seemed nonplussed and then amused by her suggestion.

'You can't be serious?'

'Never more so. What do you think?' She perched on the edge of her seat, fidgeting with her gloves as, impatiently, she waited for him to admire her spirit, her flair for enterprise, and offer his support.

Nathan did indeed feel a spurt of admiration for the way she could always pick herself up, no matter how hard she was knocked down. He considered offering some sound advice, could see how eagerly she waited, breath held expectantly. He thought how wonderful she looked, how he would like to take her home and have her waiting there for him each and every night. But then he remembered Bertie and the dream soured. She hadn't come to him at all, she'd come only for her own selfish purposes. He leaned back in his chair and, hating the stiffness of his own face, and Lily almost as much in that bleak moment of realisation, curled one corner of his mouth into a grim smile.

'You imagine that taking a few people out on a picnic in the *Faith* will solve the Clermont-Reads' financial difficulties?'

'It's a start.'

His brows twitched expressively then he continued, 'I'm taking delivery of a new steamship soon, Lily – *The Golden Lady*. Did I tell you? You must come to the launch. She's a beauty.' Getting up, he took her firmly by the elbow and began to lead her out on to the steps. Why torture himself with her presence? It did no good. 'Now you must go. I'm very busy.' Almost as if her presence in his office embarrassed him.

Stunned, she didn't immediately answer. When she did so, her disappointment was all too evident. 'Didn't you hear my plans? I need your advice, Nathan. Your help.'

'What sort of advice could *I* give? You seem to have made up your mind already.' Blue eyes narrowed, a fan of wrinkles at each corner only adding to his attraction so far as Lily was concerned.

'The Clermont-Reads are in dire difficulties. They need some new form of income.'

'What concern is it of yours?'

'I am responsible.'

'Why?'

'Oh, I can't go into all that now, but I must help. I'm a Clermont-Read too. I'm Bertie's wife, remember?'

An infinitesimal flicker of the muscles about his mouth. 'Really? I'd quite forgotten.'

'Don't be cruel.'

'Have you taken him back into your bed then?'

Lily drew in a sharp breath, somehow not wanting to reveal Bertie's failure. 'You shouldn't ask. It's a private matter between husband and wife.'

'Damn you, Lily!'

She wanted to smooth the rigid line of his jaw, to put her arms about his neck and kiss him softly upon that disapproving mouth. Only then would the chill of jealousy leave his beloved face. But aware of the curious stares of the men in the yard below, she held back, confining herself to whispering fiercely beneath her breath, 'Oh, Nathan, don't be like this, please. You know that I have a duty towards Bertie.'

Very swiftly, and shielding her from his men by the width of his body, Nathan gripped her arm to pull her close as he hissed, equally fiercely, against her ear. 'My advice to you, Lily, is to face reality. It's time we *did* remember that Bertie is your husband. And if I recall correctly, he was once my best mate. He's been in a war and suffered enough. I can't go on cuckolding him. It isn't right. Either leave me alone or leave him and have done with all of this subterfuge. You can't have us both.'

'Nathan, I...'

'Good day, Mrs Clermont-Read.' He lifted her hand, and bestowed the softest kiss imaginable. 'It's your decision, Lily.'

Her eyelids fluttered. She was almost fainting with need. It was a wonder really that her legs were still supporting her. In that moment of longing every part of her cried out in surrender. She would leave Bertie. She would go to Nathan and live with him as his wife, his mistress, his lover ... whatever he asked. If she could only spend her life with him her happiness would be complete.

Before she could form the words, he let go of her hand and made an impatient sound, very like a growl. He knew that she would never leave Bertie. All he could do in consequence was hold on to his pride. 'As for this so-called business plan, I really couldn't stand for it, Lily. You can't seriously mean to set up in competition with me?'

'Very small competition.' She tried a smile, hoping he was teasing her.

'Make up your mind and leave the Clermont-Reads to their own well-deserved fate.'

'I've explained I can't do that. Not just yet.'

'Do as you please then. You always did know how to use people, I'll say that for you, Lily.'

She was outraged by his heartlessness, yet disguised her hurt as she flung angry words at him. 'Drat you, Nathan Monroe! I'll manage without your help then, thanks very much.'

'You do that.'

As a parting shot she told him that she would be far too busy to attend his launch. 'I've more important ways to spend my time.' She almost hated him as he stood rocking on his heels, laughing as she stamped down the stairs. But she didn't see how he then turned back into his office, sat at his desk and buried his head in his hands.

It was the nearest they'd come to a quarrel and Lily could hardly bear the agony. An offshore breeze lifted off her new straw hat and sent it skimming over the surface of the lake, the wind whipping her hair to a tangle as she sat in numb misery. What should she do? Money had to be made. The Clermont-Reads must be rescued from themselves. Perhaps Nathan was right and her idea really was stupid.

Surprisingly it was here, on the ferry, that she found the support she craved. 'You'd have to charge a fair whack.'

'I beg your pardon?'

'This idea o' your'n to earn a bob or two by taking out parties in the *Faith*. You'd need to charge quite a bit to make it pay. Offer good food. Make it exclusive like.'

'How did you know about my idea?'

Ferryman Bob settled to his rowing and gave a loud cackling laugh. 'You don't need to pay for no advertising with a voice as young and eager as yours. Carried clear as a bell right over that pier. I dare say everyone in Carreckwater will know of your business plan by this time. And believe you can do it.'

Lily found herself shame-faced but somehow encouraged by the old man's stout belief in her. 'Nathan didn't seem to think so.'

'More like he were seriously concerned you'd give his new company a run for its money. Throw a spanner in the works a bit, that would.' Old Bob chuckled.

Lily laughed out loud. 'Never!' But his words gave her pause for thought, and a part of her did wonder if perhaps Ferryman Bob might be right.

Lily stuck a home-made poster on the end of pier, right next to the place the Carreckwater ferry collected customers.

EXCLUSIVE LAKE PICNICS.
EXPLORE SECRET COVES AND ISLANDS
WHERE THE BIG STEAMERS CAN'T GO.

There followed details of times and starting-off point, with a little notepad and pencil attached to a string for customers to sign and book up.

Lily decided initially upon one sailing per day, each afternoon at three o'clock. George had willingly offered to be her engineer. Since several months back-wages were owed to him, it was in his best interests to cooperate.

Each day she took the ferry to check if anyone had signed. Annoyingly, she found the notice had disappeared, torn down by the wind no doubt. In the end she painted the details on to a board in shiny black letters – and hammered this into place with six-inch nails.

'Blow that away if you can.'

But the next day the notice had vanished yet again. 'Right! That's it.'

Once again Lily strode the length of the pier and up the steps to Nathan's office, heels clicking on the wooden boards, hands clenched into tight little fists as if she might very well pop one on anyone who stood in her way. Which, to be fair, no one did. Boatmen and fishermen scurried out of her way. Watching from his boat, Ferryman Bob grinned with pride.

'Our Lily is a fearsome sight, all right, when her dander is up,' he muttered, to no one in particular.

'Why blame me?' Nathan wanted to know, denying all knowledge of the missing signs and seeming to find it amusing. 'I'm not the only person round here to make my living from the lake. I think you're naive and foolish, Lily, but I'd do you no harm.'

She wanted to believe him. He looked so wonderful that she did believe him. They hadn't spoken for weeks and the agony of their quarrel was tearing her apart.

'Then tell whichever of these tykes is tearing down my notice that I have rights too, and if someone wants a fight, I'll give 'em one.'

'I believe you would.' He grinned at her so warmly that on impulse she had to kiss him quickly to prove she believed him.

'Oh, I've missed you, Nathan. Does this mean we're friends again?' she asked, eagerness in her voice.

But he did not gather her into his arms and kiss her again, as she so longed for him to do. Instead he said, 'You know what I want, Lily? An end to lies.'

She hurried away before she was tempted to agree. She replaced the sign and when she came the next day, it was still nailed to the post and four names had been scribbled on the notepad.

'Oh, joy! We're in business.'

The *Faith* had never looked more beautiful. She shone from stem to stern, every inch of brass glowing, every cushion plumped. Edward would have been proud of her, Lily thought. Betty had prepared a picnic that would, in her own estimation, 'Lay them out if they eat it all.'

'Better too much than too little, Betty. We need to impress. You will, of course, have to come and serve it. Only the very best on our steamer.'

'Oh, crikey. In me best uniform, you mean, with the boat's crest on the bib?' She grinned so much her cheeks plumped out like rosy apples.

'Over my dead body!' Margot stood on the neatly cut lawn before her beautiful house, glowering down at them as they loaded the yacht. She looked like a small round cannon ball which might at any moment explode.

George, stoking up and listening with satisfaction to the smooth swish of the pistons, was sorely tempted to sound the steam-whistle to see if she would, but managed to resist. Lily cast Margot an anxious glance, followed by a reassuring smile. Then she hopped out of the yacht and put a gentle hand on the woman's arm. It did indeed feel like iron, as rigid as her back-bone.

'I know it's painful, Margot, but we have to face reality. Edward is gone and we've to earn a living somehow.'

'Not using his boat for common trippers, you won't.'

Lily sighed, and though it went rather against the grain, offered what reassurance she could. 'I promise that we will take only the very best people. We're charging far too much for factory girls in any case.' Trying to bring a smile to those frozen features.

Margot turned her attention to George. 'Get off that boat this instant if you value your job, man. You too, Betty Cotley. Or you'll both collect your wages and leave my house this very minute.'

It was really perfectly dreadful, Lily thought, to see a woman of such pride robbed of her power. Neither Betty nor George moved a muscle, for both of them knew that there were no wages to collect, that whatever they did now was out of the goodness of their own hearts, and nothing whatsoever to do with Margot Clermont-Read. George, nodding rather sadly, said, 'Yes, ma'am,' and went back to his stoking. Betty scurried away into the depths of the boat, far removed from Margot's glare.

Lily patted her hand and climbed back on board.

'We have to go now. We'll talk about this later.' As the steam-yacht glided silently away from the shore, bound for its first paying expedition, Margot's furious screeching could still be heard, setting the cormorants flying from the trees in a frenzy of beating wings, and quite spoiling a sunny afternoon.

The expedition was a great success. It was a perfect day for steaming, with a clear blue sky and not a cloud in sight. The Humphreys, a delightful family from Carlisle, had the time of their lives on the lake.

They explored secret islands, guddled for trout in the shallows but sadly failed to catch any, and although they didn't completely empty Betty's hamper, declared they would not need to eat again for a week. Nor had they ever tasted such delicious smoked ham in all their lives. George, doubling as butler, poured the champagne – lemonade for the two younger Humphreys – and Lily talked about the scenery and history of the locality, ruthlessly exploiting Margot's many lectures which she'd been forced to endure in the past. She found she enjoyed the task, privately vowing to read up on more of Lakeland's history.

At the end of the two-hour sail the family were deposited back at the pier with an appeal that perhaps they might tell others how much they had enjoyed their trip.

'Indeed we will, Mrs Clermont-Read. Delightful, quite delightful.' They finished off the glories of the day with a substantial tip.

Nathan was standing at the end of the pier with his back to her and Lily couldn't resist running to tell him her good news. He turned quickly at the sound of her voice, a startled expression on his face, and she saw then that he was not alone. Selene was with him.

Selene looked angelic in lemon chiffon with a cleverly twisted scrap of fabric about her blonde curls which might have passed for a hat. A long straight feather protruded from the top of this to emphasise her regal height. The vivid picture she made, with her shining fair hair and red lips, caused Lily suddenly to feel altogether grubby and dowdy in Edward's old steam coat, no doubt with smuts of soot on her nose too.

Selene declared that she'd only called upon Nathan with a message from Marcus Kirkby.

'The dear man wishes to take all his workers for a steamer ride. He is so generous, you simply wouldn't believe.'

Lily hadn't even realised Nathan and Selene were speaking again. To her eyes the pair seemed decidedly jumpy, Nathan wearing his famous scowl as he so often did when on the defensive. But this fairy story had to be believed, however unlikely a benefactor Marcus Kirkby might seem, as Lily had no wish to give Nathan the satisfaction of seeing her display any jealousy.

She blundered in with her news, which now seemed to have fallen rather flat. They both smiled at her, benevolent, condescending, indulging her as if she were a small child seeking praise.

Before she was halfway through her tale, Selene interrupted. 'How very fortuitous that we should meet like this. So much nicer to take a ride home with you instead of that dreadfully slow ferry. Why the old man cannot get a modern one, I really can't imagine.'

'He enjoys rowing,' Lily said, but her mind was not on Ferryman Bob and his idiosyncrasies. Selene was already making impatient gestures, keeping her impeccable costume well away from Lily's grubby coat.

'Do stop prattling, Lily. I haven't all day.'

On their homeward journey, Lily struggled to listen while she chattered on about poor Mrs Kirkby and how she was more and more confined to a darkened room.

'Suffers dreadful pains in her spine, poor woman, resulting in the most debilitating headaches.'

'Is she good to you? What are your duties exactly?' The idea of Selene reading to an invalid, tending her every need, serving and carrying milk puddings, seemed beyond imagination. Certainly Lily's.

'Heavens, yes, I'm much more comfortable at Rosedale Lodge. I am Catherine's companion, not her servant, dear girl. You are welcome to draughty Barwick House and Mama's moods.' Selene's lips curved into a beatific smile and, fleetingly, Lily wondered what secrets lay behind it. Were those suspicions she'd had about her all that time ago right after all?

Later, as Selene disembarked at the folly and slipped out through the kissing gate, Lily could see a carriage waiting in the lane, and caught a glimpse of Marcus Kirkby. His frowning stare seeming to devour the distance between them, bringing an unexpected shiver to her spine. A very strange man indeed. Who knew what Selene was up to? Though really Lily had no wish to know. She was welcome to him.

So many secrets and lies.

Lily, of course, had secrets of her own, and had seriously underestimated Margot. Her mother-in-law's fortune may have diminished but not her vindictiveness.

She was waiting for Lily on her return, watching silently as she assisted Betty in gathering together the remains of the luncheon and instructed George on what time to have the yacht ready next day, always supposing there were some bookings.

But as the maid scuttled into the house and George made the *Faith* secure, Margot crossed the lawn with a gracious smile painted upon her plump face and Lily braced herself for a barrage of questions.

'I take it the day was a success?'

'Yes, indeed.' But before Lily could embark upon her tale, Margot grasped her arm between pincer-like fingers and hissed into her face. 'Continue with this shameful nonsense and I shall tell Bertie your dirty little secret. I doubt you would wish that to happen, in his delicate state of health.'

Stunned by this reminder of Margot's power, Lily could think of nothing by way of response. Yet hadn't she known the woman was a world expert at using information for her own benefit? The last thing Lily wanted was to hurt Bertie. Or abandon hope of one day finding happiness with Nathan.

'Do you hear me?'

'Yes, Margot, I hear you. But if you stop my cruises, which I see as the only way of earning our bread, not *shameful nonsense* at all, then how will you and your precious son survive? Why don't you tell me that?'

The next day, to Lily's great joy, there were several more signatures on the booking pad. The week was filling up nicely.

'It's going to work,' she told Margot later that afternoon, following a second and even more successful trip with a party of six this time.

'First thing in the morning, you will take the notice down.'

Summoning all the patience she could muster, anxious not to alienate her further, Lily made no comment. The boat belonged to Margot, after all, and the last thing Lily needed was to be denied the use of it.

'I really can't imagine what the ladies at the Yacht Club will think when they discover that I have gone into trade!'

Lily forbore to remind Margot that her own husband had earned their very substantial income over the years through trade. Since his death, though the house was still stuffed with items of considerable value, certainly in Lily's terms, cash was hard to come by and Margot would make no shift to help herself by selling any of the symbols of her success.

'They'll think that we're being enterprising, I expect,' Lily said, openly cheerful.

'Didn't you hear what I said to you yesterday?'

'I heard.' She decided to come clean. 'Look, Margot, I admit there are problems, but Bertie and I are doing our best to solve them.'

'Poppycock! I knew this marriage would be a disaster from the start. You're entirely the wrong woman for my darling child.'

'With all due respect, that is for Bertie to say and not you.'

'Have you given him up? This paramour of yours?'

'I think that's my business, not yours.'

'How dare you? Of course it is my business.'

'It is not.'

'Bertie is my son.'

'And my husband. What he needs right now is time. If you're prepared to risk hurting him after what he's been through, on your head be it. I shall not be held responsible. Heaven knows what effect such a revelation might have.'

Margot's eyes filled with sudden panic and Lily felt a rush of unexpected sympathy for her. She might very well have said something soothing at this point but there was a tap on the door and Betty entered bearing afternoon tea.

Ever uncomfortable before the servants, Margot sat straight-backed, staring stonily into space, for, much as she hated to admit it, the dratted girl did have a point. Bertie had been behaving exceedingly oddly lately. She certainly had no wish to be the one to tip him over the edge.

It was left to Lily to provide the necessary chit-chat as Betty set up the folding table for tea. 'Our clients enjoyed themselves thoroughly today. What's more, I see they've left us plenty of salmon pate. How wonderful.'

Margot's eyes darted to the heavily laden tray of goodies which even now Betty was setting before her.

Tea was poured in an awkward silence, then Betty sketched a curtsey, anxious to be back in the kitchen with her aching feet on the fender. 'Will there be anything more, ma'am?'

'No, thank you.' Lily reached for a slice of toast and started to spread it lavishly with butter and pate. 'That will do, Betty.

'I have every hope,' she continued, sharing a smile of amusement with Betty as she exited, 'that this summer will prove more profitable than we imagine. I only wish we had more boats.'

After grudgingly eating some pate, just to prove that she had not entirely forgiven Lily, Margot resumed her argument. 'My permission should have been sought before you embarked upon such an enterprise.'

'You're quite right, and I'm sorry. I was afraid you might refuse.'

'I most certainly would have done!'

Lily giggled. 'Just as well I didn't ask then.'

Margot glared and considered chastising this disrespectful daughter-in-law of hers. But the salmon tasted delicious, such a delight after the dreadfully dreary meals they'd been forced to endure lately, that she was already having second thoughts. She'd watch events closely, though Lily Thorpe had a habit of getting too big for her boots at times.

Probate would be settled soon and heaven knows what new horrors that would bring. Mr Groves had assured her that the house at least was safe but the income to run it, the vast sums of money which Edward had supplied for her to enjoy, was quite gone.

'We'll see how the business develops over these next weeks,' she conceded, dabbing at a speck of butter on her chin with her napkin. 'Then I will give you my decision on the matter.'

Smiling from ear to ear, Lily reached for a second slice of toast, suddenly desperately hungry for she'd been too excited to eat all day. 'Thank you, Margot. Perhaps we might have a glass of champagne with dinner, to celebrate the launch of our new business?'

Margot's eyes brightened. Now there was a rare treat. 'Perhaps we might,' she agreed.

That first season Lily's business went from strength to strength. There was nothing she loved more than to rise at first light and walk to the *Faith* while the dew was still wet on the grass and the lake lay mirror-calm save for the odd yacht or rowing boat fidgeting at its moorings.

George was usually the one who brought a wagonload of coal from the station yard each morning, but Lily was not above helping to shovel it into the bunker. On other days they might load wood – usually birch, as she remembered it had been Edward's favourite.

The first cruise of the day took place at eleven, so, once everything was ready, Lily would go into the house, wash and change, and take breakfast with Thomas. Always a lively meal, she would enjoy simply being his mother for a while. Bertie rarely joined them. Then she would leave Thomas in the hands of his new nanny for a few hours while she donned her skipper's hat and went to work, humming happily to herself.

A stylish lunch was provided for her guests in a wooded inlet or on some island or other, while Lily, George and Betty snatched a sandwich when they could. Most of their time was spent in keeping the clients happy, pointing out dippers, coot, cheeky grey wagtails or Britain's smallest grebe, the dabchick, swimming shyly underneath banks. Or laughing at the acrobatics of a red squirrel banging away at a nut wedged in a nearby tree.

The visitors, often city folk, enjoyed these diversions.

The afternoon party usually took a longer trip, leaving at three and returning by five. It was a lovely leisurely way of life but never for a moment did Lily forget that these people and this boat were in her care. The lake was over eighty feet deep in places and cold enough to kill in minutes, even in midsummer. She acquired from the stalwart George the skills of steering, learning how to turn the *Faith* to meet the wash from other boats, negotiate a landing in wind, and how a steam engine responds instantly to the controls, giving full power at the first movement. She learned the unwritten laws of the lake, such as who has right of way, where currents made it unsafe to steam, and how two steamers must not pass each other in the narrows between islands.

On the days when a squally wind brought five foot waves capped with white foam and she could not take the boat out, Lily would chafe and fidget restlessly. Not simply because of the loss of revenue but because this had become her own private world and she loved it.

On one such day when she was confined to barracks, as she put it, Lily spent hours in an overheated kitchen preparing a dish of fudge, with her own hands this time, for Hannah and Arnie.

As she stirred the sticky sweet mixture, the smell of it brought to mind happy days in her mother's kitchen and she recalled with nostalgia the closeness she'd once enjoyed with her family. Now her own father had barred her from his house.

In her heart it did not surprise her. She had seen the knowledge of her affair in every curious eye whenever she walked out, heard the whispers as she passed by. Whether the gossip had reached her husband, Lily couldn't rightly say. But she hadn't set eyes on Nathan for months. Didn't that count for anything?

It was almost a relief that Bertie seemed to spend most of his time sitting in Edward's study with a glass of his father's best whisky at his elbow, staring blankly out the window, though it broke Lily's heart to see him that way.

He looked exactly the same. Sandy hair, soft brown eyes, round boyish face. But he was not the same. The joy in him was quite dead. He never laughed, never joked, never even smiled, except with little Thomas. And though she well knew the time was coming to be honest with her husband, fear of his response kept her silent. Such a revelation would do nothing to restore the spirits of this dear man who was her husband.

To hurt Bertie might tip him over the precipice to which he clung. Lily couldn't do it, not until he was perfectly himself again. But nor could she contemplate living the rest of her life without Nathan. Hadn't she lost enough loved ones already? First Dick, then Emma, and then her own precious Amy, the pain of which she still nursed like an aching tooth.

It was certainly true that rumours had ruined her relationship with her family. She would dearly love to heal the breach. But how?

Lily wrapped the fudge in greaseproof paper and took it to Ferryman Bob, who was to be her emissary.

'Please say, to my father's face if you can, that although I may find it hard at times, and am still falling a little by the wayside, I am trying to be respectable and responsible. My own person.'

He asked her to repeat this until he had carefully learned it off by heart, since she refused to write them down. 'That would be too formal,' Lily insisted. But he took her message willingly enough, without truly comprehending it.

She sat by the folly all the next day hoping for a reply. None came.

Chapter Twenty-Three

Winter came, holding the lake in its iron grip, an Arctic spectacle of icicles falling from every fence and tree, great banks of snow blocking the lanes and shrouding the woodlands in a sparkling canopy of white. Lily found herself growing restless from being confined so much indoors and when one day the sun came out, glinting blue-white on a fresh fall of snow, causing the ice-bound lake to glitter as if studded with diamonds, she begged Bertie to take a walk with her.

Obediently he came. He never refused her anything. 'Come and eat, Bertie dear,' she would say, and he would eat. 'Do come and sit with me, Bertie, and we'll read the newspaper together,' and he would come and listen as she read. But even during his favourite occupation of walking, he rarely smiled and never instigated any conversation on his own account.

This day proved to be different. Perhaps it was the freezing air, or the exhilaration of being outdoors again after the monotonous routine of life within Margot's over-stuffed rooms. Or the mystical glories of the ice-bound mountains glimmering enticingly in the morning sun.

He trekked happily through the thick drifts of snow with her, very nearly laughed when she tossed a snowball at him, and even tossed one back at her. She urged him to help make a snowman for Thomas and he did so, lending it his bright red scarf and woolly hat.

Lily watched with joy as something seemed to unfurl and blossom within him. It came slowly at first, his smiles stiff and unnatural. And if most of this newborn pleasure was derived largely from the lake, what of it? Frozen white from shore to shore, he told her how rarely this occurred over the years. 'Though it happens more often with the smaller lakes, like Carreckwater. People have been known to hold parties and dances upon it.'

'I doubt we'll risk it, Bertie.'

'We could go skating.'

'It might not be thick enough.'

'Thomas would love it.'

'He might drown if the ice breaks.'

But the old reckless light was back, however momentarily, in the brown velvet eyes. 'Have you ever had a ride on an ice yacht, Lily?'

She laughed. 'You know I haven't.'

'I used to do it all the time when I was a boy. You must try it, this very day. We'll check, but I'll swear the ice is thick enough along this eastern section, and there's just the right amount of wind.'

How could she refuse? He looked so bright and happy, almost his old jolly self. Lily felt a weight lift from her heart to see the anguish banished from his eyes, for even one day. 'Not Thomas, though. He's far too young.'

'I'm not, I'm not!' But though the probe Bertie pushed into the ice told of a good thickness, Thomas was placed firmly in Betty's arms and only allowed to watch Mummy and Daddy sail up and down on the ice yacht. Though he jumped up and down with excitement and shouted, 'Let me, let me,' his pleas fell upon deaf ears.

The ice heaved and squeaked alarmingly as the flat-bottomed yacht with its metal runners sped over its surface, tacking into a strong headwind, skirting the rocky base of Hazel Holme and bumping terrifyingly over frozen waves till they reached a smoother stretch and could swing about.

'Isn't it wonderful?' Bertie yelled.

'It's freezing. I can't feel my face. Is it still there?' Laughing, he told her that it must be because her nose glowed like a beacon in the middle of it. Then, daringly, Bertie reached over to kiss her as she struggled to change sides before they turned about. It was the first time he had touched her in months.

'Don't you dare,' she scolded. 'You'll have us both over.' She shuddered at the memory of another accident so long ago. A lifetime?

'You're my beautiful ice maiden,' he yelled above the scrape of blades and the roar of the wind. 'What a sport you are, Lily.'

'I'm not made of ice at all,' she shouted back. 'I'm a warm-blooded woman, and I need thawing out.'

They stopped frequently to fortify themselves with steaming hot cups of coffee, enjoying the happiest afternoon ever. With one small chubby hand clutched in each of theirs, they took Thomas out for a trial skate on a very safe thick corner of the ice. Oh, and didn't he love it? The little boy was pink with excitement by the time Betty took him inside for hot chocolate and his nap. A perfect family day.

Bertie said, 'I thought I might start designing again soon. Then I mean to build a power boat this summer while you're busy with your little business.'

Swallowing the protest that her 'little' business was meant to keep them, Lily merely smiled encouragement. 'That would be wonderful.' Perhaps soon, she thought, he would also be ready to talk, and then surprised her by doing so there and then.

'Sorry I've been such a silly ass, Lily.'

'You haven't.'

'Made a bit of a pickle of our marriage, eh? Must have driven you demented. All that nonsense with Rose and then Nan.'

'Nan?' The shock of this new information caused a trickle of cold sweat to run between her breasts. Not Nan as well. How could he? Bertie looked discomfited, hardly able to meet the expression of disappointment in her eyes. 'I was grieving, as you were, after we lost little Amy. Couldn't quite get a grip on things, don't you know?'

'Oh, Bertie.' Lily remembered Ferryman Bob mentioning how he'd ferried him back and forth quite a lot at that time. She'd paid little attention. Now she saw where Bertie had found his consolation, in a life of debauchery. She couldn't help but shudder at the thought, and Bertie couldn't help but notice.

He shuffled his feet like a naughty schoolboy, wondering how he could explain to her about his feelings of uselessness. How he'd suffered his own sense of loss and guilt for his beloved child. And how later, in London, he'd kicked over the traces good and proper, not wanting to face the future. Preferring to punish himself by living with the lowest of the low because of bitter feelings of inadequacy. No, he couldn't tell her all of that.

'I'm no good, old thing. Don't deserve you, my lovely Lily.' His voice was mournful, sad. 'The likes of Nan are all I'm fit for now.'

What could she say? Was this the moment to call an end to this mockery of a marriage? Dare she simply agree that she too was far from innocent, that they had married for the wrong reasons and, fond though she was of him, that was no basis for a lifetime together? 'I don't blame you, Bertie,' she managed, and her heart softened as he grinned with relief.

'Should've known you'd understand, old thing.'

Lily knew she should explain that she loved Nathan. She wanted an end to this farce so she could be with him. But Bertie was saying that at least they were still good friends, that they could surely start again.

'But…'

'We'll give it a try. What d'you say?' Taking her agreement for granted, he urged her back on to the ice to skate further out, now that Thomas had gone.

'Bertie…' she began, but got no further as an all too familiar figure emerged from behind snow laden holly bushes. 'Nathan?' She felt as if her eyes were playing tricks on her, forming a mirage out of the ice. But, no, he was real enough.

Bertie said, 'Ah, there you are, old chap. At last. Thought you were never coming over to see me. Didn't you hear I was home?'

The two men in Lily's life now stood face to face, considering each other. Bertie in his plus fours, Fair Isle sweater and peaked cap, and Nathan less stylishly attired in fisherman's jumper and dark trousers tucked into his boots.

In that moment it occurred to Lily that although Bertie had been home for several months, he'd never thought to call on his one-time friend either. She knew, of course, why Nathan had not come to see Bertie. But why had Bertie not gone to see him? She looked into her husband's face and saw the reason. It made her heart jump. Dear God, he knew. It was written there, plain as plain in his brown eyes.

Yet he sought a fresh start for them both. He'd accepted her forgiveness as if by right. Would he now offer his? Lily wished she could read his sad, injured mind.

Bertie opened his gold cigarette case and held it out. 'Got no Turkish left old chap. Only gaspers, I'm afraid.'

Nathan declined and, turned to Lily. 'You look half frozen. Why don't you go inside and leave Bertie and me to chat about old times?'

Nothing would have induced her to leave them alone together at that moment. Lily gave a brittle little laugh which sounded false even to her own ears. 'Why don't we all go in and have a hot toddy?'

'No, no,' Bertie protested. 'Nathan hasn't had a skate yet. Care for a race, old boy?'

Nathan met his shrewd gaze and gave a half-smile. 'Why not?'

'A mile down the lake and back, and jump the gap. What d'you say?'

The blood drained from Lily's already pale face. Close to the centre of the lake a current ran too fast to freeze and several feet of open water cut through the ice. 'The gap? You can't seriously mean to try...'

'Why not? Bit of a lark, eh? Nathan ain't afraid of taking a risk, are you, old boy? Get away with anything, he can. Luck of the devil, don't you know?' Grinning at his rival. 'Best man takes all?'

'Right,' Nathan said, in his softest voice. Unusually for them both, they didn't lay down a bet. But Lily recognised they were talking of more than a race.

Lily watched with her heart in her mouth. She couldn't believe this was happening. Why had Nathan accepted such a foolish challenge? Why had Bertie issued it? But she knew the answer, only too well. A reckless passion burned in them both, showing itself in the grim set of their faces, in every line of their straining bodies.

Skates were put on and adjusted, a distance set and agreed. 'Down the eastern side as far as the folly, then swing into the centre of the lake, jump the gap, and cross to the western shore.'

'That tall beech as the finishing post?'

'Agreed.'

'This is madness,' she said, trying one last time to stop them. 'How will you ever get back?'

'Walk around the lake, silly.'

Lily was instructed as to how to start them off. How to time them with Bertie's pocket watch. How to wave her handkerchief in acknowledgement when the first one crossed the finishing line. She couldn't even think of finishing lines. Her eyes were riveted upon the swiftly running ribbon of black water that marked the centre of the lake.

Bertie didn't kiss her as he set off. Neither man asked her to wish him luck, nor begged for a favour as the knights of old might have done. But it was a similar contest, all the same.

They started slowly, muscles straining, arms swinging, Nathan's balance less certain than Bertie's because of his stiff arm. Little by little they gathered pace and the two figures rapidly diminished as they sped away. She wanted to call them back, to wake as if from a deep sleep and find this all a nightmare.

They skated on, strong and determined.

It was perfectly clear to Lily's anxious eyes that each was putting everything he had into the race. Whatever the outcome it must be seen through to its conclusion. Though they looked like two dolls skimming swiftly away over the frozen ice, they were men, filled with anger and the desire for revenge: Bertie because of his wife's betrayal, and Nathan because he believed Lily had been treated badly.

Nothing she could say now would bring them back. She called their names anyway, just in case, but the wind tossed her voice carelessly back.

Lily had never felt so alone. The silence of the lake was broken only by the swish of blades against ice, the whisper of the wind in the trees. A dozen sensations and questions fought for supremacy in her mind. Would they be safe? Would the ice hold? Which one would win? More to the point, which one did she want to win? And if one fell ... But she could not take this thought any further.

One moment Nathan was ahead by a fraction, the next it would be Bertie. The distance to the gap was lessening and the nearer they got to it, the thinner the ice was. Lily could hardly bear to look, daren't even breathe.

They were almost upon it. Nathan reached it first and took off, leaping, legs splayed, high into the air. For an endless, heart splitting second that seemed like a lifetime he hung perilously over the rushing black water. Almost at the same instant Bertie too leaped the gap which from this distance appeared thin and narrow though Lily knew it to be five or six foot wide at least, and deadly. Then with a loud crack Nathan's blades touched the ice, skidded, rocked, swerved a little. He was safe. It needed only for Bertie to land and the agony would be over.

Something was happening. Whether it was Bertie coming down too close to Nathan, or Nathan losing his balance she couldn't quite tell, but even from this distance Lily could hear the ice splintering.

Selene had been keeping a disdainful eye upon the activity on the frozen lake as she sipped her tea in the little parlour. She was furious that Margot had forbidden her the satisfaction of revenge upon her trollop of a sister-in-law, despite the obvious goings-on which she would have loved to tell Bertie about. Yet because of his precarious state of health, she had been ordered not to.

Certainly he'd been behaving rather oddly lately. He was suffering endless headaches, moody depressions, and frequently talking to himself. He drank too much, and had recently taken to walking out late in the night, or so servant gossip informed her.

Gossip. There was another cross she had to bear. All Selene could do was to bite her tongue and suffer in silence. She'd become increasingly aware of whispers and pitying glances following her wherever she went. They saw her as the spurned woman, unwanted and cast-off in favour of another. The fact that the other woman in the case had been her own sister-in-law only made the humiliation worse. Yet there was nothing she could do about it.

She quailed at the prospect of facing her thirtieth birthday next year, still unwed. Had anyone warned her of such a fate at twenty-one, Selene was quite sure she would have expired from shock. Planning with Mama which suitor she might favour had once been a favourite sport. Now her last chance had been spoiled by Lily. A fact she intended never to forget. If she could find some means to get her own back, she would most certainly do so.

Meanwhile her mother's little tea-parties had become a veritable minefield of question and innuendo.

Mrs Philip Linden, once the insipid Lucy Rigg, now a young matron of means and mother of four children, was at this very moment pressing her hand and stifling a manufactured tear as she softly enquired how 'dear Selene' did these days.

'I do very well, thank you,' Selene responded, not rising to the implied request for a confidential exchange. At least she had the satisfaction of knowing this to be perfectly true, even if her life had not proceeded in quite the direction she had expected.

She and Marcus had developed a most satisfactory routine in which caring for his wife took very little part. This chore could largely be left to the servants, though Catherine's presence provided the cover of respectability which they needed. Privately Selene dreamed of a day when his wife was no longer a feature in their lives. But since Catherine was still a relatively young woman, and for all her aches and pains surprisingly resolute in taking excessive care of herself, there seemed little prospect of such an event in the foreseeable future.

However, there were certainly compensations to be enjoyed in the meantime.

Marcus had taken to sleeping in a private bedchamber, for the 'increased comfort' of his ailing wife. Catherine had not objected and Selene often wondered how much she guessed or if she heard footsteps creeping along the corridor each night.

'It must be so stifling for you, being at the beck and call of an invalid all the time. Poor you.' Lucy's strident voice broke into her thoughts.

'Not at all. I am her friend, not her servant. Catherine is a most untroublesome creature and I do have access to Marcus's Daimler, complete with chauffeur to take me about.'

Lucy looked momentarily nonplussed by this piece of upstaging. Even her own dear Philip couldn't run to such magnificence.

'How lovely. Although motors are such dreadfully noisome machines, are they not? Simply shrouding the landscape of the Lakes in clouds of dust.' It was the best put-down she could devise for a machine she'd give her eye-teeth to possess.

Sophie Dunston, fiddling with her spectacles and talking through her adenoids, fervently agreed. 'Almost as bad as women smoking. Quite dreadful.'

Selene, who had recently taken up this pastime, gritted her teeth and smiled. 'Oh, I don't know, a puff of a Turkish can be most satisfying.' How she loved the expression of shock on their faces. If these excessively proper ladies disapproved of fast motor cars and cigarettes, what would they have to say about her more nefarious diversions? she wondered, recalling the panting, thrashing figure of Marcus in her bed last night. There were indeed many compensations in her life, even if there were still one or two matters left unsettled. Selene gazed upon them with a pitying condescension, not least on her own mother who suffered such disappointment on her behalf.

Margot was at this moment sitting tight-lipped while Edith Ferguson-Walsh went boring on at length about how 'darling Dora' was soon to be married to a French businessman who owned two large hotels in Paris.

'So romantic. They met when Dora was recuperating after her illness. He's terribly rich and the entire family is to be invited to stay for a whole *week* for the wedding.'

'How very splendid,' Margot drily remarked, inwardly fuming at the way such a dull, plump creature as Dora could strike so lucky.

When the little tea-party was thankfully over and Selene stood by as Betty helped the ladies on with their furs and wraps, Lucy bent close to whisper yet more words of comfort.

'I do think you've had an awfully lucky escape. Did you hear how poor Captain Swinbourne has died in poverty after going to live with his sister in Harrogate? And we know who we can blame for that, do we not?'

'Do we?' Yet more gossip.

'My dear, he was not exactly old, was he, the poor man? Nor suffering from ill health so far as I'm aware. Though they do say he was an inveterate gambler.'

'Indeed?'

'A weakness taken full advantage of by that dreadful man.'

'Do you mean Nathan Monroe?'

'Who else? Worked his way up from ticket-collector through deck-hand to manager and then bought the company off Swinbourne. Though how else he came by the money if not through gambling I wouldn't care to speculate. Really, dear Selene, you should thank your sister-in-law for taking him off your hands.'

'And what about my poor brother?'

Lucy had the grace to flush and, hastily kissing the air inches from Selene's cheek, prepared to depart. 'I really must dash. The children will be needing me and Philip does so hate it when I'm away too long. Unlike you, I am not a lady of leisure. Dear me, no.' A smile of triumph and a gentle tilt of her pretty head as she swirled out of the door on a breeze of Ashes of Roses.

Selene stood on the doorstep, grim-faced, while all the ladies climbed aboard their gigs. George directed the resultant traffic jam into some order along the drive, and the clip-clop of horses' hooves, muffled by sacking wraps to prevent them slithering about on the ice, died slowly away. Her last thought before preparing herself to face Margot's usual post-mortem on the afternoon was that if money came so easily to Nathan Monroe, she could only hope that he would just as easily lose it.

Margot, however, at that precise moment, had other matters on her mind. Not wishing to brave the icy blast of the chill outdoors, she had sunk upon her favourite window seat to watch the departure of her guests through the window. From here she could also see the entire frozen expanse of the lake.

Though she could not with certainty make out the identity of the two figures, her mother's instinct told her that one of them must be Bertie. Who else but her own beloved son could skate so well, or have the nerve to take part in such a reckless act? Nor did she need to puzzle over why he was on the ice, risking life and limb in that crazy fashion, or who was to blame for his being there.

She saw the two figures collide and instantly let out a howl which grew in volume as she ran out into the snow until it was a full-blooded scream for George, for Betty, for Selene – and in particular, at that dreaded moment of possible loss, for Edward.

They were all in the kitchen, Betty and Lily bustling about with hot kettles, whisky and fragrant fresh coffee while the two men sat swathed in blankets and towels.

'I can't believe you could be so stupid,' Margot was saying, in her fiercest, no-nonsense voice. 'What were you thinking of to permit them to be so foolish? Bertie might well have been killed out there.'

It was, of course, to Lily that she directed this furious accusation. Yet Lily made no move to defend herself against Margot's rage. She didn't have the strength, for she too had never felt so angry in all her life. It was the only way to express intense relief.

'Dash it, we weren't killed, Mama. We're fine and dandy. Anyway, that's what life's all about, ain't it, Nathan, old chap? Risk. Ah, coffee. You're an angel, Betty. Sorry, even my gaspers are soaking wet.'

Lily found her voice at last. 'For goodness' sake, Bertie, what do a few cigarettes matter? Margot is right, you could've lost your lives out there. Nathan nearly did.'

Bertie looked at her, an oddly mournful expression on his boyish face. 'I wouldn't have let him drown, Lily. I saved him, didn't I?' She half expected him to add, 'for you', and was grateful that he didn't. Instead he turned to Nathan with a grin. 'We're even now, old chap, eh?'

Lily paused in shaking mustard powder into two deep bowls of hot water. 'Even? What d'you mean, even? This hasn't happened before, has it?'

'Dear heaven,' said Margot, collapsing into a chair and sending Betty scurrying for smelling salts for the second time in months. 'He means,' Nathan quietly explained, 'that I saved him from drowning when we were fishing that time.'

'That's right.' Bertie grinned. 'What a lark that was. One minute I was catching a whopper, the next I was in the drink. Would have copped it if it hadn't been for Nathan's quick action in pulling me out. So you see, Lily, old thing, we know how to look after each other.'

She looked from one to other of them and wondered, just for a fleeting second, if that were true. But they both looked so innocent it must be. Quite incomprehensible, the pair of them.

Lily was haunted by the incident. She had to admit that Margot was right for once. One of them could have died out there, and the fault would have been entirely hers. But because of Bertie's precarious state of health, and not least her own sense of guilt, she made no further comment upon the subject. They understood each other perfectly. Life would go on as usual.

She would concentrate on being a good and faithful wife to Bertie, even if he hadn't behaved quite as a good and faithful husband himself. To cheat on her with Rose was bad enough, and then with Nan as well was appalling. She couldn't bear to imagine what he'd got up to in London during all those long months after the war. Nor would she ever ask. Lily supposed she should make allowances. As Nathan said, he'd come home alive and in one piece.

Having made up her mind to stick by Bertie, it seemed imperative that Nathan should stay away. The last thing she needed was for him and Bertie to take up their old friendship. She wrote him a brief but painfully clear note.

It was obligingly delivered by the faithful Betty who carefully managed to cloak her avid curiosity.

She handed the letter to a grim-faced Nathan and scurried quickly away, not wanting to answer any questions. The affair was obviously over.

The ice finally melted and a cold winter passed into a cool spring. Saffron and gold leaves hung like flecks of fire on the black claws of still-bare trees. But elsewhere pink buds were appearing on the horse chestnuts. Bright pussy willow starred the curving bays and wooded inlets. Soon the ragged grasses on the steep hillsides would blaze with golden gorse. Change was in the air.

One day the sun would shine warmly, the next a bitter wind would blow. Rather in tune with Lily's emotions.

Little had changed in her marriage. Bertie still occupied the small dressing room, for which she was truly grateful. They continued to live their separate lives while keeping up the facade of a happy married life.

Lily threw herself into her work, anxious to keep her mind occupied rather than lingering over what might have been. Even so her eyes kept searching the horizon for any sight of Nathan, her ears constantly attuned for the sound of his voice reverberating over the water when he was out in one of his steamers. But he kept away, as she had requested.

In other ways, at least, life was improving. Money was easier, debts were slowly being settled, one by one, and suppliers were again happy to attend Barwick House. But by the end of that second summer of her operation, Lily still felt far from secure. Another long winter lay ahead which would prove a great strain on their savings with no money coming in.

She spoke about this problem to Ferryman Bob. 'What next, Bob? The *Faith* is doing well enough, but I'm not sure how much longer we can cope.'

To Ferryman Bob the answer seemed obvious. 'Thee needs another boat, Lily.'

'I suppose I do, but where from?' And then she remembered the talks she had enjoyed with Edward. '*Kaspar!*'

'What?'

'*Kaspar.* That was the name of Edward's freight boat. The one he scuttled.'

'A cargo boat won't make any money on the lake these days. The roads are getting better all the time and folk use cars and trucks and lorries now. Even the *Raven* on Windermere is coming to the end of her working life.'

A spark of unexpected excitement lit within her. 'But she was a fine boat! Edward said so. His treasure, he called her. She could be restored, altered in some way, perhaps used for some other purpose. Couldn't we find her and bring her up?'

He looked stunned. 'By heck, that sounds like a tall order.'

'But not impossible?'

Bob grinned. 'Naught's impossible, isn't that what they say? It just takes a bit longer.'

Chapter Twenty-Four

1921

It took the best part of two months. They first had to find where the *Kaspar* had settled, fortunately in a reasonably shallow part of the lake since Edward hadn't the heart to scuttle her in deep water. She lay deep in mud, the water a good foot above the cabin roof and they set about pulling her out. Half a dozen men were engaged to carry out the work, standing in six or seven feet of water, soaking wet and freezing cold despite their gum-boots and waterproofs.

'She's not going to be easy to lift,' Ferryman Bob said, shaking his head.

'But you promised we could do it,' Lily reminded him.

The boat had first to be sealed with steel plating and clay, then the sludge which had collected inside was pumped out by hand: a long and tedious task. To Lily, standing beside them in the glutinous mud and silt, it seemed little short of a miracle. As the boat was relieved of its burden it began, very gently at first, to rise. The men slid ropes underneath the keel and hauled on them until she finally floated to the surface, spewing out a pound or two of trout and char as she came.

Everyone was laughing and kissing and whooping with joy.

It was the end of October. All their grim and filthy work had been rewarded at last. The boat was caked with mud and weed, filthy beyond comprehension, gunwales awash, and already Lily was worrying over whether the timbers would hold, and whether she could afford the enormous cost required to restore her.

She was much bigger than Lily had expected. Bob measured her length at sixty-five feet, and nearly twelve in the beam. Some of her ribs were soft but most were reasonably sound. The funnel from the fire box was missing, and the boiler looked to be in a sorry state. They bailed her out, scrubbed and hosed her down, and by the time she was hauled on to dry land, Lily almost despaired at the amount of work that still lay ahead.

'Do you reckon my father would help?' she asked Ferryman Bob as they sat on the small jetty, viewing their handiwork. They were eating their sandwiches and taking a welcome breather.

He shook his head, eyes sad. 'I've already asked him. When I took round that bit o' fudge.'

Lily's heart clenched. 'What did he say?'

'I don't recall exactly.'

'Yes, you do.'

The old man looked embarrassed but Lily insisted, finally gave in. 'If you must know, he said he had no daughter by that name.'

The sandwich dropped from her fingers. Never, in all her life, had she imagined being entirely cast adrift by her own family. 'I see.' Which of course she did. Would they believe her if she now told them she'd given up Nathan for good? Only was it even true? Did she still privately hope for her marriage to fail so she could rush back into his arms? Wasn't that exactly what she would do right now if she didn't feel so desperately sorry for Bertie?

The engine was taken to pieces and cleaned. The cylinder heads were taken off and found to be good, with remarkably little sign of rust, as were the piston rings. Some parts were missing or broken and local craftsmen had to be found to mend them or fashion new. Often these were men who worked at the quarry and knew about steam engines. *Kaspar's* had been well greased before she sank so were soon in fine fettle again. But it all took time and Lily fretted that the boat wouldn't be ready for the start of the next season in May.

The boiler was sent away to be overhauled and strengthened, and while Ferryman Bob and George worked hard on the engine, Lily scrubbed and scoured and cleaned with Thomas alongside her. The little boy loved every minute of it since it meant he could get dirty without being scolded. With the boat chocked up on wedges and bogeys, it was possible to reach every part of her hull. Lily and

George scraped her clean, then coated her with oils and preservatives. This treatment had to be repeated at two-weekly intervals throughout the winter, letting it soak deep into the timbers to do its work. In the spring they would paint her, good as new.

'She looks better already,' Lily announced with pride.

'She'll need to dry out slow like. You can't rush a job like this,' Ferryman Bob warned. ''But she's a fine ship, pine on oak. She'll do.'

Lily became obsessed. She spent every hour she could on the boat. She carefully carried away any loose pieces of timber or fragments from the cabin or deck and laid them out in Edward's old boathouse to treat them there. Putting the jigsaw back together would, she reckoned, be something of a nightmare.

In addition she'd require a complete refit with a smart saloon if she was to carry passengers. Who could do that for her? And how much would it all cost?

Lily gathered all her courage and went to call on her father.

Arnie was not at home and Lily was ashamed to feel instant relief. Hannah at least welcomed her, made a jam sandwich for her grandson and gave him a bag of buttons to play with. She made no comment when Lily attempted to explain, without giving details of any kind, or naming any names, that she and Bertie had sorted things out and matters were improving between them.

'I'm glad to hear it.' Hannah had her arms wrapped about herself in that familiar disapproving manner.

Lily hurried on to outline her plans for restoring the boat. 'I need a saloon, Mam, with walnut panelling, plush seats, the lot. Only I haven't got much money. I thought Dad might help.'

'You must've been busy.'

'Yes.' She was exhausted. Lily slept the sleep of the dead each night, which was a blessing in itself, but where she would find the energy to complete her task, she really couldn't imagine.

'I wouldn't recommend you spend more time on them boats than you do with Bertie, in view of your difficulties,' Hannah warned. 'Could be a bad mistake.'

'We need to make money.'

'That's for your husband to do, surely?'

Lily was silent. She'd entirely failed to persuade Bertie to help. He refused all her entreaties on this matter. Instead he'd spent the winter back in his old ways of lazing about and drinking too much.

'I thought you loved boats,' she'd said, to no avail. Lily even found herself extolling the benefits of fresh air and exercise until he told her sharply that she was not his nurse and he'd do as he pleased. So she gave up.

Lily was beginning to wonder if perhaps Edward had been right to have so little faith in his son – a bleak thought. Bertie's mood swings continued to be difficult. Now she called to Thomas, who'd been investigating the glories of the under-stairs cupboard, and said her goodbyes.

'Ask Dad to come over, will you? I really could do with his help.'

'I'll speak to him, but I can't promise aught.'

Lily was far too tired to quarrel with anyone. She waited two weeks then reluctantly swallowed the last of her pride and stood before her mother-in-law, begging for a loan. She asked if perhaps there might be something in the overstuffed house which Margot could sell to fund the enterprise, promising a proper rate of interest in return. There was outrage, of course, at the very suggestion, denial there was anything of real value, but when Lily pointed out that she would then no longer be in a position to finance Margot's little treats and new frocks, a miraculous change of heart took place. Two Chinese vases and a few Dresden pieces were sold for a good price.

Lily found a carpenter to make the saloon and do the refit. It wouldn't be as good a job as Arnie would have done, and no doubt would cost twice as much, but what else could she do? If Bertie wouldn't help her, if her own father wouldn't help her, there was an end of the matter.

The new saloon was in the best traditional style with swagged silk curtains, plush seats and crimson carpets. A fringed canopy was erected on deck, beneath which a wind-up gramophone reposed on a table beside comfortable basket chairs, in readiness for picnics and dance parties. The paintwork shone in brilliant white with maroon trim, brass fittings and walnut panelling were polished to perfection.

'Isn't she beautiful?' Lily smoothed her hands over the cool wood, then put them to her own flushed cheeks, as proud as if she'd just given birth.

'Aye, she's right bonny,' Ferryman Bob agreed, searching frantically for a cigarette in the folds of his cap to help calm his nervousness. 'I hope that engine works.'

'She will.'

Everything was set ready. The boiler had been re-installed and filled with water. Wood, being kinder on the system as it was so clean and left little ash, was stacked ready in the bunkers. Pumps and valves had been checked; every nut, screw and bearing greased and cleaned. There was nothing to be done now but pray.

They all gathered on the jetty, despite a chill wind, on this momentous day. George and Betty were there, and Margot holding tightly to Thomas's hand. Even Bertie stood some distance away, feigning disinterest.

'What you going to call her then?' Ferryman Bob wanted to know.

There was only one possible answer. 'Lakeland Lily,' she said, smiling with delight. 'What else?'

The official launch was to be in a few weeks' time, at the end of May, but first must come the trial run.

Lakeland Lily was rolled down to the lake on bogeys. Both Ferryman Bob and Lily had gone over her inch by inch, checking for signs of any leak. There were none. She floated. She sat sound and stable in the water, looking bigger somehow, almost majestic.

Lily was the one to open the main steam valve, letting the engine warm through, just to be on the safe side. She held her breath. Would it turn? Would there be any last minute hiccups? With a hiss of steam the engine came slowly to life and the boat slid slowly, almost regally, forward. Everybody cheered. Thomas was almost sick with excitement and Lily felt sure this must be the most exciting moment of her life.

Now they could go ahead with planning the official launch. Margot was prevailed upon to send invitations to all her friends, which she did with ill grace and much grumbling about what on earth they would think of such a mad-cap scheme. Lily invited Hannah and Arnie, sadly aware that they wouldn't come, for, after debating long and hard with herself, she also invited Nathan.

Her agonising proved unnecessary since he politely but coolly declined. It hurt Lily beyond words that, for all they were no longer lovers, he refused to attend the launch even as a friend to wish her well. But since she'd refused to go to his launch, what could she say?

Perhaps carried along by this wave of joyous achievement, Betty and George decided finally to tie the knot and settle into matrimony, though not entirely with Margot's blessing.

'I do hope this doesn't mean you will be leaving us, Betty?' The war had done nothing, in Margot's opinion, to ease the servant problem.

'No, ma'am.' Betty shifted her aching feet in their sensible brown brogues and assured her mistress that she would be staying, having half expected to be turned out without a reference. 'Not for the moment, anyroad.'

'What do you mean, not for the moment? With two million unemployed, where else would you find a job?' As if she personally paid Betty's wages.

When it was blushingly explained that Betty may have to change her plans if she were to fall pregnant, an utterly scandalised Margot considered the girl with new eyes.

Plain almost past redemption, with her shiny plump cheeks, bright eyes and country-mouse brown hair held in place by a maid's cap worn low over a broad flat forehead, it was hard to imagine Betty inflaming anyone's passion, let alone that of good looking George.

'We'll discuss that particular matter on another occasion,' her mistress sternly informed her, as if George would need her written permission before he dare embark upon the idea of fatherhood. 'For now be thankful I've agreed to approve this fancy of yours for matrimony.'

'Oh, I am that, ma'am. George is too. Right grateful we are.'

Margot sniffed. 'You will live in his flat over the stables, I dare say?'

'If you please, ma'am.'

'Hm. I trust you have saved well for this marriage?'

'Oh, yes, ma'am.' Betty had been saving for little else for years. All through the war, in her stolid way she had never lost faith in George, for all they'd had to wait so long. She had a bottom drawer to rival a royal bride's, in Betty's opinion. It'd been a pity they'd had the set-back of earning no money this last year or two, but things were looking up now. 'We'd like to wed at the end of April, just before the launch of *Lakeland Lily*. If that's all right by you, ma'am?'

Margot consulted her diary, confirming that April remained, as yet, blank. 'I see no reason why not. A wedding might cheer us all up after this endless and hard-working winter. You must make your own frock, of course, and pay for the whole thing yourself.'

'Oh, yes, ma'am.' The pattern was, at this very moment, spread all over the floor of her attic room.

So permission was reluctantly granted. Betty bobbed a respectful curtsey and escaped with a grin on her face as wide as a Cheshire cat's.

The wedding took place on a beautiful sunny day in early May, and, much to everyone's delight, Betty looked very nearly pretty. There was no doubting her joy and happiness.

As ever George looked smart and handsome in his chauffeur's livery, straight-backed and proud, it seemed, to have Betty on his arm. There was such tenderness in the way he smiled into her eyes and slipped the gold band on to her willing finger that Lily's throat tightened with emotion as she watched them, envious suddenly of their loving closeness.

Everyone had a lovely time, throwing rice, laughing and joking, and afterwards eating an enormous cream tea aboard. And Betty didn't complain about her feet once.

Life seemed to be going right for them all at last. But then the night before the official launch was due to take place, Ferryman Bob came knocking on the door. 'Come quick,' he yelled. *Lakeland Lily's* on fire!'

Lily raged. Whatever manners and etiquette she'd acquired while living at Barwick House now vanished as she paced the Persian rug, face black with soot, hands scratched and bleeding and clenched into furious fists which she pounded one into the other, like someone demented. Hot-tempered Lily Thorpe was back.

'Drat, drat, *drat!* Who did this to me? How dare they? I'll not give in,' she cried. 'I won't be beaten. Damn it, I won't!'

Fortunately they'd managed to save the main hull, but the beautiful saloon with its swagged curtains and walnut panelling was burned to a crisp.

It would take weeks, months perhaps, to clean and rebuild her. A long winter of effort and expense all destroyed. Lily looked as she felt, like a caged animal ready to pounce and kill for the hurt done to a precious offspring – only to find the culprit had flown.

She swung about and faced her mother-in-law. 'Did you do it? Go on, tell me. Is this your handiwork? After all, your family is pretty heartless where accidents are concerned.'

'How dare you? Take that back at once.'

Somehow Lily managed to do so. Margot, sitting wrapped in her dressing gown and curling rags, seemed far removed from the vindictive woman who had made Lily's life such a misery in the early days of her marriage.

Stifling her rage, she drew a long breath. 'Perhaps a small port for each of us would be a good idea. Calm us down. What do you say?

Margot brightened as Lily fetched bottle and glasses, and the two women sat side by side on the sofa, going over the night's events. 'At least it was only the boat and not the house,' Margot kept saying. 'No loss at all, really.'

'No loss? No *loss? Lakeland Lily* represents our income, our livelihood. Have you any idea how much she cost to restore? Now she'll need stripping out and refitting all over again.' Lily topped up both glasses then slumped back upon the uncomfortable, straight-backed sofa, tears threatening as anger gave way to despair.

It was incredible to find herself actually fighting for the Clermont-Reads. Partly from guilt, of course, but partly to save Barwick House for Thomas, and Bertie from the threat of madness. Even Margot from herself.

Where was Bertie? Lily thought on a wave of resentment. Fast asleep in an alcohol-induced stupor, no doubt. Why was he never around when he was most needed? She felt bone weary, desperate for sleep herself, and the port only increased her lethargy. She fought to stay awake and concentrate.

Margot asked, 'How will you find the money to start again? If you continue stripping my house at this rate, Lily Thorpe, I'll have nothing but empty rooms.'

A slight exaggeration, but say what you like about the woman, she had the unhappy knack of putting her finger on any problem. Where indeed could they find the money? Oh, she'd got her revenge all right. Upon them all, herself included. Lily had bled the Clermont-Reads dry, so that now she couldn't even get together the necessary capital to launch one extra boat, let alone an entire business.

Yet she would succeed dammit, come what may. Even if someone did mean her not to succeed.

But who?

In truth Margot was an unlikely candidate, too afraid of hurting Bertie and knowing quite well which side her bread was buttered, or rather where her next dish of salmon pate was coming from.

'We could ask Selene to approach Marcus Kirkby,' she suggested, breaking into Lily's reverie. 'He made a fortune out of munitions during the war.'

Lily looked at her mother-in-law with new respect. 'Do you think she'd help?'

'I'm her mother.'

Selene, however, when the suggestion was put to her, seemed appalled at the very idea.

'Good heavens, I simply couldn't do it.'

'I'm only asking for a loan, at a proper rate of interest,' Lily told her, trying not to remember she had said much the same thing to Margot. Panic fluttered in her breast as she saw the debts mounting again.

Selene lifted her hands in a flurry of chiffon and clinking jewellery, wrinkling her pretty nose as if perplexed. 'In any case, why should he? It's not his problem. And I've no money. I've seen no sign of any inheritance from Papa.'

'There isn't any inheritance.'

'Well, there should be. Mama has the house, Lily the boats, Bertie his idle life and Pa's whisky. What do I have?'

Even Margot felt moved to protest. 'I've worked all my life for this house and everything in it, so I deserve it. Your father and I hadn't a penny between us when we started out. We achieved everything ourselves. You must do the same. Bertie isn't well because of the war, as you well know, miss.' It was a rare thing for her to attack Selene, and be so revealing about her own past life. But she didn't go so far as to defend Lily's using the *Faith,* for all it had been necessary. That would have been going too far.

'Marcus doesn't believe everything can be gone, and neither do I.' Selene patted a curl into place unnecessarily, her hair was arranged in some complex 'Greek' coiffure and tied up in a fringed scarf. 'He really has far more important projects to spend his money on. He's currently engaged in buying shares in some local company or other. In addition he has the expense of a sick wife.'

Not to mention, Lily thought, Selene's singing lessons which she had recently taken up, and extensive wardrobe. Lily thought that her beads grew longer and her flimsy frocks shorter every time she saw her. Well above the ankle now and in the very pink of fashion. She also hosted his dinner parties and had developed a taste for cocktails. Whatever her life with Marcus Kirkby consisted of, Lily judged it to be one of extreme comfort, if not highly luxurious.

Did Selene still bear a grudge over Lily's ruining her chance of marriage with Nathan Monroe? Surely not? She'd been considerably more upset by the loss of her father's fortune.

Whatever the reason she point-blank refused to help financially. 'I have my own life to lead,' she said, confirming Lily's thoughts. 'Far removed from Barwick House. And, really, I'm not at all interested in Lily's little schemes.' Or even her own mother's, it seemed. 'Besides which, I know full well who was responsible.'

Lily sat up. 'You do?'

'Nathan Monroe. Marcus saw him creeping about the place on the night of the fire. He assumed, Lily, that he was waiting for some tryst or other, therefore none of his business.'

There was amusement in her tone, and the words seared Lily like fork lightning. She had to turn away from the triumph that blazed in Selene's eyes.

Dear God, could it be true? She recalled how totally uncooperative he had been when she'd needed advice at the start of her enterprise. He had also bluntly declined her invitation to come to the launch. What was that if not jealousy? Yet this was the man she loved, the man to whom she'd felt she could trust with her life.

The next morning Lily made her accusation. She took the ferry to the steamer pier, well wrapped up in a green wool cape and matching hat, pulled down over her ears against a chill breeze. A bank of scowling clouds hung over the nearby fells, reminding her of Nathan's habitual expression, and Lily shuddered with trepidation. This was not going to be a pleasant interview.

She chose to confront him in the first-class saloon of his new steamship, *The Golden Lady*. With its twin columns and gilded Corinthian capitals between windows dressed with thick velvet curtains, the whole ship was cushioned and carpeted in the style of a luxurious first-class railway carriage. Which was a pity in a way, for its very grandeur made her own *Lakeland Lily* seem shabby by comparison, serving only to increase her sense of insecurity.

Nevertheless Lily braced herself and calmly put her accusation, then watched with growing alarm as the lines of anger deepened on his face. Still favouring his stiff arm, though there was some movement in his fingers now, Nathan thumped one fist on to the desk and leaned towards her.

'That is how you see me, is it? As a vengeful arsonist? You avoid me for months and then accuse me of this. What exactly have I done, Lily, to deserve such an accusation?'

'I would've thought that was obvious,' she declared, tilting her chin. 'You can't deny that you are the most likely suspect. For all you claim to have spent those missing eight years in the navy, and not in prison! Tell me now if that's the truth? Make me believe in your innocence.'

He glowered at her, more ferocious than she had ever seen him in her life. 'Damn you, Lily, why will you always rake up the past?'

Her legs had gone so weak with misery she longed to sit down, but, since he hadn't offered her the opportunity, didn't dare. Wishing now that she hadn't come, she longed only to turn and run.

'If you must know, before I did near seven years in the Navy, I spent two in Walton Jail, Liverpool. For stealing. The fact that I'd run away from home and fallen to theft in order to survive didn't help to lessen my sentence one bit. They were tough in those days.'

'I'm sorry,' she said, and she was. The misdemeanours of a young urchin living rough on the streets of Liverpool didn't make Nathan evil, only unfortunate. Even so ... She stared at her buttoned shoes for a long moment. 'We have proof.'

'What proof?'

'You were seen by Marcus Kirkby.'

'Kirkby?' Nathan made a sound deep in his throat. 'You'd rather believe that weasel than me?'

She looked at him then with pleading in her eyes. 'What else could I think? It couldn't be Margot. She's far too selfish, and anxious for me to provide the wherewithal for her to enjoy herself. As for Selene, she has a new life now and is totally uninterested in me, Barwick House, or even her own mother. While you – well, you were jealous of my plans from the start, refused to help, so I thought...'

'I would enjoy destroying the woman I love?'

Since there could be no proper answer to this, Lily burst into tears.

But the idea would not leave her mind. If Selene were right and Nathan was the perpetrator of this vindictive crime, then she must take care.

Yet why would he do such a thing? It surely couldn't be from simple jealousy. How could her little cruises in any way harm his big Public Steamers? One glimpse of *The Golden Lady* had put paid to that notion.

He'd refused categorically to declare his innocence, claiming that since she loved him she should trust him. Yet if he loved her, why hadn't he trusted her enough to tell her before about his prison sentence? How could she believe him a word he said?

Lily couldn't help recalling how, as a boy, he'd often made her feel uncomfortable. How he'd ingratiated himself with her family as a lodger on his return, and later had come into Bertie's life as a friend, to such an extent that each had saved the other from drowning. Or so they claimed. But how far could she trust him? And if it were all true, why would he, a friend, deliberately set out to hurt her?

Because she refused to leave Bertie?

Even as the chilling thought formed in her head, Lily fought to reject it.

1922 proved to be another hard-working year. Margot agreed to sell one of her gloomy landscapes, which, surprisingly, brought in enough money to clean, dry out and rebuild the *Lakeland Lily* and put the ship at last into operation.

The musical parties proved to be extremely popular. George would wind the gramophone, punctiliously changing needles after each record, and the Lakeland air echoed to symphonic syncopation, a jolly foxtrot, or such lively numbers as 'Ain't We Got Fun', while the bright young things danced or lounged about and chattered endlessly.

Lakeland Lily could hold fifty people easily, so birthday parties, anniversaries, and even small wedding receptions were now possible aboard her, and Lily discovered that she loved every aspect of the business. When she wasn't actively working on the boats she was devising ways to advertise them, writing to charabanc and railway companies offering runabout tickets or special day trips as Nathan had told her he'd done for his company. Then there were the accounts and an increasing number of staff to see to. She never seemed to have a minute to herself. It was a relief in one sense to be so busy as it gave her less time to think. But Lily was tired.

'I need more help,' she wailed, as she burned the midnight oil checking bookings, adding up columns of figures, and still had to be up at dawn to help with the loading of wood on to and *Faith*.

She called on Rose, much to her old friend's surprise. 'Why would you want me?'

'Because I need help and it's time you did something with your life besides sell vegetables. Anyway, you're my friend, aren't you?'

'Happen. What about Bertie?'

'He doesn't wish to be involved with my boats.'

'I meant…'

'I know what you meant. Are you interested in the job or not?' Rose shrugged. 'Why not?'

Rose was installed in a wooden office painted bright blue on the pier, which improved bookings enormously. Her bright face seen through the window seemed to draw people to make enquiries. She chalked details on blackboards and stuck them all over the place, often next to those set up by Nathan. If no customers appeared she would walk up and down crying out in a loud cheerful voice as the other boatmen did. If they dared complain, she'd give them short shrift. 'If you can yell your heads off, so can I, woman or no. Roll up, roll up. Whatever they have to offer, ladies and gentlemen, we'll better it.'

'Comfort and refreshments on board the *Lucy Ann*.'

'The luxurious *Lakeland Lily* will take you to secret islands, where those lumbering old boats can't go. Or a private picnic on the *Faith*, if you prefer. With champagne.'

'Orchestra on board to play all the latest tunes,' cried the Public Steamer man.

'Dancing and music while you eat. Cheapest fares on the lake. Roll up, roll up.'

'Cream teas.'

'Three-course dinners,' Rose recklessly offered, not knowing whether it were possible or not but determined to make it so.

Her attitude to the customers was friendly but far from servile, as if she had something very special to offer and if they couldn't see that, then the fault was entirely theirs. They'd hear her shouts and come over out of curiosity, quickly make their booking and thrust money at her. Sometimes, if a note was offered, Rose would screw it up in her hand as if this happened every day of the week and she could afford to treat it with contempt. Then when the customer had gone she would smooth it out with a licked finger and put it carefully in the box she kept under the counter.

Lily watched all of this with pleasure and saw her takings rise.

Chapter Twenty-Five

1923

Rose's presence gave Lily more time to spend with Thomas. Grown into a sturdy schoolboy now, he had become far more demanding than when he'd been small. She contrived as well to spend what time she could with Bertie. That summer they would often sit in the conservatory together after dinner, or on a dry-stone wall watching the boats on the lake. Another pleasure was helping their son with his swimming lessons, and introducing him to the joys of Lakeland.

'I'm glad we're still friends, Lily,' Bertie told her one Sunday afternoon as they walked over to Carreck Woods, Thomas bounding ahead, all long legs and big feet like an overgrown puppy. 'A real family again, eh? Isn't he making a fine young chap?'

'He is,' Lily proudly agreed, watching her young son shin up the trunk of a tree then drop into a pile of soft leaves.

There was a small silence. 'We should have more babies, don't you think? A house needs a full nursery.'

She thought of her exhausted mother and her own private vow not to end up the same way. Nor had she any wish to share her husband's bed again. Lily wondered, from time to time, whether the lack of intimacy in their marriage troubled Bertie. If so, he'd showed no sign. Please don't let him ask me, she silently prayed.

'Babies aren't so easily produced, and they grow bigger, remember.'

Bertie snapped off a twig and began to swish at the long grass. 'The more Thomas grows, the more interesting he becomes. He's learning to sail and I mean to build him a small boat of his own. I should like four children, two boys and two girls. Wouldn't that be perfect, now that we are happy together, Lily? Don't you think it's time.'

Lily looked into his radiant face and fleetingly wondered if it would be worth having a nurseryful, as he put it, in order to sustain this precarious happiness.

Then she thought of Nathan and the sacrifice she had already made, and her stomach churned at the thought.

She swung away from him, walked over to a large beech and leaned against its gnarled trunk while gazing upon the green and blue landscape framed by the overhanging branches. Fingers of sun poked between like shards of golden glass viewed through a mist of tears.

'Isn't it a glorious day?' she said over-brightly into the silence. 'Look, there's a half-sunken boat. Could we rescue it, do you think?'

'I was talking about babies, Lily, not boats.' There was irritation in his voice now. 'You're obsessed with the bally things.'

One of the Public Steamers glided slowly by, leaving a herringbone pattern in its wash and a plume of white smoke from its funnel. What she wouldn't give to own such a vessel! One that would carry hundreds, not dozens, of people. They'd make real money then.

'Perhaps I am,' she murmured, then laughed self-consciously. 'When would I have time for babies? The business must come first, Bertie. We have to earn our living now, remember.' She'd given up asking for his assistance. Accepted, as Edward had done before her, that Bertie was not meant for a working life. Sad but true. 'I've taken on Rose to help with the paperwork. Did I tell you?'

'Rose?' He sounded surprised, almost shocked.

'She's doing wonders on the pier, and it leaves me more time to order supplies and do the bills. I was getting horribly behind, and if we aren't efficient, we'll fail.'

'Does that matter?'

She stared at him for a moment, nonplussed. 'Of course it matters. Heavens, Bertie, are you mad?' She could have bitten off her tongue. She really shouldn't let his silliness trouble her. Bertie knew nothing about business. She closed her eyes, tired after the week's work, dreaming of smooth waters and soft breezes in her hair, but his next words left her reeling though they did not at first quite make sense. 'I never meant it to happen, you know. It was an accident.'

Only one accident came to Lily's mind, so she sighed, murmuring something about it all having happened years ago. 'You weren't even there that day.'

'No, I mean the *Lakeland Lily*. I only went to see what it was that kept you so fearfully busy and away from me all of the time. I was so dashed jealous. You'd no time for me any more.'

Lily's eyes flew open and she looked into his boyish face, soulful and guilty, as if he'd been found digging into his tuck box after lights out.

'Tell me what you did, Bertie?'

'Only struck a match to light the lamp, don't you know, to take a proper look. Though it was still pretty dark and I blundered about quite a bit. The dratted thing must've fallen over. Everything seemed all right when I left, Lily. Not that I actually remember too well.'

'You were drunk.'

It was not a question but a statement of fact and Bertie did not attempt to deny it. He pressed his lips together in a resigned sort of way and nodded. 'I dare say I must've been. Sorry, old thing.'

All that agonising over who might have had it in mind to destroy her, trying to decide if Selene was right in her accusation, imagining some dire plot against her. She'd accused Nathan of arson, and all the time it had been Bertie behaving like a drunken idiot! Jealous and sorry for himself at her supposed neglect of him. Lily could almost see him stumbling about the boat, cursing as he fell over, then forgetting what he was about and skulking off to bed, leaving an overturned lamp to smoulder and destroy.

She could hardly believe such wanton carelessness. True, he had not been himself ever since the war, but then few people had. If his problem had been something recognisable, like shell-shock, or neurasthenia as they were now calling it, she might have coped better with him. But a sense of failure seemed to have soured his character utterly. She'd thought since last winter that he was getting better, little by little. It seemed not.

The flare of anger quickly died and Lily's heart went out to him, and she sighed with sad resignation. Perhaps another baby would help to bring back the fun they'd enjoyed in the early days of their marriage – if she could only carry out such an act of generosity. Then again, since he was no longer the same man, what sort of a father would he make?

Whatever her motives for marrying Bertie in the first place, perhaps because of them, he deserved her care and consideration. He must be given a purpose, one that restored his faith in life, and in himself. Who better to do this for him but Lily, his wife?

She felt relieved that Nathan's innocence had been proved, but that didn't alter the fact that he was gone from her life, not for a few months or a year but for ever. Any attempt to see him again, as she so longed to do, could tip Bertie over the edge. And God knew what he would set his hand to then.

Each day at dawn, before she started work on *Lakeland Lily*, she loved to walk along the twisting lane that wound up the hill past a cluster of white-walled cottages, wisps of smoke coming from the circular stone chimneys. She liked to trail her fingers along the harsh lines of dry-stone walls softened by pads of velvet lichen, clumps of green fern and winter-flowering jasmine. Once in Carreck Woods, the silence enveloped her, making her feel whole and strong. Lily loved to breathe in the scent of damp earth, lay her cheek against the shiny bark of a silver birch, or sit quietly on one of the thick roots which erupted from a craggy knoll.

She loved this place, needed its peace and the sanctuary it offered from the turmoil which was her life.

This morning she smiled as a family of roe deer quietly surveyed her before continuing with their feeding. She made no move, afraid to startle them. Treading softly was becoming second nature to her these days.

She was alone in the woods as always. These were her private moments at the start of each day, when she could think and dream and recall happy times. Once down in her office or on the boats, there wasn't a moment to herself.

Lily hadn't seen Nathan in months, though there were times

when she felt his presence beside her like a living ghost. Even when she caught a glimpse of him going about his work, he didn't stop to speak to her, nor she to him. But the pain of living without him burst upon her fresh and raw each and every day. That last afternoon months ago, following Bertie's revelation, she'd gone to offer him an apology.

'I was wrong to accuse you of firing the *Lakeland Lily*. I know now who it was.' She'd looked into his face and wondered how she'd managed to keep away from him so long. The sun lit his dark hair to gleaming black silk and she could scarcely stop herself from smoothing back a stray curl. If only, she'd thought, I could see the expression in his eyes. They were narrowed to mere slits beneath his dark winged brows.

'Come with me.' He'd grasped her arm and, ignoring her half-hearted protests, marched her along the pavement almost at a run, forcing her into the front seat of his motor. It was a new Morris and very smart.

'I – I can't come with you. I've an appointment with the Lake Commissioners in half an hour.'

'You can spare me ten minutes.'

Lily had made no further protest. Wasn't she almost glad to be compelled to remain with him?

Once outside the village Nathan stopped the car and turned to her. His voice seemed to come from a long way off. 'You look well, Lily, if a little tired.'

'Thank you.' She remembered to this day the sick feeling in her stomach, how she'd kept her eyes on the distant mountains, veined with snow like threads of silver.

'Why?'

'Why what?'

'Don't pretend you don't know what I mean.'

Knowing he was there beside her, so close she could smell the clean soapy tang of him, feel the warmth emanating from his body, touch him if she liked, caused Lily to waver in her resolution. How could she possibly contemplate a life which did not hold Nathan in it? 'We agreed that it was over,' she reminded him.

'You decided.'

'It's for the best.'

'Best for whom?'

'Oh, Nathan, don't! Best for Bertie. For me. For all of us.' She risked a glance into his piercing blue eyes so he could see the truth of her words, and the effort they cost her.

There was a breathless, heart stopping silence, then Nathan leaned closer to press his lips to hers, softly brushing her mouth so that it opened beneath his like a flower to the sun. 'Not best for me,' he whispered.

Her heart thudded inside her chest, robbing her of breath and leaving the bittersweet ache of desire in its place. Perversely the fact that he was barely touching her made her want him all the more. Her skin felt as if it were on fire, scalding with need. Never in all her life had she felt such pain. Lily could hear her own voice begging him to let her go, to leave her alone, though he had withdrawn and she was perfectly free to let herself out of the car and walk away. Had she wanted to.

'We belong together, you and I. Don't deny it.' His fingers lightly caressed her throat, stroking its sensitive hollows, while his mouth remained tantalisingly out of reach.

'Bertie needs me.'

'*I* need you.'

Lily wanted to explain about Bertie's sense of inadequacy, his jealousy and feelings of neglect, and his heavy drinking. She wanted to defend him. 'It was the war that did it to him, and it's been worse since his father died. The manner and timing of Edward's death seemed to compound his sense of failure.' She gabbled on, needing to fill the silence with words. 'I've got him working on his power-boat plans again. He's actually started building one at last. Perhaps that will help. How could I leave him now, when he is so troubled? You were in the war, you must see that's impossible?'

If she'd hoped for understanding or sympathy, she was disappointed. Nathan was not in the mood to consider another man's problems, particularly when that man possessed the woman he wanted for himself. 'The war hasn't turned me into an arsonist. I'm the one you need in your life. Admit it.'

Lily beseeched him with her eyes not to press for any such admission while Nathan let his gaze trace every beloved feature of her face, as if memorising it for all time. The stubborn purity of her blunt chin, the soft flushed cheeks, a cluster of curls on her brow that never quite stayed in place. And those bewitching hazel eyes, so wide open and honest, utterly frank and appealing. They could make an angel of most men, except perhaps the devil that lived within himself.

'You are mine, Lily. Always have been. Always will be. Deny it as you will.' Then he'd pulled her into his arms and in the gloriously crazy moments that followed, Lily proved him right in everything he'd said. Loving him as she did, how could she deny it?

Later, when he'd returned her to the pier, she caught a glimpse of Selene, and guilt came, acid sour in her throat. Hastily she tucked escaping curls beneath her hat, smoothed rumpled skirts and attempted to cool her cheeks with the back of one leather-gloved hand before sneaking from his motor and appearing before her sister-in-law, as if from quite the opposite direction.

It was only Lily's newly discovered passion for her steamboat business which had kept her sane since that day. She'd found an ambition inside herself that she hadn't known existed. If it was by way of compensation for her lost love, so be it. Thinking, planning, working with the boats kept her from dwelling on how badly she'd messed up her life.

Only last week they'd uncovered two more scuttled craft and she was busily negotiating for their lifting and restoration. In September she'd bought the remains of a sad neglected vessel for under fifty pounds.

So many people now worshipped speed that enthusiasm for power boating had quite taken over. The leisurely days of steaming were considered far too old hat and Edwardian. Yet the visitors didn't seem to think this way, or they wouldn't queue in their dozens to sail on one of Lily's boats. Any number of steam launches had been dismantled, sold for scrap, or simply left to rot. Her fleet was small as yet, but if she continued to buy them up at this rate, as she intended to do, then in two or three years she would own half a dozen or more.

She dreamed of how one day she might build a much larger ship. A Public Steamer to rival *The Golden Lady*. Then what would Nathan say? She almost smiled at the prospect. If she couldn't have him as a husband and lover, why not as a business rival? It was better than nothing. And what would she name such a ship? *Lakeland Lily II*? Of course.

She laughed at the thought, the lilting sound carrying over the distant valley. Now where would she get the money to build herself such a vessel? She who'd been born and brought up in the mucky Cobbles. Lily Thorpe who couldn't at one time afford an apprenticeship to a humble dressmaker.

'Getting above yourself again, lass?' she scolded as she gazed about her at the dome of a midnight blue sky, shading through paler blues to a pink horizon where it lit up the dark mountain peaks as if with a rose-tinted lantern. Pockets of wispy mist stubbornly clung to the hollows and beneath these lay the lake, a shimmer of silver in the ghost light of early morning.

But the sky was brightening and soon a clamour filled the air: the merry call of the peewit, the soaring song of the lark. The dawn chorus had begun. Smiling, Lily got to her feet and went to work.

It was a week or two later and Lily sat in Hannah's front parlour. Their fragile reconciliation proceeded with painful slowness and, as always on these visits, the silences between them were long. They sat, a picture of unacknowledged guilt and disappointment, only the boy playing at their feet oblivious to the suppressed emotion in the small shabby room.

Lily tried, as so many times before, to say that things were better, that Bertie was slowly coming out of his depression. Even if this was an optimistic view of his state of health, she felt it necessary to keep up a front. She wanted them to see her as a respectable married woman with a flourishing business. Longed for them to be proud of her, to say they understood. And to forgive the grievous sin of adultery, though Lily knew that to a non-conformist Puritan like Hannah it would have been better had she died. Her fall from grace still lay between them like an unbridgeable gulf.

Arnie sat slumped in the corner, saying nothing, sunk in problems of his own.

Hannah said, 'Not thinking of adding to your family yet then?' her eyes on the boy.

Lily fidgeted in her seat, smoothing her barathea wool skirt. 'Not just yet. There's plenty of time.'

'It goes quick enough.'

'Too quick,' Arnie said. 'You're near thirty.'

'I know.'

'Are you happy, love?' The softening in her mother's tone brought a rush of tears to Lily's eyes. She dipped her head, tucking her son's shirt more firmly into his shorts, so Hannah couldn't see her face. 'Why shouldn't I be happy? I've got what I wanted, haven't I? I've escaped from The Cobbles. Have a fine house, good husband, healthy son, and a growing business. I should think anyone would be pleased with all of that. What else could I want?'

A coal shifted in the grate. Nobody spoke or moved.

Then Arnie stirred himself from his corner seat, and tapped Thomas's head. 'How about you, young man? I dare say you'd think a twist of liquorice more interesting than talk, eh?'

'Ooh, yes, please, Grandpa.'

'We'll walk down to Mrs Robbins's shop and see if she's got any, shall we? Our Kitty used to love bull's eyes, but she's a fancy young woman now. Seventeen and courting. Too big for toffee. You're not, though, eh?'

The two went off happily together, Lily smiling as Thomas asked, goggle-eyed, 'Was it a real bull's eye, Grandpa?'

Hannah folded her hands and remarked in her stiff, best-behaviour voice, 'Well, it's good to see you again, Lily. We're allus pleased to have you call. And the little lad'll cheer Dad up. He's been a bit down in the dumps lately.'

'Why, what's wrong?'

Hannah told her how the fishing was down to almost nothing, how boat building work remained unreliable and Arnie was growing ever more worried and depressed.

'I wish he'd come and work for me,' Lily said. 'I'm rescuing more and more scuttled boats. I could give him enough work to keep him going for years.'

Hannah shook her head. 'Thee knows your father's pride as well as I do. He'll not take work from his own daughter.'

'He would if *you* asked him.'

But no amount of argument would change Hannah's mind. In the end Lily was forced to admit that her mother was probably right. Arnie would take help from no one, least of all his own daughter.

Margot had to admit she was bitterly disappointed with life. It had not turned out at all as she'd expected. Britain now had its first Labour Government, for goodness' sake. Ramsay MacDonald was Prime Minister and had even taken working men into his Cabinet. What was the world coming to?

As she sat with her friends in the little drawing room, enjoying morning coffee on this sunny June day in 1924, not for the world would she admit to the very real disillusionment she felt over her daughter Selene, who simply hadn't made the progress she'd expected.

Bertie, too, grew ever more gloomy and unpredictable. One day he might be deeply engrossed in bits of wood and glue, the next he would shut himself in his room for hours, or disappear for days on end. What he got up to half the time Margot didn't care to consider, but she knew who to blame for his misery: his wife. Admittedly that dreadful affair of hers was long since over, but the damage it had done was beyond belief. How could poor Bertie ever trust her again?

The chit certainly gave little thought to her marriage, spending every waking moment on her precious boats.

And although she was making good money and fast repaying the loan, Margot deeply resented the fact that her daughter-in-law scrutinised every penny the household spent. Nothing escaped her notice, insisting they must save. For what Margot couldn't imagine. Typical working-class attitude! She even had the nerve to prevent Margot from buying the clothes she needed. Lily Thorpe might be content to go about in last year's fashions but that was not something Margot had ever been forced to endure before. Quite intolerable!

'How is young Thomas?' Edith Ferguson-Walsh politely enquired, sipping her tea and expecting the usual bland reply. Instead, Margot's lip curled and she almost spat out her answer.

'Boys will be boys, I dare say. Behaves like a young urchin half the time.' If she'd been certain he was Bertie's son, Margot might have forgiven him this childish failing.

'Aren't they all?' sighed Edith. 'Now my own...'

But Margot had no wish to hear about Edith's brood. 'That woman has started taking him to The Cobbles again, which only adds to the child's lack of discipline.'

Edith clucked sympathetically. 'It's the war, of course. The lack of a father's influence during those important early years.'

Margot couldn't help but agree. She found it increasingly difficult to come to terms with this rapidly changing world. And poor Bertie wasn't fit for anything now, least of all fatherhood. She woke in the night in a sweat sometimes at the prospect of no genuine heir for Barwick House. 'The war has destroyed everything. What it hasn't ruined, it has worsened. Everybody thinks they're somebody these days. I cannot imagine what we're coming to. Heavens, I was forced to pull up my own weeds yesterday because Betty declared she hadn't the time. The very idea!'

Edith tilted her head sympathetically, and tutted. 'How perfectly dreadful. Did I tell you that my...'

'What did we win the war for, that's what I'd like to know, if not to hold on to our standards, now so sadly under attack?'

'Quite. My own dear Dora has two darling children. Did I mention it?' Edith said, managing to get her say at last.

When her guests had gone, Margot vented her spleen upon Selene, as she had longed to do all afternoon. 'Why are you not married? Well past thirty and still a spinster!'

Selene winced at the word.

'What is Catherine Kirkby thinking of? Why she has not introduced you to someone suitable by this time, I cannot imagine.'

'She is an invalid, Mama.'

'And that man – he works you like a slave. Look to your future, gel. Would you stay a companion all your life?'

Selene merely smiled, assuring her mother that slavery was not Marcus Kirkby's style and she was, in any case, perfectly content, thank you very much, husband or no. 'The ones I've seen so far have really been perfect drips. Quite second-rate.'

'Rich?'

'Not even that, dear Mama.'

Margot lapsed into dissatisfied silence, though not for long, for she always liked to have the last word. 'It won't do.'

'It will have to do. The war has robbed me of all hope of marriage, Mama, as it has many girls of my age. Do you expect me to live like a nun?'

Margot went quite white and felt the stirrings of panic in her breast. What was Selene trying to say? Surely she had misheard? 'Nonsense! See you keep your wits about you, gel. You aren't turning into one of these fast pieces, I hope? And pray don't cross your legs, it isn't ladylike. I can almost see your knees in that skirt.'

Selene demurely put her knees together and tugged at her skirt as Margot peered closer through her *pince-nez*.

'That isn't rouge on your lips, is it?'

'No, Mama. It's lipstick.'

Margot looked shocked. 'A gel would never have used such a thing in *my* day. We can't have you losing your reputation, which is perfectly possible even in the house of a gentleman. Men being what they are. That would certainly ruin your chances of a good marriage.'

Sighing, Selene pecked a kiss upon her mother's furrowed brow while rolling her eyes in Lily's direction. But her words at least agreed with her mother's sentiment. 'I'm sure you are right, Mama.'

Chapter Twenty-Six

Selene made a point of telling Lily, as they strolled along the shore afterwards, while Margot slept off a substantial luncheon, that she considered the new business project perfectly splendid. 'Don't let Mama bully you. Someone has to settle her debts and keep her pantry filled, otherwise she'd be destitute in a matter of weeks.'

'So long as it isn't you who has to deal with the problem, eh?'

Selene had the grace to smilingly concede this to be the case. 'What a fusspot she is! I swear she grows worse.'

'She's only concerned for you.'

'I'm perfectly capable of running my own life.'

'Or ruining it, according to your mother.' Both girls laughed. A sort of truce, if not exactly friendship, had grown between them over the last few years; nurtured, surprisingly enough, more by Selene than Lily.

'At least she's accepted you at last?'

Lily cast her a sideways glance. 'I wouldn't exactly say accepted. We rub along.'

'Perhaps young Thomas has won her round. I think she's rather fond of the little lad despite her grumbles. She prattles about him enough to Edith Ferguson-Walsh. He's a little charmer, so why not? And handsome, like his father, eh?'

Lily felt a tightening inside her.

'Do you see much of Nathan Monroe these days?' Selene asked, confirming the thought processes which led to this question as she idly hooked an arm through Lily's with a feigned air of innocence. The gesture rather took Lily by surprise and she took a moment to collect herself before answering.

'No,' she said, 'I never see Nathan Monroe at all. Why should I?'

decisions didn't come quickly to him. Only he'd been chewing over this particular problem for some time.

The question was, should he speak to Lily first?

She was fair bouncing with energy and ideas, that lass. Never still for a moment, and bonny as a picture. But underneath the surface he could sense a deep sadness, like brooding rocks under the glassy lake. He thought about this for a while, forgetting his hunt for the match.

Happen it was time he did put his oars up. Maybe let somebody else have a go. Somebody who could run a proper ferry that would take more people than the half dozen he could manage. He'd had long enough to make up his mind. Yes, it was past time he put the solution into effect.

His fingers produced a match, as if by magic, and struck it on the steel tip of his boot. The cigarette flared as he lit it, and his thoughts were tranquil as he drew the smoke into his old lungs. Then, eyes creased against the thread of smoke, he untied the painter and climbed into the boat. Enough thinking. It was time to make a move. And best, he decided, that it come direct from him.

'I can't quite believe it,' Lily said, grinning at Rose in open astonishment. 'My father has actually agreed to join us! Mind, he's going to lease a steam boat from me to use as the new ferry. Can't buy one and won't borrow.'

'Fair enough,' Rose said. 'We all have our pride.'

'And he might agree to do a bit of joinery for me, if he can spare the time.'

'Everything's coming right at last.' Very slowly, Lily's laughter faded.

'More or less.' She remembered how she'd looked in on Bertie before going to work that morning. He hadn't been in his bed but had lain, unconscious and fully clothed, on the floor, as if the effort of getting into it had been too much for him. 'Considering.'

'Good.' Rose busied herself tidying the small booking office, little more than a wooden hut. Straightening papers that didn't need straightening, locking things that were already locked. 'All right if I go now?'

'Of course.' On a sudden impulse, thinking of yet another dull evening ahead listening to Margot's moans, Lily suddenly said, 'Why don't you come round for supper tonight? Like the old days.' She watched as a slow crimson flush spread over Rose's cheeks. 'Made other plans, eh?'

'Aye, you could say so. I'm sorry, Lily. Some other time.'

Now Lily looked at Rose properly she seemed different somehow, not exactly smart but certainly more glamorous. She wore a peacock blue frock with a dipped hem and a flower pinned to the collar. And she'd bobbed her hair quite short. 'You've got a new boy friend. Who is it? Does he live in The Cobbles?'

'He used to.'

'Anyone I know?'

After a moment Rose said, 'No one you know well, anyroad. I'll be off then.' And she picked up her coat, a smart new red one, Lily noticed, and fled.

Margot sat on a hard chair in the overheated bedroom, adjusted her face into a suitable expression of compassion and prepared her attack. She'd come ready to let fly but one glance at the pasty-faced woman lying limply between the starched sheets had tempered even her virulence.

'So you see, my dear Mrs Kirkby – or may I call you Catherine? – Selene is in danger of staying on the shelf which would never do. The poor girl will very soon be past her prime.' She mouthed 'Thirty-three', as if by not speaking it aloud she could deny the shameful truth about her daughter's age. 'She deserves a good husband and children of her own to cherish before it is too late, as I'm sure you'll agree. I rather thought, when she came here... Not that I blame you in any way, of course, dear Catherine. After all, how can you ... in your state of ... But I'm sure you'll understand now if I ask, nay, insist, that I take my daughter home. As a good mother, what else can I do?' She made a helpless little gesture, meant to unite them in the conspiracy of womanhood. Only then did Margot pause to allow her listener the opportunity to reply. She did not.

Whether Catherine Kirkby would ever have risen to the occasion was hard to say, for at that moment the door opened and Marcus himself entered. Margot had quite forgotten what a tall man he was, and how very forbidding. Particularly in the confined space of the airless bedchamber.

'Mrs Clermont-Read. To what do we owe this honour?' His smile, she noticed, was not especially welcoming. He seemed stiff and formal, not even extending a hand in greeting.

'I was passing.' The lie brought a flush to her cheeks and again he smiled, though not a muscle flickered around his eyes.

'Charming. Had you thought to telephone first – you do own a telephone – I might have saved you the trouble. As you can see my wife is not up to callers.'

He was already grasping Margot's elbow, ushering her to the door. 'In fact, she abhors being disturbed. I'm surprised the housekeeper didn't warn you.' His voice indicated that he would have something to say to the woman on the subject, even though the housekeeper had not yet been born who could keep Margot from a course of action she was set upon. Certainly not the skinny woman with the sour face who had tussled with her at the foot of the stairs.

'I would've thought a little company would cheer her,' Margot persisted, attempting to regain control of her arm. 'Doesn't do to languish.'

As if she would never dream of doing such a thing.

Despite her protests, her furious attempts to remain, or even bid the silent patient goodbye, she was entirely thwarted. Within seconds she found herself not only out of the stuffy bedroom but standing on the slate doorstep of Rosedale Lodge, her host thrusting her coat and umbrella very firmly into her gloved hands. Naturally she had not removed her hat.

'Thank you for the kind thought,' he was saying, and almost had the door closed before Margot collected herself.

'I came for Selene. I wish her to return home at once.'

This time there was no smile, only the coldest, fiercest glare Margot had ever encountered.

'Home? You mean to Barwick House? I don't think so, Mrs Clermont-Read. This is Selene's home now. And always will be.'

'Indeed it is not. I mean to find her a husband forthwith. Make her give me grandchildren…' But Margot's last desperate words met only with the solid oak door.

As she stamped down the drive, shoes crunching on the splinters of slate underfoot, she well knew who to blame for this dreadful state of affairs, for the reason her darling Selene had never married. Oh, yes, indeed she did.

Marcus Kirkby sacked the housekeeper on the spot. Within half an hour she was following Margot down that long empty drive. Then he very thoughtfully took a cup of hot chocolate up to his wife, together with a small sleeping draught to calm her. He sat with her till she slept, like the adoring husband he was.

Next he collected Selene from the parlour where she'd been napping, in between reading one of her favourite magazines, and took her to his bed where he pumped out his fury into her yielding body, making her scream with pleasure and pain. Since there was no one of any account in the house to hear, what did it matter?

Power. That was what Marcus enjoyed, nay, thirsted for. More and more power. He certainly could not tolerate overprotective mamas interfering with his life, which was, in his opinion, very nearly perfect. He never relinquished a prize once he had won it. And there were other prizes that he had long had his eye on.

Selene smiled, as if reading his thoughts. Reclining naked upon the silk coverlet she gazed adoringly up at him out of kohl-lined eyes, hoping she resembled one of the heroines in the Ethel M. Dell novels she read so avidly. She certainly had the figure for it. Nice girls, of course, didn't have bosoms. But then, Selene did not consider herself a nice girl. She'd shingled her hair, crimsoned her wide mouth, even pencilled her eyebrows. She was a vamp, wasn't she? Much more fun.

'We've just been honoured by a visit from your mother,' Marcus informed her. 'She has grown strangely protective of your virtue lately.'

This so amused them both that they felt bound to devise a silly game where Selene dressed as a child in long stockings and garters and ran around the bedroom whimpering and pleading for him to be a good daddy to her, while Marcus chivvied and chastised her, telling her to run faster, till eventually she allowed him to catch her and make her be a good girl.

Later, as they lay damply entwined, he quietly outlined his plans. 'I think we have been patient long enough, don't you, my sweet?'

'Indeed I do. Have you found someone?'

'Everything is in place, my dear. It needs only my word.'

'Good,' Selene inserted a cigarette into a long, tortoise-shell holder. Marcus lit it, and one for himself.

'Your stupid brother confessed to the arson, silly oaf.'

Selene frowned. 'I didn't even know that he'd visited the *Lakeland Lily* that night. Drunken fool!'

'We certainly deserve our pleasantly indolent life in the Lakes.'

'Otherwise what was the war in aid of, if we achieve no reward for our effort?' Selene agreed, smiling.

'Quite.' He rubbed his hand over her hot skin and squeezed one breast, hard, making her close her eyes in ecstasy. 'I believe it's time for us to take possession of what is rightfully ours, now they are both fat with success. First one and then the other.'

'For *my* revenge.'

'And your inheritance.'

'Quite.'

'But softly.' He nuzzled into her soft flesh with his mouth, then pushed open her legs, preparing to enjoy her again. 'So no one hears us retrieve it.'

The very next morning Marcus Kirkby called upon Nathan and made an offer to buy him out, lock, stock and barrel. He pointed out that he already owned a substantial part of the Steamship Company, having secretly acquired the remaining shares still held by Captain Swinbourne's widowed sister, who had been more than eager to get her hands on some ready cash.

Marcus told Nathan he had always held a longing to spend his declining years in the Lake District. How he was a romantic at heart, seeking only a business to amuse him, something to 'play with' now that he had made his fortune.

'Highly diverting, what? That I, Marcus Kirkby, businessman and entrepreneur, should find myself untroubled about making more money.' He laughed, a deep booming sound that held no mirth in it. 'I have all that I need and my offer, you will admit, is generous.'

Nathan made no comment. The news that Marcus Kirkby owned such a large share in the company had come as a shock. Drat Swinbourne! A cheat even in his business deals.

With commendable restraint he showed Kirkby the door. The Steamship Company, he declared unambiguously, was not, and never would be, for sale.

'Pity,' said Kirkby, smiling while inwardly cursing. Had he mistaken Monroe's character? He'd thought the man a rogue, ready enough to turn in a nice fat profit, without favour or sentiment. 'Do think about it, at least. It wouldn't do for you to suffer regrets later.'

'There will be no regrets, and no question of a sale. The boats are my life as well as my livelihood.'

'But your profits are down.'

Nathan's eyes narrowed. 'Who told you so?'

'My dear man, any fool could guess. I have seen the queues on the pier. Lily's exclusive little steamboats seem extremely popular.'

'Then why would you wish to buy what you see as an ailing business?'

'Perhaps I feel that I could take on the competition from *Lakeland Lily* in a more objective and businesslike manner.'

Nathan held open the door. 'Good day to you, sir.'

'Should you change your mind, as I'm sure you will when you've had time to reconsider, you know where to find me.'

Nathan had no intention of doing any such thing and followed

Kirkby out on to the steps in order to tell him so. But he never quite found the words for his attention was caught by the sight of a familiar figure. He would know that Fair Isle sweater and those baggy plus fours anywhere. The man was leaning into the booking office talking to Rose, and as Nathan watched, oblivious of his recent visitor's irritation, he saw Rose close the shutter on the little window, lock the door and, slipping her hand under the young's man's arm, walk briskly with him across the wooden pier.

Seconds later Nathan too locked his office door, climbed into his Morris and drove with his foot hard down on the pedal right around the twisting road that circumnavigated Carreckwater, straight to Barwick House.

Kirkby sat in his Daimler and watched him leave, and then instructed his chauffeur to follow.

Lily was not in. Betty, in sorrowful tones, informed Nathan that she had gone down to Preston in search of a new engine. He declined to leave a message but felt disappointment and vague irritation as he left. He'd simply have to wait until she came back.

Later, he wondered about the wisdom of going up to the house at all. Perhaps it was wrong to interfere. Hadn't he tried several times before and she'd either ignored, or returned, every one of his notes? If Lily didn't want to see what was going on, why should he care? Because he did. He cared a great deal.

A bleak emptiness grew within him. Why couldn't he forget her? Lily didn't belong to him any more. Hadn't she made that abundantly clear? She wanted to be a respectable married woman and successful businesswoman, at whatever cost to her happiness, in order to prove that she'd climbed out of the gutter.

On second thoughts, perhaps it was just as well she hadn't been in. Much better that he keep his nose out of her affairs. Let fate resolve the matter as it surely must, then he couldn't be blamed if things went wrong, could he? He must try to forget her, learn to live without her. Though God knows how.

At least no harm had been done by his visit. Betty would probably forget to mention he had even been in the neighbourhood.

Betty did not forget. She thought Nathan Monroe real matinee idol material, with a sort of lurking danger in his face, rather like Rudolph Valentino in *The Sheik*. She eagerly related his visit to a startled Lily, aware her mistress feigned disinterest while drinking in every word.

Lily, however, had other matters to concern her. Her latest acquisition had been found half sunk at its moorings, a steel plate having been bent and buckled sufficiently to permit water to flow in. Could this be another of Bertie's drunken binges?

He was so affronted when she accused him of it that she found herself apologising for even considering him capable of such a dreadful act.

'As if I care about your bally boats!' he said, aggrieved.

She'd found him, as so often these days, in the conservatory. When she had finished begging his forgiveness, he returned to reading his newspaper, a half-filled glass of whisky at his elbow. It was eleven o'clock in the morning.

'Aren't you going to work on your power boat?' she gently enquired. 'You don't seem to be making much progress.' He turned a page as if he had not heard.

'Bertie.'

'You can't rush such a delicate operation. It needs painstaking precision.'

'Yes, but I would've thought you were eager to sail in her.'

'You *drive* a power boat, not *sail*.'

'Sorry. What I meant was...'

'I know what you meant.' He sighed and laid down the paper with a gesture of impatience. 'Why must you always be checking up on me, Lily old thing. Can't a chap take a morning off once in a while?'

Lily glanced at the glass and at his bloodshot eyes, not quite focusing on anything so that she wondered if his reading the newspaper were a sham. She smiled brightly. 'My mother always said the devil finds work for idle hands to do.'

'Are you accusing me of being in league with the devil, Lily?'

'No, I meant only that work – real work – keeps us happy and young. Don't you think so?' she ventured, on a note of forced brightness. 'Better to be busy than bored, eh? And you won't finish your boat sitting here.'

He smiled sadly at her, as if it were all out of his hands. 'Best for *you* to be busy. We all know you were brought up to work, Lily. I was not.' He shook out the pages of his newspaper with an angry rustle and buried himself behind it once more.

Defeated, Lily turned to go. She was almost out of the door when she heard the splinter of glass. With a cry she saw that he had hurled it to the floor. Shards of it sparkled on the green slate tiles. He could as easily have thrown it through the window, she supposed, such was the angry flush on his face.

'Don't worry.' He was pushing past her. 'I'll *work*, damn you, since that's all you care about. I'll finish the dratted thing – prove I'm as good as you. I'll build the fastest bloody power boat on this whole bally lake. You see if I don't!'

When he had gone, scattering pages of *The Times* in his wake, Lily was left with a disturbing sense of unease, wondering exactly what she had unleashed.

Nathan was waiting for her by the folly. He knew she came that way and couldn't help himself. He had to see her.

The sight of him, calmly and patiently leaning against the mistletoe-cloaked stone, as if he would wait for her all day if necessary, was so unexpected it shook Lily badly.

He was, in her opinion, quite the most handsome man in all the world. How had she imagined she could contemplate life without him? How could she hope to get him out of her system just because of her own sense of guilt over the damage she had done to the Clermont-Reads? An emotion she was beginning to see as entirely misguided in view of the way the family were determined not to help themselves in any way.

So long as he kept his distance, she could survive. She could cope with Margot's pettiness and Bertie's selfish idleness. She would serve her penance for daring to enter their rarefied portals and damaging their lives. For the sake of Thomas, at least, and her own sense of justice.

But if he touched her she would be lost. Lily knew this instinctively. As she approached he took his hands quickly from his pockets and stood up straight. He spoke her name, making her toes curl with pleasure, but she let him go no further, unleashing upon him the full power of her temper.

'How dare you call at my home and pester me?' As he opened his mouth to protest she rounded on his again. 'No, don't trouble to deny it. Betty told me. Nor do I want any more of your silly love notes. You promised to stay away. so please do so. Is your word meaningless?'

With miserable satisfaction she watched the blood gradually drain from his face, his jaw tighten, eyes narrow till they were dark and forbidding. He took a step towards her and a crisp stem of bracken cracked as loud as gun-shot beneath his boot. Lily jumped.

'They weren't "love notes", but something I reckoned you should know about.'

She raised her eyes in disbelief.

'I thought you and I had trust at least, Lily?'

'All that is in the past. I never think of it now.'

'Don't you?'

'No. It's over, our ... our…'

'Affair?'

She'd start it again now, if he asked her. 'I'm a respectable wife and mother, and businesswoman, with a reputation to consider,' she announced.

He gave a bitter laugh. 'And how important that reputation is to you. Worth more than our happiness, or even honesty in a marriage.'

Lily felt as if she were falling. She longed to deny this, yet he was right in a way. Her marriage had begun in dishonesty and fed on it until it was now a festering sore. The only saving grace in her quest for revenge had been the fact that once Bertie had been entirely sweet and charming. Now that was no longer the case, she felt she'd no right to complain but must live with the results of her own folly. Bertie needed her. And Nathan, by obsessively refusing to let her go, was only making matters worse. She told him so now.

'You mustn't keep holding on to me.'

He looked at her almost with pity in his eyes, perhaps seeing the shine of tears in her own. His voice, when he spoke again, was gentle. 'How could I, when you've made it clear that I've no right? I wanted only to help, Lily. I reckoned there were certain matters that you should know.'

She wished he wouldn't keep saying her name in that soft way that made her toes curl. 'What sort of matters?'

'What your newly reformed husband might not tell you himself.'

For a second she was caught wrong-footed, but, Lily being Lily, she leaped at once to Bertie's defence. 'He might be to blame for the firing of *Lakeland Lily*, but he wouldn't hurt me. We've made a fresh start.'

He was staring at her with open sympathy in his eyes and she felt her iron control start to slip. If he didn't go soon she would fall into his arms and burst into foolish tears. When he put out a hand to her, she flinched away as if scalded. 'Leave me alone, Nathan. Get out of my life. I don't need you.'

'I think you do.'

She shouted at him then, the old Lily, hot and fierce. 'You're a bloody nuisance, Nathan Monroe. And a liar.'

'I'm telling you the truth.'

'As you did when you denied ever having been in prison? Well, I wish you'd never come back from there, or whatever hell hole you sprang from.' She regretted the words almost the moment they were out of her mouth, but it was too late.

They stood in stunned silence, both breathless, as if they'd run a race or fought a battle, which in a way they had. But the anger in her was spent, and in its place had come need, sweet and dangerous.

He was so close he was almost touching her. He looked so handsome in his dark suit, smooth and close-fitting over his perfect man's body, and a shirt of palest cream with a cravat of navy blue silk, she noticed. Lily's fingers itched suddenly to untie it, to peel back the shirt, and she very nearly, in that fleeting second, laughed out loud as this startling burst of desire clenched every muscle within her. If she had done so, if she had reached for him, perhaps everything might have been different. But he was speaking again and as the words penetrated, the laughter died in her throat, stillborn.

'You're the one who lies and cheats, Lily, not me. I've done nothing to be ashamed of. I haven't married someone I don't love. I haven't set out to take revenge on anyone. But I might, damn you. I just might.'

He was shaking her by the shoulders, almost lifting her off her feet in his fury. Then he let her go so abruptly that she lost her footing and very nearly stumbled.

'If you won't listen to advice, to hell with you! And if you want me out of your life, so be it.' Whereupon he swung on his polished heel and strode away.

Lily stood with one fist clenched tight against her chest, watching till he'd plunged through a thicket of willow and hazel and vanished from her sight. Then she put the hand to her cold cheeks and found them wet.

Chapter Twenty-Seven

The *Lakeland Lily* lay low in the water, rails and funnels brilliant white above the maroon of her hull, flag flying, a lily proudly embossed on her prow. She was a fine, neat little steamer, quick to respond to the lightest touch and easy to handle in a fractious wind. She began work at ten each day and steamed for twelve hours taking passengers up and down the lake, even continuing till midnight if a private party was on board.

Lily herself often skippered her, steering through the channels with practised ease. She'd learned to land without bumping, had become accomplished at the task and held no fear of it. Though when she'd first started she'd been perfectly hopeless, missing the pier entirely while the boatmen had laughed and shouted out to her, 'Shall we fetch the jetty over for you?'

Now, despite the way the dales could funnel the wind from two different angles at once, she could manage the boat well, whether it be light or dark. Lily knew she could sail out in sunshine and as easily return in thick mist, and that the light could play tricks with the eyes, presenting a mirage of hills that did not exist. But Ferryman Bob and George had trained her well and made sure of her skills.

Now Lily had every confidence in herself. She took care to remember that there was more behind than in front of her. She could shout 'Throw more wood on', or 'Send it on', when the cruise was about to start as loudly as the rest, proud to be a skipper.

There were other rules to follow on the lake, of course, and it was essential that they be kept. There were currents and shallows, and underwater rocks to avoid. When two vessels met they were expected to pass on the port side, altering course well in advance in order to do so. Lily had learned all of this.

371

She helped to load the wood and coal in the mornings, pump out the bilges, check that everything was shipshape with ropes neatly coiled, fire buckets to hand, the correct pressure in the boiler. There was nothing she wasn't prepared to do for the sake of her lovely boats.

Best of all Lily liked to mingle with the passengers, taking their tickets or, as today, relaxing on the buttoned seats, hearing the swish of the water creaming behind them and enjoying listening to Ferryman Bob tell one of his many yarns. This one was about Charles Fildes who built the *Fairy Queen* and used to take out her boiler and engine each winter to use in a miniature locomotive in his garden. At least this was one of his true stories, related to entertain the passengers.

The sun was shining from a wide blue sky with not a sign of a cloud. Close by the shore a heron stood in the shallows collecting its breakfast before lifting powerful wings and taking off low over the sparkling water. Grand houses peeped shyly from behind thick foliage, and the steep green flanks of the surrounding mountains were pencil sharp in the clear air – as if a child had drawn them and coloured them in with her brightest paints. Lily sighed with happiness. Life on the water here was so peaceful, as her home life could not be, which somehow added to her pleasure.

She was helping a small girl up on to the seat for a better view of Hazel Holme when the shout went up.

'Damned fool, what does he think he's doing?'

She glanced up to find *The Golden Lady* steaming towards them at full speed. Her blood ran cold and she was on her feet in seconds, running to George whose grey face spoke of his fear.

'Where the hell he thinks he's going, I'm sure I don't know, Miss Lily.'

'Dear heaven, she's too big for these waters, let alone ... She shouldn't even be here!' One of the unwritten but hard and fast rules was that no two steamers must pass in the narrows between islands. There simply wasn't room because of the way the land extended beneath the surface of the water around each island, creating dangerously narrow channels. 'Isn't she going to stop or change course?' Lily cried, stunned as the ship steamed relentlessly nearer, leaving *Lakeland Lily* with no opportunity to get out of the way in time.

'What do we do?' George asked, panic rising in his voice. Lily didn't know. Put her in reverse? Try to turn her? While she hesitated, *The Golden Lady* came inexorably on.

George and Lily together wrenched the *Lakeland Lily* round as best they could and she rocked crazily in the water as a result. But she didn't stand a chance.

The small steamer could go nowhere but plough through the shallows right on to land. She drove aground with a terrible grinding and tearing of her hull. *Lakeland Lily* was very firmly beached on Hazel Holme with half her screaming passengers falling over like skittles on deck.

Dear God, Lily thought, would this battle for vengeance never end?

Lakeland Lily stood in dry dock and business was looking grim. She must be brought back into service with all speed if Lily were not to lose the best part of the season.

Nathan rang with his apologies and some tale of its all being an accident, caused by a new skipper. She put down the phone without even troubling to respond. Then she sent the family solicitor, Mr Groves, to see him. He stood before a grave-faced, tight-lipped Nathan and issued a formal warning.

'Any more trouble of this nature and Mrs Clermont-Read will have no hesitation in taking the matter to court.'

Nathan's frozen glare said it all.

Groves handed him a written warning, lest he be in any doubt that she was serious. 'I would advise you, Mr Monroe, to stay well away from Mrs Clermont-Read and her steam launches in future. Is that quite clear? Do we understand the situation?'

'We understand it fully. Tell her nothing on God's earth would induce me to come anywhere near her. Not ever again.'

It was exactly the reaction Lily had requested, yet somehow it offered no comfort whatsoever.

From that day on it was as if open warfare had been declared between them. After four frantic weeks of effort *Lakeland Lily* was back in the water.

Lily instructed Rose to shout all the louder on the pier, and put up more blackboards. She rented a small cafe nearby and served refreshments to those waiting to board. She organised bargain runabout tickets with the railway and charabanc companies who brought people from Bradford, Leeds and Halifax, or Liverpool, Preston and Blackburn. She hired a band to outplay the ones on board the *Lucy Ann* and *The Golden Lady*. She even offered brown ale on her picnics, something which Margot hated. And her efforts paid off. The number of customers doubled, packing her fleet of steamboats with gentlemen in moustaches and gaiters, ladies in cloche hats, and children in sailor suits.

And they loved it. Some thought they could sail all the way to the sea in one of Lily's boats and Rose rarely disabused them. So long as they handed over their shillings they could think what they liked.

Finally, Lily put in an order for a large steamship. She had paid off her loans, had a fair amount saved and would beg or borrow the rest from the bank, bully Margot to sell more pictures, steal the money if she must, but she would not be beaten. Certainly not by foul play perpetrated by Nathan Monroe. She would work every hour God sent, and make her fortune in no time.

Margot had taken to her bed, and this time it looked as if she meant to stay there. Barwick House had never seemed more depressing. The lamps were shrouded with squares of black linen, the green window blinds drawn, and Betty and George tiptoed about the place, afraid to disturb the all-enveloping silence.

It was as if the last of Margot's energy had seeped away. She would receive no visitors, talk to no one. She had stopped her constant criticising, never interrogated Lily on her routine, didn't even utter a single complaint if her luncheon was late. She just lay in bed, staring out of the window or flicking through old magazines without reading any of them, growing older by the minute before Lily's eyes.

When Lily begged her mother-in-law to get up and take tea in the parlour she simply sighed and looked away. Her life, she said, had served no purpose. She had been a complete failure as a mother. Neither of her children had come up to scratch, so the fault must be entirely hers. 'What did I do wrong?' she asked pitifully.

Lily took a more prosaic view. 'It must be the way of the world for parents to be disappointed in their children. Certainly mine suffer exactly the same sentiments over me.'

Margot looked at her askance. 'How can you say so? You've gone up in the world. You have married into one of the finest families in Carreckwater.'

Lily smiled. 'There are some matters which cannot be measured in terms of money or class. Certainly my mother thinks so.'

Margot frowned, clearly not believing this to be true, but Lily had no wish just then to go into the question of morals. To open Margot's eyes to whatever pranks Bertie had got up to in the past, or risk hinting at what Selene might be up to now, would be too much for her to absorb. So she tucked in sheets, plumped pillows and said no more.

'I wanted only the best for them, and neither cares a scrap about me,' Margot wailed.

'I'm still here,' Lily gently reminded her.

Tearful eyes looked up into hers. 'Why?'

Lily could only chuckle as she slid a fresh hot water bottle beneath the covers. 'You always told me I was born daft. Happen you were right,' she said, in a return to her old accent. 'Now, Betty has made some lovely oxtail soup. I'll go and fetch us a bowl each, and we can take lunch together up here. Then I can see you drink every drop.'

'Harridan!' Margot called after her, but Lily didn't mind. Her mother-in-law was a sad creature now, not yet sixty but old before her time. Perhaps she had good cause. Lily felt almost sorry for her.

Nor did Lily feel quite her old optimistic self. She too had changed over the years. Grown a little wiser, a touch calmer and more patient in her dealings with people – Nathan Monroe notwithstanding.

And was perhaps more realistic in her expectations of life. Sadly, on the other hand, she had also lost a little faith and trust in the people she loved. Lily now believed that she could rely on no one but herself.

Certainly living with the betrayal and hurt caused by the man she loved had proved to be more painful than even she could have imagined. The days and weeks following the near collision were the worst she had ever known. How could he have done this to her? How could he have been so cruel? Was this the proof of his love? Of his mindless, heartless obsession?

Competition, however fierce, was surely healthy. But not this. Selene had warned her that Nathan was jealous of her success. She hadn't believed it then, and still couldn't now. There must be more to it than that.

As for sending those mysterious little notes, trying to put the blame on Bertie, that left her utterly breathless. Could Nathan truly have staged an 'accident' on the lake. Why would he? There could be only one reason: to punish her for refusing to leave Bertie.

Tears shone in her hazel eyes.

Nathan Monroe was selfish, rotten to the core. Always had been, always would be. And she really was much better off without him.

It was the end of another long and tiring day. Lily had worked late at the office. Now she wearily rang for the new steam ferry, glad at least of the opportunity to see Arnie. It pleased her to see her father happy and content at last.

'You like this job, don't you?' she said as they sat together in the bow.

'Aye, suits me grand. I know I was a bit cussed about it at first, but I'm right grateful to you, and to Ferryman Bob.'

As he handed her out at the folly, he said, 'I'm proud of you too, my fine daughter. Right proud.' The two smiled into each other's eyes and on impulse Lily kissed him, the old animosity at last dead between them.

'And I of you.'

As she approached Barwick House, Lily saw Bertie striding towards her down the path. Thomas was skipping beside him, chattering and asking questions as he so loved to do. Too big now to lift, and knowing how he hated to be kissed, she contented herself with ruffling her son's hair and asking if he'd had a lovely day.

'Dad's finished his boat,' he told her excitedly. 'Can I go out in it?'

Bertie had worked like a man possessed for weeks. Lily could hardly believe it. He'd even taken all his meals in Edward's old boathouse, and was rarely home before midnight. In no time the jig-saw pieces had been assembled into a sleek craft. She didn't dare utter a word of protest when he'd spent a small fortune on a splendid engine and all the other necessary bits and pieces he needed. She was too delighted to see a finished boat at last.

'When are you going to try her out?' she asked him now.

'Soon. Then you'll see how fast she goes. I intend to race her, don't you know? Make her as famous as your boats, Lily.'

She sighed, pleased he had done so well but not wishing to compete with her own husband. 'Isn't Daddy clever?' she said, hugging Thomas.

'Let me come too, Daddy. I want a go in her.'

Lily laughed. 'Later, darling, when you're older.'

'I'm older now.'

'Course he is. Proper little man.'

Lily glanced at the sky, which looked ominous. 'Not this evening, in any case. There isn't a breath of wind.'

'For God's sake, Lily, how many times must I tell you that you don't need wind for a power boat?'

'I meant only that the weather seems uncertain. The wind has dropped and it might rain.'

'Mummy, *please!*'

The last thing she needed after a tiring day was an argument so she simply smiled and put a finger to her lips. 'We'll see, shall we? Now it is suppertime. Don't stay out too late, Bertie dear.'

But he wasn't listening, already striding away. Lily watched him go with sadness in her heart, the rain starting in earnest before he had even reached the folly. He was a jealous fool, but what harm could he come to? He could handle boats.

The next day brought a clear, rain-washed sky with that clarity of light which could only be called translucent. Perfect weather, Bertie decided, for his first trial run.

He called Selene, telling her to be there prompt at two, and to bring Marcus if she wished. He urged Margot to rise and watch him. She agreed to watch from the window of her bedroom.

There was another minor tussle over whether or not Thomas should be allowed to be on board for the trial. In the end it was agreed that the first run at least, should be Bertie's alone.

'She's a fine boat. You'll see, Lily.'

'I'm sure she is. You must be so proud of her.'

Word must have quickly spread because by two o'clock several small craft had gathered on the lake to watch the trials. Lily and Thomas, with George and Betty, stood on board the *Faith,* which made a good vantage point. Some distance away, across the lake Lily could see Selene with Marcus on his own power boat, and Arnie aboard his steam ferry with a sizeable group of interested passengers.

'What will you name her?' Lily called to Bertie, but he only shook his head.

'Tell you later.'

She was eighteen feet long with narrow decks and clean vee-shaped lines. Very elegant and, he claimed, fast. Bertie took her out gently, heading for the centre of the lake. There he drove back and forth, gathering speed at a most impressive rate, creating a fine spray in her wake.

'Isn't she tremendous,' Thomas cried.

Lily could only agree. The boat seemed steady enough, handling well. So thrilled was Lily for Bertie's triumph that she blew the steam whistle for him by way of a salute, which set off other whistles and klaxons, a whole cacophony of noise from the myriad small boats which made up the group of curious onlookers.

When Bertie came alongside he shouted across to her. 'How about that? Didn't I tell you I'd make you proud of me?'

Lily laughed. 'And didn't I always say you could do it, if you put your mind to it?'

'Will you let Thomas come now? Just for a little spin.'

Did she trust her child to this new boat? Thomas was jumping up and down with excitement. 'Another time perhaps,' she said. 'Come and have tea first. You must be worn out.'

Tea was a jolly affair, washed down with champagne as Selene and Marcus Kirkby came to join them for the celebrations. 'Fine performance, Bertie. You can be rightly pleased with yourself. Is she for sale?'

Bertie's face was bright with joy, eyes dancing, sandy curls springing wildly about his head. Almost his old self again, Lily thought with pleasure.

He said, 'No, dammit, she isn't. Did you see the speed she revved up? Engine got a bit overheated at the end, and the propellers took a bit of strain. Maybe they should be bigger. I'll look into that, but she held her course well, eh?'

'I thought everything was for sale, at a price,' Marcus said, turning to Lily. 'How about your business, for instance?'

Taken aback, she laughed. 'What are you suggesting?'

'That I'd give you a fair price and clear this lake free of other – shall we call them? – encumbrances.'

Lily stared, puzzled for a moment before understanding dawned. 'I think I can deal with the competition myself, thank you.'

'I believe nothing has quite gone right for you lately, Lily. I would've thought you'd be more than ready to give up.' He regarded her with a smile that somehow made her uneasy.

'Then you heard wrong. I love my boats, and can manage them very well, despite recent difficulties.'

Selene said, 'Oh, Lily, do stop being so selfish and stubborn. You know that Nathan will win in the end. Why don't you sell to Marcus instead? He'll deal with him so much better.'

Bertie, still deep in his own thoughts, said, 'I might consider an offer. Depends what it is. I could always sell you this little beauty, Marcus, and build myself another, better model, eh? What d'you say, old sport. Like to try her out?'

'I wouldn't mind.'

When Selene protested, she too was generously offered a ride.

'No, thank you,' she said, rather sniffily. 'It would quite ruin my hair. I shall stay here with Lily while you boys play. I'll persuade her to change her mind and sell up.'

Lily laughed, hazel eyes sparkling. 'You won't succeed.'

'These were my father's boats in the first place, remember. I think I deserve to have them back, don't you?'

Lily was astounded. 'That's not true. Only the *Faith* was worth anything in the beginning. The *Lakeland Lily* was originally the Kaspar, and cost more to recover and restore than her actual scuttled value. It took nearly two years before she was properly paying her way. I'm only now making any real money, through my own efforts.'

But Selene would have none of it. 'You took advantage of Mama, forcing her to sell pictures, *my* inheritance.'

'I beg your pardon but I've kept Margot in comfort, *and* paid off her debts. Repaid her loans ten-fold.' Which is more than you have done, Lily could have added.

'By rights, everything should be mine. I know my father felt sorry for you, but he wouldn't have wanted *you* to inherit, Lily, a nobody from The Cobbles.'

Selene still knew how to inflict a wound, and leave Lily too stunned to answer.

'Of course, we all know how you do so love to steal my possessions, you naughty girl.' The point of this remark did not escape Lily either.

She would have liked to protest further, to say that it was *she* who had built the boat business up, not Edward; that *she* hadn't run away when the going got tough. But Bertie was falling into sulk again and she had no wish to spoil his day. 'We can discuss this another time. Enough business talk for today. Let Bertie enjoy his trials.'

As he set off again, this time with Marcus Kirkby as crew member, Lily helped put away the tea things. Her irritation over the conversation that had just occurred made her clumsy and a cup slid from her fingers to smash upon the deck. Cursing beneath her breath, she went for a brush and dustpan but Betty took them from her, saying she'd do it herself while they still had some crockery left.

Perhaps, Lily thought, she did owe Selene something. Perhaps it wasn't enough to have paid off their debts and saved Margot from bankruptcy. Should she have paid Selene something for the boats? Oh, dear, why was everything so complicated where the Clermont-Read family was concerned?

The boat had completed one lap by this time and it was only as Bertie swung it round for a second full run down the lake that Lily realised there were three figures on board. Bertie and Marcus Kirkby in the front, and a third small figure behind.

'Who ... ?' Horror-struck she guessed what had happened. While she and Selene had been arguing about the justice or otherwise of her claim, Thomas had sneaked aboard his father's boat.

'Dear God,' Lily prayed. 'Let him be safe.'

The boat started well, skimming over the waters while Lily watched, heart in mouth. In another moment or two Bertie would realise Thomas was with them, slow down and bring him safely back. But he didn't slow down, he went even faster. Lily prayed fervently that his confidence in the new power boat was justified.

The boat gathered momentum, the sound of its engines filling the lake valley, reverberating off the mountains and sending birds flying up in alarm from the trees.

They all heard the thud, as if someone had punched a solid wall, and then the boat started to snake. Lily watched in terrified horror as the front lifted and the craft somersaulted into the air.

The engine had once again overheated and the strain on the propellers had apparently been too great. These had come off, the boat spun out of control and finally broke into pieces. All three passengers had been thrown clear. Marcus died instantly on impact.

Bertie lay half conscious for a week and then slowly and painfully came back to life. Thomas, perhaps because he was young and small, miraculously survived with hardly a bruise. Thank God!

He proudly told his mother how his swimming lessons had paid off.

'I could've swum right back to shore if Grandpa hadn't picked me up in his ferry boat.'

Lily went down on her knees and thanked her maker for this gift of her son's life.

Selene was inconsolable. Not so much, as it turned out, because she grieved for Marcus Kirkby, but because her own future was now thrown into turmoil. Tied to two women now, she could either continue looking after Catherine Kirkby, without the delightful compensations her husband had offered, or remain at home and take care of her invalid mother. The spinster daughter's usual lot in life.

Lily felt certain that she, for one, would never wish to go out in a boat again. When she told Bertie this, he only laughed. 'It's the shock, old thing. It'll pass.'

'What are we to do, Bertie?' she asked him one day when he was well enough to sit by the window of his room. 'I could sell to Nathan. It's presumably what he wants.'

'Is it what you want?'

'I don't know.'

'Then if in doubt, don't sell.'

She was silent for a moment, but the question had to be asked. 'What about us, Bertie? You and me.'

He didn't even glance at her, keeping his eyes fixed on the distant mountains. 'I'm thinking on that, Lily.' And since he would say no more, she crept quietly away again.

Then one morning George came to her with a small fragment of the power boat in his hand.

'I think you should see this, Miss Lily.'

It was the boat's name plate. It read, *Sweet Rose*.

Bertie was packing when she went to his room later that afternoon, which somehow did not surprise her.

'Leaving?'

He folded a silk cravat and laid it on top of the shirts in his portmanteau. 'Don't be cross, old thing. Rose is my sort of girl. As you'll have realised by now.'

'I see.'

'I always felt a bit inadequate beside you. Not your fault, don't you know, that you've so much energy. Mine really, for being such a useless ass.'

'You're being unfair to yourself, Bertie.'

He smiled. 'And you've a heart of gold, Lily, but you're better off without me, old thing. Rose and I mean to go to London and start a little boat business on the Thames.'

'How will you manage?' She meant for money.

'Mama will see me right.'

Same old Bertie, not even realising his mother no longer had any money. It wouldn't last, of course. He'd soon tire of the effort involved, and it would be herself who would finance his indolence. Lily knew she'd never be free from that responsibility. Nor would she wish to be. She watched him for a moment, then gently laid a hand on his arm. 'I'm sorry. I'd no right to involve you in my revenge for Dick. It was wrong of me.'

Bertie grinned, then seeing the tears in her eyes, put his arms about her and held her close, awkwardly patting her shoulder. 'Don't weep, old sport. We gave it a go. Fun too, some of it, eh? Apart from losing our little Amy.' He was silent for a moment, offering her his hanky, helping her dry the tears. 'You'll let Thomas come and visit?'

'Oh, yes, of course.'

He beamed. 'I'd like that. And we can still be friends?'

'Always.'

'Don't blame Nathan for that near-miss business. Blame Marcus Kirkby and my fearfully selfish sister. She put him up to it, never having forgiven you for spoiling her engagement. Though I doubt he'd ever have married her. Nathan always loved you, not Selene, and she knew it. Pay her off and start afresh, Lily. Time you left Barwick House in any case. All debts to the Clermont-Reads are cleared, as, I hope, are ours to you. There's a new world dawning where class ain't so important. Make what you will of it, Lily, your life is your own.'

It was the most profound speech she had ever heard him make, and for a moment they gazed upon each other with warm compassion, wanting to say so much more but not knowing how.

'I'll do the decent thing,' he said at last. 'Give you the divorce and so on. Be happy.'

Then he kissed her cheek, said he would send George up for his luggage and walked out of the door, and from her life.

Lily stood for a long while with her hand clasped to her mouth, unable to move, unable to take in what had just occurred. She was free. The trap had opened.

Debts paid, he'd said. And they were. Hers to Margot and Bertie for using up the last of Edward's money on The Cobbles. The Clermont-Reads' to her for killing Dick. She'd lost little Amy, her darling first child, but she still had Thomas, strong and healthy. Time at last to put the past behind them and go forward. Time to grasp happiness with both hands.

But would he still want her after all the hurt and the accusations? 'He'll hate me.'

'It's true, he might, Betty said, as she helped mop Lily's tears with a corner of her apron. 'Since you never believed a word he said and he were telling the truth all along. But you won't know for sure unless you go and ask, now will you?'

'Dare I even try?'

'I'll pack your things, just in case, shall I? And Master Thomas's, while you go and find out where your future is to be. You can telephone me later.'

'Oh, Betty.'

'Go on with you, while you have the courage.'

Lily didn't wait for the ferry. She drove herself in the *Faith,* not wanting to talk to Arnie or anyone at this moment. Making the steam-yacht fast at the pier, she ran along the slatted boards, not pausing at his office for dusk was already falling and she knew he wouldn't be there. She passed the boathouses without a second glance, ran up Fisher's Brow so fast she nearly expired for lack of breath at the top of it. Oblivious to the curious glances of people who stopped to watch her pass, she ran on, one hand pressed to her aching side. Only when she reached Mallard Street did she slow to a walk, and came at last to Drake Road.

Perhaps he had heard the sound of her hurrying feet, the clip of her heels on the cobbles. Or perhaps there was a more mundane reason, such as Betty telephoning to say she was coming. Whatever the reason, he was waiting for her at the door, and all she had to do was walk into his arms. Oh, it felt so good to be home.